Kempton's Journey

SCEPTRE

Also by Valerie Blumenthal

Chasing Eagles
Knowing Me
Benjamin's Dream
Homage to Sarah
The Colours of her Days
To Anna: About whom Nothing is Known

Kempton's Journey

Valerie Blumenthal

SCEPTRE

Copyright © 1997 Valerie Blumenthal

First published in 1997 by Hodder and Stoughton
A division of Hodder Headline PLC
A Sceptre Book

The right of Valerie Blumenthal to be identified as the Author of
the Work has been asserted by her in accordance with the
Copyright, Designs and Patents Act 1988.

10 9 8 7 6 5 4 3 2 1

All rights reserved. No part of this publication may be
reproduced, stored in a retrieval system or transmitted
in any form or by any means without the prior written
permission of the publisher, nor be otherwise circulated
in any form of binding or cover other than that in which
it is published and without a similar condition being
imposed on the subsequent purchaser.

All characters in this publication are fictitious and any
resemblance to real persons, living or dead, is purely coincidental.

A CIP catalogue record for this title is available
from the British Library

ISBN 0 340 67492 X

Typeset by Palimpsest Book Production Limited,
Polmont, Stirlingshire
Printed and bound in Great Britain by
Mackays of Chatham PLC, Chatham, Kent

Hodder and Stoughton
A division of Hodder Headline PLC
338 Euston Road
London NW1 3BH

Acknowledgements

Thanks to:

Richmond Tourist Office.

Tracy Alexander, Kempton Park Racecourse.

Douglas Driver, Richmond Slipways.

Mrs R. Kadir, Petersham Farm. Richmond.

Penguin for permission to quote from *Reveries of the Solitary Walker* by Rousseau, translated by Peter France (Penguin Classics, 1979) © Peter France, 1979.

Starters' Orders

The sound of gunshot, swiftly followed by another sound from over the brow of the hill. A roar. No, more like the rolling of drums. Thunder? The thunder of hooves. And to his horror a herd of stampeding horses is bearing down on him. He starts to run. But his legs are leaden and he can only run on the spot. Closer and closer they come. Hundreds of them. The noise is colossal. The valley reverberates with it, and with his own deafening heartbeat. They are almost level with him and he stops trying to run and bends double like a shell to protect himself. Catches a glimpse of hooves and legs and burning eyes. And jockeys. What is this? They are all being ridden by jockeys, whipping their mounts, urging them on.

'Get out of the way,' the cry goes up; and they part like the Red Sea round his defenceless island and hurtle onwards, over the horizon.

'For chrissake!' Kempton wakes up yelling. Sits bolt upright in bed and fumbles for the lamp. It crashes to the floor, taking with it a glass of water and several books. He feels for it on the carpet, fingers making contact with the switch. Then There Was Light. Oh and the relief. His heart settling down. He retrieves the books, the empty glass, and lays some Kleenex on the wet patch. Writes in the notepad he always keeps by the bed: phone doctor, sleeping pills.

How many years is it, Kempton wonders, since he last sat in a doctor's waiting room? It must be at least six or seven, when he had back problems after a single humiliating experience as the only male at an aerobics class. His face compresses into a grimace at the recollection. Nine o'clock on this Tuesday morning, and he feels ill at ease and twitchy. For most of the others waiting, the health centre – festive with orange and green paper decorations traversing the ceiling, sprigs of artificial holly, and a bauble-studded tree in one corner – is apparently a social meeting place where regular attendants compare afflictions in grisly detail and mothers earnestly discuss potty training whilst casting indulgent glances towards their older children playing Let's-Be-Thugs. Enough to deter anyone from parenthood, Kempton reflects, observing with an expression of distaste. Tiredness makes him intolerant. Perhaps at heart he is a bit of a misanthrope? Kempton, who goes out of his way to say the apposite thing, covers up for other people's rudeness and apologises to someone when *they* bump into him.

He riffles through a mangled *Reader's Digest*, but his glasses are on the passenger seat of his car – he has an image of them lying in their case there. He holds the journal at arm's length from him, but can make no sense of the blurred print and puts it back on the table disconsolately. Decrepitude playing the game of Grandmother's Footsteps. And he's been waiting more than half an hour. At this rate he won't be at the office before mid-morning. An image of Pitman springs up before him, consulting his flashy gold watch – and the blond hairs sprouting around the strap; his belly like a slab over his belt. And all Kempton wants is a decent night's sleep. He had thought it could be arranged over the phone – Sleeping badly? Nightmares? A written prescription . . . Collect it, a quick trip to the chemist, and to work on time. No explanation required to Pitman.

The elderly woman next to him kneading her features, kneading her handkerchief between arthritic fingers. What does she fear? He has the fleeting urge to soothe her by laying his hand over hers. His father might have done that sort of thing. She reminds him of his landlady at Oxford. In fact everyone, however obscurely, reminds him of someone he knows: an expression, the hairline, face-shape, a feature, a gesture. Not a doppelgänger likeness, more a passing similarity that recalls to mind someone maybe not thought of for years. The game helps whittle away the time.

And what might they make of him? The baggy sleep-deprived brown eyes of a man in his mid-forties, beneath heavy, inverted brows set into a longish, olive-toned face, a seam running down either cheek; a nose like a promontory; and a mobile, full-lipped mouth – buckled now in contemplation – the whole topped by thinning dark hair. When he gets to his feet (self-consciously) in response to his name finally being called, he is immensely tall and powerfully built. There is something faintly rumpled about him. And he walks with a head-down apologetic lope. He lopes down the corridor now, past various numbered doctors' rooms; murmuring comes from within.

The door to room number four is ajar, and hesitantly he enters. A man of about his own age half rises from behind the desk and waves vaguely for him to take the chair across from him. As Kempton does so his feet accidentally kick a child's truck beneath it. He is awkward and dry-mouthed. Lack of sleep makes him constantly thirsty.

The doctor tapping the computer keys. His own name flashing up in green.

'Prévot. Is that a French name?'

• Kempton's Journey

'Yes. My grandfather was French.'

'And your christian name. Have we spelt it right? KEMPTON? Not KENTON?'

Everyone makes the same mistake. Often he doesn't bother to correct it. Marked out for ever because of Minnie's thoughtless eccentricity.

'No, that's correct.' He feels obliged to offer an explanation, just as he always does. 'My mother's a racing fiend. Kempton Park was rather handy for where she used to live. It could have been worse. I could have been named after a horse,' he jokes. The standard, churned-out joke.

A small boy dragged round racecourses. Saturdays spent under the brim of her trilby. Noisy crowds, the percussion of hooves, the smell of excitement and beer; the steaming-flanked horses and bright-capped jockeys aloft. The mysterious tic-tac men with their sign language. The ecstatic voice of the commentator over the Tannoy. And how many times would he end up separated from Minnie, and the loudspeaker would relay the message: 'Would Mrs Prévot come to the winners' enclosure please. We have a young boy . . .'

'I see,' the doctor says. Of course he couldn't possibly. Minnie is beyond definition or comprehension.

'So what can I do for you?'

'I shan't take up your time, doctor,' Kempton tells him briskly. 'I only want some sleeping pills. I had some Halcion a few years ago. When I had a bad back. They were excellent. You know – you didn't get that hungover feeling the next day.'

'Halcion was withdrawn from the market two or three years ago.'

The doctor's steady gaze disconcerts Kempton, and he shifts about in his chair. 'Oh? Why?'

'It was considered to have unacceptable side effects. In fact there was a programme on television about the controversy a while back.'

'I didn't see it. So what were the side effects?'

'Aggressiveness. Mood swings. Depression. Persecution complex. That kind of thing.' A glimmer of a smile on his thin, sallow face. 'In the States a man was acquitted of murdering his wife, blaming his action on the fact he had been taking Halcion at the time.'

'Good God, he got off free?'

'Well the charge was changed to manslaughter.'

'Good God. Only in America! What a great excuse. If you want to murder your wife, that is. So what can I take instead of Halcion?' He is parched with thirst now. Looks longingly at the cup of half-drunk tea on the desk. Is anxious to be gone; can clearly see Pitman pacing his mahogany panelled office. That was once his own.

'First things first, Mr Prévot. Why do you want sleeping pills?'

He'd have thought that was obvious. 'I'm having a problem sleeping. Look—'

'How long have you had this problem?'

This man apparently has all the time in the world. Doesn't seem perturbed by the thought of the spilling-over waiting room. December 19th, and it's beginning to snow outside. The big-flaked kind that settles. Through the window he can glimpse the maroon roof of his company Carlton becoming speckled with white. Snow. Austria. Vanessa in her pink skiing salopettes, flaunting herself about.

'A couple of weeks or so,' he says vaguely, watching the white spread and link up. He focuses his attention once more on the man opposite him. 'Except for that time with my back, and then another time, nearly three years ago—' (and with good reason then) '—I've never had any trouble sleeping. In fact I can usually conk out anywhere. On the floor, in an upright chair, in the bath. It's quite a joke with people, actually, my ability to sleep wherever I am. Then recently I had a spate of nightmares and that was it. *Adieu* sleep. Look, I really don't want to take up any more of your time. I've seen the hordes in the waiting room, so if you could just—'

'Is there anything on your mind, would you say?'

This catches him short, the directness of the question slashing across him. He shrugs and pulls a dismissive expression.

'No, nothing in particular.' More a general malaise he does not care to analyse. 'I mean, I'd say I was a reasonably well-balanced individual on the whole.' A typical Libran, according to his daughter. 'I can cope with things. I can deal with the odd hiccough fairly well.'

'What sort of hiccough?'

'Oh you know . . .' Unsure about the way the conversation is going. He should get up and leave now, pills or no pills. But doesn't; sits firm in his chair, urged on by the doctor's little peck of a nod. 'I was widowed almost three years ago. She – no, it doesn't matter. Then nearly two years ago my business virtually went bust. Well that's nothing new in a recession. I sold the company. I'm now an employee. Well, I consider myself fortunate. Let's face it, it could have been worse. You only have to look out there. I've got a daughter. Cat. Short for Catriona. She's great . . . Just after the business episode she had a climbing accident. Look, the main thing is she's alive and healthy. She's got a limp and her leg's badly disfigured, but she's been very plucky. No, everything's fine. Really it is. We have fun, she and I, when she's down from Oxford. A good life. I've got a lovely house . . .'

Within him an extraordinary surging up. Spears behind his eyes. A geyser thrusting up from his stomach to his throat, blocked by a bar. And vainly he struggles to keep his features in order, keep the smile on his face. But he has no control over his facial muscles, which are tugging downwards – it's as if he is wearing a rubber mask that is being dragged in a conflicting direction over his eyes, his nose, mouth and jaw. His entire body is resisting him. The bar across his throat disintegrates. His body ceases to be his own and collapses. Suddenly Kempton is convulsed in sobs, stifling them in the serge crook of his arm, hiding the wreckage of his face in shame. One minute a normally self-contained, dependable man, the next this sob-wracked heap. And the worst of it is he can hear himself and see himself from some detached vantage point, yet cannot stop himself. What a debacle.

And all he had requested, such a benign request, is that he be given a prescription for some pills so he can have a decent night's sleep.

Eventually, with Herculean effort, he pulls himself together, acutely embarrassed. And mustering up the dregs of his dignity and malehood, he starts to bluster apologies. Tries to resite a grin on his face; his mouth gaping in a painful rictus. The doctor does not grin in return. He sits perfectly still, his eyes spilling sympathy.

'It's all right you know. You've no need to be ashamed.'

'Of course it's not all right,' Kempton says vehemently. 'A grown man behaving like that.' He is shaken by his own outburst. A man of his sort of upbringing; unused to public displays of emotion. He plucks a pen from a selection in a mug on the desk and toys with it, pushing the button at the base so that the ball-point pops up and down. On the mug the words: Please don't try my patients. Briefly he wants to laugh.

He is being assessed – which does nothing to make him feel more comfortable; rotates his shoulders a few times within the confines of his coat.

'Look, I really don't want to take up more of your time Doctor—' Has he already said that? '—And I'm getting a bit late myself actually. You know – no longer my own boss, etcetera—' Here he attempts a lighthearted laugh, but it comes out like a creaking door. '—So if you could just give me a prescription.'

'Christmas is a bad time for you, I imagine,' the doctor interrupts him. 'Would you consider seeing a counsellor in the new year?'

A counsellor? Every woman he comes across nowadays seems to be a counsellor or training to be one. Once it was interior design (Vanessa had been an interior designer), now it's counselling. It goes with the tennis set, as he calls it. With women who feel guilty for sitting around, who want to be able to say, when asked on the cocktail party circuit, that they do something valuable.

'I don't think so.'

'Why not?'

The guy gets full marks for persistence. 'Well, I don't feel the need. I'm fine.'

'With respect, Mr Prévot, I wouldn't agree that you *are* fine.'

That awful welling-up within him again. This time he masters it, his battle witnessed by the doctor, whose deepening frown forms a node between his eyebrows.

'OK, maybe I'm not as fine as I thought I was. I'll consider what you said.'

Bartering compliance for a prescription – although of course he has no intention. And he is rewarded: two weeks' supply. The prospect of a fortnight's sleep; the sweetness of Fauré's *Sanctus*. Presumably the doctor trusts him not to consume them all in one go, that he wouldn't deliberately leave his daughter orphaned. But the doctor doesn't know the half of it. It is tiredness that is making him react like this. And who wouldn't be a bit out of sorts with a nightly quota of three hours' sleep, interspersed with nightmares? It is important to remain *rational*. Kempton has spent a lifetime being rational. His epitaph will read, 'He always did the right thing.' Or possibly, 'Where are my glasses?'

He masks his awkwardness with the confident parting handshake of a self-assured man, and draws up his coat collar in readiness for the cold outside. That man who had striven for a normal family life – which was all he had ever sought – and who had established his own successful business. A man who is now an employee of no great rank and loathes his bosses – who he knows are dying to get rid of him; is strained with his colleagues, who were once *his* employees; hates the whole shitty kow-towing degradation of it. And, yes, Christmas *is* a bad time for him. Without Vanessa. Hates her for what she did. And watching Cat limp, with that beacon grin of hers. And Peter for seducing her. And Minnie for just about everything. And himself most of all. And no, it is not merely tiredness. He has had it up to *here*. There is no one with whom he can discuss his turmoil, because he is too self-contained. Anyway, his male friends would shy away in discomfort. Besides which Peter is – was – his closest friend. Over the years Peter, a self-confessed roué, has kept him entertained, boosted his flagging spirits, introduced him to women, got him drunk, partnered him at squash, supported his choral society's events. And now swiped his daughter.

Out of the building Kempton lopes – the snow has become sleet after all – and sits glaze-visioned in his car for several minutes. Before starting the engine and heading, not for the office in Mortlake, but home, from where he will phone and put an end to Pitman's pacing by claiming to be struck down by food poisoning after last night's Chinese.

Over the hill and far away. But not far enough. A white Georgian terraced house in a plane-tree lined road off Richmond Hill. And his sweet lass down from Oxford is with her lover. Probably screwing at this moment. He seethes at his own imagery.

Mrs Jakes' morning. He had forgotten; acknowledges

surprise then dismay as she opens his front door at the sound of his key in the lock.

'Holy Mother, you startled me,' she exclaims, hand to her pinafored breast as he brushes off the damp glistening on his coat. Helps him take the coat off and drapes it over the bannister.

He had wanted to be alone, closet himself in his study and howl lupine howls. 'Food poisoning,' he says. 'I was at the doctor's. Excuse me Mrs Jakes, I've got to phone the office.'

'Lucozade,' she says predictably, following him. 'You should be tucked up warm.' She has been with the family thirteen years.

Kempton's study: colour-scheme and fabrics chosen by his wife as deemed appropriate for a man. A maroon paint with a speckled effect on the walls, maroon and cream striped curtains. There her concession to masculinity ended, with a complex arrangement of swags and tails and tassels. The entire house decorated as though he did not exist. Recently he has noticed the house is beginning to have a faded look (like himself); but he wouldn't know how or where to start with getting it decorated. Anyway, there is no money. Added to his other worries Kempton has financial problems. The house costs a fortune in bills and maintenance, which was just about viable when the business was his own and doing well. Lately he has been seriously considering taking a lodger. Or selling.

He takes the cordless phone from its cradle to the armchair and sits down without looking. A squawk from Spike.

'Kempton here,' he tells Pitman, hoisting the affronted cat onto his knee.

'What happened to you then?' The other's nasal East London voice grates into his ear. This is a man who wears a pink shirt and co-ordinating pink-and-purple diagonally striped tie.

'I've got food poisoning. Must have been last night's Chinese.'

'You've got to be kidding. What a time to go and get ill. When are you coming back?'

'A couple of days maybe.'

'Well that's great. Bloomin' great.'

'I'll do some phoning from home.'

'Yeah, yeah.' Hangs up, leaving waves of animosity twanging.

Sorry you're ill, mouths Kempton. Hope you'll be better soon. We'll manage. Don't hurry back. He grits his teeth against subordination.

Mrs Jakes has obviously been listening outside the door for him to finish on the phone, gives a token knock and enters with a tumbler of Lucozade; makes it plain she intends to linger. But he is firm, ignores the reproach in her broad, Irish face and actually locks the door – inaudibly – behind her. Her presence in the house inhibits him. Only when the Hoover starts up does he relax a little. He must remember to buy her a Christmas present. Add it to his list. A man governed by lists; clinging desperately to the routine of responsibility. And does Mrs Jakes secretly blame him for what happened? On her own in the house twice a week, lovingly dusting the furniture, vacuuming the carpets, washing the kitchen floor, shrines to Vanessa's impeccable taste, does she wonder if he drove her to it, or at least could have prevented it in some way?

He wonders this himself, with monotonous frequency. It treads on his heels barely a pace behind him. Vanessa's mother – with whom she had always fought – had blamed him. Over from the States for the funeral, she had assuaged her own guilt by transferring it onto him: weeping and

• Kempton's Journey

recriminating ostentatiously. Then had returned to Florida where she was safely shacked up with her fourth husband.

('What's another word for "families"?' Kempton, doing the quick-crossword one evening, asked Peter. 'Clutter,' Peter replied.).

The awful gut-wrenching urge to cry has gone. Incompatible with Mrs Jakes' singing over the Hoover. And in the kitchen: Radio 2, and Ken Bruce. And up Kempton gets to turn on the gas fire; stands over it watching it leap into indigo then yellow ribbons within its mock-Adam pine surround; goes to his pedestal desk – *his* choice; a solid, Victorian piece of furniture in faded mahogany. Gradually he has started to make the room his own: a pair of Art Nouveau lamps, a bronze hound on a marble base, bronze figurine of a woman. Collecting Art Nouveau is a comparatively new hobby, already becoming quite absorbing. He collects old records too. And old journals and magazines, stashed away in a hide trunk. His study is becoming satisfyingly crowded.

His listless gaze meets the sleet outside the tall, paned window. And a woman is tugging her spaniel on one of those retracting leads past the lamppost with the sign saying that owners of dogs fouling the pavement would be fined £100. Vanessa's spaniel – definitely not his – had disliked all men. It had been found run over the day after her death.

He no longer feels the desire to break down and sob. But something else is happening to him, this Tuesday morning, six days before Christmas. A very great anger and sense of injustice are seeping into the buttoned-up heart of this normally sanguine man.

Beyond the window through which he broods and blames, preparation for the festivities gets underway with or without him, and in an inspiring crystal-flash he can see it all: the lit-up shops and music playing from within; feet skimming along wet pavements; busy florists, and

• 12

husbands selecting flowers – guilt tokens – for their wives, compensation for the past year's misdemeanours; and the restaurants resounding to the laughter of office parties, and businessmen in paper crowns blowing cardboard trumpets at giggling secretaries. At the Richmond Theatre the posters advertise Lionel Blair as Buttons in *Cinderella*. In Dickins & Jones a Falstaffian Father Christmas perpetuates childhood dreams (he was never permitted them) . . . The river dissolving into the mist, the silver sleet; the jammed bridge and the block of buses . . . In the park the wary eyes of deer concealed among the oak of Sidmouth Wood. And in Mortlake, in the cellars of Prévot, Pitman & Saunders, boxes are being loaded onto pallets, and Hamish, the cellar manager, is doing a fair imitation of Goering.

Kempton's wonderful cellars that he used to wander round inspecting just for pleasure; his lovely dimly-lit, cool cellars – subsequently modernised, half the wine auctioned off and the space restocked with pallet loads of crap. The galling thing is the stuff sells in gallons. And who is responsible for selling it? Who's got poor old Mike Chandler's job? Kempton – sales director of Prévot, Pitman & Saunders, purveyors of crap and paint-stripper, previously the respected Prévot Fine Wine Company, est. 1925 (by his paternal grandfather, whose spasmodic importing of a lethal pear liqueur laid legitimate claim to the company's nascency; no matter that a generation was skipped-out in the interim). Prévot, Pitman & Saunders: a spawning of Pitman & Saunders Construction. A builder and an accountant turned wine merchants. They've retained Kempton's surname to fool his few old, loyal customers that they are still buying quality. And he enacts the bluff, that's the worst of it.

'No room for sentiment,' says Pitman. 'You've got to think commercial, Kempton.' (Ke-empton, he says in his flat accent). 'That was your trouble. You didn't think big. Look how we've turned this business round. Profit – that's the name of the game.'

His clichés make Kempton writhe. His sentences are littered with expressions like 'scenario', and 'in terms of', and 'game', and 'basically'. Pitman thinks Uncle Vanya is a racehorse, and Duke Ellington the Queen's first cousin.

At their army-surplus desks the minions keep Pitman's (managing director) and Saunders' (financial director) clockwork in lucrative motion. Kempton's office had been the domain of Mike Chandler, fired on some trumped-up pretext, but really because he was gay. And also to make room for Kempton in his new, demoted role. So Kempton, who is still in touch with Mike, occupies his chair. And this morning that chair is conspicuous in its emptiness. On the wall to one side of it Vanessa and Cat laugh down from their frame, perfectly encaptured one summer's day a few years ago, perched on the low wall, swinging their bare legs. Oh ache, ache, maybe he should remove it. On his desk, clamouring for his attention: the white computer printouts of sales figures, the pink ones of orders, the blue of delivery, the green of customers who owe money; the letters of complaint, the letters of query, the rare one of praise; the lists of newly-opened restaurants, the list of this month's special offers; the rep's reports, the memos, the catering journals, the faxes from suppliers, the diary appointments . . . The, the, the. *His* business. But not any longer. He created it from nothing but a bottle of pear liqueur, then allowed it to die. God's hubris. And now he is no archangel to Pitman's and Saunder's combined mightiness.

He knows they are right: he was not commercially-minded enough to ride a recession. And if Vanessa hadn't—? But his business had been his hobby. It had been pleasurable. It had been gentlemanly and run on trust. The places he was supplying and offering extended credit to were falling victim, one after the other: restaurants, catering companies, independent off-licences, clubs. The wines he was shipping were too specialised, too expensive for today's requirements. Irrelevant that his won medals and awards and high praise in the newspaper wine columns. And French and Italian wine sales were affected by strong opposition from other countries. '– You've got to move with the times, Ke-empton.' His concession was to stock a couple of Californians – a red Zinfandel and a sweet semillon, and a riesling from Coonawarra, Australia; but people wanted names they knew. Kempton no longer understood his business. He still receives phone calls from some of the small French growers who used to supply him; and a powerful nostalgia courses through him as they converse in French. Promises to visit . . . And have you heard? Madame Richard's husband has died and she is struggling to keep the business going on her own. They are all struggling.

Kempton has never been particularly ambitious – Vanessa's voice, high with frustration, following him about; criticism in an eroding trickle that twice drove him elsewhere. But he has always had integrity, always been reliable. It comes of being a schoolmaster's son. And as a reaction against his mother. To date, his whole life has been a reaction against Minnie's influence, he realises now.

Jimmy Young's theme is blaring cheerfully from the kitchen radio. What is Kempton going to do all day? He can't just hang around in his study. He *should* do some business phoning, make appointments, cancel appointments. But a sudden perversity grabs at him, pushing him back into his chair as he is about to get up and dutifully fetch his briefcase. Something else is happening to him, besides his anger, besides his sorrow, pumping an alien kind of energy into him. It shoots through him in exhilarating gusts. He has never experienced anything like it before: the heady, reckless adrenalin of rebellion. No, I'm not going to make those calls. Let the customers phone the office and complain. Let all hell break loose. He would not be there to see it, to deal with it. Time for a showdown. He is fed up of their patronising attitudes. Do they think he doesn't know the snide remarks they make behind his back? that they call him The Blot (on the landscape)? And his colleagues pity him. What humiliation! And he has permitted it to happen. Well, he will leave the answer-phone on and not take any calls from the office. He will take tomorrow off and the day after that; in fact the whole week if he feels like it. He will go to the recycling bank and chuck all his bottles and cans and papers into the appropriate containers (the rewarding splintering of glass). He will do all his Christmas shopping; walk in Richmond Park; browse round the antiques centre; go to the library; perfect that tricky passage in *The Creation* when Harry, the choir master, claps his hands and shouts, 'Baritones,' in a pained voice, looking directly at him ... And barricade himself in the house against Pitman and Saunders. They can't get rid of him. He has a year and two months of his contract left to run. He cares not an iota about the business anymore. It is no longer his responsibility. He has severed the blood ties, as it were.

A curious amalgam of emotions jostle within Kempton, triggered by his crisis at the doctor's. And now he gets up and puts an old recording of Ella Fitzgerald on the player. Cole Porter's 'All Through The Night'. 'The day is the enemy, the night my friend,' undulates her molasses voice. Not true, not true, as his body and sheets entangle in bitter conflict night after night. Ella drowns out Jimmy Young and Mrs Jakes and the Hoover.

Back at his desk, Kempton is pensive. He senses that this morning is of immense importance, although in what way he does not know. He takes his fountain pen from its stand, positions the A4 pad squarely in front of him, puts on his glasses, pauses and chews on his lower lip, does an elaborate doodle of hearts and crosses and eyes in the margin, downs the glass of Lucozade, then writes a heading which he underlines heavily:

LIFE LIST.

2

The Runners

His life list is growing like a knitted scarf; first the various personae, then particular incidents; and these ignite a shard of memories – where? When? How? Why? Oh yes, that was the day we . . . An assault course of reminiscences, thoughts and emotions shunting each other for space; revived feelings of injustice or resentment, the softness of joy. The mind is not an orderly thing and he scrawls everything down as it comes to him, in no chronological sequence. The unlocking of Kempton. And he is completely engrossed – doesn't even notice Ella has stopped singing – still wearing his pinstriped suit as though about to attend a meeting, bent over his note pad, turning the pages as fast as he can write, barely able to keep up with the galloping memory chain.

'I'm off now.' Jerked back to the present by Mrs Jakes outside the door. Her feet creaking.

'OK.' He gets up reluctantly and opens it. She purses her lips at his wild appearance, his burnt cheeks and mussed hair, wisps on end from where he has been grabbing at it.

'You don't look well,' she says, wagging her finger. 'I'd go to bed if I was you.'

'I probably will,' he demurs, to keep the conversation brief. 'You found the money by the kettle?'

'Of course. As usual,' she says stiffly. And he knows she's thinking that they see each other so rarely – he's always at work when she comes – that he might at least chat a bit. He's not very good with small talk. Perhaps he should discuss the Irish problem with her, but that's a bit heavy, and emotive. And he doesn't know her views. He could end up inadvertently offending her and losing her altogether, and then where would he be? He settles on, 'Will you be with your daughter over Christmas?'

'Yes. There'll be ten of us. I'm going there Christmas Eve. We'll go to mass. I'll be along on Friday then.'

'Yes. And if I don't see you, have a first rate Christmas. I'll leave an extra envelope by the kettle.' He is struck by a sudden idea. 'What perfume do you like, Mrs Jakes?'

She chortles – a smoker's guttural sound – knotting her scarf into the beige collar of her coat, settling her jowls into it. 'I've worn 4711 all my life.'

Finally she leaves. The whole house to himself. Three storeys of it, of Vanessa's input and manic energy and peremptory disregard for his opinion. A tall, skinny house, too big for just him. He only uses bits of it; the other part he sort of creeps around in. And, like every other Tuesday, there are clean sheets on his bed, with hospital corners, and his shirts warm and pungent from the iron, hanging in his wardrobe, the sleeves ruler-creased. Christmas cards grouped on windowsills. And what a farce they are: 'This year we really *must* get together'; having said the identical thing last year and the year before that – though at the time, in a mood of bonhomie, one genuinely meant it. This year several are from lone, predatory women. No one he really fancies though. Damaged women.

The sepia-toned day, the venal branches of skeletal trees; and he feels like a schoolboy playing truant. Winces thinking about the spectacle he made of himself at the doctor's. He would cross the street to avoid seeing the man again. He wishes he could forget about it, but he can't dismiss it. He feels scraped-skin raw, his emotions dangerously close to the surface. He exchanges the Ella Fitzgerald for an old Callas record and goes back to his desk; tears out a clean page from the notepad and writes 4711 (do they still make it?), then adds: gloves and smoked salmon, Minnie. Cat – watch? Book? CD? Go, Asian Emporium? Tree. Puts one of his agate weights on it – amongst other things he collects semi-precious minerals – and turns back to his original list.

The personae. Minnie first, naturally. And what a deliberately coy soubriquet for such a big, dominating presence. Out of Minnie by Edmond, he thinks, to use her own jargon. Hmph. He smiles, imitating her in his head. Hmph. Her character hewn from a thousand race meetings. Not a photograph of her without her briar pipe.

His father, a history and French teacher: tall and turkey-necked, stoop-shouldered, a high, domed forehead and receded hairline, and the hair which remained, white interspersed with wings of washed-out yellow. The face, the big, gleaming head and doleful brown eyes (Kempton's) of an intellectual – and also an aesthete: lover of beauty, of the arts, of fine silver, exotic bow ties and fancy waistcoats; erudite and gentle and ponderous-mannered; finally, demolished.

Himself, Kempton: toe-the line acquiescent boy, purposeful young man, mostly-dutiful husband, doting father. Widower.

Vanessa: the beautiful young woman whom men and women alike turned to stare at, the coquette, demanding wife, mother; manic-depressive.

Cat. His Cat: his nature-child, as he called her when she was a little girl, philanthropic, dreamy, humorous and stubborn; champion of causes; liberated woman. And now? And now. Peter. Grudgingly, he goes on the list: self-confessed dilettante, restaurateur, writer, polo-player, seducer.

He adds Pitman, Saunders in brackets, and draws a squiggle underneath. The eight runners in an arduous race who have had an effect on his life. There are others, but their impact has not been lasting. The past leans hard on his shoulder, challenging him.

He holds Minnie at least partly responsible for his father's death. Remembers helping pack up the house when his parents separated. His father on his knees in the library, heaping books into crates. 'What am I going to do with them all? Where'll I put them? I've no room. Why's she doing this at our time of life?'

He was sixty-five, newly-retired – eleven years older than Minnie. He had been forty-five when Kempton was born. And Kempton, on summer vacation from Oxford, said inadequately, 'Well, you know what she's like.'

'Yes, but not this. Not *this*.' He gestured helplessly. 'We ticked along. We didn't interfere in each other's lives. I never prevented her from doing what she wanted. It's such a – such a wrench, such an – upheaval, you understand.'

The kitchen table was piled with rusting cake tins, old potties, antiquated electrical gadgets with greasy cords, plastic containers, tins of tobacco, copies of the *Sporting Life*.

'So hard to know what to salvage,' his mother said when he wandered into the kitchen. You never know what you might need. Hmph.'

'It all looks disgusting. You should chuck the lot,' Kempton said bitterly, stalking out of the room.

'Oh dear, dear, dear, someone's got the hump,' came her taunting after him.

Her wedding dress on the bonfire. For a moment, filled with air, it developed a body inside, and then, as though speared, it deflated and caught alight: the ivory crepe de Chine and lace darkening and curling before being engulfed. Minnie in her felt gardening hat whooping in delight. She was cruel, Kempton thought, hating her. And from an upper window his father's wan face pressed to the pane.

'It's absurd how much importance people attach to their possessions,' Minnie said as she fed the bonfire with the accumulation of years.

'Don't you care about Father's feelings?' Kempton asked, peering up at the flat darkness of the window where his father had been (and what about his own feelings?).

'I never noticed that caring about people's feelings got one very far, Kempton,' she said; and took her matches from her tweed greatcoat pocket to relight her pipe.

'I never noticed that you tried,' he countered.

He disappeared gladly to France for the summer, through to the end of September. It was then, grape picking for money under a lowering sun, he decided on the direction of his future. Not history after all. With typical thoroughness, he began establishing contacts during his Bordeaux sojourn; made lists; planted the pips.

His father died two years later in his drab flat in Hammersmith overlooking the railway – he to whom the surrounding environment had always been so important. And the river not in sight. 'But he used to walk there every evening,' his neighbour told Kempton. 'Fed the gulls and ducks.'

His mother was late for the church service; smelt of whisky when she slid into the seat next to him; her brown trilby hat askew. Her racing hat. She had slotted in the funeral between *races*.

So the books were never unpacked. Kempton has them

all now. A prize collection of first editions and limited editions worth a great deal of money. His favourite: Johnson's life by Boswell. Hears his father's tones, reverent, quoting from it.

Yet he can't ever remember his parents quarrelling.

'You can't quarrel if you don't converse,' Minnie said.

'Then why didn't you converse?'

'About what?'

'Gardening. Archaeology. You shared those.'

'Oh the primroses are coming up nicely dear. And I would date that piece of pot from the second century AD, not the first BC.'

'You know what I mean.'

'And you, Kempton, have no idea what *I* mean.'

Himself and Vanessa bickering; her shrilling and himself retreating – which enflamed her more; which drove him further into stubborn silence. Vanessa claimed he didn't try and 'get into her head'. That was a stupid, overused expression, he countered. She would be riled because he never displayed any jealousy, worse, apparently never experienced it. Provoking him, flirting outrageously, sobbing at his detachedness, at his indulgent smile. And himself wearied by all the show of passion, trying to laugh her out of it. Sometimes they would be visiting friends and would have to leave early on some pretext because her mood would have swung from one extreme to another within a couple of hours. He dreaded a week of elation when she gave her all, scarcely went to bed at night – needed no sleep – whirled faster and faster, buoyed up like a child at a party – I'm so happy, everything's worth it to feel this happy; it always ended in desolation.

'You can't imagine the pain inside you. It's a solid, evil, blackness,' she said once, trying to describe it to him after one of her bad spells. 'Ghastly, ghastly despair. It doesn't matter how anyone tries to reason with you. You don't care about anyone around you. They don't exist. There's nothing but the agony inside you.'

In between the vacillations she was loving and loveable, warm and effervescent and generous; tactile and impulsive. Would do anything for anyone. Loved to entertain. Wanted to please everyone. A magnet to all who met and knew her.

Vanessa's black-lashed grey eyes. Vanessa in her black stockings, clawing his back when they made love, beside herself – Oh God, oh *God* – drawing him into her with her strong muscles, pouring her wetness around him.

Beautiful, beautiful Vanessa, refusing to get out of bed, languishing there; monotone voice. Nothing, she stated. Pointless. Nothing and no one can fulfil me. He would spoon-feed her through the day from his phone in the office: '. . . Darling, listen to me, go and fetch the cordless phone from downstairs . . . Please. For *me*. Just that one thing. I'll hang on.' Waiting interminably – what was she doing? Then her voice: 'Kempton?' 'Yes, I'm here. Now you're up, don't go back to bed. Go into the kitchen, put on the kettle, tell me as you're doing it . . .'

Everything he could to keep her going when she threw away the lithium. Could he have done more? He felt so inadequate.

And other times he might phone and get the answer-machine. Where was she? Fear rising in him. And off home he would tear, clammy-palmed with terror. He couldn't keep an eye on her every second though.

Failure. Kempton is a failure. And nobody, but nobody, unless they have been through the same thing, could know what it was like. Is like. And all he ever coveted is ordinariness. Other men yearned for the heights; not Kempton.

Gossamer, Minnie referred to her nastily. 'The only thing Gossamer and I have in common is our ability to miscarry,' she told Kempton.

'Thank God you've got nothing in common. I didn't marry Vanessa to have a replica of you,' he replied.

She knew nothing of Vanessa's sickness. Kempton would not give her the satisfaction of thinking their relationship was anything less than perfect. After the deed he had similarly fooled himself. Theirs had been a perfect marriage; how could she have done it? His jagged grief – even that could not be straightforward. Cat sequestered away within her own dreams and silences. Where is Cat now to rescue him? He feels betrayed by his daughter, betrayed by his wife, betrayed by his mother. Perhaps he isn't a misanthrope, but he would have every right to be a misogynist. But Kempton loves women. Not in a philandering way; he loves and needs female company. Likes the other perspective, as he puts it. And they seem to find him attractive.

I don't want to live alone. I don't like living alone. It's unnatural.

Stringing out the days. He didn't know how to deal with Cat's sorrow and his own simultaneously. He could give her his arms, but not his voice or ears. Sitting down to silent meals cooked by his daughter – and up she would suddenly spring and walk, very upright and deliberate, from the kitchen.

'Let her stay with me for a bit,' Minnie, who adored Cat, suggested.

And on his own, about ten days after the event, he staggered downstairs, early-morning sludge-visioned, to the kitchen to fix himself a coffee, taking a mug at random from the cupboard. Black coffee: like inexistence, he thought. He shuffled in his pyjamas across the tiled floor to the table; clasped the mug, damp-hot between his hands that had lost their meaning, that had stroked intimate places. He raised it to his lips, and then he noticed it: her lipstick stain, alive on the rim. For seconds she was trapped there, in the cameo of his tears. Vanessa was on the mug, in his mouth.

In the dirty-linen basket in the bathroom were a pair of her knickers: ivory, silky, flimsy things; the gusset slightly marked where it had nudged between her legs. He held them to his nose and inhaled the faint odour of her, slept with them under his cheek. And the bedclothes were the same ones they had shared, and he would only change them when they became too filthy to leave any longer.

Going through the contents of her handbag – make-up, brush, wallet, keys, cleaning docket, scrunched-up Kleenex – he came across her diary, and there marked for the day she did it was a business appointment at a client's house. 'Take swatches,' was scribbled by it. It should have been an ordinary day for her. And the next day, 28 February, was marked, 'My birthday?!!! Big O. Yuk'.

Gradually the days took a pigeon's steps towards normality. But the nights became worse. He would lie awake, rigidly still, in resistance to his body which was guiltily alive. It was the longest he could remember going without sex and his erectness tortured him. During his marriage making love had been so integral that he had forgotten the separateness of the body and mind. Now they were opposing factions: the one craved and the other repelled. He was ashamed of his body's audacity with its detachment from grief. Ashamed, even as he necessarily satiated it.

The house was like a florist's. And the water grew stale and stank with the gases like human excrement. The fridge was sour with its contents. All the rooms were washed in stillness.

Incidents – a shred here, a nibble there; meandering reminiscences; Kempton's sizzling close-to-the-edge mood. The steady heartbeat of the longcase clock just outside in the hall. Spike purring on his lap, claws grating back and forth against his thighs. Rower's thighs. He had rowed first for his school then his college. And the phone ringing makes him start in his chair so that Spike leaps down from him, ears pinned back, and flees the room. A thin coating of grey fur clings to Kempton's suit.

Over the answer-machine comes first his own recorded message then Peter's voice: 'Well hello there—' fake American drawl. 'It's your old chum here, if I still qualify as that. I phoned your office to order some paint stripper for a staff do, but your secretary said you were at home ill. Sorry to hear that. How about, when you're better, meeting up for a drink? I think we ought to talk. Cheers.'

'No I don't think so,' Kempton mutters. Peter with his need always to clear the air. The only man Kempton has ever met who embraces, even kisses on either cheek, another man. Completely without secrets. Impossible to insult or shock or rile.

But Kempton's thought flow is disrupted, and upstairs he traipses to change out of his business suit. His mufti consists of beige cords (he doesn't get on with jeans: they always go like concrete after being washed and he ends up sweating and irritable as he struggles to squeeze into them), the nearest shirt in his wardrobe – which happens to be a blue stripe (presses it, sweet-smelling, to his nostrils for an instant), Aran pullover, Argyll socks (he has long big toes which invariably poke holes in them), brown suede lace-up shoes. He finds getting dressed rather a chore. So if Peter phoned him, where is Cat, he wonders, surveying his own drooping brown eyes in the mirror (theatrically lit all round: Vanessa's make-up place), as he washes his hands and splashes water on his face. Tips his head forward slightly to inspect his hair, fingering through it. No more seems to have disappeared in the last month. He has resigned himself to frontal baldness in the not too distant future. But – just two things. If this has to be the case, don't let his head be like his father's glossy dome;

and please, no curious tuft like a ram's curl left behind in the front as a kind of mocking token. He would shave it to match the rest if that happened. Meanwhile he sites a 'logger's' hat on the vulnerable area to protect it from the elements.

He takes his sheepskin jacket (his last present from Vanessa) from the hall cupboard, his umbrella, braces himself for the sleet, the crowds, and out he goes to rejoin life. He barely budges from Richmond nowadays, he realises – waving at a neighbour, then swiftly following that, the owner from the small garage two roads away. he hardly bothers with London at all. There is everything he needs locally. Set-in-his-ways Kempton ('God you can be boring,' Vanessa levelled at him). He must go to the cemetery. He hasn't been for a while. For the first year he went every day.

Kempton, loping down Hill Rise into the Christmas-y town. Peers into the antique market on the way; it is packed, tempering his urge to browse. Past the Salamis Taverna – and the celestial aromas of spices and herbs evoking Greek island holidays, wafting through the door as a customer pushes it open. The owner, whom Kempton knows, spots him and waves, shouts cheerfully in his earthy accent, 'Good afternoon Mr Kempton (never having grasped the complications of his name), and Kempton, lifting his hand in a reciprocal gesture, glances at his watch and sees that it *is* the afternoon; almost one thirty. Another couple of hours and it will be growing dark. For God's sake, it's dark already. Today never got light to start with. Past Beeton's; and Joe's Bar and Grill. His haunts. His saliva glands starting to activate with the heady mix of odours. For someone with food poisoning he's pretty hungry. This makes him smile. Two fingers to Pitman. Kempton will show him he will not be chucked about. In fact he may even take himself off to the cinema. See *Babe* and join the veggie set. No chance of that.

• Kempton's Journey

The novelty of rebellion sends little waves of glee through him, and he hums to himself, that elusive passage from *The Creation* – ah, nearly had it then – is experimenting with the long run without taking a breath in the middle when, wham, he collides with someone. There is a sickening crash of glass or china as bags tumble to the ground, accompanied by an anguished shriek, followed by a high-pitched tirade.

'I'm sorry. I'm terribly sorry.' He crouches down, his hat meeting the sopping woollen one of the woman's bent head, and helps her pick up bits of yellow china.

'Why didn't you fucking well look where you were going?' she says, furiously gathering fragments and throwing them in the Dickins & Jones carrier.

'I'll pay for everything.'

'You're fucking right you will.'

They stand up simultaneously.

'Oh, hi Kempton.' Suzanne Harrison, one of his two past transgressions. Wife of a rather sanctimonious solicitor. He hasn't seen her for at least two years – and then it was briefly, at the Orange Tree theatre. Brecht's *The Good Woman of Setzuan*. In the bar, while her husband was ordering drinks, she cornered Kempton by the lapels and pulled him towards her. 'If ever you want a good woman you know where to find her.'

They hug. Her cheeks beneath the wet hat are cold.

He grins delightedly. 'It's great to see you.' Runs his hands up and down her thick coat, beneath which he recalls a spectacular body.

'You too. Stranger,' she adds accusingly.

'Well you know . . .' He shrugs. Looks hopeless for a moment.

'Yes,' she says, then her tone changes. 'No, actually that's not true. I couldn't know. Nobody could.'

He stares at her.

'The new me,' she explains. 'I'm training as a counsellor.'

Kempton starts laughing. He has a loud, slow, from-the-depths-of-a-cave laugh which tends to make other people smile.

'What's so funny?' Poking him in the back with her gloved hand.

'Too complicated to explain.'

'I'm also breeding bloodhounds. My bitch has just had her second litter. I could sell you one if you like.'

'You're jok-ing . . .' And even as he says it his face undergoes a transformation. His features clear and seem to lift (and isn't there perhaps a slight resemblance in Kempton's crumpled, irregular features between him and a bloodhound?). Why not? Why on earth not? He can already see himself, training it, taking it for walks in Richmond Park, resting his feet on it beneath his desk at the office.

She studies him, lips in a moue. 'I take it that's a yes.'

'Let me think about it.' The pragmatic man takes over.

'Oh come on Kempton, you've decided already. You know you have. In the last five seconds you have just become the proud owner of a bloodhound with a pedigree as long as your face. They're the most amazing dogs. Terribly intelligent. Loving. Think what fun you'd have.'

And think of it: an affectionate companion that didn't nag, didn't suffer from depression, would revere him unquestioningly.

'I don't know . . .' Standing on the pavement in the rain, surrounded by her shopping and broken purchases; her grinning face freckled with rain. Feet skirting around them. 'Pluto would be a good name wouldn't it? Isn't Pluto a bloodhound?'

'I believe so.'

What an extraordinary day.

They end up in Dickins & Jones together. The china department is heaving. She replaces the broken jug and dish.

'How do I know you're not ripping me off?' Kempton says, writing out a cheque for £43.98. 'For all I know the stuff that broke only cost £10.99.'

'For all you know maybe it did.' She folds the cheque and puts it securely in her wallet; hands a card to the salesgirl.

'Who pays the account, you or your husband?' he asks Suzanne suspiciously.

'Stop being so picky, Kempton.'

'A deposit on a puppy then,' he barters.

'Not on your nellie.'

'Services rendered then?' he murmurs, raising hopeful eyebrows at her.

'Why aren't you at work?' she answers.

He takes this as affirmation. Something to look forward to. But first she helps him get into the Christmas spirit: she picks out suede gauntlets for Minnie. The 4711 for Mrs Jakes. A green crushed-velvet scarf for his secretary. For Cat, a chrome watch as starters. Nothing for Peter. Normally he would give him a bottle of Taylors and something else; a CD perhaps, or a book. He buys himself a food hamper.

'Who's that for?'

'Myself.'

'Really?'

'Yes.'

'That's healthy.' She gives a sequence of slow, thoughtful nods.

'What do you mean?'

'Treating yourself. Liking yourself. Or at least trying to.'

'Oh for God's sake Suzanne. Cut the counsellor bit.'

But maybe there's a smidgen of truth in what she says.

Kempton's bedroom. All Vanessa-frills and roses in full chintzy bloom. Prints hanging from bows. Draped and canopied bed.

'Fucking hell.' Suzanne emits a kind of hiss through

her teeth. He had forgotton how irritating she could be. He is beginning to go off her and to wish he hadn't made his remark about 'services rendered'. Their previous sessions, about five years ago, had taken place in her house. Remembering them makes him feel aroused again.

She pulls off her ghastly hat, and her long beige hair straggles out, damp and crumpled. She is really quite plain, but endearingly unselfconscious, and her eyes are lively and intelligent. And her body; it makes up for everything. Really voluptuous. Layers of unflattering clothing before he can get near it. Eventually they stand by the edge of the bed naked.

'Your body's fantastic.' He circles his hands slowly around her shoulders then cups her breasts.

'You're in pretty good nick yourself.'

'I'm losing my hair,' he laments, kissing her.

'Only on your head,' she says against his mouth, moving her hand downwards. 'You're still the hairiest man I know.'

'Not on my back.'

'No. I have an aversion to hairy backs.'

'So I'm in with a chance?' He moves her backwards so that she is against the wall and pins her there.

'You just might be . . . Oh fuck that feels good.'

The nice thing about sex with Suzanne is it's so uncomplicated and comfortable. No question of love or grand passion. No demands or jealousy. Just vigorous, wholehearted, straightforward, this-is-fun-let's-forget-our-problems sex. But afterwards he becomes pensive.

'Did it mean I didn't love her – when you and I had our thing? I mean that bothers me now, that I was unfaithful to Vanessa. And there was another time—' He has the need to confess. 'I had another fling.'

'I know.'

'How?' He props himself up on an elbow and turns to her astonished (how odd to be lying beside her in this frothy bed).

'With Janet Ridley. She told me.'

'She *told* you?'

'Sure. Don't look so aghast, Kempton. Women talk to each other. Yap-yap. Don't you know that by now? You really don't know the first thing about women do you?'

Kempton shakes his head dismally.

And did they compare notes, he wonders. Glancing at her he can tell from her expression that, yes, they did.

Cat driving to Richmond from Wimbledon in her Ford Fiesta with its Disabled badge. Thinking: her poor father with food poisoning, thinking that perhaps that's what's wrong with her. Or perhaps not. And if not, how to tell him, as there is one thing Cat would not contemplate. Cat belongs to Pro-Life.

'I promise I'll pick out the best male for you,' Suzanne says, pulling her thick brown polo-neck over her head (hair flattened and electric, eyebrows upside-down). 'He'll be ready at nine weeks. That's just after Christmas.'

'Couldn't I have him for Christmas?'

'All I want for Christmas is a bow-wow,' she chants. 'No, I'm very strict about that. Not a day before he's nine weeks old. And he'll have to have another inoculation at twelve weeks. And be wormed.'

'Oh God, I'm really not sure.' Back flood the misgivings. All the hassle. Puddles. Shit everywhere. Newspaper. Torn cushions – and feathers everywhere. 'Maybe it's a crazy idea.'

'You and Pluto are made for each other.' She appraises him, sucking in her lips. 'You even look a bit bloodhoundish.'

At the front door she hugs him, then stands back. 'By the way Kempton, it *doesn't* mean you didn't love her.'

'She could be so – difficult.' The relief of admitting it.

'And you loved her in spite of that. But it wore you down.'

'Yes.'

Extraordinary tears threatening the backs of his eyes again. She gives his hand a firm little shake and leaves – at the same moment as he sees his daughter's car draw up. Talk about timing. And Kempton, physically spent, mentally bewildered, rather battered and shattered after his day, looks appropriately pallid; as though he just conceivably has been ill with food poisoning.

3

Favourite

Something past six, and the sky is a graduated black, the road beneath glistens patent. The street light nearest Kempton's house throws out a wide globe of illumination that encompasses Cat. Her ungainly, lopsided progress towards him from the road, up the short path then the three steps – with that huge radiating smile of hers – still makes his stomach contract in anguish. But he knows better than to help her, in the same way one does not complete a stammerer's sentence for him. She will get there in her own time. A bunch of daffodils rests diagonally across her chest, a splurge of yellow Spring brightness against the black of her coat, contrasting with the wiry darkness of her hair (in a plait), the paleness of her Modigliani face. Her little vanity case – her mother's – bangs against the side of her good leg: so she's come for the night? To look after him? Sometimes he feels weak, so filled with love for her is he.

'What a lovely, lovely surprise. It's smackeroo to see you,' he says, opening his arms to her when she finally makes it to the doorway. They have a whole vocabulary between them of words or expressions she invented over the years.

'I expected you to be in bed,' she says, kissing him on the lips. She is tall, and sapling slender.

'I revived.' Drawing her into the warmth of the hall, one arm still around her, then into his study where the fire is making patterns on the wall. The answer-phone light flickering with the wrath of Pitman. The desk spilling over with the chaotic signs of a flurry of activity.

Cat takes it all in. 'Dad, you haven't been *working*' – settling beside him on the sofa, trailing a finger down the line carved into his cheek.

'Not really. Not proper work.' He captures her finger and kisses it, and she swivels round slightly, studying him shrewdly. He smiles under her scrutiny, detonates one of his single loud drum-bursts of laughter.

'Kempton, I don't actually think you're ill.'

'Well—' hesitates. '—Not *ill*, ill.'

'God that sounds cryptic. Shall we play Twenty Questions?'

'No. I'll tell you later.'

'Peter said your secretary sounded harassed. And he could hear Pitman yelling in the background.'

'That would be par for the course. So to what do I owe this pleasure?'

'I was worried, what do you think?'

'And you were prepared to leave your *boyfriend's* side for the night?'

'Dad, if you're going to start, I'm leaving this second.'

She detaches herself from him, making ready, grasping the edge of the sofa as though about to stand up. But he puts his hand on top of one of hers to restrain her.

'OK. I won't make one sarcastic comment, I promise.' But she can't tether his thoughts.

He gets up to put a record on. 'I think something jolly,' he says. Her eyes follow him affectionately. Poor Kempton – he does have a lot to contend with. He certainly looks rather dishevelled this evening. And as he fingers through his selection of records on the shelf – 'This one? No. Ah, what about – no, too heavy. I know, maybe . . . Ah, this would be different' – she wants to rush up to him and embrace him. Her father can be so *cute* (he can't stand her telling him that, so she does it to annoy him: Oh Kempton you are so *cute*). He can also be unimaginative, prosaic and intolerant. And narrow-minded. How is she going to tell him? She could tell him now. She could prepare him; say, 'Dad I think I might be—' rather than, 'I am.' The *fait accompli*. But he looks particularly vulnerable. And she doesn't want to ruin Christmas, which is going to have its let-downs for him as it is. Is there ever a good time to impart bad news?

Her father is in the midst of placing Lee Wiley – 'Night in Manhattan' – on the turntable, when a shrilling comes from Cat's coat, which is draped over his desk chair.

'Good God, what's that?'

'My mobile.'

'Your *what*?'

'Wart bought it for me. He says it's dangerous for any woman driving alone not to have one.' Wart is her nickname for Peter, whose good looks do not impress her.

She stretches across the sofa to fish the phone out of the pocket. A strip of pale, narrow waist is exposed as her skimpy jumper rides up. She always seems to wear the wrong clothes for the season.

'Hi Wart.'

Cat grinning down the phone. Cheshire-cat Cat. Twin rows of big white teeth. Like breeze-blocks, she jokes about them. Like Kempton's in fact. He watches her, listens to her furiously.

'. . . I'm OK. Stop *fussing* . . . I will too . . .'

Can't stand hearing her sounding womanly and warm; her throaty wood-pigeon voice. A giggle laced with sexuality. Knowing it's Peter the other end. 'He's fine,' she says,

• Kempton's Journey

and glances over to him (still squatting by the record player, Lee Wiley gliding round and round silently), and he glares back and stomps into the kitchen, unable to listen to any more. He paces round, Pitman fashion, for a bit then calms down slightly, stoops to open the fridge to see if there's anything for dinner. The shelves reveal a wedge of Cheddar that has gone like chalk in its opened packet, a tub of Flora, one and a half tomatoes, two sausages, a half pint of milk, one egg, six chocolate mousses – he's got a nerve to phone her here, he really has. Buried in the fridge and in thought, Kempton is startled by a pair of arms enveloping him from behind.

'Give me a shnuggle,' Cat says. And when could he ever resist her? He stands up and obliges her.

'There's no food,' he says, gesturing to the fridge. She peers inside. 'See what you mean. Anything in the larder cupboard?'

'I don't know. A packet of pasta I think. You know, those twirly things. Brown rice. I'm sure there's some brown rice. And some tins of tuna.'

'I could make a sausage and tuna risotto.'

'Or we could go out. I'll take you out. I'd like to do that. I haven't taken my daughter out in ages.'

'I can see that reproachful look coming on Kempton.'

'No, no,' he protests quickly.

'You know what I'd really like?'

'What?'

'To go to the cinema. To see *Babe*. I noticed it's on down the road. Wart refuses to see it.'

'I'll take you,' Kempton says immediately. One up on Peter. 'I'd been thinking about going anyway.'

'Popcorn,' she says, linking her arm through his. 'A giant tub. Followed by a four-cheese pizza.' Ravenous suddenly, having starved herself throughout the day.

* * *

Really, he could punch people the way they stare at Cat and then avert their gaze as she limps, head up, across the restaurant to their table. Completely different from the way they would look at her simply because here is a refreshingly natural attractive young woman. And once they are seated there are more surreptitious glances, and now it is obviously their relationship that's in question. He could conceivably be her lover: there is no real resemblance except for their height and smile. Her eyes are her mother's: grey irises with brown rims, a thick black wedge of lashes, but steady, with a wryness in their expression. Vanessa's were always on the move. Is this how it is for Peter when they go out together? If anything, Cat looks young for her age, which is not quite twenty. And she rarely wears make-up. Lecher. Peter is nothing but a lecher. I'm her father, Kempton wants to stand up and shout to the room. *I'm* not like that.

'Lots of extra mushrooms,' Cat is saying. 'And garlic bread.'

She never seems to notice other people, Kempton marvels. Is quite content cloistered away on her own little patch. He turns his attention to the wine list – his glasses are half way down his nose, settled on its bump. 'There's a decent looking Barbaresca here. Let's spoil ourselves and have a bottle of that.'

The waiter comes over to take their order.

'I think we'd better have the garlic bread now,' Kempton says. 'The young lady's hungry. And the wine at the same time. Number 32.'

The waiter bends over the wine list, following Kempton's finger pointing to the Barbaresca Riserva 1985.

'I'm afraid that one's deleted from the list.'

'What are you talking about? It's printed here. You're staring at it.'

'No, I mean we don't stock it.'

Kempton makes an exasperated sound in his throat. 'I

don't believe it—' he had been really looking forward to it. 'Why don't you stock it?'

'We don't sell enough.'

'Then why have it on your list?' Kempton snaps.

'Steam, Dad,' sings Cat sweetly – her code word for whenever he gets het up, which he tends to do about little things – and makes a twirling gesture round her ears, to imply smoke coming out of them.

'OK. We'll have the Barolo '91. Do you have *that*?' Gives an exaggerated sigh.

'I'll go and check.'

Kempton rolls his eyes upwards as the waiter disappears.

'You get so wound up Dad. It's such a tiny thing to get so wound up about.'

'The point is they're supposed to be running a—' He breaks off. Who is he to accuse anyone else of inefficiency in running a business?

'Point taken,' he says.

The waiter returns. 'We have it. Well actually it's the '92 now.'

'Don't worry. That's fine. We'll have that. I'm sure it's just as good.' Kempton, contrite and magnanimous now.

The Barolo duly arrives. Cat watches her father swilling the wine around in his mouth, his cheeks puffing like a guinea-pig's. He takes it so *seriously*. She resists the urge to smile, winks instead at the young waiter. On the table: a basket of hot, herby bread oozing with the garlic butter melted in the centre of each round chunk; black, squidgy olives surrounded by thick green oil; a small white saucer of fat peanuts (they look like embryos, thinks Cat. Oh God); and Kempton, having approved the wine, crams a handful into his mouth.

'I can't stop thinking about the film,' she says. 'The piglet's face. It was so cute, so human. It really seemed to smile. And its little beseeching eyes. Wasn't it cute?'

'I'm a little concerned that you use the same word to apply to a piglet as you do to your father,' Kempton says.

'Aw, Kempton.' Blows a kiss at him.

'Anyway, I'm afraid it won't stop me eating pork.'

'Cold-hearted man.'

'But I *am* in favour of kinder conditions for livestock. You know that.'

'Yes I know . . . And I loved the noise the duck's feet made as it padded about inside the house. Plap. Not *F*lap. Definitely plap-plap.'

'Silly.' He reaches forward to tweak her chin.

Sometimes she can be such a child still, that's what hurts particularly. And this evening he has noticed her gnawing her index finger quite a lot, which she does when something is preoccupying her.

'Plap – So, Kempton, what's up?' she says briskly, throwing him, as she always does, with her abrupt change of mood and manner. To Cat her sudden pronouncements or actions are normal and not abrupt since in her own head she will have been mulling over whatever it is for some while.

'What do you mean?'

'Well you didn't go to work and you haven't got food poisoning. You said you'd tell me.'

'It's hard to explain.' He crumbles a chunk of garlic bread between his thumb and forefinger.

'Try. I'm a good listener.'

And there – this is the paradox in her: the wise, mature Cat versus the childlike one. The transition is not yet fully made, nor is it ready to be. I don't really know her, he realises with a jolt. Oh, on one level, but not another. Is that all one can hope for – all of us, ever, to know each other up to a point and not beyond it, though we call ourselves close?

The waiter heading towards them with plates of pizzas

aloft; setting them down with a flourish. Then the black pepper ritual. Cat waiting for Kempton's response, patient-expressioned.

'I went to the doctor this morning,' he tells her when they are alone. 'I haven't been sleeping properly. So I wanted some pills. But the doctor wouldn't dole them out just like that.'

'No of course not. That wouldn't be responsible. He'd want to know why you weren't sleeping before he gave you anything.'

'Yes, that *is* what he wanted to know.'

Cuts into his Mexican pizza – melted cheese in long skeins from his fork. He winds it round. No he cannot tell his daughter what happened this morning. It is far too humiliating – he is still smarting from it. And he is supposed to be a strong, solid figure who protects her and looks after her, even lies to her to shield her if necessary. It would not do to let her know what happened. She has been exposed far too much, with her mother, without being exposed to his weaknesses. He feels frequently that he has let her down badly as a father, that he hasn't protected her enough, or given her enough guidance. She seems to have brought herself up somehow, without assistance from either of her parents. And is this just one of the reasons she has latched onto Peter? As an alternative father figure?

'Dad?' Her tender, brushed-grass voice. Her hand reaching across the white tablecloth (already tomato-stained) to cover his that is gripped tensely round his fork. 'What is it?'

And with the sweetness in her tone, her beautiful, generous, grey eyes, it is almost too much for him again. He nearly – but with effort just contains himself – so nearly finds himself in danger of blubbing again. What is wrong with him? Like a menopausal woman. The male menopause; is that what he's going through?

Cat observing her father's clenched features, his reddening eyes, his valiant effort not to cede to his emotion. She waits for his face to resume its composure; leans back slightly, lightening the pressure of her hand.

'I've had rather a lot on my mind, that's all,' he says finally, in a normal voice. 'I suppose everything's caught up with me rather.'

'You mean Mummy?'

'Yes. Of course, yes. But other things too. My business. And—' Looks at her gravely. Her eyes don't waver.

'Me?'

He makes a succession of clicking noises with his tongue against the roof of his mouth, as he decides whether to discuss it or not. 'Yes, he says then. 'You. Your accident. It was quite ghastly for me. I feel selfish saying it. But as a father, I can't—'

'I know Dad. It's all right. I do know.'

'And now – seeing your poor leg, your lovely legs . . . You're so brave. It kills me. I don't know how you're so brave.'

'I've got no option. Anyway, it doesn't feel brave. It's really not that important.'

'You say that . . . So, well I thought I was used to all these things. And now there's your—' Twists his lips into a tight bud.

'My affair with Peter.'

'Yes.'

'I can't make any of these things better for you, Dad. You have to do it yourself.'

'And don't you think I'm trying to? I have been trying to.'

'No Dad. You've been blocking yourself, that's all.'

'That's probably as good a way as any. So, what about you and Peter? How am I supposed to make that better for myself?'

• Kempton's Journey

'You could be glad I'm happy.'
'Happy.' He repeats it, rolling his eyes skywards. Gives a small, disparaging laugh.
'Yes,' she says. 'Happy.'
'For how long?'
'How long is happiness ever for?'
And that gets to him. For several minutes they eat in thoughtful but not acrimonious silence.
'I started doing a kind of life-list today,' Kempton tells her suddenly.
'What do you mean?'
'You know – people, memories, events that have affected me.'
'Minnie must feature pretty strongly.'
'Let's say it's more than a walk-on part . . . But you see, darling, I realised something else. It was extraordinary. It occurred to me that all my life I've always done the right, the expected thing. And today something in me snapped. I had the oddest urge to rebel.'
Cat studying her father with that penetrating intensity which always makes him smile. She is reading psychology at St Hilda's – wants to be a criminal psychologist, of all things.
She twists round to get something out of her coat pocket – she rarely carries a bag.
'Not your mobile phone,' he says, putting his hand to his forehead in mock horror.
'No. It's an extra Christmas present for you. I saw it today in a bookshop. I haven't wrapped it, I'm afraid.'
'Darling it's another six days to Christmas. Won't I be seeing you?'
'Yes of course. But I think it makes sense to give it to you now. A propos of what you were saying, I think you might get something out of it.' Hands him the small package.
He opens the Waterstone's bag: 'Jean-Jacques Rousseau, *Meditations of a Solitary Walker*,' he reads out loud. 'Thank

you darling, that's very kind.' Leans across the table to kiss her.

'It's taken from his *Reveries of the Solitary Walker.*'

'You're a very thoughtful girl.' Slightly bewildered by her choice.

'It's just I think it could be particularly relevant now.'

'Why?'

'You'll see.'

He transfers the mini book to his own jacket pocket, and broaches the subject that has been bothering him for about a week.

'And speaking of Christmas—' he has to be careful, Christmas always seems to stoke up passions, '—um – we haven't discussed arrangements. What are your plans?'

Now don't come on all heavy, he warns himself.

And Cat, too, is aware that she must tread equally carefully. Since the onset of her relationship with Peter – six months, but Kempton has only been cognisant of the facts for two – it seems they are continually trying not to upset one another. Skirting round the little issues to avoid the major one. So hard for the father letting her go, and for the daughter, extricating herself without hurting him any more.

'Well Christmas Day with you of course.' She flashes him a chirpy smile.

'That's the good news,' he says dryly. 'And the bad?' But he knows it. He knows that for most of this Christmas break he will be on his own. It will not be like Christmas at all. He will be one of those pathetic creatures fending for himself. At this moment he hates Peter with every one of his bodily bits.

'Well I must spend Christmas Eve with – Peter.' Uses his full name this time, with respectful gravity. Conscious of her father's sucked-in lips and pained eyes.

'Will you be staying over at all? At home I mean. I mean with me.'

He sounds so awkward, getting himself all knotted in his attempt to be diplomatic, and her heart goes out to him.

'Yes. Christmas night itself, if that's all right—'

'Of course it's all right.'

'—And I'll come in plenty of time in the morning to do lunch together with you. So we'll have a really nice time.'

She sounds as though she is offering encouragement to a child, trying to chivvy him, and that child knows he's being given a duff deal: I'm giving you £1 instead of £100, aren't you a lucky boy? Yes, thank you.

'That will be great.' He can hear the hollowness of his own voice. 'And the rest of the holiday?'

'I said I'd spend a few days with Melissa.'

'Great,' Kempton says again. And wasn't that what Pitman said to him this morning? Great. Really great. 'No, I mean it,' he says, nodding hard, baring his teeth in a brave smile.

Magnificent Melissa, as he calls her. And if he's honest doesn't he fancy her and lust after her like mad? Is he therefore no better than Peter? The thought only just occurs to him and, in his head, Kempton immediately tries to justify his own position to himself: he has always quashed his urges, instincts, desires – call them what you will – when she has stayed in their house. And it hasn't been easy, in the face of her flashing everything she's got; which is plenty. And when she playfully tried to pull down his swimming trunks that time a few months back, in the Richmond swimming pool . . . He has only ever been respectful to her, not uttered so much as a word with innuendo in it. But how he has sometimes wished. And imagined. So, Kempton wonders, *does* that make him as bad? And Peter is only more honest, doing openly what all or most men would like to be doing? Having a relationship with a girl young enough to be his daughter?

No, he will not be compared.

'I'll stay some days with you, Dad,' Cat is saying. 'I promise.'
'Only if you want to, not because you feel you have to.'
'No, of course I want to.'
'And I'll be fine,' he tells her. 'I've got lots to do anyway.' What? Gaping time stretching uncertainly. Then remembers: 'Oh, I forgot to tell you. I'm getting a dog.'

And tonight, back home: the pleasure of seeing her wandering about in her ancient pale blue towelling robe, her feet long and bare, and pink from the bath (the scarring hidden from sight), hearing her gargling, the pipes belching and vibrating, the loo flushing. Kissing her goodnight outside her bedroom door across the small square landing. Then knowing she is tucked up in her old bed – on her own, his child – for the night.

'Kempton,' comes her voice, faint from within as he is about to close his own door.
'Yes darling?'
'Stop castigating yourself.'
That catches him short. She has a knack of doing it. He goes into his own room, through into the bathroom. Starts up the waterpick and swills out the garlic from his mouth. He fills a glass of water and swallows a sleeping pill. What a strange day, what a strange day – clambering into the untidy bed, sorting out the pillows and duvet and covering up the stains. And isn't it fortunate Cat didn't wander into his room and see the evidence of how he spent the afternoon? How does Suzanne get away with her affairs? How does she justify infidelity to herself? Or maybe she has no need to. Doesn't her husband suspect? Or maybe Kempton is her only lapse. But he is not so arrogant as to believe that. Perhaps there is an understanding between her and her husband. Others' lives! '. . . And the Spirit of God moved upon the face of the waters. And God said, "Let

there be light." And there was LIGHT!' The opening of *The Creation* flashes through his mind, the chorus blasting their heads off. Harry's feverish baton coming down like a scythe, severing them as though severing the light itself.

The hall clock's docile midnight chime, and will he have the strength to stick to his decision not to go into the office in the morning? A test of his grit. He must. He will. Bolstered by the propsect of a leisurely breakfast with his daughter. He will make them both scrambled eggs – oh, he remembers, only one egg and half a pint of milk. But there's a tin of powdered milk in the cupboard, and a box of porridge oats. What better than hot porridge with a pool of golden syrup on top, on a cold wet day? He is ridiculously happy knowing she's just a few feet across the landing. The whole house seems to have meaning again. He recalls an incident when she was a very young child, no more than four years old. They were walking back to his car, her hand engulfed in his (he can remember the feel of it, so small and sweet, and fat and warm: an oyster in a shell), and he had stopped at the edge of the road waiting for the lights to change. In the gutter was a dead bird. He can remember thinking, please don't let her notice. But Cat's eyes were ever sharp.

'What's that?' she asked in her funny, husky voice.

'It's a stone,' the father answered, to spare her grief.

'No it's not,' she said, shaking her head firmly. 'It's a dead bird.'

The lights turned to red and, confounded, he led her across the road. The bird, the reason for her testing him, were not mentioned further. Even then, he muses, rolling over onto his side and rubbing his feet together for warmth, she was ahead of him. She has always had a way of seeming to be on another plateau, as far as her sense of logic is concerned. She absorbed the ordinary and took it a stage further. Laterally.

Cat returning from school, and her mother in bed with

depression. Knowing instinctively, from tiny childhood, when to make herself scarce; and this was it: Cat was instinctive. And later on *she* was like the mother, and Vanessa the child. Vanessa, half her height, weeping in her daughter's arms. Cat preparing dinner; taking it up on a tray to her mother, then having hers with her father in the kitchen or in front of the television. And she would relate her own news, but only up to a point. Never beyond it. And one got nowhere by asking: a half smile, a downward sweep of the eyelashes, but nothing else.

Images flicking like snakes' tongues in and out of the preliminary rungs of sleep. His head feels oversized. An elephantine head lolling on top of a body that is without substance, that is dissolving. Cat's baby hand tucked in his. And Vanessa – when he first met her he noticed her exquisite hands constantly on the move, fiddling, gesticulating, coming up to the centre of her mouth, playing with her full upper lip, the deep cleft above it, touching the tip of her tongue, or running through her heavy fringe – and behind its straight-cut shield, a fine, clear, pale forehead.

His father's age-spotted hands. He can remember going to visit his father not long before he died, in his last year at Oxford (what was his girlfriend's name at the time? What *was* it? He had been crazy about her. How could he forget? 'I'm not ready for a one-to-one relationship,' she told him kindly.). He was shocked at his deterioration. He looked seventy-seven, not sixty-seven, and he didn't seem to know what he was doing anymore. He smelt. His clothes were stained – his father who had always been so meticulous. The waistcoats, the bow ties ('I don't seem to be able to tie them anymore') were packed away at the bottom of a trunk. He reeled off names of people, of places that Kempton had not a clue to what or to whom he was referring: an endless, rambling verbal barrage, as though

• Kempton's Journey

he had not spoken to anyone for months and had saved it all for Kempton. And in the bedroom, on the table next to the bed, was a book on the Restoration period, closed, and with a thick layer of dust on its jacket which Kempton wiped his finger through, leaving a waving path. But most poignant of all were his pyjamas – paisley-patterned and folded into a square on the pillow, just as he had always done all his life. In the midst of the disarray, the hopeless staleness, the bemused air, the disconnected speech, there were his pyjamas as a symbol of perpetuity and discipline and habit. And utter, complete aloneness.

Kempton took the bus directly to his mother's house. She was in her garden; appeared blissful filling a metal pail with brussels sprouts.

'You've got to do something about Father. How could you let him get like that?'

'Like what?' She stood up, arching her back. 'He's not my responsibility Kempton.'

'You selfish cow.'

Left again directly. Turned round once, to see her shrug, before she went back to pulling the brussels from their woody stalk.

He contacted the social services himself; but his father had a heart attack a fortnight later.

Kempton falls asleep; dreams that he has to take Gabriel's role in *The Creation* as the singer has fallen ill. 'But that's a soprano part,' he protests to Harry. 'Yes I'm fully aware of that,' the choirmaster replies. 'So I can't do it,' Kempton says. 'But you *are* a soprano.' They all gather in the nave of the church, except it is a palatial room decorated in Rococo style and turns out to be Hampton Court. All the other singers are there. The woman who was supposed to have been Gabriel calls out, 'Hi Kempton, you were great in be-e-ed,' trilling the word operatically. Nobody looks in the least shocked (every one of them is wearing horn-rimmed glasses), and he takes his place in front of them. Finds himself standing beside Saunders. 'I'm singing Gabriel,' Saunders tells him. 'No I am,' Kempton corrects him. 'Neither of you is,' says Harry, brandishing his baton. 'This is an extermination camp. You're going to be made into sausages.'

This is a nightmare. I'm having a nightmare. But he dreams he is saying it, and Harry, who is Henry VIII, is bearing down on him with the baton, which has transmogrified into a pair of red-hot tongs, and only then does he wake up.

Shit – what a dream. He'd rather not sleep than experience one like that again. He turns on the lamp and fumbles around on the chest of drawers next to the bed for something to read: *The Times*, yesterday's *Evening Standard*, *Gramophone*, *Private Eye*, *The Vineyards of France*. Nothing, it occurs to him, the least indicting or risqué should he ever be found dead in his bed. But the sleeping pills have kicked in and he is only half way through Londoner's Diary in the *Standard* when his eyelids keep sliding forward. He barely manages to switch off the lamp – halleluia, sleep – before he is out.

Cat being sick in her bathroom. He can hear her.

'Darling, are you all right in there,' he calls, realising immediately how daft the question is: of course she is not all right. Knocking on the door, which she has locked. 'Can't I come in? I could—' What could he?

'No Dad. Leave me.'

'I'll phone a doctor.'

'No! I'm OK.'

Stands outside, listening to her retch, feeling useless.

She joins him downstairs half an hour later. Very pinched. Grey-encircled, grey eyes. Huge owl eyes. Her lips have dissolved into the pallor of her face.

• Kempton's Journey

'Cat you must let me phone the doctor; you look terrible.'

'Gee, and I thought I looked great,' she jokes, Peter fashion, in a Texan drawl.

'It's not funny.'

'No, I know.' And no it isn't. 'But it's probably just the pizza, I mean I really did pig myself last night – that makes me think of *Babe* – and I drank a lot for me.'

'Well, if you're not better later—'

'I will be,' she says with certainty.

'But if you're not.'

'Then I'll go to the doctor,' she says to shut him up. 'And talking of tummy upsets – are you going into work today?'

'Nope. I'm going to the supermarket for a bumper shop and to dump the bottles and papers. Then for a swim. I'm going to finish my Christmas shopping. Buy a tree. You know, generally get into *l'ésprit*. Will you spend the day with me? At least let me look after you?'

'No. I have to get back.'

'Why?' he says, against his own inclinations. 'Why do you have to get back?'

'I just do.' Cat trying not to wave the red cape.

'*He* can wait a day or so, can't he? Treat 'em mean, keep 'em keen,' he adds harshly.

She ignores him. 'I've actually got an essay to write. And all my books are there . . . I'm going to make myself a tea. I can't face coffee this morning.'

'I'm sorry. I'm sorry.' He is contrite. 'Let me do it. Let me at least do that.'

'Kempton, I'm a big girl.'

'Yes, but just this. I want to pamper you a bit when you're ill. I bet Peter doesn't pamper you.' He's done it again. Incapable of going a couple of sentences without mentioning *him*, and ruining the atmosphere between them. And he had been so looking forward to making porridge for them both.

'He wouldn't be Peter if he did. And I don't need pampering. But he's very caring.'

'I don't want to know.'

'You asked.'

'I wish I hadn't.'

The kettle comes to the boil, and he pours the water over a teabag and is about to add milk, when she calls out, 'No milk.'

'It's quite fresh, even though there's not much left.'

'No I don't think I should have it. I'm still a bit queasy.'

Breakfast is a strained affair. Him munching away at his cereal (it sounds amplified in his head), fighting back sarcastic comments; Her sipping at the black tea, fighting back nausea. Each yearning to be friends with the other.

The phone rings.

'Well we know who that is,' Kempton says.

'Let me answer. I'll tell him I'm here looking after you.'

'Brilliant. That's a brilliant idea.'

Cat rescues the phone just as the answer-machine message is about to cut in.

'Hallo? Oh Mr Pitman – it's Catriona. How *are* you? Yes I can imagine it's frantic—' Turns to wink at her father. 'No I'm afraid he's really bad. That's why I'm here. He's throwing up all over the place.'

One of Kempton's deep guffaws bursts from him and he stifles another. Makes a silent, clapping gesture with his hands and gives his daughter the thumbs-up sign. How he loves her. Please God (or whoever) don't let me drive her away. Let there be a way for her to finish with Peter without damaging our relationship.

Also, if the truth be known, he misses Peter. If it could come to an end soon then he might, just conceivably, be able to forgive him and resume their friendship.

He sees Cat off: 'Please take care of yourself. I'll phone – no, you phone me tomorrow and let me know how you are.' He rarely phones her. Peter might answer. He waves her off in her little red Fiesta that for some reason she has named Deirdre. Feels forlorn watching it disappear down the road.

But the day is planned, and he will fill it accordingly. And tonight is choir practice; and as usual afterwards a crowd of them will go to the Lamb and Flag. He will amuse them with his dream. That should be good for a pint.

He goes round to the back door, to collect the box of newspapers. About a fortnight's worth. On top is the *Richmond and Twickenham Times*, open at the entertainment page. And quite a large, boxed advertisement catches his eye: 'Bereaved through a partner's suicide?' This is in bold print, but the rest is a blur. He fishes his glasses from his pocket (such a nuisance not being able to read things impulsively anymore), and reads on. 'There are more of us about than you would think. Social meetings held fortnightly, on Thursdays. Also events and outings. For more information . . .'

Kempton stares at it thoughtfully, re-reads it, then carefully tears out that part of the page and goes into the kitchen, where he tucks it under the phone.

He makes a couple of journeys to the car, first with the bottles, then with the paper-box, which he balances against his chest while he unlocks the boot. Although he has a garage he keeps the car in the street and has, at great expense, invested in a resident's parking permit. The garage is empty, except for a few sheets of plywood. Unused. A neighbour asked if he could rent it. Kempton refused. It is locked for good.

4

Outsider

Another decent night's sleep; but he should have set the alarm. It is impossible for Kempton to sneak into his office unnoticed since the refurbishment. The two rooms once used for storage, and a dingy reception area have been transformed into a spacious open-plan area with four girls in it and five computers. Kempton brags that he is computer illiterate. In his day there were just two computers which he never went near. One for orders, stock control, and customers accounts – all handled by Brian Bingham, now in charge of purchasing; the other for the cellars. The bookeeper – an elderly woman called Gladys, now retired – used one of those old-fashioned desk calculators. His secretary, Julia, seemed perfectly happy with an electric typewriter and handed him immaculate carbon copies of all correspondence. It worked quite satisfactorily. He never sent a memo, and when Jim Masters started circulating them Kempton asked him what he was thinking of.

'Morning Mr Prévot,' the female chorus greets him. Julia jerks her chin in the direction of Pitman's door and gives a thumbs-down sign.

• Kempton's Journey

And the man himself emerges from his office, having heard the girls. 'Oh you've deigned to turn up have you? I want a word with you.'

Kempton adjusting his shoulders, setting his jaw. Resentment swelling within him. And the door to Jim Masters' room is open. He'll be rubbing his hands. Kempton had been on the point of sacking him when Pitman had bailed out the company and promoted Jim to marketing manager. Pitman's Pet. The Pit's Bull. A smarmy, smart alec . . . Indignation fermenting in Kempton's heart. The gnashing teeth of rebellion.

'When I get a chance,' he says calmly (with infuriating calm, as far as Pitman's concerned). Strides loftily to the end of the corridor and his own office. Oh God, his desk. It has grown. Sighing with the weight of two days' post, memos and matters pending. And before he can sit down the phone rings.

'It's only me,' says Julia. 'I just wanted to remind you it's the Christmas lunch today.'

'Oh God. Where?'

'Madre's.'

A jolly. He can't, simply can't, face the prospect of an office jolly. But a jolly only for the hierarchy. Seventeen of them including the reps. The half dozen or so others – the drivers, warehouse staff, the grafters who sweat it out twelve hours a day, organise their own. When Kempton owned the business the entire staff numbered nine and there was no Upstairs Downstairs divide.

Vanessa and Cat smiling down at Kempton as he sifts through the piles on his desk. Amazing how much post can arrive in the space of two days. He bins most of it straight away. He wishes with all his heart that he hadn't come back. Had taken sick leave until after Christmas. Better still, ad infinitum. And one of his best customers, a small hotel chain, has been taken over and his chances of getting in there are slim. In fact they are supposed to be tendering today, now he comes to think of it. Oh shit. Kempton begins rummaging with mole-like frenzy on his desk for his hand-written list. Papers scattering, pens, paperclips, leaflets raining down (fleetingly he recalls games of Pelmanism as a child). And at this point in his search, Pitman enters.

'What the hell's going on in here?'

'I'm looking for something.'

'Well quit looking. What the hell have you been playing at for two days?'

'I've been ill.' Kempton leans against the vandalised desk. His hair looks like a punk's from his frantic hands.

'Yeah, yeah. That doesn't stop you lifting the phone. I left a dozen messages yesterday—'

'I must've slept through them.'

'Oh sure . . . So where's Grove Estate's list then? It's got to be in by today and we couldn't find it on the computer.'

'It's not on the computer.'

'Well where is it then?' Pitman twirling on his heels in frustration; his beefy complexion becoming marbled with white.

'That's what I'm looking for.'

'I don't believe it. You mean it's not been printed out? What do you think that Two-and-a-half grand machine is sitting on your desk for? Fun?'

Kempton playing deaf. He had years of experience at it with Vanessa. Pitman's rantings are caught only in snatches. But everyone else can hear him. Tongues will be whispering. And those in his camp will feel sorry for him, which is as bad as those in the other smirking.

Ah there it is! Kempton espies part of a sheet of paper and the letters, -STATES. Somehow the list had become sandwiched in a health farm brochure. His immense relief serves as a catalyst for the release of his anger. While quick to become irritated, it takes a lot to incite rage in him,

• Kempton's Journey

and then it is not Kempton's tendency to shout. His rage manifests itself first in the drawing in of his stomach and thrusting out of the chest, then a sequence with the eyes – a widening and fixing on their target, then narrowing and shooting out rays of frying heat, this followed by an almighty banging down of his fists on the nearest available surface.

Pitman has barely time to shrivel under the fearsomeness of Kempton's gaze, before he is deafened by the thunderclap of his hands meeting the desk. And then finds himself being grabbed by the neck as Kempton's fingers tighten on the knot of his lilac and white spotted tie.

'Don't you ever speak to me like that again, you jumped-up creep,' Kempton hisses. 'Now will you please get out of my office this second. *Comprenez-vous*?' He lets go of his employer and sits back in his chair. There is a zinging in his ears; tom-toms pounding in his chest. He wonders if he is going to have a heart attack.

The other man gawps for a few seconds. 'Hey, Ke-empton,' he says finally, wheedling.

Without a word Kempton gets up and goes over to the door; opens it and waits. And Pitman makes his exit, his ears red-rimmed, ox-neck, scarlet. Half way down the corridor he turns and glowers.

'I won't forget this.'

Kempton's jubilation lasts a couple of minutes: he cavorts round the chaos of his office, trampling on papers, yelling out silent 'yippees'. Dervish-crazy. Then, suddenly enervated, he sits down and slumps over his desk, head in hands. How long can he endure this for? Is this really to be his lot for the rest of his working days?

He extricates his proposal for Grove Estates and switches on the computer. The menu flashing on the screen. Dozens of fluorescent possibilities. He tentatively moves the cursor to Draft Wine lists, and a new square appears with about fifty names. At the end of these he spots Potential Business, and again moves the cursor. Presses Enter. Miraculously an empty square comes up, except for the heading, Customer's Name.

'Grove Estates,' he types out with an excited finger.

> 'At Prévot, Pitman & Saunders we pride ourselves on the following: 24-hour free delivery within the London area, 48 hours within a radius of 50 miles. We can offer you wines under your own label, print your wine lists and provide covers and maps. And of course our excellent quality and value is well-known.'

Lies. But then Grove Estates, as a property company, is probably no more discerning than Pitman. ('You have no commercial vision, that's your problem Ke-empton' . . .)

> 'Nor have you any need to phone in with your order, for on an agreed day *we* will telephone *you*. Your local sales representative will even stock-take for you if required. He or she will be delighted to offer any advice and will keep you informed about new lines, special offers, bin-ends, and of course vintage changes. They will also provide you with promotional material such as tent cards, posters etc.
>   My proposed list, tailored to your requirements, is as follows . . .'

He is determined to get this account. At any cost. Further slashes prices which he had carefully worked out. Recklesness seizing him: Macon Rouge, listed at £4.20 a bottle, originally discounted by him to £3.90 (giving them thirty percent profit), he now reduces to £3.30. As the wine costs them £3 a bottle and they need to make a minimum of twenty-five percent, taking into account all their overheads, a ten percent gross profit amounts in reality to a fifteen percent loss on the Macon Rouge. And the Fleurie. And the Bulgarian sauvignon. What fun. Kempton feels quite manic, laughing out loud as he juggles about with the figures, his hands – three fingers on each now – whizzing gleefully across the keyboard. Finally he remembers to press the 'save' button, prints out two copies and takes one through to Julia to fax to Grove Estates immediately.

'You used the computer,' she says disbelievingly.

It will be several weeks before his actions come to the light of Saunders' attention and the proverbial hits the fan. And meanwhile he has made it just in time for the office shindig where, at Madre's, he fully intends that The Blot will get absolutely blotto.

Seventeen of them around two tables pushed together. His hat is a red cone with a gold circle the size of a fifty pence in the middle. At first he resisted putting it on. The only hatless person there. An aperitif (vodka) and two glasses of wine later, it is sited lopsidedly over an eye. On his left, Anna, one of the reps, has undone a couple of the top buttons of her cream satiny blouse, and he tries to keep his glance from straying in the direction of her lacy half-cup bra. For ease Pitman has settled on a fixed menu. Scraped melon skins now rest on plates, like shored boats. Two or three people have left their Parma ham. And Pitman, jovial, scoops up his secretary's – Linda – who pretends to slap his wrist then gives a simpering smile. Alcohol, Kempton thinks, the great equaliser. The awfulness of these annual events made bearable only by copious quantities of it. Theirs is one of three office parties in the restaurant: The same types, the same clothes, same pettinesses and antagonisms masked – or unmasked – by the same jokes, followed by the same laughter and blowing of paper pipes. And Brian Bingham, normally a reticent, shy fellow, is blushing and stuttering his joke:

'. . . And so this guy says to the Chinese man, "When do you have elections?" And the Chinese replies, "Whenever I see pletty girl."' Gales of laughter from their table competing with hoots of delirium from another where the orator is actually standing up on his chair.

'What did the horse say to the sheep when it moved next door?' reads Julia from the little slip enclosed in a cracker.

'What?' call out a couple of voices.

'Now we'll be neigh-baas,' Julia says. Peals of more laughter – and groans – greet this. Actually it's rather sweet, Kempton thinks, pouring himself and Anna more wine (Chianti, what else?). Cat would like it. Cute, she'd remark . . . From time to time he catches Pitman's eye and glares very deliberately at him; doesn't want him to think he has softened in any way.

'I got a card from Mike Chandler,' says Tim Isaacs suddenly on his other side. Tim is the area sales manager, a man in his mid-thirties. If Kempton were not around he would certainly be sales director. Or maybe he would leave. He has more or less told Kempton he has only stayed on from loyalty to him. But jobs in the wine trade do not abound, and he knows no other life.

'I did too,' Kempton says.

'Did he tell you what he's doing?'

'No. You?'

'Yep. He's writing a novel. And cleaning windows to finance himself.'

'Shit.'

'Why shit? He says he's never been happier.'

That sets Kempton brooding, and for all his intentions of becoming paralytic the wine never seems to come his way after his fourth glass, and he observes the various members of his table with almost sober distaste: Saunders, whippet thin and raisin-eyed, nodding as though struck with Parkinson's, non-existent lips split in a stupid grin; Pitman, with his Tenerife tan, never looking so much like a road mender as he does now – Kempton can picture him with a pneumatic drill vibrating under his hand; Jim

• Kempton's Journey

Masters – fair, crew-cut hair, the look of a fifties marine – leaning across Saunders' PA and winding her long hair round his mouth like a moustache; David Black, credit controller and keen body builder, lolling in his chair and blowing kisses at Julia, whose face is set in a forced smile. What a bunch. What a farce. He would like to leap up and yell that: what a farce! Urgently craves more wine to enable him to get through the rest of this torture. The bonhomie, the uproarious behaviour is already degenerating into less good-humoured slanging, bawdiness and personal jabs. These sorts of events can end in tears. He has seen it happen. And suddenly he remembers a conversation with Vanessa, after a friend's party. Vanessa driving because he had drunk too much.

'I knew it would be atrocious,' he muttered.
'Well why did we go then?'
'I thought you wanted to.'
'Not if you didn't want to.'
'You see you *did*. You wanted to flirt. You were in your element.'
'Well you don't take any notice of me.'

He pretended to snore, and she pressed her foot down harder on the accelerator, seemed prepared to kill them both.

The truth is he could never refuse a party invitation because as a child he had been to so few. Cannot recall Minnie ever giving one for him. Decades later it still rankles.

Back at the office he is making some headway with his 'In' tray when Julia comes in bearing a fax from Grove Estates. 'Thank you for your proposal,' it says. 'We have pleasure in accepting the terms as set out by you.'

'That's good news, isn't it? Keep him quiet for a while.'

She swivels her head in the vague direction of Pitman's room.

'"For a while" being the operative phrase, Julia.'

She tilts her chin quizzically. He shakes his head and returns to clearing his desk. And to thinking about Mike Chandler, Master of Wine, up a ladder swishing a soapy wet shammy over windows.

The traffic is appalling; and whichever lane he is in is the wrong one. It is quite extraordinary how the second he has moved from one to the other (incurring V-signs and glares), the traffic in the original one will put on a sudden spurt and a dozen vehicles will glide past him. It's the same at supermarkets. He always picks the wrong queue. The definition of a loser? Eventually he gives up lane-hopping for the simple reason a police car is on his tail and he is way over the alcohol limit and doesn't want to draw attention to himself. Checks that his lights are on. In front of him a juggernaut is blocking his line of vision. He loathes juggernaut drivers, the way they swing their ruddy great vehicles round corners, Goliaths perched in their cabin, wheels always just over the white line. Omnipotent. Has taken down the registration number so many times he has lost count – boiling with fury, then doing nothing about it.

It takes nearly three quarters of an hour to crawl the distance between Mortlake and Richmond and he is fit to explode by the time he arrives home. A lewd joke Pitman told towards the end of lunch, concerning a big-breasted girl and a farmer, keeps replaying in his head. He has allotted this evening to decorate the tree he bought yesterday. He had been tempted by one of those Norwegian jobs which did not shed and somehow propagate in every room, spiking your bare feet; but the cost was prohibitive. The high point of the evening: dressing up a tree.

So what has befallen his social life? Hit by a mysterious

• Kempton's Journey

ague. One dinner party to go to: the usual Spare Man stuff (he should charge a fee); but he has already done the rounds and hostesses have moved onto fresher quarry. He should push himself more. Not that he feels inclined to be sociable at the moment in his present frame of mind. Come to think of it he has never really been sociable. However, a tiny flicker on the horizon, the minutest ripple to interrupt the uniformity of a straight line would be agreeable. It is hard not to compare then and now. Not the 'then' of Vanessa days, but afterwards, when things had settled a bit and he could enjoy having Cat to himself. She was in her A-level year at school. He had grown used to having her around in the evenings. There was an easy harmony between them. She seemed to like it also, doing the cooking (she loved to make meringues), taking on the domestic, almost wifely role. And on a Saturday morning they would go to the supermarket together, consult and tick off the list. There was a certain piquancy in the situation: having his daughter housekeep for him. And the rare occasion a woman stayed the night, Cat was no-questions-asked diplomatic and would arrange to stay with a friend. But there was no special boy in her life, and he sometimes teased her, secretly glad nonetheless. And when she had her climbing accident and he was in pieces, crazed with worry – practically living at the Hammersmith hospital for two months as bits of bone and flesh were grafted from here to there on his precious daughter's beautiful leg – who was more of a help than anyone? Peter. Just as he was when the business collapsed, and after Vanessa's death. Peter, with his off-beat humour and cynicism, whose crude motto used to be: *Vidi, Vici, Veni*. One of the few people who could behave naturally in the face of bereavement or tragedy. Peter, who rolls his own cigarettes with Russian tobacco, claims to be an atheist yet goes to confession three times a year, suffers from asthma, is the proud owner of a VW camper and thinks this entitles him to vote Labour, despite his navy blue Aston Martin in the garage.

'Hypocrite,' Kempton levelled at him.

'Show me someone who isn't, to a lesser or greater degree,' Peter replied. 'I'm not hurting anyone.'

But now he is.

'What about Augusta?'

'What *about* Augusta?'

'As a name.'

'Too die-hard Tory.'

'Ouch.'

'Lucy,' Cat says. 'Nothing cringe-worthy for when she's older. Marc for a boy. With a "C."'

'Do I have a say in this?'

'If you let me get on with my essay.'

'"The Power of Unconscious Thought,"' he reads, bending over her. '"Starting from the premise that thoughts are an integral part of our minds, we then have to divide the process into two factions: unconscious thought, which is spontaneous, i.e. impressions which flit in and out of our minds of their own accord, and conscious thought, which we deliberately manifest. These can further be divided into positive and negative thought, and sub-divided, amongst others, into good and bad. Assuming *un*conscious thoughts to be the truest reflection of our inner selves, by trapping them immediately it should be possible to channel the 'positive' and 'good' elements beneficially, thus taking control of our 'true' self.

'"As a case study I would like to cite David, a convicted murderer . . ."'

'You're a deep little thing, aren't you, sweetheart?'

'Don't patronise me, Wart.'

• Kempton's Journey

'OK. But Mar*co* if it's a boy. Compromise.'

She contemplates it for a few seconds. 'All right. I like that actually.'

'And for a girl—' His eyes alight on a book of Freud amongst the others on the floor surrounding her. '—Sigmunda.'

She throws her fibre tip pen at him. A squiggle of black on his sleeve. 'Disappear. Go and write your play. You haven't touched it for two days.'

'It's in here.' Taps his forehead. Observes her for a moment, sprawled on the dhurrie in one of his shirts. Her leg, scarred from three inches above the knee to just above her ankle, is a couple of inches shorter than the other and resembles a gnarled vine. He strokes the patchwork of misshapen flesh. 'What does it feel?'

'Numb mostly.'

'I fell in love with you when you were in hospital . . . Where's the wee-wee tube. I want to see it again. The most glorious mediterranean blue glinting through its little porthole.'

'On the kitchen table.'

'I'm going to have a glass box made for it. Pass it off as a Damien Hirst. If we get married old Kempton will be my father-in-law. What a hoot. Dad! My Son, welcome into the family!'

'Poor Kempton,' says Cat.

Kempton sets down his briefcase in the hall and hangs his coat over the bannister. Monotony, habit, he adds mentally to his Life List. Do something about. Join bereaved partners' group? Join dating agency? Start going to wine bars. Finances: sort out. Accidentally he brushes against the tree and a shower of pine needles rains down. And what has happened to carol singers? Nobody seems to bother anymore. Remembers himself standing on doorsteps as a boy with a group of others. 'And – now!' his father would usher them in. 'The-e fi-irst No-el . . .' The porch light illuminating their faces.

Into his study and Spike, shut in there all day, greets him with a quivering snake-tail and rattling purrs. The acrid odour of cat urine and faeces permeating the room, which Kempton traces to behind the sofa. The answer-phone flashing.

'You old fraudster,' says Peter. 'Still, glad to hear you're not at death's door. Look, I don't know why you're so fazed about Cat and myself. You should be glad. She could be involved with some guy on crack, or a train spotter. Or a Jehovah's Witness. Imagine tha—'

Kempton fast forwards the tape – Peter's voice sounding like a demented Cantonese; and then a woman: 'Hi Kempton, it's Suzanne. I've weakened. What's in a few days? You can have Pluto Christmas Eve. That's Sunday in case you didn't know. Providing I don't hear to the contrary I'll deliver him around six-ish in exchange for services rendered.'

He laughs, suddenly cheered. Double whammy. Two things to look forward to. A flicker *and* a ripple. Into the kitchen. Humming as he opens a tin of liver-and-kidney-flavoured Whiskas. Cuts it up on the plastic plate – 'How will you like him, eh Spike?' – Puts it on the Garfield mat. He is really quite excited about the dog. He'll have to get a basket – glances round him for a suitable spot for it – and a brush and comb. And some toys. And how does Suzanne manage to escape from her family on Christmas Eve? On a Sunday, Christmas Eve, for Chrissake? But that's her problem, not his. Nonetheless he is curious. Realises he knows very little about her. Somewhere along the line he seems to recall there are at least two children around Cat's age. But he can't remember what gender they are. He ought to ask. It's pretty remiss of him not to know. To go to bed with her, bonk her and not know something like that. But on the other hand he is reluctant to probe. It's not that he doesn't like her or that he is not interested. It is simply easier this way. Pleasant. Light. No hassle.

Three minutes before six. Just time to clean up Spike's mess before his ritual vodka and the news. Then he will sift through his *Bachelor's Cookbook*, a gift from Peter. He resents the flippant title, the implication that every male on his own is a carefree bachelor; not a careworn, asset-stripped divorcé, or a grieving, strapped-for-cash widower. 'The Hungry Lone Wolf.' Now that would be a good title ... A pasta probably. Linguini with prawns in a tomato sauce. There are some prawns in the freezer. He has nearly learnt to do that without referring to the book. And afterwards he will delve about in the cupboard under the stairs (must be careful not to bang his head as usual); try not to think of this time last year when Cat and he did the tree together, or three years ago: Vanessa and he trying to disentangle the lights and ending up screwing on the carpet. It will take him hours to disentangle them on his own and find out which is the rogue bulb preventing the whole lot from working.

And so another evening will bite the dust.

5

Novice

The cemetery, this bleak, swept-sky morning, is a busy place. Guilt, thinks Minnie. It's the time of year for it. Twelve months' guilt crammed into the space of a few days. She comes here once a week, to the same spot. Has done so for twenty-six years. She has created a minature shrubbery on the grave, which everyone stops to comment on. There's very little that needs doing to it this morning, but she trowels around a bit between the various heathers, scatters some more fine pebbles from a bag on top of the wet soil; picks off a branch of dead Rosemary. In all it takes her no more than ten minutes.

'Morning Mrs Prévot.' Jonathan, the caretaker, blind in one eye but vigilant in the other, doffs his cap on his rounds.

'Good morning to you Jonathan.'

'Don't look too promising.' He stares up at the sky. Drizzle landing on his upturned face.

She joins him in gazing upwards. The pair of them united by the murky ceiling of cloud.

'No it doesn't, does it?' She has a clipped, upper-class

• Kempton's Journey

accent. Her eyes are an extraordinary blue, like barely tinted glass; running now from the cold.

'What do you reckon about Kempton on Monday then? Will it be abandoned?'

'In the lap of the gods I'd say Jonathan, hmph.'

'You putting on One Man in the King George then?'

'Haven't decided yet. I'm waiting to see what the weather will do. Monsieur Le Curé may be long priced but he likes the mud.'

'I'll bear that in mind.'

'Happy Christmas then Jonathan.'

He can take a hint – senses she wants to be alone. 'You too, Mrs Prévot.' Doffs his cap again and continues on his rounds. They always have a similar conversation: either racing or gardening.

She settles herself onto her shooting stick, huddles into her quilted layers of clothing and yanks down her trilby further. Her hair, drawn back in a chignon beneath it, is a faded auburn banded with ash-grey. She is nearly eighty and could still be termed a handsome woman, although the texture of her skin has become coarse and lined and rather weather-beaten. She can feel that her nose – a strong, prominent nose – is red; can feel a drip on its end. Rummages about in her pocket for her linen handkerchief to dab at it, and comes into contact with the flask also in there. Ah, what a good idea. She pulls it out and unscrews the stopper; takes a swig of port. Instant soothing warmth fanning through her.

'Here's to you, dearest.' Gives a chin-jerk towards the grave, then her eyes linger nostalgically there. 'Remember Crete.' She sighs deeply. 'Always, always, always.'

She fiddles about in her other pocket for her Swan matches to relight her pipe, impervious to the stares and nudging from a group a couple of tombstones away; is tranquil and at home here, her bottom cradled by the shooting stick seat moulded into her form by constant use; warmed by the Grahams and her pipe; surrounded by fresh air and memories nothing can sully. And the *Sporting Life* at her feet. She bends to pick it up.

'Now who shall we put our money on this afternoon dearest?'

At least she has been spared Alzheimer's. Her memories, if anything, become sharper.

Kempton in the petshop, like a child parachuted into Hamleys. He manages to spend getting on for ninety pounds there. Into the large wicker basket the assistant arranges a fabric collar (complete with engraved disc) and lead, a squeaky Christmas pudding, a squeaky John Major, a ball with a bell inside, a rubber pull thing, three metal bowls, a large bag of dried puppy food, three packets of frozen tripe, special rusks, four chew sticks and an owner's handbook about bloodhounds. For good measure, fixing her stern and pointed glance on him, she throws in a free sticker for his car that says, 'A dog is not just for Christmas.'

He staggers out of the shop to his car parked outside with the hazard lights blinking. A traffic warden by it writing nonchalantly in his pad.

'Aw no,' protests Kempton. 'Too late. I've started now,' says the warden. I've started so I'll finish, Magnus Magnusson used to say.

'How do you expect me to cart this lot more than a few yards? I had to park here.'

'You're causing an obstruction—' he gestures to the cars stacking behind to overtake. 'The law's the law.'

• Kempton's Journey

He continues writing without lifting his eyes from the page.

'Oh come off it.'

'Look, if you object then explain to the authorities. I've got my job to do.'

'I vas only obeying orders.' Kempton rests the basket and contents on the car roof and gives a Nazi salute.

The warden ignores him; slaps the twenty-pound ticket on the windscreen. Kempton wrenches it off and screws it up in front of him. The other man shrugs. 'It makes no difference. You get another in the post.'

His pleasure of a few moments ago is tainted and he drives home in an angry mood. Steam, Dad. He can almost hear Cat saying it and smiles, his knuckles relaxing on the steering wheel. And it is true: the man *was* only doing his job. And what a job for a man in his fifties to be doing on a freezing wet Saturday before Christmas. Kempton is almost inclined to turn round and seek out the traffic warden; apologise for his rudeness. Let's go into business together mate. You hate your job, I hate mine . . . But he does not have to worry about his for another five days. And no doubt the man has developed a coconut husk after years of insults. Perhaps he does not hate his job at all. Perhaps he really is a megalomaniac who gets high on wielding his power, a vengeful pleasure from watching motorists dance with helpless rage as they wrest their ticket from the windscreen.

Animo et fide, Cat has written in her Christmas card that arrived this morning and he has stood on the kitchen dresser. 'By courage and faith,' she has translated beneath the Latin ('In case you didn't know'). But he does know. His father used to quote the little motto. Much good it did him. She has also drawn a cartoon illustration, of a man battling his way up a mountain and wiping his forhead. A 'phew' written by his mouth. He should be so grateful to have a daughter like her. Is so grateful. Often thanks God or whoever for her. But, but, but . . .

Kempton fetches a spare pillow from the airing cupboard – goose feather – and a thick white bath towel – Harrods – with which to pad out the basket. It looks homely under the table. He places the squeaky John Major in it, and finds a cardboard box for the rest of the toys. Puts it by the back door, along with a pile of newspapers in readiness. The trio of bowls next to Spike's. Then he goes into his study with a mug of coffee and his new book.

'Your puppy should have his first meal at about 8.00 a.m. consisting of Farex, broken rusk or Weetabix soaked in warm milk with brown sugar or honey.'

Farex! Rusks! Weetabix! He will have to go out again to buy some.

'For luncheon, at around midday, ox heads, sheep's heads, horsemeat, whalemeat, kangaroo meat and tripe are all suitable, if cubed.'

What is this? Kempton turns in disbelief to the front of the book and sees it was first published in 1958.

'Eyes: The Bloodhound's eyes are considered by some to be unattractive, because of the apparency of the third eyelid, the haw. This can also cause the eyes to be runny, inflamed, and can sometimes lead to infection.'

'Oh no.'

'They have very independent natures, are affectionate, usually docile, are loyal, somewhat reserved, always dignified, but have a tendency to disobedience.'

Why bloodhounds? Why can't Suzanne breed labradors or retrievers? Something normal.

'Some bloodhounds develop the habit of baying at night. This is an extremely eerie sound that your neighbours might not appreciate.'

Oh God, what has he let himself in for?

'And don't forget,' the author warns cheerfully, 'a bloodhound puddle is more of a lake.'

The word harebrained shoots through his mind. I must be mad ('Well done Ke-empton, one of your better ruses,' Pitman sneers in his head. 'Why didn't I think of bringing a puppy into the office to defecate all over the expensive new carpet?'). He gets up from the armchair and goes over to the phone; turns it over and over in his hands, debating whether to ring Suzanne (the computerised voice cutting in: 'Please hang up and try again'). But her husband is bound to be at home. There again, presumably he knows she is selling Kempton a dog. 'I bumped into Kempton Prévot the other day. He's taking one of the pups,' he imagines her explaining. Or perhaps she's not mentioned his name at all. But it could be awkward. And he has never been much good at bluffing. Sucker. Oh Kempton, you are a sucker. OK, so she will just have to come by with the puppy on Sunday, as planned, and take it away again, even though it will probably mean sacrificing a bonk. He will not be swayed.

Back into the kitchen to retrieve his receipt from the petshop. The basket neat and expectant there. A sudden pang grips him, a feeling so powerful he likens it to female broodiness.

'Shit,' he says out loud. He has never been good at decision making. Another of Vanessa's criticisms.

Oh imperfect man.

Christmas eve, the radio blasting out 'Oh Come all ye faithful', and Kempton's baritone in powerful unison as he sorts out the best china for the next day. And how much china did they get through with Vanessa's tantrums? Then there was the occasion she ran out of the house naked, on a manic high. His thoughts turn and turn again to her. The good, the beautiful, the bad, the hideous. It seems to be getting worse, not better; in the early days he had blocked his emotions, repressed his memories, bolstered himself with anger at her deed. Will there come a time when an entire day, or days, will pass without a single visitation from Vanessa?

'I may as well learn to repair what I destroy,' she joked one day, and enrolled for porcelain restoration classes. A year later she expanded her interior design business to offer it as an extra service to clients, and made one of the upstairs rooms into a studio. She was always enterprising and purposeful, once she had decided something, would never be deflected, and would set about whatever task it was with a frenetic zeal. Dynamic, compared to her husband's pedantic plodding. There was so much energy in her. So much apparent strength. But her strength was all on the surface, with no plinth to support it. And that final act, did that take strength? Did she have doubts before she did it? Regret? guilt? pity for those she was about to desert and leave flailing in the molasses of the aftermath? What crossed her mind? Was there fear? And he will never know. That is almost the worst of it. In all logic he realises that he will gradually become used to her absence, that he has already become more so, that – he hardly dares think it, so guilty does he feel – life is more peaceful without her, living at his own whims and not in constant dread of her mood swings; but: those last thoughts of hers as she orchestrated the end of her life and the destruction of several others, he will never be able to draw any comfort from. The loose strands waving in the air can never be linked.

'Good King Wenceslas . . .' Resolutely, he adjoins the King's College Choir, sorting out the silver cutlery now. Must dip the forks; their prongs are dung coloured.

A knock on the kitchen window from the patio startles him, and he stops singing, his mouth frozen mid-motion. Suzanne's happy round face pressed to the glass. She is holding up something that looks like a folded-over bean bag.

'Hang on,' he calls, smiling back at her, running to open the door.

'Hi. I rang the front door bell but you didn't hear. No wonder. Singing away. You've got a nice voice, actually. Meet Pluto.' She reaches up on tiptoe, and he bends his head to receive her kiss on the lips. She tastes of a curious mixture of garlic and peppermints. The one, no doubt, intended to counteract the other.

'He looks like a bean bag.' Taking the puppy from her and dangling it.

'Careful, you have to hold under his bum.'

He has never held a puppy. Their spaniel was at least two when Vanessa got him from Battersea. The puppy's face is a mass of toppling skin, its eyes buried deep within, its nose like a black doorstop. The jowls and dewlap, disproportionately long ears and domed head give it the appearance of an elderly bewigged judge. The short-haired black-and-tan coat is porpoise-sleek. Kempton is instantly smitten. He remembers Vanessa passing Cat into his arms. This feeling is almost akin to it. Total, unconditional, immediate capitulation.

'The point of no return,' murmurs Suzanne, watching him.

The puppy smells of milk and a baby sweetness. Its paws are enormous, with strong claws.

'He's so floppy.' Kempton bends his face towards the dog's, and a small pink tongue shoots out to lick him.

'He's weed on your patio, so he's safe to plonk on the floor for a bit.'

'You're an hour early. I haven't laid out the newspaper yet.'

'Sorry. Things – you know.' Waves her hand vaguely, and he assumes she means something to do with her husband.

'Anyway, I can help you with the paper. Put him down, Kempton.'

As Kempton crouches down the little dog wriggles then slithers from his arms; proceeds to dart round the kitchen, nose to the ground, ears sweeping the tiles, tail wagging.

'Stern,' Suzanne informs Kempton, on her knees with him on the floor, arranging the newspaper sheets. 'A bloodhound's tail is called a stern. I brought some food for him, by the way, to start you off. He puked up in the car, so he might not be hungry. Also they do go off their food in new surroundings. And I've got his papers. Oh and he's likely to whine most of the night as he's bound to miss his mother and siblings. You've got to realise it's quite traumatic for him. You might have to have him in your room for the first night. So what are you doing tomorrow?'

'I've got Cat and Minnie – my mother – coming. And you?' He stands up, stretching his back. She follows suit.

'Oh the usual. You know. Family.' It strikes him how evasive she is. Probably embarrassed. Although she never seems anything but relaxed. 'Can I put the kettle on?' she asks.

'Yes . . . I've forgotten about your children. Have you got two or three?'

'Four.' She fills it; presses down the switch. 'Where are the mugs?'

'In that cupboard by your head. Here. I'll do it. Good God. Four. I mean, your body's so good.'

'Thank you.' She pretends to curtsy. 'Is the coffee in this cupboard?' Points towards the one with the glazed door through which tins and packets are visible.

'Yes. Sorry. I'm just dumbfounded.'

'Why? What's so remarkable about four children? Unless the father's name is Herod.'

He misses the joke. 'I don't know. No, of course not. Nothing remarkable. It's just that everyone I know has the usual one, two or three maximum. How old are they?'

'Well the twins are nineteen. They're at East Anglia and Manchester.'

'Twins,' he reiterates in surprise. 'Are they identical?'

'Well one's a boy and the other a girl, but apart from that – Kempton, what is all this sudden flurry of interest in my offspring?'

He spins round on his heels before sitting down. The puppy – *his* puppy, he reminds himself – is exploring every niche; has already lapped up Spike's milk (where is Spike?). Kempton, who has always been contemptuous of people who put on stupid, baby voices, has the extraordinary urge to do just that. A whole odd, gurgling new language rises to his throat as he watches the dog. Suzanne's presence deters him. She puts the mug of coffee in front of him, and a jar that says 'sugar' on it. A carton of milk from the fridge. 'Make yourself at home, Suzanne. Yes I will,' she says, sitting down next to him and pushing her lips forward into a quizzical expression. 'So?'

'Well it's just that I realised I don't know anything about you really, apart from your husband being a solicitor. I mean it seems wrong. Cheap, if you like. Not fair on you. Ungentleman . . .' His voice tails off when he notices her deepening frown.

'What? To screw her and not know the names of her kids, you mean? And you think then you'll know all about me, because you know my kids' names.'

'I didn't mean tha—'

'Julian, Vikki, Tina and Sophia,' she says, striking the names off on her fingers. 'Tina is seventeen and Sophia fifteen. Four fairly normal kids. So now you know everything.'

'You're cross.' He looks at her mock pleadingly, and she gives an exaggerated sigh and sits back in her chair, rocking it on two legs. Her eyes are a light hazel with darker flecks in them which seem to be dancing, echoing the freckles on her short, broad nose.

'Do I look cross?'

'I don't know. I need to look more closely.' Peers intently into her irises, pursing his mouth as he feigns concentration. Her face breaks into a smile. Her teeth are her best feature: very white and even.

'Let's keep this simple for the moment, hm?'

'Yes I agree.' Relieved, he moves his face away, and sits back once more.

Pluto lying on his back in the middle of the floor, paws dangling in the air. Kempton carries him, asleep, over to the basket beneath the table, pressing the wrinkled face against his evening stubble, inhaling the milky, puppy odour. Transfers him to the basket. A small, dark, kidney shape against the white pillow and towel.

'Funny to think one day he'll fill the basket,' Suzanne muses.

'I love him,' Kempton says abruptly, suddenly choked.

'Have you got any massage oil?' she asks, as he is doing his utmost to hold back from coming while she gyrates on top of him.

'No.'

'I'll bring some next time.'

'Shit. Why – did – you – have – to – say – that?'

He finds lying next to Suzanne after sex very companionable. In fact everything about her is companionable. He can't remember ever having felt this comfortable and easy with a woman.

He gives a sudden shout of laughter. 'I've just got the joke,' he explains, when she looks puzzled. 'You know, what you said about Herod. It's really funny.'

'My God Kempton, that was really quick off the mark. Welcome to the land of the living.'

'OK Ms Sarcasm. So I was preoccupied.'

'Now you've gone defensive.'

'Not at all.' Stroking her tummy, circling his hand beneath the bedclothes.

'That's really nice.'

'Good. We aim to please.'

'You're quite tactile, aren't you?'

'Am I? I suppose so. It's so much easier, touching rather than speaking sometimes, isn't it?'

'I know what you mean.'

She smells nice. Her skin has its own wholesome, sweet odour, even after making love. He likes the way she is at ease with her body and unselfconscious.

'You know,' he says, thoughts going off at a tangent, 'people don't think of a man on his own as being vulnerable. Men are supposed to be stoic and strong. Never cry.' Still recalls his performance five days earlier at the doctor with shame.

'Well that's rubbish,' she says forcefully. 'Women are far stronger mentally than men. They need us more than we need them.' Lying there beside him with a challenging half-smile, waiting for the indignant contradiction.

In fact he agrees with her. He has known several divorced men; they have all leaped headlong into a new relationship on the rebound. Two of them had, anyway, left for another woman. The divorced women he has met have taken their time. Thinks of himself, and of his father.

'I daresay you're right. My father went to pieces when he and my mother split up. It certainly wasn't anything to do with love. I never saw any love between them. He just couldn't exist alone. I think the next generation is different. Our kids have been brought up differently. But I suppose it depends on the individual. And the situation.'

'What about you?'

'I cope OK,' he says evasively.

'That's not what I meant.'

'I – don't like it.'

'Do you miss someone, or Vanessa herself? You don't mind my asking, do you?'

And strangely he does not. He has never discussed Vanessa with another woman, let alone his feelings about her. Several reasons: one, he has not been that close to anyone else; two, it might have offended the person concerned; three, as a rule Kempton is not a man to reveal his innermost self. Perhaps it is the fact she is married, but the boundaries with Suzanne seem less defined.

After a considered pause he says, 'Both. Some*one*, and Vanessa. I miss her terribly sometimes. It's like a—' he strives for an analogy. 'My throat is gagged with pain sometimes, even after almost three years.' And as he speaks the gag is there, stifling his throat, and his voice cracks. Kempton takes control of himself. A deep intake of breath, slow releasing of air. Suzanne's sympathetic eyes; her hand stroking his upper arm.

'It comes in waves. At unexpected times.'

'I know. Something will suddenly spark a memory. What about when you're making love with another woman?'

'Not very often nowadays—' chance would be a fine thing. '—It hasn't with you,' he says quickly.

'I wouldn't be offended. It would be natural.'

'Well anyway it's true.' Reverts to the original conversation: 'I mean the normal Vanessa was so loveable. The other one . . . It was very hard to live with. You want to know something? No, I don't miss the manic Vanessa. She drove me crazy sometimes. There were times when I almost disliked her.'

Out they come, the words he has never admitted to anyone, least of all himself; constrained as he is by his sense of failure, that he mishandled everything, that perhaps he even brought out her dark side.

'The depressive Vanessa – God you've no idea how powerless you feel, listening to the talk of dying. All that torment going on inside someone you love. And you can't help them. Then they turn on you.'

The last time she miscarried, at five months.

'Don't you think I care too?' he shouted in desperation, when weeks had passed and it was as if he did not exist.

'You can't compare what you're feeling with what I am,' she said. 'I was the one carrying him.' A boy. It would have been a boy . . .

'But you don't like being on your own.'

'Not really. I don't think I was designed for it.' Pulls a rueful expression.

'Is it that you miss the attention of a woman?' She raises herself up, scrutinising him. One freckled breast – heavy, mango-shaped, large-nippled – erotically exposed out of the bedclothes, at variance with her counsellor-mood.

He brushes the tip of her nipple with his fingers, smiling. 'You could say that.' Voice larded with innuendo; then, seriously, 'Actually I miss the giving part. Almost more than anything. That probably sounds an odd thing for a man to say. As *you* said a moment ago, women don't seem to need us men anymore. There was this programme on TV last night. A woman journalist was being interviewed. I don't know who she was. Anyway, she was so hard-bitten and self-sufficient. Rather terrifying. Women seem afraid to be feminine. As though it's wrong.' Vanessa, the most feminine of all.

'Well the guidelines have changed. The parameters,' she says. 'It's bloody hard being a woman today.'

'Actually it's bloody hard being a man.'

'It's bloody hard being a human being,' Suzanne goes one better. 'Everybody's confused, scattering in different directions. They want a point of view they can rely on, and there isn't one. No government they can trust. No God. No family life. No rules. Women don't trust men, men don't trust women, children can't trust adults. Everything is competitive, selfish, experimental. There's nothing to focus on. Everyone's clamouring out of time with each other, with louder and louder voices to make themselves heard.'

A channel of warmth between their bodies. Heat radiating from his. The pleasant floating sensation of his limbs.

Kempton regards her in astonishment.

'Well, what do I say to that?'

'Why do you have to say anything?'

'No, I mean you're right. What you said makes sense . . . I must admit, this makes a change from the usual bed talk.'

'What is the usual bed talk?'

'Well, you know . . .'

They are both silent for a bit, he pondering over what she said. He would like to tell her about Cat and Peter, but suspects her response would be a 'so what?' which would only get him riled. He would also like to ask about her husband, but feels that would be inappropriate. Asks instead, 'What about you? Could you live alone?'

'Don't forget I've got four children.'

'No, I mean without a partner. Could you?'

'Yes,' she replies without hesitation.

'You wouldn't be lonely?'

'There's nothing lonelier than living in a loveless relationship.'

He glances sharply at her, but her pale-lashed eyes give nothing away. An image of his father and mother sitting at the dining table without speaking, flashes before him; and himself, a child, his food seeming to stick in his throat. Those awful mealtimes.

'A relationship shouldn't be a remedy,' Suzanne says. 'It should enhance what you already have in your life.'

• Kempton's Journey

He tells her about the group he's considering joining.

'I suspect the only thing you'll have in common,' she says with typical Suzanne dryness, 'is that your partners all topped themselves. You'll compare guilt and anger. But try it anyway.'

'I shall do,' he retorts, irritated. Just when he is beginning to feel a real rapport with her, she goes and says something which annoys him.

At the front door she rummages in her capacious bag and hands him a tiny package. 'For you. For Christmas,' she says.

'I didn't buy you anything.' He shakes his head regretfully. Puts Pluto down and takes the gift. Pluto shoots towards the kitchen.

'It's nothing. Don't start with the guilt thing. Anyway, you've just given me a £300 cheque for the puppy.'

'Oh I forgot that. He's much more placid than I expected,' he says, kissing her goodbye, running his hands down her bulked-out body.

'Don't be fooled. I'll come and see you both soon,' she adds quickly. 'Now don't be all morose over Christmas.'

'I'm dreading it,' he admits, thinking how strange it is the way she has re-entered his life. Does she merit an inclusion on his list? He switches on the outside light for her. 'Be careful not to slip. It's really icy.'

'Yes.' She hugs him.

He watches her get in her car – her swaddled beige shape easing itself into position. The window opening and her hand waving outside. He feels a deep sense of satisfaction within him. Tranquillity pervades the small street of terraced houses. Everybody is indoors. A frozen mist hangs in the air. The parish church bell chimes the hour. And from an open window of a house drift the sounds of someone practising the violin. He recognises it as part of Bach's Double Violin Concerto. Over and over again. Such diligence.

He goes indoors, to get ready for Christmas, and to bond with Pluto. Who has disappeared. After a frantic search, a yapping and yowling on the patio alert him to his whereabouts: the puppy must have followed Spike through the cat flap and now the two are confronting one another a few feet apart; the one with arched-back fury, the other with excited curiosity. Nail-up cat flap, Kempton writes mentally on his list as he scoops up Pluto. Buy cat litter. Eventually he bribes the cat inside with food and, pinioning its paws to avoid being scratched, holds it up to let Pluto have a sniff. Spike struggles in his arms, hissing, and with an extraordinary contortion of his body, manages to break free – scratching Kempton's hand, which starts to bleed. A line of little red bubbles appears. The puppy hurtles after the fleeing cat towards Kempton's study and almost immediately there follows the noise of splintering glass.

Spike sitting like a Buddha on Kempton's desk. Around him and scattered on the floor, the fragments of Kempton's small Art Nouveau mirror. He lifts up the puppy before it can cut itself and shuts it in the kitchen; next he carries the cat into the sitting room; then he sweeps up the mess with a dustpan and brush. Seven years bad luck? he wonders. He is generally impatient of superstition, nonetheless he feels a slight sense of ominous foreboding.

And as he bends to pick up a shard of glass on the carpet there is the sound of rending fabric, and a sudden chill up his bottom. Rests his hand there. His trousers. He has split his favourite cord trousers.

6

Stakes

Twelve forty-one. One seventeen. One fifty-seven. Two thirty-three. Three forty-two. At these intervals Kempton trudges downstairs in response to the plaintive whining which penetrates his sleep. And each time finds a new puddle which has somehow avoided the map of newspaper sheets. Pluto flatteringly thrilled to see him. Between that hour of three forty-two and six forty-eight he falls into a catatonic slumber, to be awakened by thuds as though the bailiffs have moved in. For a few minutes he lies there in bed, the awnings of sleep shading his comprehension. The thuds amplify, and with a grim presentiment, Kempton drags himself up from the bed. He puts on his slippers, shuffles back down to the kitchen, and turns the door handle with dread. Stands, arms akimbo, surveying the devastation, closing his eyes then opening them slowly in the hope this is a Temazepam-induced hallucination. Not. Never has he seen anything like it. The kitchen looks as though it has been vandalised. It *has* been vandalised. And the puppy dancing round him with apparent pride. 'I'm only tiny and look what I've done all by myself,' it is as though he is saying.

Spike cleaning himself with an air of insouciance on top of the table. The activities of the last few hours seem to have effected an inexplicable truce between them. The newspaper has been largely eaten; puddles and atolls of shit surround the remaining sodden pieces. The basket has been similarly feasted upon, and sticks of wicker are scattered about. The cat litter tray is upturned, and Kempton's shirts, which had been drying on hangers suspended from the units, are trailing through this unsavoury mess in tatters. The vegetable rack is on its side, with its contents – potatoes, brussels sprouts, carrots – dispersed amongst the legitimate toys. It also appears that most of the wooden cupboard knobs have been gnawed; and one drawer has been tugged open, expelling paper napkins, candles, doilies, silver foil, cocktail sticks, an unravelled ball of string . . .

'Wicked dog, wicked dog.' Kempton grabs him and takes him on a tour of his misdemeanours. The dog licking him delightedly. 'Wicked Pluto,' he repeats, pushing his nose first towards a puddle then a chewed knob. The dog wags his stern.

Belatedly Kempton recalls the handbook's advice; can almost hear the author's hearty tones: 'Do move all temptation from within your puppy's reach. To him a silk slipper and an old discarded one are identical. Only gradually will he learn what is his own and what is not. And remember: dogs are not born with a conscience.'

He resolves to empty the lobby of all its paraphernalia and confine Pluto in there tonight. He goes in there now and unhooks his waxed jacket, steps into his wellingtons – they are freezing – and tucks his pyjama trousers inside. Can already feel the cold whooshing in through the gap under the door.

'Walkies Pluto.' Gives a two-toned whistle; rather likes it and tries it again.

He gathers the dog into his arms. It is so soft. He loves the squashiness of its loose-fleshed face against his own. And the moist cool blob of a nose. And the unquestioning readiness of the little creature to commit itself, to transfer all its reliance and allegiance onto him, Kempton. What – as a surrogate mother?

'I've been rejected all my life,' he tells the counsellor who has manifested herself in his head. 'My mother, my wife – the ultimate cop-out – and now my daughter. Please not my dog.'

'Would you say you are a weak man Mr Prévot?'

The scene fades. Into the silent, frozen twilight of his small garden he carries the dog. Sets it gently on the ground. The Arctic air catches him in the chest, bites his ears, lances his eyes, forcing tears from them. The grass crunchy beneath his feet; and his boots leave imprints in the silver. Overhead: the pale remains of a pot-bellied moon in a sky slow to relinquish night. Kempton thrusts his hands into his jacket pockets and breathes deeply. Everything is uncannily still: a silver and charcoal stage set into which he has strolled as the sole member of the cast. The houses either side are in darkness, and he can just make out their hulks. If he ignores lights from the windows of other neighbouring properties he can imagine that, except for the dog, he is alone, caught in the turnstile of existence. He has a sense of oneness with it that brings to him simultaneously calm and contentment, yet also a longing and profound sorrow.

That feeling of exposure, of rawness, that lately he has been experiencing, returns to him; and now he is accustomed to the prickling behind his eyes which will take him at any time, without warning. It is as though there is another self within him who, like a jack-in-the-box, will not be suppressed. To Kempton there is something ethereal about this early Christmas morning. He could almost believe in God. Right now he would like to be able to attribute everything around him to some greater order that has nothing to do with logic. For perhaps the first time he is conscious of the scale of immensity outside of him; and he feels a twinge of excitement.

Last night he fell asleep with the lamp on, reading the book Cat gave him. 'A great change which had recently come over me, a new moral vision of the world which had opened before me, the foolish judgements of men, whose absurdity I was beginning to sense . . .' wrote Rousseau, 'and finally the wish to find a less uncertain road for the rest of my career . . . all this impressed on me the long-felt need for a general review of my opinions.'

The paragraph comes back to him now, the gist rather than every word (Pluto darting about with his odd gait and exploring nose, trailing ears and jaunty stern); he can relate it to himself. How extraordinary that Cat should have chosen this book at this time. But he is still on the brink, not quite open to receiving, reluctant to recognise what is not instantly accessible, gripping on, from habit, to the familiar patterns, quibbles and anxieties; and the pressing imminent problems – well, one mainly – that no amount of rationalising will ever, so Kempton assures himself, resolve.

What would Vanessa have said about it? She used to flirt with Peter herself. Perhaps a situation of mother-daughter rivalry would have arisen, giving a twist to the tale. And one of those unforeseen, painful hankerings for his wife yanks at Kempton with such force that he groans out loud.

'Christmas is a bad time for you I imagine . . .'

Oh and it is.

Remembering: her love of surprises. She would hide things around the house. And she elevated gift-wrapping to an art. That largesse of her nature, her childlike excitement, her wholehearted enthusiasm, would illuminate the house and encompass everyone around her. And they all basked like cats in the sun of her mood. But the mood could not be sustained. He remembers their last New Year's Eve.

'Marriage is unnatural. Two people staying together for ever,' she proclaimed over the dinner table where three other couples were also present.

Kempton, a little surprised by her statement, nevertheless took up the gauntlet wholeheartedly, expanding on the theme. 'Women think men are the same as them bar the physiology,' he said. 'They don't realise men are just not designed for monogamy and that fidelity is a deliberate and conscious effort which goes against the body's instincts. The French have the right outlook.'

He did not notice her sharp look, and there followed a spirited discussion, with Vanessa, the instigator of it, becoming more and more silent. At midnight the host put the television on, and to the chimes of Big Ben they all stood up to toast each other, kissing and hugging and laughing. Kempton embraced his wife.

'I hate you,' she said. 'If you only knew how I hate you sometimes.' And her eyes shot out venomous rays.

'What have I said, what have I done?' he kept asking, in the car and when they were home.

She shook her head, weeping, eye make-up streaked down her cheeks, red lipstick smeared. 'Even the dog hates you,' she said.

She lay beside him in bed, inconsolable, pushing him away when he tried to comfort her. An hour or so later he was woken up by her shrieking in his ear. 'You have never loved me. You've lied to me. Our marriage is a lie. Everything is.'

'Ssh, you'll wake Cat.'

'I don't care. She's old enough to know the truth.'

'You can be really selfish you know.'

'Oh here we go again. Your stock word. Selfish. You're the one who's selfish, Kempton. Boring, lying, cold, selfish, shallow, unfeeling. You don't ever—'

'Shut up, or I'll go into the spare room.'

'You see. That's all you can think of. *You. Your* feelings. You don't even *know* what you did wrong, you're so insensitive.' Sobbing loudly, beating her fists on the bedclothes.

'What *have* I done wrong? If you'll only – let me switch on the lamp.'

'Don't you dare. I don't want the lamp on.'

He found his wrists tightly clamped by her; shook himself free. 'Right, that's it. I'm going into the other room.'

And now her hand tried to restrain him, to grab him back, grasping his sleeve. 'Don't go. You are *not* going. Bastard. *Bastard.*'

He pushed her away, stumbled in the dark over various obstacles in his path, fumbled for the door and went into the spare room, pursued by her. He slammed the door and locked it, while she pummelled on it the other side. Five or ten minutes later he heard her retreat into their own room, crying in there; and put the pillow over his head to buffer the sounds.

Later she explained that her remark at the dinner party had only been the part of what she was intending to say: that having made that decision to marry, the couple should be physically faithful. He, however, had interrupted her before she could finish, and implied that it was every man's right to have affairs within a marriage.

'So I take it you've been unfaithful to me,' she said.

'No of course not,' he lied forcefully.

Oh God, he hates thinking about that evening; wishes the bad wouldn't keep rearing up, filling his head with sourness. Quarrelling with Vanessa had been like pushing a melting snowball along that never got anywhere. Their rows were emotional, destructive and exhausting;

and achieved nothing, were founded on nothing. But at least they did not quarrel the night before she did it, or the morning itself. He could never, never have lived with that.

And the truth about the spaniel, he reminds himself with a sense of malignment, was that its previous, male, owner had beaten it within an inch of its life and subsequently it had had a dislike of all men.

Poor, lovely, Vanessa – who was so untechnical that the only time she had fixed on a plug she rang him at work, she was so proud. How had she known what to do with the car? he had wondered at the time. And then it had come to him: from the novel she had been reading. And sure enough, there it was, a long passage graphically detailing the procedure. Kempton wrote a furious letter to the author via his publisher. 'I hold you responsible,' he said in it. The author wrote back. 'And what about drugs, muggings, murder, rape, etc, that you can read about every day in the paper? What about TV. and cinema? I am extremely sorry about your wife, but we can only be responsible for our own actions. There are thousands of ways of choosing to live and thousands of ways of dying. Only a few people will choose how they die, and that is their decision and theirs alone. Might I suggest you stop blaming and find a therapist?' Kempton threw the letter away.

After Vanessa died people didn't know what to say to him; their condolences were tempered with awkward self-consciousness. Suicide was a taboo subject. Words jammed in their throats. He believed that everyone was whispering. He felt disgraced. She had cast a slur on his character. He thought that everyone was judging him. This was exacerbated by the comments of several well-intentioned people: 'She always seemed so bright and vivacious' – or words to that effect. What they were really implying, so he thought, was, 'What did you *do* to her to drive her to such an act?'

And yes, that was how people remembered her; *he* likes to remember her: warm and talented, creative, articulate, sexy, beautiful. An exceptional woman. And himself so ordinary. Sometimes Kempton feels so ordinary. More than that. Spectacularly ordinary. Spectacularly unspectacular. He will leave not the titchiest print mark behind him.

I still miss her . . . Do I? Do I? Do I?

Pluto chasing back to him, pressing himself close to Kempton's legs.

'What am I going to do, eh Pluto? What am I going to do?'

Pluto squats and wees.

'Good boy, good boy,' Kempton praises him enthusiastically, patting him, about to carry him indoors, when the dog squats again, his flanks quivering. He is a tiny, dark, hunched-up form against the pale frost and lifting sky.

'Good boy, good boy,' Kempton shouts joyously this time, almost overcome with paternal elation; and now does pick him up to carry him indoors, where the arduous task of cleaning up the kitchen awaits him – Happy Christmas Kempton – and there are the brussels to peel and the table to lay; the church service to listen to on Radio Four; the presents to arrange round the tree. And he has just remembered his torn corduroys. And he has to psyche himself up for Minnie. He will not become irritable today or stalk from the room in a huff. He will at all costs retain his humour. Will not rise to Minnie's bait. Will not make a single acerbic remark to Cat about Peter.

'I feel so sick. I've never felt so sick,' Cat moans.

'Poor little love.' Peter, crouching beside her, supporting her body.

'There's nothing left in me to throw up. It feels like I'm going to throw up Foetus.'

'I swear you won't. Foetus is well entrenched in a different zone.'

She laughs, then immediately retches again, several times; afterwards leans back against him weakly. 'It's OK. I'm OK now.'

'You can't possibly go to Kempton's like this.'

'I can and I am.'

'I'm coming too, then.'

'Wart, you *can't*.'

'I can and I am.'

Minnie, her hands in sheepskin mittens, despondently scraping the ice from the windscreen of her 1954 Austin Princess. The hearse, her son refers to it. A fine Christmas this promises to be, with Kempton Park almost sure to be called off tomorrow. She doesn't ask a lot out of life, doesn't expect happiness to show its face her way again, let alone love; she doesn't interfere with anyone and no one interferes with her; her gardening, her archeological digs and racing events are the mainstays of an existence in which she partakes with no great pleasure. Boxing Day without Kempton Park to enliven the ghastliness of the Christmas period is unimaginable. She will have to endure the whole stupid, infantile charade – which not a soul she knows enjoys – with nothing to look forward to

• Kempton's Journey

as her reward for good behaviour. No sniping at her son. She has a certain fondness for Kempton which she realises he would never acknowledge. Not the usual maternal feelings; nevertheless she does understand him better than he believes she does. For instance, she understands that in marrying Gossamer he picked a woman as far removed as possible from herself. And he really thinks she didn't know about his wife's sickness. His denseness over this is quite funny. He credits her with no insight whatsoever. He is judgemental, and inclined to be pompous. Whenever she offers peace overtures he rejects them: to help sort out the chaos of his garden, to take him shopping and update his wardrobe, even to have him accompany her to the races – which she recalls he enjoyed as a small boy, although God forbid he should admit that now. Poor Kempton. He looks like a camel with a deflated hump, with the burden of all his problems. And she knows all about these too, including her granddaughter's affair with Peter – of which she does not disapprove. Peter is one of the few men she likes.

'So, dearest,' she says out loud, buffing the windscreen then the headlights with a cloth, panting a little with exertion and from the emphysema her doctor has recently diagnosed, 'what do you say, shall we emigrate? We could go back to Crete. Get away from all this hypocrisy.'

But the grave is here. She cannot bear the idea of the grave being left unattended. Could it be moved? And what about Kempton Park?

After almost three years of widowhood Kempton still does not regard the kitchen as his natural domain. The machines intimidate him – he has never used the Magimix, nor the liquidiser, and the coffee grinder is a waste of time. He did try the juice extractor once, but the liquid shot over the top. Some of the utensils baffle him also. What is one supposed to do with a mortar and pestle? And there is a drawer-full of smaller implements: complicated looking slicers, peelers, wooden-handled objects with strange protuberances, one with tiny scoops either end, another with a serrated wheel, and one with a sort of ridged tongue. He has never used the rolling pin; and for the life of him he cannot understand the need for half a dozen different whisks when one – or even a fork – does everything. But he is proud of the way he can wield the lemon squeezer and garlic crusher; sometimes becomes rather carried away with the latter. Peter is a genius in the kitchen; but then he is a professional: often steps in, in an emergency, if one of the chefs in his trendy Wimbledon restaurant is ill or throws a tantrum.

Doesn't want to think about Peter and ruin his Christmas. Midday, and Pluto, having weed outside again – by luck rather than design – having eaten his plate of tripe, and Spike's tuna, and another kitchen unit knob, is asleep, sprawled between the cooker and the fridge. Kempton has to keep stepping over him. The oven is on, with the turkey, potatoes and parsnips inside, at a hundred and eighty degrees centigrade. The dish of ready-prepared stuffing, and ready-prepared bread sauce are in the smaller oven above, which is switched off. The pre-cooked Christmas pud is awaiting entry to the microwave. The table in the dining room is more or less laid. And where is Cat for the finishing touches? She had promised to be early, to help him. He tries to quench the incipient niggling anger before it becomes full-blown outrage. Oh but he knows. He can perfectly envisage the scene: Peter and her exchanging presents in bed. All lovey-dovey. Thank you darling, it's lovely darling. Screwing. Oh God look at the time. I'm going

• Kempton's Journey

to be late. Dad will go mad. And yes he will. Is beginning to. Steam.

Into the sitting room, where a bottle of Champagne is resting on a bed of ice inside its bucket. But suppose she has had an accident? His stomach clenches. He pictures her car trundling innocently along; Cat's smile; overnight bag on the seat next to her, and probably some presents. A cassette playing. And closer and closer they draw to that invisible freezing patch. Then she is upon it, the little car pirouetting on its wheels and his little girl – he clasps his head, shaking it briskly to rid himself of the frightful images.

He will phone her. But first he puts on a record. Eartha Kitt. Purring into action. Speaking of which, at that precise moment there comes from outside the throaty purring of a powerful engine and a car drawing up in the road. The engine cutting. Two successive thuds from heavy doors. He recognises all these sounds; but he must be mistaken. He bounds to the window and stares out incredulously and with gathering fury. And at the point when his features are squeezing themselves into a livid contortion, Peter spots him from the pavement and waves cheerfully.

The gall, the gall. Kempton dashes to the front door in readiness – collides into the tree and jolts the fairy lights, which immediately fuse. He can feel pine needles in his hair.

'Shit.' He shouts it, almost dancing in his rage. He cannot recall ever having felt so incensed, so provoked. Yes he can. Just a few days earlier by Pitman. And he is normally so phlegmatic. Or he used to be.

He flings the door open, blocking the space with his bulk. Barely glances at his daughter, or the basket containing parcels, which she and Peter are holding together, one handle each.

'*You're* not coming in.' He glowers at Peter.

'Happy Christmas, old chum,' says Peter.

'Get out of the way.'

'That's not very hospitable.'

'Get *out*.' He tries to haul Cat inside and push Peter out simultaneously.

Cat tries to placate him. Puts down her end of the basket and stretches her arm towards him. 'Dad, please. I wasn't well. Wart drove me here. I wouldn't have been able to come otherwise.'

'It would have been better if you hadn't.'

'Dad, please.' She attempts to hug him but he holds himself rigid.

'That's a bloody thing to say to your daughter. You really are being a bit of a berk, Kempton.' Peter edges his foot inside.

'Right, that's it. I've had all I can take. Cat, this was very, very wrong of you.'

'Dad—'

'*Wrong* of her? Why won't you listen?' Peter starting to become angry now. 'She was ill. She—' Cat flashes him a warning look, and he breaks off.

'Wart's not just my chauffeur,' she says. Her lips have gone. She is trembling; and attempts again to embrace him.

'I'm fully aware what else he is besides your chauffeur,' Kempton says, his own hurt and anger making him cruel, swelling inside him, suffusing him. He forces his daughter's hands from round his neck, ignoring her ghostly face, tearful eyes. He is blocked from her by his sense of very great injustice and something demonic, almost like hate.

'I won't have you talking to her like that.' Peter tries to barge his way past; but Kempton is taller and more powerfully built. And charged with adrenalin.

'*You* have no say in this.' Kempton's face is an inch from his old friend's, his fist up threateningly. 'It's all your doing.'

• Kempton's Journey

'I can't stand this, I can't stand it,' screams Cat in a tone reminiscent of her mother's.

'Baby—' Peter makes a move towards her.

'No. She can come in on her own.' Kempton bars him with his arm. 'I will not have you in my home, contaminating it, ruining my Christmas.'

'You've done that yourself already, mate. You're being ridiculous.' Peter stands back now, shaking his head in disbelief and making a frustrated gesture in the air with the flats of his hands.

Cat, silently gazing at the floor.

'I think not.' Kempton turns to his daughter. 'Cat, you come inside please. Now.' Imperious.

'No Dad.' She says this very softly. Steps back, and links hands with Peter.

Kempton staring at her, shocked, rent apart by an implosion of pain. He doubles up with it and leans against the wall. For a moment they are blurred: Peter – raised eyebrow, stern mouth, penetrating blue eyes; Cat drooped against him, chewing her finger; then they are once more in sharp, wounding focus, the pair of them a united front against himself.

'Well?' Peter says.

'Cat?' Kempton questions her. 'It's up to you.'

She stops worrying her finger, but leaves it resting at the corner of her hips. 'Dad, even the Germans and British had a truce at Christmas, across the trenches. Please let us both come in and talk for a bit.'

'I'm not having a filthy old lecher in my house.'

'That's it. There are limits,' Peter says, turning to go.

'*Wart.*' Cat captures his arm, but he shakes it off and starts walking away.

'Wart – Peter – Wart,' she screams. 'Now look what you've done. You're so stubborn. So stupid,' she shouts at her father, as Peter heads for his car.

At the sight of his retreating back, Kempton feels a slight relaxing of tension. He makes to kiss his daughter's head. 'Darling, let's you and I—'

She ducks. '*No* Kempton. Oh you really are . . . You really are – unreasonable sometimes. And archaic.' She pushes the basket towards him with one foot. 'These are for you and Minnie.'

'Stay. For Chrissake, stay. It's Christmas. You can't *do* this.'

But she can. He watches despairingly as she limps away down the path, to the car, where Peter is holding the door open for her.

'I love you, Dad.' Her voice, gentle and sad, floating across the iced winter air, breaking up into fragments, drifting away down the empty river.

'No you don't. You just proved that by your choice,' he calls back with a viciousness he does not feel.

In this study he slumps onto the sofa. A dry sob escapes him. Right now he would truthfully be glad if someone said that today would be his last day on earth. No more decisions. No more sorrow ripping through him – vacating him for a bit then returning with a vengeance, playing cat and mouse with his emotions and mental stability. Is this what Vanessa felt? This exhaustion draining you of the energy to cope anymore, and one suddenly thinks: enough. I've had enough. How could Cat do this to him? And her basket and contents a lonesome reminder in the hall.

The roasting odours of the turkey. He had so wanted to make a nice Christmas. Was it too much to demand? a loving, harmonious Christmas. For a few minutes he sits there in a stupor, until Eartha comes to the end. Then he lumbers up, and with a leaden heart goes to the kitchen to baste the turkey. Everything has lost its meaning. And Minnie will soon be here. And the fairy lights have fused, and what is, what is, what is the point?

• Kempton's Journey

Pluto stirring, wagging his tail at the sight of Kempton His wholehearted affection is almost too much. Kempton feels as though he is being throttled.

'Hello little chap.' Skims the dog into his arms as it is about to squat sleepily on the spot, and carries him outside immediately.

'Wee-wees! Good boy,' he congratulates Pluto, repressing the wave of pain that rises to his throat. I have to get away. I need a holiday he thinks. I can't take much more.

Remorse is seeping into him. Perhaps he could have handled the situation better. But how, without capitulating? There was no way he would have invited Peter in. Therefore he was right. A case of impasse. But – she was ill. Only now does this register. They had said Cat was ill. And he can picture her wan little Modigliani face, owl-eyed. Oh God, what's wrong with her? Perhaps he was too rash. His rage had obliterated everything else. He'll phone; discard his pride and phone. Oh he wishes she would come back. At this moment he would even let Peter in, just to see her. Perhaps they have only gone a few yards down the road to alarm him and are right now heading back; parking . . .

Races round the side way with Pluto in his arms, to the front, to inspect the road. But the only cars drawing up are visitors' for his neighbours, and Minnie's hearse.

He watches her park, and waits by the door for her to get out of the huge black car – delving about in its depths; the back of her camel coat, the crown of her pull-on tweed hat visible – then she emerges with a large amount of paraphernalia: shooting stick (what on earth does she need that for indoors? he wonders, already irritated), ancient leather bag, hoisted by its worn strap over a shoulder, and a large basket not unlike Cat's. He ought to help her, but Pluto is in his arms.

'What are you cuddling a beanbag for?' she asks as she approaches. Her nose is crimson from cold.

'He's called Pluto.' Kempton is taken aback. 'I said exactly the same. That he looked like a beanbag.'

'You see how alike we are dear. Hmph.' She pecks him on the cheek after a second's hesitation, noticing but not remarking on, his harrowed and dishevelled appearance. The dog struggling in his arms trying to reach her and lick her.

'He's adorable,' she says. 'If we could just go indoors Kempton—'

'We'll have to go round the side. This door's locked. I'm sorry, I can't carry anything because of him.'

'When did I ever need male assistance?'

You said it. But he doesn't speak the words out loud. He is in no mood for battle. He doesn't know how he is going to get through the day. The quarrel is replaying in his head. His own remarks. He said terrible things, didn't he?

He sets Pluto down on the kitchen floor. The room is littered with toys. John Major's skull has been ripped open. The newspaper, much of it wet, is all over the place. The sink is full of dishes, the work surfaces crowded with saucepans.

'Well I must say, it's an improvement on the usual.' Minnie, taking off her hat and coat and laying them across the table. 'Almost like a home. Something smells good,' she adds hurriedly, remembering her good intentions, before he can snipe back and the conversation degenerate.

'Thanks. Sherry?' The circumstances hardly warrant the Champagne.

'Of course.' She hauls Pluto onto her lap and he tries to clamber onto her face as she is about to light her pipe. 'Yes, who's bootiful, who's bootiful,' she cooes in a way he has not heard before. They never had pets when he was a child. It occurs to him only now to wonder the reason; when she was so obviously the type.

'This is most unlike you, Kempton.'

'What is?'
'To buy a puppy.'
'I was persuaded. Against my better judgement.'
'I'll have him whenever you can't look after him.'
'*Really*?' he asks, pouring her a Fino sherry and himself a vodka.
'Any time.'
'Why didn't we have a dog at home?'
'Your father was allergic to them. And cats.'
'I never knew.'
'There are lots of things you never knew. Hmph. Where can I put the presents?'
'Round the tree in the hall.'

She follows him, pursued by the puppy, who stalks and pounces at her trouser-clad calves.

'You forgot to switch the lights on,' she says, arranging several parcels round the tub.

'I didn't. They fused. I'm fed up of them. I spent hours going through them. I had them working brilliantly, then I tripped over them. They're a waste of time. I'm not bothering with them next year.' Next year? Next year he will be far away. Disappear for the whole of the Christmas period. Join the émigré set. Except they all seem to play golf or bridge, both which are anathema to him.

'So where's Cat?' his mother asks, walking into the primrose rag-rolled sitting room, whose tall, festooned, sash windows look onto the frozen landscape of his neglected garden; which makes her itch to get stuck into it every time she sees it. The frost, the icicles still hanging from the roof of the small shed, remind her: no racing, no racing.

'Been and gone,' he answers tersely, forming his lips into a silent whistle, in an attempt to look nonchalant. Wanders up to the baby grand and runs his fingers in a glissando along the keys.

'What do you mean?' Minnie's eyes, pale above the

sherry in its cut glass, survey him. Her long legs are neatly crossed on the primrose damask sofa; her narrow feet in dark brown brogues, ankles just visible beneath her beige slacks. Her hair is in its usual strawberry-roan chignon. Her nose is back to its normal colour now that she has thawed through. A good-looking woman for nearly eighty.

'She turned up with Peter. I won't have that man in the house.'

'So you turned your own daughter away?'

'No I turned *him* away. It was her choice to go with him. I wanted Cat to stay of course.' He doesn't mention about her being ill. But in fact he can hardly think of anything else. He needs to speak to her, to phone her. This second.

'You can't have expected her to stay without him.'

'Look I don't want to talk about it. Right?'

'You put her in an impossible position.'

'They put themselves – and me – in it, by his coming with her. Peter knows my feelings on the matter. It was thoughtless and very crass.' Stubbornness vying with his conscience. Cat's entreating voice: 'Dad, please. I wasn't well.' And Peter's: 'She was ill.'

'Anyway, you're a fine one to talk,' he accuses her. 'Parental responsibility is hardly your strong point.'

She shrugs, uncrosses her legs and gets up.

'Where are you going?' Alarm in his tone. Perversely he does not want her to leave. In the absence of any other company, she is better than nothing when he is feeling like this. He is terrified of being left alone.

She had been on the point of leaving, but his obvious distress tempers her exasperation with pity for him.

'To make the gravy. I can't stand turkey without gravy.'

Relief swamps him. Gratitude. He almost runs into the kitchen in front of her in case she changes her mind. 'I'll show you where everything is . . . What do you want?

Flour – here.' He brandishes the storage jar. 'Bisto? Stock cubes? Here.'

'The turkey. I always make the gravy in the roasting tin.'

'Oh yes.'

'So I'll need to transfer it to a carving dish or something.'

'Sure. Anything.' He starts whistling. Hyperactive, eager to please.

The rare sight of his mother cooking in his kitchen. Pluto at her feet, watching her. And Kempton disappears into his study to dial Peter's number. He gets the answerphone, and hesitates, but can't bring himself to leave a message. He replaces the receiver despondently.

He cannot remember the last time he had a meal alone with his mother. On this basis, seated opposite each other at the dining table, which she has made an attempt to look festive – holly from her garden, a poinsettia, gold crackers and brightly patterned paper napkins, all which she brought with her – it would not be right to indulge in the usual ping-pong of insults.

Over the soup – cream of watercress from a carton – they attempt to keep up a neutral conversation. The soup itself provides a reasonable starting point.

'It's really excellent isn't it? I mean it tastes quite home-made. I live off these,' Kempton says.

'I must admit it's not bad.'

'And the mushroom one is also delicious.'

'I'd have thought you'd have learnt to cook by now, Kempton.'

'Oh it's not really my scene. Too fiddly. I'm getting quite good at pasta though. And roast lamb. I do that really well. Cat showed me. You stud it with rosemary and cloves of garlic. Dribble olive oil over it . . .' Why did he need to mention Cat? Maybe Peter has had to take her to hospital. Maybe they had been trying to explain that to Kempton, and he had not given them the chance.

'How's the business?' Minnie asks.

'Fine. Well actually it's ghastly. I can't tell you what it's like working for Pitman.' He relates about the office party to her, and about the doctoring of Grove Estates' wine list. She laughs in approval.

'Maybe it's time to up sticks,' she says.

'I've got just over another year of my contract to run.'

'Does that matter, all said and done? They'd have to pay you something.'

'In point of fact they wouldn't. Not if I left voluntarily. I might get a few months' goodwill pay. And my pension. Big deal. That wouldn't go very far. I mean there's this house for a start.' Sweeps his arms wide in a gesture that encompasses the room.

'Couldn't you do something else?'

'Like what? Mike Chandler, my ex-sales director, if you recall, is cleaning windows.' But what about the novel he is also writing? And according to Tim Isaacs, Mike is happier than he ever was. The spark of hope – hope born of alternative possibilities – kindles within Kempton. A man of single purpose, tunnel vision: what would it be like, he wonders, to perform an act one day that was truly Promethean?

He asks her about her next dig.

'I can't go on them anymore,' she tells him. 'Not with my emphysema.'

'Oh, that's a real shame.' He knows how she used to enjoy them.

'One of those things. Hmph. And there are still group trips.'

'Oh well, that's something.'

An awkward pause in the conversation, which he fills by dutifully asking her about her racing.

'Kempton Park's almost certain to be called off tomorrow,' she says.

'That'll be a blow for you.'

'Well it will really. It's been a ritual for as long as I can remember. You know – the same old crowd meeting every year. Hmph. It'll be strange not to go.'

He remembers going with her. Everybody had made a fuss of him. There was one woman in particular: he had been bursting to go to the toilet and she led him to the members' enclosure. She had huge black eyes and very black hair. A slight accent. Who was she?

He tries to see it from Minnie's point of view. What is he so passionate about that were an event to be cancelled his disappointment would be similarly great to hers? Nothing, he realises. The choir, playing squash, are not in the same league as her racing or, once, her archaeological digs. As a student he had loved rowing and had certainly taken it very seriously. Most of his leisure time was taken up with it. Practising in all weathers. Straining thighs wet and pink from rain and cold. Aching arms. Cox screaming, '*Pull* for God's sake.' And, yes, perhaps that had been comparable. But it was a long time ago. There is not one thing nowadays about which he is passionate.

'You're cold,' Vanessa once accused him. 'There's nothing you care about.' 'I care about you and Cat,' he said. 'Doesn't that count?'

'Hmph . . .' Minnie breaks into his thoughts. 'Kempton, I just want to say one thing.'

'What?' Immediately defensive.

'Cat's got a sensible head on her. And she could do worse than Peter. Twenty something years age difference isn't unusual nowadays. He's younger than you, anyway.'

'Four years, for Chrissake. He's my friend. Was. I've seen him in action. I know what he's like.' *Vidi, vici, veni.*

'Maybe she's tamed him.'

'For ten minutes perhaps. Look I've told you I don't—'

'I've said my piece. Shall I carry these out to the kitchen?'

'Please,' he says stiffly.

Pluto whining from the lobby when he hears them.

'Good boy, good Pluto,' Kempton calls. 'It seems so mean,' he says to his mother as there now come the sounds of paws scraping the door.

'It's kinder in the end.' Minnie, running the soup bowls under the tap before stacking them in the dishwasher. 'This way he'll be used to it for tonight. You can't expect him to survive eight hours in there alone without breaking him in gradually.'

He knows she is right, but it is all he can do not to go into the lobby and pluck the puppy out and cuddle it. He is like a besotted new father; had felt quite jealous when Pluto was responding to Minnie's fussing. He had wanted to tear the puppy away from her.

He carves and serves everything in the kitchen. Minnie observes him pensively. He is very precise the way he dissects the turkey. His bent head shows its thinning patch. He is middle-aged. Extraordinary to think of that son she used to cart round race meetings – her husband taught on Saturdays – extraordinary to think of that small boy who had sheltered under the brim of her trilby, as middle-aged. When he was very young he had seemed to like coming with her and had yelled with the best of them, peering through his own binoculars she'd bought him, from a raised vantage point. At Kempton, which was so flat, they always stood at a particular spot by the track and his face would light up when the horses thundered past. She had begun to appreciate his company, and to think it was not so bad having a son. Then, almost overnight, he had changed, had become reluctant to accompany her. He had become disdainful and more introspective. And he made it clear he was embarrassed by her.

'It's the first big meal I've done on my own,' Kempton announces with some pride when he sees the food in colourful dollops on the plate. 'Except for your gravy of course.'

'Jolly good. Hmph.'

But back at the table the seat next to him, where Cat should be, is empty. Her place setting has been removed. Confronted with his full plate, he hasn't much appetite. Prods the brussels desultorily (Minnie has brought another bagful from her garden; he does not know when he will use them), and picks uninterestedly at the turkey. There is something wrong with it. Too bland. And dry, despite the gravy.

'I didn't salt it enough. And it's overcooked.'

'It's not too bad,' she says generously, chewing hard so that her jaw aches and she questions the anchorage of her crowns.

'The chestnuts are like bullets. And the sage and onion stuffing has gone crusty.'

'Maybe you didn't add enough water to it. Or an egg. Did you beat in an egg?'

'No. I didn't know you had to.'

'That's probably it then. But it's edible.'

His mother is being really pleasant. In fact it is quite unsettling how they are both being so civil to one another. Normal action will be resumed in the new year . . .

'Decent wine at any rate. Is this something your company stocks?'

'You're joking. *Did* stock. It was part of my old stock. I bought the bin ends for myself. Pitman didn't want anything to do with them. What would he do with a Château Lascombes?'

He is unable to swallow his food. Pushes the plate away. He has to track down—

'Hello.' Cat standing in the doorway, in her coat. Vanity case by her feet. 'I came in the back way.'

'Oh God, *darling*.' He leaps up, knocking his wine over.

Minnie rights the glass and mops up the spillage with a paper napkin.

Kempton enveloping his daughter in his arms. The relief of holding her. 'I've been so worried. I've been so worried.' His mouth against her hair.

'We went for a walk.' She nestles in the hollow beneath his jaw.

'Are you on your own?' Gripping her tightly as he asks this in case she tries to pull away.

But she doesn't flinch. 'Yes. Peter's fetching me in the morning.'

'I can take you back.'

'No, it's arranged. I promise he won't come in.'

She does not want to have to rely on her father tomorrow. By tomorrow her father will be cognisant of certain facts. Who can gauge what his mood will be then?

Kempton is about to apologise for earlier, but changes his mind quickly. After all, they did put him on the spot, didn't they? He holds Cat at arm's length, enabling him to look into her eyes. Heaves out a great exhalation. 'If you *knew* how glad I am to see you . . .' His joy is so overwhelming that at this moment he would even be civil to Peter. No. Perhaps that would be going too far.

'I do know.'

'Love ya, sweetie-pie.'

'Love ya too, Kempton.'

'So what's this about being ill then?'

'Oh it's nothing. A bit of a tummy upset, that's all.' Waves her hand dismissively, and leaving the enclave of his arms, goes up to her grandmother to hug her.

'Happy Christmas Minnie.'

'Hello dearest one.' Minnie, still seated, hugs her back. 'The same to you.'

She knows instantly what is wrong with her granddaughter. After six pregnancies, all except one of which ended in miscarriages, she should know. And how will her son react? Poor Kempton. Feels a fresh pang of compassion for him as she observes him fussing around his daughter, unable to do enough for her, laying her place at the table again, putting in front of her a plate piled high with food that he does not notice her gaze at with repugnance; ablaze with bonhomie, garrulous with love and a happiness that she fears will be very transient indeed.

Pluto, released and exuberant, darting about while they open their presents round the tree. A 1960 recording of Ronnie Aldrich and the Squadcats' 'St Louis Blues' drifting out of Kempton's study. At last it feels like Christmas day.

'I'm sorry, my wrapping leaves a lot to be desired,' he says.

Minnie, pipe dangling from the corner of her mouth, is otherwise regal as she bestows the gifts. She tries on her gauntlets appreciatively, while Cat slips on the chrome watch, exclaiming over it. Kempton wrestling with the gold twine round Cat's gift to him. He opens the paper finally to reveal a wooden box containing a pyrites crystalline, a geode and a rose-quartz, to add to his collection of minerals.

'They're beautiful. Thank you darling. Very, very much.'

'And this is also for you.' She fishes an envelope from her basket and hands it to him. 'Hey, does this dog ever stop licking? Ploo-to-to. Who's a licky poglet?' as he scrambles over her lap.

'So what's in here then?'

'Open it and see.'

Minnie screwing up her eyes to read the writing on her packet of smoked salmon, without her glasses. 'Eust . . . It's no good, what does it say dear?' she asks Cat.

'Finest smoked salmon soaked in ten-year-old malt whisky.'

'I need my glasses too. What on earth *is* this?' Kempton, trying to decipher the wording and illustration on one of the newspaper cuttings from the envelope. His glasses are on his desk in his study, and he disappears to put them on; reads: 'Holiday in the Lot et Garonne region of France the old-fashioned way. Take a horse-drawn Romany caravan and explore the beautiful countryside. Forget time and all your problems; feel your tension slip away as your horse plods gently along the quiet lanes amongst chestnut groves and lush pasture, dissected by clear-water brooks . . .'

The second torn-out page is an advertisement for art classes held in small groups in an experienced artist's private studio.

'Learn to paint without feeling self-conscious,' runs the heading. And beneath: 'Tuition to suit all abilities. Individual guidance at your own pace. Hours to suit you. Three-hour sessions. All mediums taught.'

Romany holidays in France? Painting classes? What is Cat thinking of? He returns to them in the hall. Cat has the ruched silk scarf he bought for her wound round her neck, and is lying on the floor, poring over his main present to her: an early twentieth century book, handbound in brocade and with an enamel clasp, of translated Indian poems, exquisitely illustrated.

'I've never seen anything like it.' She gets up with difficulty, bolstering herself first on one elbow, to kiss him. 'Where did you find it?'

'At the antiquarian bookshop in King Street.'

'I love it. It's quite the most beautiful book I've seen.'

'Good. I'm glad. But will you please tell me, what are these in aid of?' He holds out the two cuttings.

'To inspire you.'

'*Inspire* me?'

• Kempton's Journey

'Yes. You need a holiday. And you're rather good at painting. Well, drawing.'

'Don't be silly, I've never done any. How can you say that?'

'You're always doodling.'

'Adorning women with beards and spectacles in magazines, you mean. Filling in the O's and A's in headings. Sure. That makes me a Picasso.'

'No, seriously. You're always drawing houses and trees.'

'That must tell you something about me. Go on. You're the psychologist.'

'Houses equal security, I suppose. Trees? Love of harmony? Or perhaps the subconscious desire to branch out. Oh yes. that's it.' She laughs. 'Got you in one. Anyway, they're really *good* Kempton. If you went to classes you could be good.'

'I'd feel an absolute berk.'

'That's why I picked out that particular advert. I thought you might be a bit self-conscious somewhere like Richmond Adult College.'

'Hmph,' Minnie interrupts. 'This is for you Kempton, from me. Oh and there's one other small present left by the tree. I don't know who that's from.'

Suzanne. 'To the proud new father,' she has written on the little card attached.

'I'll open it later. Thanks Minnie.' Taking her gift.

It is an encyclopedia of Art Nouveau. He is touched. 'That's very thoughtful of you. Really very kind.'

She is standing very straight-backed and authoritative by the tree; and Kempton hesitates, then makes a move as if to go over to her and perhaps kiss her. But at that point she turns abruptly; and his arms, that had been raised, fall and hang slack at his sides.

'Clearing-up time,' she says briskly. 'Cat and I will do it. You did lunch.'

'OK, thanks.'

He cannot remember her ever having hugged him. One day, he vows, he will tell her that. And he will bring up the fact she never gave him a party. But he is pleased with the book. He will read that in bed tonight. Less intense than the Rousseau. He is not in the mood for introspection. He is rather worn-out from today, actually. Sapped. Like he used to be after dramatics with Vanessa.

In the privacy of his study he opens Suzanne's present. Inside a small box is a key ring with a pewter bloodhound dangling from it. 'Couldn't believe it when I saw this,' says the enclosed note in large spiky writing. 'I had to get it for you. Hope he's behaving. With unchaste thoughts and lustful hugs, Suzanne.'

He fingers the little object, smiling. Whenever he thinks of Suzanne he feels like smiling. ('Why did you laugh?' she said the other day, after he had found some remark, or maybe a gesture – he can't remember what – amusing. 'I didn't. I smiled out loud,' he replied). He wonders what she is doing now, presumes she is surrounded by her family; tries to picture her in the context of her home, which he only remembers hazily. Is already looking forward to seeing her again. Whenever that will be.

In the kitchen Minnie says to Cat, 'Stem ginger in warm water, dear heart. It's excellent for morning sickness.'

'What?' Cat's hands frothing about in the sink become instantly still. The saucepan she had been holding slips from her grasp, back into the water. 'How did you know?'

'Experience?'

'I'm not getting rid of it,' she says, slightly defensively.

'No, I didn't think you would. How does Peter feel about it?'

'He's thrilled. You should see him. He's like a kid himself.'

'And you're happy with him?'
'Extremely.'
'Then that's fine, isn't it. Hmph. So when are you going to tell your father?'
'Tomorrow morning. When I've finished throwing up. It's amazing he doesn't suspect anything. I mean I was really bad the other morning when I was here.'
'You know what your father's like.'
'Yes.'

'So Christmas turned out all right in the end,' Kempton says, kissing his daughter goodnight in her bed. Trying to ignore the men's pyjamas she is wearing.

'It sure did.' She feels like an executioner; in a few hours he will be a crushed man. And he seems so vulnerable at the moment, looks perpetually bemused.

'Thank you for coming back today darling. I don't know what I'd have done . . . Anyway, let's not talk about that. Minnie wasn't too awful today, was she?'

'No. I thought she was on good form.' But Cat never thinks of her grandmother as awful.

'I wish I knew what made her tick.'

'Do you really?'

'Well—' ponders for a moment, 'well it would be interesting, I suppose. I don't know much – well, nothing really – about her parents. My maternal grandparents.' He is thoughtful for a bit. Cat smiles, then rolls over onto her tummy and huddles her head into the crook of her arm so that her face is invisible to him. 'What?' he asks her, prodding her shape beneath the duvet. 'What are you smiling about?'

'Nothing. Night-night then Kempton.'

'Night, sweetie-pie.'

'And don't chuck those pages I cut out.'

'Dotty. Eccentric. You are, you know.'

'Aquarians always are.'
'Sleep well.'
She knows she won't. 'You too.'
He kisses the wiry sorrel crown of her head and leaves her room. Happiness is his for another nine hours.

7

One-horse Race

Not quite seven thirty. And it is bitterly cold. No racing for Minnie. But Kempton has other matters to concern himself with. For a start there is Pluto, who emerges from a vortex of feathers to welcome him. The cushion cover is shredded into bandages. Bits of the basket are scattered about. A small area of the door has been gnawed. But the general damage is limited. There is just one puddle, partially soaked up by the feathers. Kempton fastens the collar round Pluto's neck and opens the door to the garden. The dog immediately zooms outside and performs. Kempton praises him and strokes him in an abstracted way. Pluto rushes off to explore. He is becoming bolder by the hour, adapting to his imposed routine, even showing preliminary signs of developing a conscience. Rolls now on the hard ground, giving small squeaks of pleasure.

The plastic guttering creaks under its heavy layer of ice. Still, serene early morning. But Kempton is far from serene. He has left Cat being sick in the house. He is knitted-browed and meditative by the flower bed of shrubs and weeds and spiky thistles – mysterious in their silver coating. Oblivious of the cold, despite the fact he is wearing only his pyjamas, dressing gown and slippers. His hair is on end, fine like antennae, and beige bits of scalp gleam through. A seam runs diagonally across his cheek, from the top of one ear to the edge of his mouth, from where his face was pressed into the pillow. 'Not a pretty sight,' Kempton often remarks out loud when he has that first unlovely glimpse of himself in the mirror in the morning. Who'd want to wake up with that? A deterrent for all but the most genuinely committed of women. But this morning he has not glanced at himself. He went straight to his daughter in the bathroom to offer his assistance.

'This isn't right. You must see a doctor' – As she retched into the toilet. Feeling useless and anxious, watching her.

'Please Dad. Not now. Please leave me,' she said, when she could speak.

So downstairs he came. And here he is in his bleak little garden. And a horrible thought is inveigling its way into his brain for the first time, and settling there. Memories of Vanessa vomiting every morning when she was – He cannot even frame the word to himself. A sour taste flowing into his mouth. The syncopated accelerando of his heart as – ah no, oh God, oh shit, please not that – the deplorable possibility dawns on him and takes root. Fool. Is he retarded or something, not to have seen it earlier? Kempton, you're a *fool*. He punches the air several times.

Indoors he sweeps up the feathers. They swirl everwhere, taunting him, it seems to him, deliberately; drifting gently over his head or just out of reach; landing – only to float upwards again. The dance of the feathers, he thinks. And the Sugar Plum Fairy theme plays in his head, which is pounding. When he touches his left temple he can feel a raised vein there, beating with a life of its own. Perhaps he will have a thrombosis.

Pluto waiting for his Farex and milk. His pulled-down

eyes like Kempton's own. And this done, Kempton creeps upstairs, past the closed door of the other bathroom, and into his own via his bedroom. Confronts his dark-stubbled, creased-cheeked, crumpled face and wild sparse hair in the mirror with which Vanessa ill-advisedly told the decorator to cover the entire wall above the bath. He can't avoid seeing himself on the toilet either, which is most off-putting. He tries to turn sideways or look between his knees, but invariably catches his reflection, nonetheless; his face, red and bulging-eyed. How basic we all are, it will strike him. One day he will wrench the mirror down himself. But this morning, as it is several days since Mrs Jakes was last here, it has accumulated so many smears, streaks and blobs that you can't see a thing unless you squint deliberately. And grant you, his body is in very fair shape. And once he has shaved, cleaned his teeth, thoroughly washed out his mouth, and brushed back his recalcitrant hair – careful not to damage a single precious strand – well, he scrubs up good, as Vanessa used to say.

He longs for his cords. He is so used to plucking them from the back of the chair without thought. Tomorrow he will make time to buy another pair. Meanwhile his beige twills will have to suffice; along with his checked Viyella shirt over which he drags a thick, ribbed maroon jumper he seems to remember Peter gave him for some birthday. But it's bloody cold and why cut off his nose? Brushes his hair flat again. Goes downstairs to make the first coffee of the day and read the paper (always surprised that it should be delivered on Boxing Day), while he waits for his daughter; who appears about an hour later, parchment-frail, finger up to her mouth, wearing black leggings and a man's shirt which hangs down beneath her own long grey cardigan. The scarf which Kempton gave her. A high pony-tail. Bare feet and, obscurely, one red-varnished toenail: her big toe. Oh my darling daughter.

• Kempton's Journey

How has it happened? How has everything happened? If they are all products of their environment, following, conforming to, or rebelling against known patterns, then he has only himself to blame. And Vanessa. But the dynamics of family relationships are far too perplexing, and Kempton has never been good at – or perhaps bothered with – dealing with issues not immediately accessible to his comprehension.

He can hardly look at her. Is suddenly afflicted with a fit of shivering. He cannot behave as normal; as though he is not bursting to know the truth, unpalatable though it is bound to be. He cannot even ask her if she is feeling better.

He turns away from her. 'Tea. I'll make you some nice tea.' Occupies himself with this, and starts to prattle inanely – about Pluto, the feathers, how odd that there should be a paper on Boxing Day, and poor Minnie with Kempton Park called off; and he must buy some more cords tomorrow – has he told her he tore his old ones? – he is quite lost without them . . .

'I gather you've sussed it then,' Cat says, when he finally breaks off and puts the mug of tea in front of her (her own mug with the aquarian sign of the water-bearer on it).

'Tell me you're not. Tell me. Just tell me.'

He makes it so difficult for her, she thinks resentfully. With his preconceived, stereotyped ideas and hang-ups he is entrenched in another era. And right now she needs his paternal support. She has asked so little of him over the years. That annoys her also: that he doesn't even realise it. But he is suffering; of that there is no doubt. His expression is anguished.

'I am. Six weeks.' Looks back at him steadily, with a hint of defiance.

Kempton stumbling to his feet; pushing his chair back so violently that it falls to the ground. He kicks at it there.

'You stupid little bitch.' He does not shout; in fact she

has hardly ever heard him shout. But this soft-voiced fury is worse. It makes her shrivel inwardly. 'You stupid, stupid, *stupid*—'

He stares down at her for a moment, his complexion devoid of all colour.

She is silent, fighting against tears. He has never spoken to her like that. Her stomach is knotted as she watches him making an effort to control himself – taking deep breaths and making 'phwoo' sounds, circling his neck several times. He makes a fist of one hand and slaps it repeatedly into the palm of the other. This goes on for a few minutes.

'You're in plenty of time to have an abortion,' he says eventually from his position by the lobby door, some distance from her.

The insensitivity of this remark makes her gasp. Knowing as he does, her views. A deliberately cruel remark. She is seeing a side of him she has not done before, and does not like it. Has a sudden insight into her mother's character. With another kind of man her mother might . . .

'I didn't hear that, Kempton,' she says with a gritted-lipped tightness. Cat, who has marched for her beliefs, started petitions, lobbied in the street, held meetings; written hundreds of letters to medical bodies, women's groups, schools, politicians, judges, heads of nations and religious bodies; incurred the wrath of feminists – yet she would classify herself as one; polarised herself from some of her fellow students; and spent six hours in a police cell.

'I said you're in—'

'If you repeat it I shall leave the house this minute and walk all the way home, I swear.'

And he does not doubt her.

'OK, OK. Oh God.' He clasps his head. What else? What else is there that can go wrong? It is as though there is a vendetta against him. Hee-hee, let's target old Kempton,

Cat thinking, he can't see that it isn't against him,

that none of this need hurt him. She gets up from the table and goes up to him, wraps her arms around his waist.

'Hey Dad.'

He does not resist her and, encouraged, she nuzzles her head against him, squeezes him tighter, her arms long and strong. She feels his whole body give; and her own antagonism dissipates.

'I need you. I really do, you know Dad.'

She feels him tense again, as though he is about to contradict her, pour scorn on her remark. But she holds on to him resolutely, and once more his body relaxes.

The fierceness of his anger ebbs, and is replaced by a sense of heaviness. And briefly the thought occurs to him: how would he feel if it were not Peter she was pregnant by, but a boy of her own age? Dismisses this from his mind immediately. And what is she going to do? What are her plans? has she thought it out?

He asks her these questions, pulling away from her; but not roughly.

'Sort of,' she says. 'I mean I'm definitely not dropping out of university or anything. No way.'

'Well I suppose that's something.'

He returns to the table, dragging his feet. There is too much to adjust to. He needs to sort through the rubble of his emotions.

She joins him at the table, taking his hand which is fiddling with the fruit in the bowl. 'It'll be all right, you know.'

'What makes you think that? That's an incredibly glib thing to say.'

'A hunch.'

'For Chrissake. You can't live on a hunch.'

'OK. Wart and I have a great relationship, if you want to know.'

He doesn't. 'You're a child, Cat. Darling you're still a child. I don't mean to be insulting but—'

'Then don't be. How old was Mummy when you married her?'

'I don't remember.' Brooding into the small whorl in his coffee; fingering round the rim of the mug.

'Li-er. She was my age. You know bloody well she was.'

'Well OK. And look how immature she was. With respect.'

'But I'm not her. I don't have the same expectations.'

What are her expectations? What were Vanessa's? What were his?

'That's an interesting comment.' But he doesn't ask her to elaborate; he is not in the mood for lengthy analysis. But her reply has set him thinking. There he is labelling her a child when, typically, she floors him with one of her remarks. She is such an idealist – he often teases her for being quaint; yet in some ways she is more of a realist than he. More in touch, anyway. In touch with what? he then asks himself. Kempton has the sense of an anchor being pulled from underneath him. Of bobbing out to sea.

He nurses his coffee mug between his hands. There are so many questions he wants to ask, but they are still only half-formed. Cat sips her tea, occasionally taking sidelong peeps at him to see what his expression is doing.

'About the – baby. What sort of a future will it have?'

'A good and secure one, I hope.'

'But it wasn't planned. Was it?'

'No.'

'So it's not really wanted then. You're having an unwanted baby because of your moral stance.'

Her eyes glinting in a way her mother's used to.

'Of course it's wanted. You talk such crap sometimes—' (he winces) '—Just because it wasn't planned doesn't mean it isn't wanted. I fail to see the connection. Actually I'm really thrilled if you want to know. I couldn't be happier. If you weren't trying to ruin everything that is.'

She is twisting the issues – like her mother did (do all women do it?) – trying to put him in the wrong. And with this reversal of the card hand he is on the defensive, without the initiative. Utterly inept in this situation into which he has been propelled.

'I'm not. But this fling with Peter—'

'Oh here we go again—'

Vanessa's expression. Even the voice pitch. He has never really noticed Vanessa in her before today, and is taken aback. Extraordinary. And the *déjà vu* of his own inadequacy rises within him.

'—When will you accept, Kempton, that this is not a fling?'

Round and round they trawl, until they are both shattered, and Kempton feels he has aged ten years in the past hour; and my God, it just hits him, I'll be a grandfather. Bring out the zimmer frame.

There is a further matter he has not mentioned. A dreadful prospect that he may as well broach now. Compound the bad tidings.

'Are you going to marry him?' Peter would be my son-in-law. And he wants to laugh hysterically.

'Not for the moment.'

Kempton, who has always been vocal about his opinions on children born out of wedlock, experiences a surge of gratitude for this small mercy. And perhaps she will miscarry. After all, it must be in her genes – her mother; Minnie. And then he is filled with horror at his own thoughts. What kind of a man, what kind of a father is he, who would wish something so terrible to befall his own daughter? Please let her be all right. Please let the baby be all right, he says in his head to make amends.

Cat goes into the garden to play with Pluto and he

watches them for a while from the window. Cat, in her outsize overcoat; her ungainly leg movements at odds with the grace of her arms. Can see her laughing as the puppy tugs one end of the dog-pull with his teeth and she tugs the other, and Pluto is gradually hauled along, his bottom sliding on the ground. Yapping excitedly when she prises the toy from his jaws. Kempton watches as she pushes him down into a sitting position; can hear her ringing voice – 'Sit. *Good* boy. Sit.' – while her hand holds him down.

He turns from the window, physically hurting. At this moment he believes he has lost her irrevocably. He trails into his study, where he spreads out the newspaper on the coffee table.

She finds him in there. 'He can almost sit,' she says. 'He's really bright.'

The cold from outdoors on her cheeks, in her shining eyes, glistening on her hair and on the fibres of her coat.

'Dad, Wart will be here soon. I told him I'd keep an eye out for him.' Standing awkwardly behind his chair and laying a hand on his shoulder.

'I hate him,' Kempton mutters into the photograph of Tony Blair grinning like a toothpaste ad. 'I can never forgive him.'

'I assume you don't mean Tony Blair,' she says lightly. But she can feel that tightening-knot sensation in her again.

'And as for *him*. How can you trust someone with so many teeth?'

Cat refrains from saying that he's a fine one to talk; what about their own breeze blocks? But he is beyond humouring.

'A foreigner could mistake his mouth for the white cliffs of Dover. Hah!' A clap of laughter at his own joke.

She feels weak from all the vomiting and from emotion. Weary from trying to appease him, and from the sleepless

• Kempton's Journey

nights leading up to telling him. Her cheeks ache. She glues her face to the study window and longs for Peter's car to draw up. Simultaneously feels guilty.

Kempton plotting how he would fix Peter's brakes, were this not likely to endanger his daughter. How much would it cost to hire a contract guy with a gun?

'He's here,' Cat announces softly.

In the front door entrance they cling to each other.

'Now you take care. Have a lovely time at Magnificent Melissa's.'

'Oh I'm not going,' she says. 'I'd be throwing up all over the place. Not very considerate to her mother.'

'No, I guess not.'

She smiles. 'So – see you soon?'

'Yes of course.' How soon? And will it be like this from now on? Always this constraint between them?

Peter's car a tactful few yards down the road.

'Kempton.' Cat pausing on the uppermost step. 'Don't forget the bits I cut out for you.'

'What bits? Oh *those*. For Chrissake darling,' he says, sounding like his old self.

She blows him a laughing kiss and makes towards Peter's car.

Sometimes children mimic her gait. Kempton has been with her when it has happened on a couple of occasions. The second time he grabbed one of the children, a boy of about ten, and almost lifted him off the pavement by his collar.

'One day you might hurt your leg and walk in a funny way,' he told the boy, with his face close to him, and enunciating each syllable with exaggerated clarity for the others to hear. 'And everyone will laugh at you and copy you. You'll like that, won't you?'

The kid, struggling to keep his heels on the ground, tilting his face away from Kempton's, shook his head, terrified.

'You don't need to protect me Dad,' Cat said to him afterwards.

Did it not occur to her that he might also be protecting himself? Yes – thank God she is alive. Yes – thank God she didn't have to have her leg amputated. Don't think he isn't grateful. But she had such beautiful, straight, slender, powerful and useful limbs before she was marred for life.

'Hi Wart,' she says brightly. 'He'll come round in the end,' and bursts into a fit of sobbing.

'It's all right baby. Hey little love, it's all right.' Peter's leather-clad arm around her.

'We're fine, aren't we?' she says into his chest, inhaling the leather, and Russian tobacco.

'Very fine. Together we can take on the world.' Repeats it, making a ditty of the words.

His face is pressed against her head, and she can feel him smiling.

'He makes me question everything. Everything I feel. I end up going over and over things in my mind, validating them to myself.'

'Well that's no bad thing.'

'He makes me feel like a child.'

'That's understandable. Come on, you know that. What parent can accept that his child is adult? And let's face it you *are* very young – no don't get cross,' he adds as her head raises as though she is about to make a retort. 'You *will* change. We all did, do and shall do.' He wipes her cheeks with his fingers, then licks his fingers. 'Could do with more salt.'

She smiles briefly. 'Kempton tries to trap everything in a time warp, that's his problem,' she says. 'He resists all change. I've got this image of him forcibly trying to hold back a wall, like Atlas.'

'He'll have the last laugh yet,' Peter says. 'In fifteen or twenty years time, when you're still young and beautiful and I'll be heading for senility.' He puts on a wavery, old-man's voice.

She ignores this. 'He thinks it's a fling. He calls it a fling. He credits me with no maturity of judgement . . . Tell me Wart, if I weren't pregnant, what do you think the chances of our staying together would be?'

'No different,' he answers assuredly. 'You?'

'The same.'

'Nunc scio sit amor.'

'What does that mean?'

'It's Virgil. Look it up.'

He starts the engine. Cat straps herself in. 'He only has your welfare at heart, Cat. Remember that. Nobody will ever have your welfare so much at heart as him. Not even me.'

Kempton standing in the doorway. Why are they still there? He can see their dark forms merge and remain merged. Tries to muster up his rage, but is too tired. How Peter must be gloating. The entire episode has, as far as Kempton is concerned, become like a competition; with his daughter as the trophy. But it is a one-horse race. Peter has impregnated her – the word Kempton uses to himself, his lip curling in disgust. Planted his obscene,

I've-been-around dick deep inside her and left his seed behind.

His life list. At his desk Kempton adds the latest events to it. Cat goes in one column, Peter another. Her plusses outnumber his minuses. Kempton's love for his daughter is mightier than his hate for Peter. This presents an interesting situation that he is not prepared to rationalise yet. He then draws a line for another column. In here goes an imaginary boyfriend. He is damned from the start as Kempton invests him with every possible disadvantage, including impecuniosity. This perennial student is living off the state whilst doing his fourth degree. He shares a squat with three other like-minded souls, talks with great knowledge of green issues, and is disparaging about his parents, who scrimped to pay for his education . . .

Come back Peter, all is forgiven. Never. Kempton draws zig-zag lines through his fictitious creation. And now he tries an academic exercise: how much is he worth? He lists in order his savings and investments (heavily dwindled), his life assurance policy value to date, the approximate value of his house, a few items of furniture, such as the Georgian sofa table, Queen Anne tallboy, Regency chiffonier, the set of eight early nineteenth-century chairs; a couple of decent paintings; some porcelain 'finds' of Vanessa: an eighteenth-century Sèvres chocolate cup and cover, a pair of Meissen figures. And then – he hesitates here, pen poised – he jots down a sum of money that he might get, were he to leave the business of his own volition before the expiry of his contract. Six months' salary? And a pension that is hardly here or there. Against his assets he must put his car, restaurant bills, half the phone bill and private health scheme – all provided at present by his employers. Then there is the building society loan to offset against the price of the house. He stares at the final figure and draws several boxes and circles round it in surprise. OK, he is hardly catch of the season, nonetheless on *paper* he is not poor. If he were to realise his assets instead of live in them or be surrounded by them . . . What does he need a house like this for, furniture like this for? All alone with the trappings and the accompanying hassle. An encumbrance. And for whom? Not for himself, that's for sure. So what does all this prove?

'The status quo,' he writes as a heading. Ponders over this for a few minutes, then adds simply, 'It cannot continue. Therefore: change it.'

A swirling upwards within him. He draws a house with shutters, partially shades them to throw light on the other half; a tree: the wide boughs of an oak, its branches spreading to the edge of the page, with dozens of offshoots, and intricate leaves like curly kale. Branch after branch, after branch.

That afternoon, with the aid of half a box of puppy choc-drops, he continues Pluto's education. Almost bursts with tenderness at the sight of the small plump body sitting to command, the disproportionately large, spare-fleshed paws, the wise old head and lugubrious eyes.

That evening, lies with his feet up on the sofa in his study, Pluto curled on the carpet beside him; half watching television, half reading his bloodhound handbook. He can concentrate on neither. His thoughts keep drifting. Cat, aged three or four, announcing to her parents one Sunday lunch, 'When you wanted me to be born Kempton dug me out of Mummy's tummy with a spade, didn't he?' Where the hell did she get that from? He can recall their laughter now. Smiles, remembering.

A few years on – and Cat, then about eleven, asked him one day when they were in the garden, 'Dad, what does going down on someone mean?'

Oh God. Vanessa was out shopping. No lies. He had always vowed: no lies.

'It means . . . It means . . .' he said.

His daughter regarding him, patient-eyed beneath rather thick brows.

'Anyway, where did you hear it?' Playing for time.

'One of the girls in my class told a joke. We all laughed, but I didn't know what it meant. Some of the others didn't either.'

'Then why did they laugh?'

'Well it's rude not to laugh at a joke, isn't it?'

'Yes of course.'

'So?'

'So. OK. So it means – it's when someone kisses another person upside down and they have no clothes on.'

'Their toes you mean? How disgusting.'

Oh God. 'No, not their toes.' Vanessa where *are* you? 'Between the – er – legs.' He turned his back on her and started to whistle nervously.

For a moment she looked blank, then she let out a shriek. 'Yuk. That's revolting. That's absolutely, disgustingly, horribly, horribly revolting.' And dashed indoors.

Later that afternoon she had a friend round for tea. Kempton could hear the two girls pealing with laughter in Cat's bedroom. 'Aagh that's so gross,' he heard the other child shout. And then in lowered voices, he caught snatches of their conversation: 'Do you think our parents . . . ?' 'And what about the teachers at school?' 'Mrs Plunket! Can you imagine Mrs Plunket?' 'And Mr Evans, he's so old and hideous, and his willie must be like string. Yuk, yuk.' 'Does everyone in the world go down on everyone?'

And now look at her.

Nobody had ever told him, not even in a joke. He had found out for himself. Hot instinct, aged sixteen and a half, with a girl eighteen months older. Had thought he was so bold and original, and had guarded his secret until he discovered that he was not original at all.

The liberated sixties. He seemed to waft through them, on the fringe of them, as it were. He doesn't remember them as being particularly great or even very liberated; until he went up to Oxford. Then, when the decade was in its final throes, Kempton hit the trail with a vengeance. Nineteen sixty-nine is lodged in his memory as the most exciting period of his life. Over the following years, decades, it has accrued ever more glowing enchantment, so that were someone to ask him to pick any time he would like to relive, he would, without a second's hesitation, plump for that first year at Oxford. Apart from visiting Cat, he has hardly been back since he graduated. Once he had wanted to live on a narrow boat on the canal there. With the break-up of his parents' marriage, then his own sober and calculated decision about his future, bourgeois respectability had held sway instead. He has lost touch with most of his Oxford colleagues. His closest friend, Paul, a physics student, had died of a brain tumour.

And what about more recent friends? 'Couple' friends, with whom he and Vanessa had used to socialise? They seem to have faded away gradually. Several men he knows have lost their businesses or gone bankrupt, thanks to Lloyds, or to banks reining in, or to fleeing debtors. One acquaintance built a small, exclusive housing development, only to have it disappear into the ground virtually overnight: solicitors' searches had failed to reveal that the site had once been a quarry. And what about Vanessa's female friends? Come to think of it, she had not really had any special friend as most women seem to. She butterflied from person to person, drew people to her, but herself was quickly restless. Friendships remained on a superficial level. Perhaps, too, other women did not trust her. Kempton remembers her telling him that: other women don't trust me. Another time she confided to him that she had the need to destroy; that when life was running smoothly or things were going well, she had the urge to jeopardise them.

'I can't explain it,' she said. 'It's as though I fear it will happen anyway, so I'll take charge and realise my worst fears sooner rather than later. And then I'll want to run from what I've done.'

Sometimes the need to see Vanessa again is overpowering in its force. After all this time he can still be seized with a longing to hold her, be held by her, make love to her, have her sleek-skinned legs in a necklace round him, lie with her in his arms – finally tranquil and serene; still cannot quite believe he will never see her again. Then, lancing across his memories comes that other one. And there he is, running to the garage, unlocking the door with out-of-control hands.

He gets up and wanders into the kitchen to open a bottle of red wine (a cabernet from the Friuli region of Italy), and pour himself a glass. And isn't it a miracle he is not an alcoholic? He could easily be in his line of business. Pluto following him sleepily. Me and my shadow. And what on earth is he going to do about the dog tomorrow? Is unutterably depressed at the prospect of returning to work.

'Do you want to come with me then, eh?' he says. 'Sit, Pluto. Sit.'

The puppy sits, and Kempton rummages for a choc drop in the box. 'Oh you're so *cute*, so cute,' he says, mimicking his daughter, hurting because of her. Has an image of her face twinned with Vanessa's. He wishes he could phone Suzanne for some female company. He must buy her a belated Christmas present. Jots this down on a scrap of paper. Also jots down 'new cords,' and 'choir practice,' lest he forgets, as Christmas has made the week go haywire. So what should he buy Suzanne? What is she interested in? Does she like to read? What kind of books? Or music. He could buy her something if he knew her taste in music.

There again, does she have a CD system or cassette? Or maybe she has some hobby and he could get something connected with that.

I know absolutely nothing about her, he realises again. Recalls her wry comment, when he asked about her children, 'And you think then you'll know all about me, because you know my kids' names.'

But she is somebody else's wife, and it is not for Kempton to become involved. Otherwise he could buy her some underwear – if he knew her size; or perfume – if he knew what she liked.

Kempton, you are a dead loss with women.

He decides he had better practise the last part of *The Creation*. The performance is this Saturday, the thirtieth, and he still has a problem with the tricky runny bits. He has always been poor at sight-reading. He refills his glass and takes it into the sitting room, where he makes himself comfortable on the piano stool. Turns to the relevant page in the score and picks out a few notes on the piano.

'The great work is comple-e-ted, the Creator looks upon it and rejoi-ces,' he sings. And suddenly there comes an unearthly mournful sound joining in with him. Pluto, with his head tilted upwards like a wolf at full moon, jaws wide, howling, baying in apparent agony, as Kempton lets loose his baritone into the winter evening's biting stillness.

8

Ladies' Race

Kempton fixing on his bow tie for the grand performance this Saturday, the thirtieth. His cummerbund next – and the satisfaction of finding that it fastens as easily as it did three years ago, the last occasion he wore a DJ. He is on pins. Anyone would presume he was a soloist, not a lowly member of the chorus. But he is afraid of letting the side down. At rehearsal on Wednesday evening he had at one point entered two bars early, along with the sopranos, his deep voice as egregious as a foghorn above tinkling cowbells. He had cringed with realisation just as Harry had clapped his hands in irritation. The suppressed laughter of other members of the choir plunged him back to his schooldays. The problem, Kempton realises, is partly due to his eyesight. With his glasses on he can see the score but not Harry; without them he can see Harry but not the score. So tonight he intends to be less zealous and take the lead from the other baritones. His future in the choir, Harry has hinted, is in jeopardy, and whilst Kempton only joined in the first place to enhance his social life, or more truthfully, to meet a woman, and has benefited on neither front, nevertheless he does quite enjoy the weekly sessions.

It is so cold that he decides to drive to the parish church. Shuts Pluto securely in the lobby with a selection of toys. It has been a strange few days, what with one thing and another. On the work front, Pitman has been off with flu, and Saunders on his own has never been a real issue. He is a nervy but bland sort of individual without Pitman to back him up. But he has a spitful streak which shows in his secretive little brown eyes. He is not to be trusted.

Kempton had arrived at the office on Wednesday deliberately early, twenty minutes before Saunders' usual scheduled time, his briefcase under one arm, a wad of newspapers under the other, and Pluto dancing about on the end of his lead.

'What on earth's that?' said Jim Masters, before disappearing into the gents.

The delighted squeals and exclamations from the girls. Offers to walk him. Pluto playing up to the adulation.

Kempton went into his room, closed the door behind him and tied the puppy to one of the desk legs by his lead; laid the newspaper and toys all around him. And about an hour later Saunders knocked on the door, entering with an incredulous expression.

'Well, this is a bit of a surprise,' he began uncertainly, scratching his head, scattering more dandruff onto his shoulders. 'I'm not sure it's a good idea.' Fuse-wire lips compressed in doubt as he stooped to stroke Pluto.

'He's already almost house-trained,' Kempton said. 'And he's very placid.'

'That's not really the point . . . Though I must say he is rather charming,' Saunders demurred, after he had knelt down and Pluto had clambered onto his lap to lick him. 'What is he then? A Fred Basset?' He straightened again. Knees creaking audibly.

'A bloodhound.'

'Ah . . . So he'll be sniffing out any trouble then.' He gave a thin laugh, and Kempton joined in politely. 'How much did he set you back then?'

'Why, would you like one?' Kempton had no intention of telling him. 'I could get one for you if you want.'

'No, no. Well I must be getting on. So had a good Christmas, did you then?'

'Fine. You?'

'Quite jolly, thanks. Quite jolly. Ate too much of course. By the way, I see Grove Estates have placed their first order.'

'Oh have they? I haven't been through the orders yet.'

'I must say you did well to get the account. To be frank neither of us thought you would.'

'Life is full of surprises,' Kempton said.

And how long before the truth emerged? Could they force him out because of it? Could he claim unfair dismissal and angle for a better financial deal?

And meanwhile, the rest of the week was made bearable by Pluto's presence at work and Pitman's absence; and by the fact that he has seen Suzanne. He sneaked off for the afternoon and they walked in Richmond Park. Suzanne's gloved left hand tucked firmly inside Kempton's gloved right one, inside his deep pocket. Pluto stopping in his tracks, quivering at a group of deer, pressing himself between Kempton and Suzanne. Kempton buzzing with rare contentment. And he has discovered a few more things about her: she paints a little, and likes poetry – even writes it. She swims at the Old Deer Park, where he does (How come I've not seen you there? he asked. Do you go at eight in the morning? she replied). She would choose Schubert's Piano Trio in E flat as her one record on a desert island, *Gulliver's Travels* as her book, and a combined razor and tweezers as her luxury. 'So I can prune all my bits in case a rescue team arrives and mistakes me for a gorilla,' she said. He has established that she does have a CD player; and thus informed can now buy her a Christmas present.

'You don't need to,' she said when he told her.

'I want to.'

In bed, after their walk, he said to her, 'I suppose I feel that Vanessa couldn't have loved me or she wouldn't have done it.'

'Loving or not loving you had nothing to do with her killing herself. The despair of depression overtakes everything else. It obliterates reason. It literally consumes the person concerned.'

'Is this something you're quoting from one of your counselling text books?' he asked rather nastily.

'No.' Suzanne pulling at a stray hair just above her nipple. 'Ah, got you, blighter. Do you want it as a keepsake, Kempton?'

He took it from her and blew it away.

'I take that very personally,' she said.

'So how can you be sure?' he said, refusing to be deflected.

'Well, of course I can't. Every case is different. And the trigger is different in each instance. But it was like that in my mother's case.'

So he has discovered that about her, too. She has offered only the barest snippets so far; but he is learning, learning.

On the smaller scale of things, he has bought a new pair of cords. But nothing seems to be straightforward at the moment, and when he was about to put them on in the evening, he discovered the plastic anti-theft tag was still clipped to them. He knew how it had happened; the salesman and he had somehow got onto the subject of dogs, and it transpired he had also just acquired a puppy. They had compared notes and progress, and while he was folding and packing the trousers the salesman was telling Kempton that his girlfriend insisted on having the dog sleep in their bedroom.

'It's becoming a problem,' he said. 'If you know what I mean.'

'Yes I can imagine,' Kempton sympathised.

So the tag had slipped the salesman's notice.

At first Kempton debated whether to take the trousers back to the shop, but then he thought he would try and remove the thing himself, otherwise it would be yet another task to do the following day. Besides, he wanted to wear them now. His first attempt was with a pair of nail scissors, but these achieved nothing and broke into the bargain. So he took the trousers downstairs into the kitchen where he fished out his wirecutters from the tool box. He laid the trousers on the table and made a second attempt. The cutters worked; however they not only severed the wire but unavoidably punctured the plastic tag. From this, like blood spurting from a vein, shot out a stream of turquoise dye onto the trousers, the table, the apples in a bowl on the table, Kempton's white shirt, his hands and Pluto's nose.

The salesman, the next day, was apologetic. 'And we don't have any others in your size,' he said. 'But one of our other branches is bound to. If you come back tomorrow I promise I'll have them in. Oh and I did what you said. I put my foot down. The puppy slept in the kitchen last night. My girlfriend told me it was worth it. If you know what I mean.'

'I've a fair idea,' Kempton said. Man-to-man laughter. And finally he has his cords.

Now here he is, arriving at the parish church, having parked a few yards down the road. And other members of the choir, along with various musicians, are arriving simultaneously, stamping their feet or thumping their hands together against the cold, heading inside. 'Jeeze I

• Kempton's Journey

hope it's warmer in here.' 'Nervous?' 'A bit.' 'You'll be fine.' 'Just keep an eye on old Harry . . .'

It's quite odd, Kempton muses, how they all seem to wear glasses; but then most of them are of a certain age. And meanwhile the audience is gathering in the pews; the place is rapidly becoming packed out: a couple of hundred people, maybe three hundred. A sea of faces. Most of the choir are old hands, but this is a first for Kempton, and he feels awed and rather thrilled. He is also a little peacock-vain of his appearance in his dinner jacket. And it is at a time like this that, unbidden, a sudden pang for Vanessa spikes him in the thorax.

The audience is now assembled, and the choir files in. Kempton is in the middle row, towering above the two diminutive men either side of him, occupying twice their area. In front of him the short gold hair and pale nape of a young soprano. He has the urge to place his index finger in the small hollow. The organist takes her place, then the other half-dozen musicians shuffle in, smiling rather apologetically: two violinists, a cellist, viola player, oboist and clarinetist. Finally Harry. Everyone applauds. Kempton scans the faces in the pews. There are several that he recognises. And several that are more familiar still: Cat – wearing a red beret – and Peter a couple of rows from the front; and beside Peter, Minnie. He had no idea they were coming, and feels touched and confused, as well as self-conscious. Another face then springs into focus a few rows further back, on the other side. Suzanne, flanked by two girls. Oh God. He fumbles for his glasses in his pocket and brings them out – attached to a large, crumpled, checked handkerchief which he quickly stuffs back inside. Sites the glasses on his nose. Except for the score in his hands, everything is mercifully blurred, including Harry; who lifts his baton for the orchestra to come in with the introduction: 'The Representation of Chaos' (Kempton has

• 144

thought recently that this would be an apt description of his mental state). The soft notes of the organ then herald the entry of the bass soloist singing Raphael's recitative; and next it is the choir's turn. The sopranos lead in, followed by the others.

'And the spirit of God moved upon the waters. And God said, "Let there be light": and there was *light*,' they all sing at the tops of their voices; Kempton sings for all he is worth, his chest thrown out like a rearing mallard's, jubilant.

The anarchy that had made up their rehearsals has miraculously given way to this structured order with all the singers and musicians in perfect unison. Kempton can rarely recall such a sense of exhilaration. He is part of this combined powerful sound that is filling and echoing within the vaulted walls of the church. He forgets the audience, forgets his intention to take the lead from the other members, but enters spot-on every time, his expression fervent, mouth shaping round every word and syllable. Just let Harry dare try to dismiss him. This is too, too marvellous. So much so that at one point his eyes fill.

But afterwards, with the burst of applause, with his glasses off and the audience leaping into recognisable perspective once more, his elation mutes somewhat. He wonders how he can make his escape without having to greet anybody; whether he can manage to sneak away. It was kind of them all to come and support his cause – Cat now clapping enthusiastically, catching his eye and raising her red beret to him – but he has no desire to confront Peter, whom he might just conceivably punch in his good-natured, handsome face; also, it is a bit embarrassing Suzanne being there with her daughters. At least he presumes that is who they are.

He lopes out with the others from the choir to fetch his coat. Excited conversation among them: 'Didn't it go well?' 'There was just one part . . .' 'I fluffed my recitative'

(Gabriel). 'You were great. You're too self-critical.' 'Who's coming for a drink then?'

If he hangs back long enough, maybe they will give up waiting for him. He wishes they had warned him they'd be coming.

In the street he tries to sandwich himself between a bunch of others; but his height and bulk make him conspicuous. Suzanne is first on the scene.

'Hi Kempton. That was terrific. I really enjoyed it.'

'Hello. Oh thanks.' Glances at the two girls. Suzanne's complexion is yellow under the street lamp. Her eyes are dancing; the whites gleam.

'You were pulling hysterical faces when you were singing.'

'Oh thanks a million.'

She always manages to take him down from whatever summit he might briefly be poised on.

'Everyone was. They all looked incredibly constipated and fervent.'

'Mum, you are so *rude*,' says one of the girls.

'Well, I said I enjoyed it and I did. Kempton these are my daughters, Vikki and Tina.'

'Hi,' they say in quick succession.

He forces a smile. 'Hello.'

'So you've got Pluto.'

He looks at the girl in surprise; the older of the two, he surmises, small and thin, with fair hair and a lot of eye makeup. 'Oh you know about Plu—'

And then Cat arrives and Minnie – thankfully no Peter to be seen – and there are introductions all round. Kempton seems to have shrunk in stature, can feel himself concertinaing into the pavement.

'I sold your father Pluto,' Suzanne tells Cat.

'Oh *did* you? He's cute, he really is. So squashy.'

'The most sensible thing that Kempton's done in years.

Hmph,' Minnie lighting her pipe. Does she really have to do it here? Kempton is sure she does it to spite him.

'How wonderful, a woman smoking a pipe,' says Suzanne.

'Hmph. I've smoked one for as long as I can remember. My father used to let me smoke his as a child—' This is news to Kempton. '—My son thinks I do it to shame him.'

And she and Suzanne start discussing dog breeding.

'I lerves your hat,' drawls Kempton, hugging his daughter, plucking her beret from her head then putting it back. '*Très Français*. So how're things darling?'

'Well, I'm fed up of being sick the whole time.'

The other two girls look at her interestedly.

'I'm pregnant,' she explains.

Kempton closes his eyes.

'How's the essay going?'

'I'm about half way through.'

'You *are* getting on with it?'

'Of course.'

'It's important.'

'Dad, I *know*. It's not a problem.'

'Well it is if you can't work because you're—'

'Kempton.' Warningly.

The girls begin talking amongst themselves and Kempton is left hovering superfluously amongst them.

'Well, I said I'd join the others for a drink,' he lies.

This is ignored, so he announces it again, slightly more forcefully, which provokes more of a reaction.

'Speak to you soon,' calls out Suzanne.

How can she be so open in front of her children? 'You mean about the dog,' he says, to cover her tracks and his own. But she doesn't respond; is deep in conversation again with Minnie – who turns fleetingly to give a goodbye nod to Kempton.

But his daughter's arms are suddenly around him in an embracing hug. And he bends his face to hers – it is soft, icy – half knocks her beret off so that it slides over her eyes.

'You see, it went fine didn't it?' She knows how apprehensive he was about the performance.

'I loved doing it. I can't describe how it felt. It felt—' He seeks an appropriate word. 'I don't know. Uplifting.'

Her expression tender; loving. When she has that expression how can he doubt their relationship? From it he draws reassurance however momentary.

'I could tell. It showed in your whole face.'

'I didn't look stupid?' Thinking of Suzanne's remark.

'No of course not. You just looked as though you were really enjoying yourself, and believing in what you were doing. Very dishy in fact, in your black-tie. And you dwarfed the others. If you hadn't been my father I'd have fancied you.'

Which sets in motion a complex chain of Freudian questions as he walks slowly back to the car; he has no intention of going to the pub. His head is reverberating. The music, the elation are still there, but already consigned to a past corner. The glory has faded too quickly, ceded to the episode outside the church, which now dominates the forefront: Minnie and Suzanne nattering like old friends; Cat's nonchalant pronouncement to the other two girls – 'I'm pregnant' – as if it were the most ordinary thing. So they will inform Suzanne who will no doubt come forward with some uninvited viewpoint. And Cat will enquire about Suzanne. And Minnie will probably voice her approval. And the brief interlude will add yards of complications to the already over-burdened load.

The car has been scratched – deliberately, it would appear – all along the driver's side by a sharp object. He stares at it with resignation. It is not his problem, he consoles himself. It is not his car; it is leased to the company. And it is a minor problem, a mere flick of aggravation when pitted against everything else.

I'm going to be a grandfather. She's throwing her life away. The words form a weary threnody to Haydn's music. Ke-empton, you need a holiday. Why don't you take a little holiday? he imagines Pitman saying. And don't come back, there's a good fellow.

New Year's Eve. And at the rather chic dinner party near the Hurlingham Club there are two unattached women and one unattached man besides himself. Kempton's rival in chance is about fifty, short and blondish, with a jolly face and the unfair advantage of being a surgeon with three homes and a list of royalty whose flesh he has carved over the years. Kempton's more dubious advantages are height, seductive eyes, a few years on his side, and the strange but proven drawing power of his widowed state. Of the two women, one is also around fifty, and a certain type: a Harbour-Club woman, a Royal Opera House woman, well-groomed, a lot of costume jewellery, a good figure, immaculately made-up. Kempton has never cared for her sort. The other, to his right is probably mid-forties, tall and big-boned with an open, wide-cheeked face and a mass of curls. Both women are dark and dressed in black, and, confusingly, both are called Annie. He chats up the Annie on his right for most of the evening, almost totally ignoring the other one; discovers she was once an opera singer but damaged her vocal cords in a road accident and is now a 'head-hunter'.

'A bit different,' Kempton says.

'Very. And much more lucrative.'

Midnight. And for good measure he kisses the other woman too. Everyone cheering and singing. A few minutes of undying friendship. The surgeon is well and truly gone. Slurring his words. Bloodshot eyes meeting in the middle of his head. Not a chance pal, Kempton thinks, smug. Looks for a scrap of paper to write his conquest's number on it, trying not to make it too obvious. But he fails to find anything, and he doesn't want to ask the hostess now and appear too keen.

The best part of being married, Vanessa remarked once, in the early days, is not having to play games anymore.

Yet she did, didn't she? She never stopped.

'What's your resolution?' Annie number one asks.

'To change everything in my life,' he answers. Shoots her one of his dark, meaningful looks that he has gathered over the years appeals to women.

Kempton, I think you might have struck lucky there, he says to himself in the car on the way home.

The Annie on my right, he tells his hostess when he phones to thank her the following day. The attractive one.

Oh yes. The hostess obliges him with the phone number, which he immediately dials. Annie sounds surprised, but gratifyingly pleased to hear from him, and they chat about the usual banalities before getting to the point and arranging to meet later in the week.

A lull in trade after the holiday period. No frantic last minute orders or complaints. But Pitman is back, in robust health. And barges into Kempton's office without knocking.

'You lost your marbles over Christmas then? Dogs aren't part of your contract. Get that thing out.'

He is, it transpires, canophobic, having been mauled as a child.

'See this?' he says, tilting his jaw for Kempton to inspect the white line stretching round its spongy perimeter. 'This is thanks to somebody's so-called pet.'

'He's a puppy for Chrissake. He's two and a half months old.'

Kempton kneels, protective of Pluto, who is straining at

his lead to get at Pitman and lick him. Pluto's stern, his whole back section, is wagging in his enthusiasm. He emits a series of small piercing yelps. Kempton strokes him to try and calm him.

'Get him to stop that bloody rack—'

Pluto's tail catches the water-bowl, which upsets and spills.

'You see? Now look at the bloody mess. And it stinks in here.'

'That's not him. It's his tripe.'

'I don't effing care what it is. It reeks. Get him out. This isn't an effing zoo.'

Kempton grinning at a sudden mental picture of Pitman as an orangutan behind bars.

'And get that stupid grin off your face,' yells Pitman.

'It's my room.' Kempton straightening up to face him.

'And it's my building.' Pitman's eyes bulge. He plants his legs in a goalkeeper's stance. 'I pay the rent here. Every bleeding, over-priced square inch of it. What I say, goes. You are no longer in charge.'

Which strikes home like nothing else has. Kempton stares at him with utter loathing. Pitman stares back.

'What is it anyway? It's quite revolting-looking. Like a sack of decaying potatoes,' Pitman says, half way out of the door. 'In fact you and it—' he appraises Kempton for a few seconds, starts to laugh – a whining sound like a clock being wound up, then shakes his head and goes from the room, still laughing.

In the end Saunders, who has succumbed to Pluto's charms, proposes a compromise. A week's stay of execution. Kempton will worry about what to do when the time comes. But relations between himself and Pitman are at an all time low. They no longer even feign civility. Saunders is more concerned about the car, when Kempton tells him about the scratch along the wing.

'I'll have to take a look at it to see whether it's worth claiming off the insurance,' he says.

And Kempton immediately regrets having mentioned it. Hopes Saunders doesn't glance inside and see the damage to the interior: the chewed seat trim, loose-hanging wires, teeth marks in the automatic gear knob and shredded door-padding.

Thursday evening, and Kempton is crossing the bridge to join the rest of the traffic making for central London. He has arranged to collect Annie from her house in Chelsea and take her to the Brasserie St Quentin for dinner. His first date for – he can't even remember the last occasion. He sucks an extra-strong peppermint as he drives around Redcliffe Square looking for her number, and parks. Finds himself outside a smart, navy door with gleaming brass furniture and flanked by two miniature conifers in tubs. Nervously circles his neck and eases his shoulders into his coat a few times. He hadn't expected her to live somewhere like this. A house like this must be worth a fortune.

The door opens. 'How nice to see you,' she says, ushering him inside.

And he fixes the smile on his face, tries not to let it waver and die; tries not to let his shock and dismay show, or his tone falter as he says, 'Yes, you too. Thanks. What a lovely place.'

It is the wrong Annie.

Oh Kempton, this could only happen to you.

He realises how the confusion arose: His hostess had been sitting opposite him at dinner. *His* right had been her left.

He is intent on getting the evening over with as quickly as possible. Ferries her to the restaurant directly, without accepting her offer of a glass of Champagne.

'What a strange smell in your car,' she observes.

'I've got a puppy. He was sick in it.'
'Oh dear. They're worse than children.'
'Yes.' Remembers his manners. 'Do you have children?'
'A son and a daughter. They've fled the nest now.'
'What do they do?' Churning out the standard questions.
'Paul's a banker.' Of course. He can predict what is coming next. 'My daughter's a full-time mother. Well of course she has a nanny.'
'So you're a grandmother.' On cue.
'Yes. I can't quite believe it.' A high, frilly laugh.
'You don't look old enough.'
'How very sweet of you. Do you mean that?'
'I never lie.' Kempton the smoothie.
'What about you? Do you have children?'
'Yes, a daughter. Nineteen. Well nearly twenty,' he says with some surprise.
'It must be hard for you.' The oily thickness of female sympathy homing-in on male vulnerability.
'We manage,' he says firmly, clamping his lips on any further information. 'So how long have you lived here . . . ?'

At the table at the restaurant, recklessly he tells her to order whatever she wants. She chooses king prawns on an expensive-looking bed of ice, parsley and lemon slices to start with, followed by quenelles of pike.

'Number twelve,' he says importantly to the wine waiter, to disguise the fact this is the house wine.

'The house wine, you mean sir,' says the waiter.

The dreary evening drags on. Kempton is almost hypnotised with boredom; hears half of what she says. She has never had a job, has no opinions that haven't been fed into her; plays golf and bridge. Between each lengthy course she re-applies her coral-red lipstick, and every so often she swivels her head to examine and pout at her reflection in the mirrored column behind her.

The bill, including desserts, coffees and petits fours, and

a Cointreau for her – 'As I'm not driving,' she says, leaning across and breathing fish towards him – comes to ninety-one pounds with service.

He drops her back at her house and escorts her to her front door.

'Would you like to come in? For a coffee or brandy . . . or something?' she says pointedly, giving a small coquettish pout.

'I'd love to but I've got a really long day tomorrow. Meetings all morning. You know.'

'Oh you poor man.' She is rather tipsy, and has gone girlish and giggly.

'So – well – I'll be in touch.'

'Oh yes. *Please*. It's been a wonderful evening. So much to talk about. I'll cook you a little something here next time. Would that be nice?'

'Great.' Pecking her on the cheek as she proffers glossy lips. Before fleeing.

Drives off as fast as possible, knowing he's way over the drink limit, but not caring. Anxious only to be home as soon as possible.

He can hardly phone the hostess again who gave the party, can he? It is not as if he knows her well. And he doesn't know the other Annie's surname to look her up. Perhaps she will contact him. But to be frank, he has lost interest.

It wasn't destined Dad, Cat would say.

And what a laugh he and Peter would once have had about it. He misses that. Male laughter. Male friendship.

But on his answer-machine is a message from Suzanne. He hears it with relief. She sounds so sane, so familiar. So Suzanne-ish. He wishes he could phone her now; that she could come over. He doesn't even feel particularly horny. He would just like to lie in bed next to her, holding her and talking with her. When she isn't annoying him she talks with a great deal of sense. It's rather like going to bed with a good friend, he thinks, as he pours himself a brandy. And she makes him laugh. What does she get out of their relationship – if one could call it that? Only sex? And, oddly, this bothers him.

He presses the 'play' button again and sits down on the chair to listen. Pluto tries to clamber onto his lap, his claws scratching Kempton's legs.

'No, that isn't allowed. You know it isn't. Suzanne says I mustn't let you.'

'Hi. It's me,' Suzanne says. 'We didn't get a chance to chat properly the other evening. I really enjoyed the performance, and you weren't really pulling hysterical faces . . . Vikki told me to say that. Actually you were—' Kempton gives a burst of laughter '—Teasing. I'm winding you up. Anyway, I phoned to say a belated happy New Year. And seriously, Kempton—' sober dropping of her voice '—I do hope it *is* a good year for you. You deserve it. Speak to you soon.'

He replays the message several times. And each time, smiles.

Walks Pluto, gets undressed, goes to bed, falls asleep, thinking of her and smiling.

9

Over The Sticks

'... At the outset I found myself plunged into such a labyrinth of problems, difficulties, objections, complexities, and obscurities that I was repeatedly tempted to abandon everything and was on the point of giving up my fruitless research and relying on the rules of common prudence in my deliberations without trying to find new rules in the principles which I had such difficulty in disentangling. But this prudence was itself so foreign and I felt so incapable of attaining it ...'

Kempton finds himself becoming quite excited when he reads this passage. It could almost have been written with him in mind. Much of what Rousseau describes does not apply to him; the ostracising by society for a start. Although he feels alienated, certainly; out on a limb. And the resultant confusion, his orbiting emotions which crave a resolution, albeit a different one from Rousseau's, he can easily recognise.

Kempton has already taken three positive steps in the past three and a half weeks. He has sent off for a brochure about the horse-drawn caravan trips in France; has phoned about the art classes and is having his first lesson next week. And he has just returned from the third thing. Well at least he can now strike the whole disastrous experience off his list. She was right. Suzanne has a habit of being right. And he knew the second he walked through the door into the room that this was going to be the case.

The flat where tonight's meeting was held was in one of Twickenham's shabbier side streets.

'Welcome to our little gathering, I'm Janice.'

The hostess, hugely fat, clad in some sort of tent and shawl, crushing him in the boughs of her arms. Her face tumbling into a waterfall of chins. And like a canary stuck on top of this fleshy pyramid: the spikey yellow of her shorn head. Each of her podgy fingers was adorned with a ring, and in her ears were several more. She was sucking – rolling her heavily mascara'd eyes upwards as she did so – on a pungent-smelling cigarette that even Kempton in his ignorance realised was not ordinary tobacco.

'Hello.' He gave a short, nervous laugh, like a single rev from a car, longing to bolt as he was hauled by her – her unconstrained breasts pressed like a bolster against his chest – into the room. It was surprisingly large and furnished entirely, it seemed, from a Middle-Eastern bazaar.

'Everybody, this is Kenton.'

He did not bother to correct her.

'Hi.' 'Hello there.' 'Greetings.' 'Salaam.' 'Watcha pal.' 'Good evening.'

Half a dozen or so individuals were seated round a tiled-top table, their faces a cursory blur. Four women, including his hostess, and three men. And now himself. And maybe they were drawing their own conclusions about him (middle-class, awkward, conventional, tense, staid; a shaving nick above his mouth), while he was assessing them.

A mug of coffee was thrust into his hand – help yourself to bits (digestive biscuits and a bowl of peanuts) – and he was bade sit down; squashed next to a woman and a man on a brown dralon sofa with a beaded 'throw' over it.

'Hi,' he said to his direct neighbours, to get in the swing of things, cricking his neck as he swivelled to face them properly. The woman was slender, pretty, rather like a cross between a gazelle and Grace Kelly, but hard-looking with tight features. And wearing stockings. Her short black skirt had ridden up, revealing the lacy tops. And extraordinarily Kempton could feel himself getting a hard-on. It was two days since he saw Suzanne and he was aroused by a stranger's stocking tops (the trouble with him is that frequent sex increases his libido).

Don't stare Dad. Cat is always telling him that. He removed his glance to the man: small and sinewy, tortoise-neck springing from patterned jumper; very little, very black eyes – like rat droppings – and he kept dabbing at the corner of his mouth with his forefinger, as though a stubborn crumb lingered there.

'Right everyone.' A bearded, bald man sprang up suddenly from the depths of a sagging armchair. His belly rippled loosely beneath a thin T-shirt, which bore across it the words, 'I'm a twice a night man.' '. . . As the founder of the organisation, if I may call it that, I'm going to ask everyone, myself included to go through the usual routine for the benefit of our two newcomers.'

Clearing of the throat. Casting of eyes professionally round the room.

'So – I'll start. I'm Malcolm. I'm a printer from Kingston. My wife committed suicide with an overdose six years ago. She had become depressed after losing both her parents and her sister in the space of a year. How did I feel then? Lost. Lonely. Sad at the waste of a life. Inadequate. I'd go and sit in the local pub and brood over the thinness of my life . . .'

He must have rehearsed this or said the same thing a dozen times, Kempton thought. It came out too pat.

• Kempton's Journey

'. . . How do I feel now? Well, the negative feelings have gone. I'm ready to start afresh.'

And who'd want you? Kempton addressed him silently as Malcolm sat down. But he identified with the sense of inadequacy.

'I'm Nadine. From Sheen. I'm unemployed,' an anorexic-looking young woman with a bitter mouth announced. 'My husband used to beat me up. Did you know that ninety per cent of violent crime is committed by men?' Her voice rising, and gaze stabbing into Kempton as though he bore sole responsibility.

He shook his head vigorously, pulling an appeasing expression.

She continued, 'He committed suicide a year ago by hanging himself. How did I feel then? I was relieved. Free. I couldn't stop talking. On the tube I used to chatter away to strangers. They must've thought I was round the twist. I probably was. How do I feel now? I – mixed-up. I keep thinking maybe I did things that made him violent towards me. That it was me. I used to contradict him. He couldn't stand being contradicted. And after he'd hurt me he was always upset, like he couldn't believe what he'd done.'

She started to weep, and Malcolm got up to embrace her.

'Good girl. Let it out. That's what we're here for. We're all friends here, aren't we?'

Loudly to the room in general; and everyone chorused 'yes' in rousing unison.

'I'm Sue. I'm a nurse from Kingston. My husband . . . My . . . He committed . . . He threw himself under a train six months ago.'

Kempton was appalled. A shock wave ran through him. The others had presumably heard it before, judging by their sympathetic but unsurprised expressions.

'I didn't know he was unhappy. I thought we . . . What did I . . .'

And she also burst into tears. This time Janice comforted her.

A man called Dave next. His wife had slashed her wrists. To punish him, he said. To make as much mess as possible.

Janice's husband had been a transvestite.

Kempton becoming more and more depressed. Let me out, let me out. Trapped in this zoo of miserable humanity. The room becoming stifling. A fan heater blasting noisy stale air round and round. Janice passing round another joint, and the smell sickening him.

One by one the other sorry tales were related in exactly the same manner. It transpired that the woman on the sofa beside him was the other new member. And now it was her turn.

'I'm Cherry,' she said in a flat tone, picking at her metal watch strap. 'I'm from Barnes and I own a PR company in Putney. My husband was a surgeon. I didn't know it at the time but he was being sued for negligence and malpractice. He committed suicide nearly two years ago with the car exhaust.' Kempton glancing at her, startled. 'He drove to Scotland to do it. Spent the night with a couple of tarts, then he did it. How did I feel then? Furious. Bloody furious, if you want to know.' The flatness left her tone and she almost shouted. 'How do I feel now?' Her voice dropped again and took on a note of defiance. 'Sometimes I like being single. I like the piquancy of the phone ringing. I like going out with different men. It feels like I'm getting my own back.'

Slow, deliberate, uncrossing and recrossing of the legs. Stocking tops flashing. Competing with her husband's last fling. Kempton debated whether to get her phone number later. But his keenness had died. Killed by gloom.

And now it was him, and he felt the blood of embarrassment singeing his cheeks.

'I'm Kempton,' he intoned into the multi-coloured

• Kempton's Journey

dhurrie. 'I'm in the wine trade. I live in Richmond. My wife was, er, she was manic-depressive. She – committed suicide—' how hard to say these words in front of other people. They sounded so stark and brutal. He supposed that was part of it: the confronting of that aspect '—nearly three years ago. With the car exhaust.'

Turned briefly to Cherry to see her reaction. But there was not a flicker in her set features.

'. . . The day before her fortieth birthday. In our garage. I found her.'

His tone thickening. Pain in his throat. Oh God please don't let him break down here, in front of this motley bunch. Everybody's gaze pinned intently on him. Hungry for his capitulation. For him to be one of them. He saved himself with effort.

'How did I feel then? I was distraught. I hated her for doing it. I felt culpable. And like – Malcolm – I felt inadequate. That I hadn't been able to prevent it. Look, I still sometimes think that if she'd really loved me she – but that's not the point. And then I think, well perhaps I didn't give her enough attention. If I had . . . So, well I don't know . . . What do I feel now? I—'

He broke off and took a considered breath. He was reluctant to let these people into his privacy. Yet conversely had the need to vocalise his inner thoughts.

'I realise I'm not to blame. I've come to accept our marriage wasn't perfect and I couldn't provide her with or be everything she wanted emotionally. I've stopped blocking myself from the reality of our relationship as it was. I don't – I mean I don't miss the constant vacillations of moods and not knowing what to expect. Sometimes I used to dread coming home after work. I feel disloyal saying that. I shouldn't have said it.'

And immediately he longed for Vanessa, to throw his

arms around her: Sorry, sorry. I didn't mean it. You're perfect. I love you.

He gave a self-conscious blast of laughter into the cloying hush of the room. What had come over him, spouting on like that? Yet he could have gone on; torn between shame and confessional need.

Afterwards they talked amongst themselves. Dave was a religious freak. Janice spoke about the 'escarpments of life', and used the expression 'chilling out.' Everybody there had read The Celestine Prophecy except him. The woman with the stockings frightened him. There was something vengeful about her. He decided definitely against asking for her number. No one else interested him, and he wondered when he could take his leave without causing offence. He began to itch with claustrophobia. At last Malcolm rounded off the evening with the week's 'thought'. He clapped his hands for silence.

'Here it is everybody,' he said (some of them had their notepads ready). 'Happiness is a strange emotion compounded of so many elements that it is impossible to sustain them all. You are fortunate if you experience it occasionally. Happiness is not an entitlement. It is a bonus. Survival is a question of chiselling out your life – a chunk of happiness here, a chunk of sadness there. Only, you are not doing the chiselling. You are being chiselled and sculpted. But you can note what is going on. And something good, however tiny, will happen each day. Not a day will pass when something good doesn't happen – it might be a bird on your windowsill or a letter from a friend. Dwell on it.'

They all embraced each other goodbye. A ritualistic hug, then a firm handshake, followed by a kiss on either cheek. Love and caring was the message. You might hate yourself, but we love you. And we hope to see you again, Kenton. And he went out into the street, into the neon-lit slanting

• Kempton's Journey

rain, the odours of hamburgers and fish and chips, and sounds of sirens, with relief.

Now in his own bed, reading the Rousseau, pausing for reflection from time to time, he admits that, yes, he *has* made some progress recently. Perhaps you are becoming a better, more tolerant man, Kempton? But only within limits.

Kempton in his office, munching his way through prawns and lettuce with mayonnaise sandwiched in springy granary bread. Phoning Suzanne at the same time. He is taking a slight risk but assumes her husband will be at work. He misses Pluto by his feet. In fact it is Pluto that he wants to discuss. Well, it is a reasonable pretext. His fingers are fishy and slippery with mayonnaise and he avoids holding the receiver too tightly. It slides out of his hands and dangles from its curly wire, sweeping papers and pens across the desk and into the bin.

'Oh God,' he says, picking it up.

'Actually it's Suzanne,' she responds.

'Oh sorry. I dropped the phone. All my papers have fallen into the bin.'

'Best place.'

'It's Kempton. Can you talk?'

'I know it's Kempton. I can sort of talk. I'm reading up for the course I'm going on at the weekend, that's all.'

'What course is that?'

'A bereavement counselling three-day workshop.'

'Oh.' Chewing the end of his pen. 'Where?'

'Oxford.'

'God, I wish I could join you.' Vivid recollections tug at him, spilling in luscious, aching colour. And to return there with Suzanne, to go to all his old haunts, listen to chamber music in the Holywell Music Room and have a pint in the

Turf Tavern (although his head brushed the ceiling there). And he might bump into his daughter.

'You could.'

He is astonished. 'How could I? What about your husband?'

'It's no big deal.'

Really, her marital situation confounds him; but he has made a pact with himself not to discuss it with her.

He is so tempted to take up her offer; then imagines himself cited in a messy divorce. And her husband a solicitor.

'Maybe it's not a brilliant idea.'

He can almost hear her shrugging.

'Look I'm only trying to be practical,' he defends himself.

'I haven't said a word.'

'No. Well. I don't know how you can be so casual, you know, about – Anyway you'll be working all the time you're there.'

'Not at night. Velvet, decadent, debauched night.' Her voice glutinous with sexual promise.

'Don't. You're getting me going.' He cradles his hand round his pinstriped crotch. Murmurs, 'Ooh.'

'To what do I owe this pleasant little chat then?' Suzanne asks.

'Well it's Pluto. He's doing something so – I mean it's so disgusting I don't even know if I can tell you.'

'Is he eating his poos?'

'How did you know?'

'It's very common in puppies.'

'Aagh. I can't tell you how it makes me feel. I mean I like him licking me. Now I can't let him lick me. It's really put me off him.'

Suzanne's smothered laughter down the line, like a horse blowing down its nostrils.

• Kempton's Journey

'Why do they do it?'

'I'm not honestly sure. But they nearly always outgrow it. Do you get cross with him when you catch him? You must let him know it's horrid. Although to him it isn't. The problem is that we impose human qualities and conditions on our pets.'

'Well, it's too bad. I'm not having him do that. I yell at him, if you want to know. And I confess I gave him a smack the other day. Only a tiny one. I mean it's disgusting. He carries them round the garden before eating them.'

Suzanne's laughter peals out. 'Oh you're so funny. You're so funny without meaning to be. God, I can just picture the pair of you.'

'OK. OK.' Kempton joins in laughing. He has a sudden urge to see her. 'I wish I could see you this evening.' He says it softly.

'We-ell.'

'I know. It's impossible. I shouldn't have said that.'

'It's not impossible actually.'

'You mean you could? You're husband's going out?'

'Yes.'

'So you could get away?'

'Yes.'

'Let's do something. The cinema and dinner? I'd really like that. I've never taken you out. We could go somewhere you don't go with your husband. Anywhere you want.'

'That would be lovely.'

They arrange a time and hang up. Kempton extricates the papers and pens from the bin. Humming in his head. A bit of Mozart's *Requiem*, which is the choir's new project.

Pitman strides into his room, wearing his overcoat and carrying his briefcase. About to set off for Heathrow and thence skiing in Verbier for a fortnight. He slams a memo onto Kempton's desk.

'I can't deal with this now. I'm already late. You'd better

have a bloody good explanation, that's all I can say. Meanwhile I've told the order department not to accept any further orders from them.'

He stops briefly at the door to shake his head and gnash his teeth. The room reverberates after him.

'Re – Grove Estates,' the typed memo says. 'It has only just come to my notice that resultant of unrealistically low prices quoted by yourself for the above account – namely, Lodge House Hotel, Bilton Manor, The Mucky Hen Inn, Old Chantry Hotel, and Lakeside View – Prévot, Pitman and Saunders has been trading at a substantial loss with Grove Estates since the onset of our business dealings with them. I wish to inform you at this point that if no reasonable explanation with regard to this matter is forthcoming upon my return from holiday, I will feel bound to sever the contract between our company and yourself.

Signed, A.P. Pitman.'

And beneath the irate black splurge of a signature, a c.c. D.F. Saunders. And beneath that, in Pitman's left-handed, sloping back writing: 'What the hell are you playing at?'

Kempton bins the memo. Starts wildly laughing. A schoolboy who has engineered his own expulsion. And it will be all round the office before the day is over. Pitman's secretary has a colander for a tongue. And he had better ring his solicitor, pre-emptively, who will tell him what he already knows: that legally he will not be entitled to a penny; but he could make a nuisance of himself and they might give him a year's salary just to get rid of him quickly and quietly. And he must also ring one of the large auction houses and organise to flog some furniture. Not the porcelain. He is sentimental about the porcelain.

'Look what I found. Look what I got today . . .' Vanessa dragging him by the arm excitedly to show him.

He feels exultant, challenged by the unknown horizon

he has pitched for himself. He is dismantling the orderliness he had been at such pains to construct; stripping the layers until all that will be left is Kempton himself. Even as he experiences it, he is aware this exultation cannot last. But for the moment he dismisses the twinges of doubt, of apprehension, and the small lone voice of reason.

No point in hanging around. He may as well go home now. Rescue Pluto from the lobby. Teach him how to walk to heel; at three months, the book says, he is the right age. Kempton will show off later to Suzanne: 'Watch us.' The proud father. And a new list. He must make a new list. Out with the old.

Grasshoppers cavorting inside him. A man in his mid-forties about to join the ranks of the unemployed. And should he telephone an estate agent? How would Cat feel about his selling the house? But Cat's home is Peter's now. But Kempton refuses to see silver linings which have nothing to do with the fundamentals of that particular issue.

Pluto refuses to walk to heel. He either tugs at his lead or sits and refuses to budge. He is developing a rather stubborn side to his nature, as warned in page eleven of the handbook. He is also indicating few further signs of any conscience, as mentioned on page twelve.

Kempton and Suzanne in Richmond Filmhouse. The film is *Il Postino*, and towards the end he slides a glance at her profile. Her chin is quivering. She is sniffling. He takes her hand and strokes the palm, rests it on his thigh with his hand firmly on top. To tell the truth he is finding it hard to stop his own eyes from watering.

'It was so sad. Why the fuck did it have to be so sad?' she says angrily, blinking in the harsh foyer light afterwards, rubbing her eyes with her knuckles.

Kempton does not help by telling her that the actor, Massimo Troisi, died after making the film.

She dashes to the ladies, and while she is gone he spots a woman he knows – and once fancied – and quickly turns his back.

'You're looking furtive,' comments Suzanne, recovered, having washed her face – and half her hair too it would seem – under the tap.

'I spotted someone I know. I thought, well, with your being married.'

'Absolutely.'

They go to a Chinese restaurant in Twickenham that Kempton has heard about. It turns out to be one of those large white and black places with a lot of granite. Single white carnations in spindly white vases on every table. Black cloths and napkins. A trendy clientèle. And Suzanne with her wet hair smarmed across her freckled forehead. But when the waiter takes her coat she is wearing an attractive black dress. At the cinema she had kept her coat on.

'You look nice.'

Vanessa: 'Don't ever use that word with me. It's the most meaningless word in the dictionary.' 'So what should I use instead?' he asked. 'Anything. I don't care. There are a dozen more imaginative words.'

'Thank you.' Suzanne combs her hair back from her forehead with her fingers in an unusually self-conscious gesture he finds endearing.

'Everyone's so fucking chic here.'

She always swears more when she is disconcerted, so that even when she appears to ooze confidence he knows this is not the case. In fact he has come to realise recently that she is far less confident than he had first thought. And this, too, endears her to him. It makes him feel protective. He is starting to care about her. Is this bad?

He leans across the table to tweak her chin. 'I'd rather be sitting here with you than with any other woman in the restaurant.' And means it.

Whoa, Kempton.

'You're really quite gallant sometimes, Kempton.'

After choosing from the menu and ordering, they discuss the film, and Neruda's poetry. He resolves to buy her a book of his poems. For his belated Christmas gift to her he bought her a book of Robert Graves – instead of a CD – which had delighted her.

He tells her about last night's awful gathering. Instead of saying I told you so, she nods understandingly.

'And actually it sounds as though you *did* get something out of it.'

'What?'

'Well, you publicly acknowledged the flaws in your relationship. That couldn't have been easy.'

'No. But once it was out I felt—'

'Cleansed?'

'Maybe. Yes, maybe.'

She is more proficient than him with chopsticks. In the end he alternates them with a knife and fork, and spoon.

'God what a mess,' he says, looking at the squiggles of red, yellow and green on the black tablecloth. 'Like a Jackson Pollock.'

'What do you think of that kind of painting?'

'I hate it, loathe it, detest it. What about you?'

'The same.'

'Good. Because otherwise I would have called you pretentious, and you would have called me limited, and I'd have left you with the bill and walked out ... Talking of bills and impecuniosity, I'm about to join the dole queue. Shall we breed bloodhounds together?'

At home he plays his messages. Cat first, back in the benign environs of St Hilda's. Then Annie, the one he took for dinner. Kempton and Suzanne on the sofa, her hand down his trousers, his down the unbuttoned front of her dress. Pluto shut outside the study door, whining.

'Who's that then?' she says, prodding his penis.

'Ouch that hurts. That isn't funny. No one. It's no one.' His erection shrinks. He gets up to fast forward the tape.

'Sorry. I didn't mean to do it quite so hard. She sounds terribly pukka, my deah.'

'She's ghastly.'

He lifts his finger from the button. 'Bye-bye for now,' says Annie.

'Byee,' sings Suzanne.

He remains by the machine. The final message is a series of grunts. They continue for about a minute before the receiver is replaced.

'What on earth was that?' Kempton feels chilled.

'You have the oddest friends.'

'No, really.' He stands regarding her, with his trousers half falling down.

'Kempton, it's just a weirdie call. A variation on the heavy breathing theme. Come back here.' She undoes her bra, cups her breasts at him.

'I don't know. It sounded different. You listen.'

He replays it, turning the volume louder. There are the distinct sounds of muffled wheezing and half-choked breathing.

'Shit.' He stares at her, rubbing his chin.

Her eyes look frightened. She does up her bra again. 'Dial 1471,' she says, just as he is thinking the same thing.

He does so. Writes the number down as the computerised voice enumerates it. It is his mother's.

When he tries dialling it the line is constantly engaged, and he rings the operator.

'I'm afraid the phone has been left off the hook,' she says.

Suzanne is insistent on coming with him.

'Your husband will be back.' Running to the car. Unlocking it, and setting off the alarm first.

'He's away.'

'For the night?'

'Yes.'

Kempton is shaking. His hands are shaking. He can hardly get the key in the ignition. The rain is teeming down. Wavy stripes down the windscreen. The creaking wipers. The roads awash with puddles. The two of them in tense silence all the way to Ham Common. Kempton flashing other drivers, blasting the hooter, shooting lights, screeching round corners; his knuckles glistening on the steering wheel. No time to analyse what it is he fears.

His mother's two-bedroom Victorian cottage at the end of a long lane is a far cry from the large house surrounded by high rhododendron bushes where he grew up. He never thought to question the reasons. He was too resentful of her to be curious. Now, standing outside the bright red front door in the driving rain, finger jammed on the bell, then lifting the lion's head knocker and banging it down, he wonders what happened.

'We should call the police,' Suzanne says.

He doesn't answer. A light is shining through the curtains of the downstairs front window, but when he tries to peer inside he can see nothing. The curtains are drawn tight. The heavy rain is needle-sharp in their faces, plastering their hair to their skulls, dripping down their necks. He turns back to Suzanne. 'Perhaps you should wait in the car.'

'No.'

'Really I—'
'No Kempton.'
'Well I'm going round the back.'
He holds her elbow securely as they follow the little wicket-fenced path round. It almost feels like two children playing a game, he thinks. And this sense of unreality is exacerbated when they see the back door swinging open. By it are Minnie's black wellingtons and a trug containing bulbs and a trowel. Her shooting stick.

The pressure of dread in his lower stomach. Strobic images of that evening nearly three years ago. And then he becomes conscious of Suzanne.

'I'm taking you back to the car.'
He shepherds her back protesting, and tells her to lock herself in. Gives her the car keys in case she needs to drive off.

'Put the heating on and get yourself warm,' he says.
He picks up Minnie's shooting stick and enters the cottage cautiously. He is not afraid for himself, but of what he will find.

The kitchen has been trashed. All the cupboards and drawers have been wrenched open and the contents thrown onto the floor. The sitting room has been similarly upturned. Ornaments lie smashed on the ground.

Kempton feels extraordinarily calm; and the surreal sensation persists as he creeps through the house, clutching the shooting stick with the sharp end pointing outwards. This isn't really happening, he thinks. This isn't really happening; tiptoeing upstairs.

Minnie is in her ransacked bedroom, lying on the floor with her hands and legs bound; gagged and blindfolded. The phone is just by her, the receiver not properly on the cradle.

'Minnie, it's all right. It's me. Kempton.' He kneels down to unfasten the gag first of all. She is almost choking

• Kempton's Journey

through it, her cheeks scarlet. His feeling of detachedness has deserted him, and he is trembling so that he fumbles with the knot uselessly.

'Bear with me. Be patient . . . You're going to be all right. Just keep calm.' But he is no longer calm himself.

The gag is eventually off, and immediately Minnie starts to gasp; colossal, wheezing gasps. Spluttering and heaving and coughing. He props her against him and massages her back. It is bony and thin. Her spine is prominent. And he still thinks of her as such a big woman.

'I – the—'

'Don't try and speak. I'll get you a drink in a minute.' He tackles the blindfold next. But the knot is too tight.

'Oh God, I'm sorry. It won't undo. I'm going to get some scissors.'

He goes back downstairs to the kitchen, to search among the devastation there. And how will Minnie react when she sees the havoc that has been wreaked in her home? He suddenly remembers Suzanne, and runs outside to the car to explain what has happened.

She phones for the police while he attends to his mother.

The bindings have bitten into her wrists, scoring the flesh; chafed and bruised her ankles. Trussed like a turkey. And the indignity of her skirt lifted high, her pale wrinkled thighs exposed, and her knickers. Did they touch her sexually, an old woman? He can't ask her that. He supports her head while she sips whisky. Her eyes are Dracula-red with broken vessels from the pressure of the blindfold. And when she has the strength to speak, it is in a hoarse tone of utter grief.

'My ring. They've taken my ring.'

Weeping as she looks down at her bare fingers.

'Your wedding ring you mean?' he says gently.

'No. Not that one.'

And he remembers she always wore a ring on the fourth finger of her right hand. A ruby – or maybe it was a garnet – in an antique setting.

She leans against him sobbing. Her hair, unravelled from its chignon, is long and ragged round her face. She looks like a witch. Shocking and terribly old.

'My ring, my ring,' she moans repeatedly. Sobs and moans like a peasant woman in mourning. While her son strokes her hair, and Suzanne watches them in silence with tears in her eyes. Until the police turn up.

Nothing else seems to matter to her. She betrays no sense of fear or shock, no pain from her injuries, no anger at her ransacked cottage or the loss of her valuables. She tells the police how she managed to reach the phone by rocking her body backwards towards it. She had dialled 999 first, counting the pads with her fingers. She had hoped they might trace her. When nobody came she made the phone call to her son, similarly feeling the pads. Ever logical, she had reasoned he would dial 1471. No, she had not been particularly afraid for her life. There were two of them. Hooded. They sounded young. Wore gloves. Were both of medium height and unarmed. They had not been unduly cruel, nor had they threatened her. But she had thought she would choke with the gag.

She is sitting on the sofa downstairs, drinking her second whisky. And throughout this report to the police she keeps shaking her head in disbelief and repeating, 'My ring, my ring,' in an anguished refrain.

'We'll do our best to get it back, Madam,' one of the policemen says.

Minnie looks at him despairingly, and massages her bare finger.

* * *

• Kempton's Journey

She stays the night at Kempton's. In Cat's bed. Suzanne in his. They do not make love. They hold each other close and hardly speak. And the next morning Suzanne drives off home and Kempton phones the office to say he won't be coming in. Doesn't bother with an explanation. It's not worth it. Helps his mother begin clearing up.

10

Race Card

A tissue-frail sun auguring an indigo sky. Clusters of snowdrops stoically making an appearance this Friday, February 16th. And the front page of the paper is full of Fergie's debts and the Queen's refusal to bail her out.

'Meanie Queenie,' Kempton mutters to Pluto. 'What's a couple of million?' Pluto compressing one of his squeaky toys in his jaws. It has long since lost its squeak, and releases gentle wheezes, like a cushion being sat on.

Unemployment is down another consecutive month, Kempton notes with interest, standing over the table reading, holding his bowl of bran flakes in one hand. In the centre of the table, either side of the fruit bowl and a half-dead potted ivy, are two valentine cards. One is home-made and has an illustration of a spider with wings dangling from the end of a thread. Beneath it are the words: The spider wanted to be a fly so that it might fly away from its own web ... and wish you happy Valentine's Day. Within, Suzanne – for she presented it to him in person ('It's supposed to be a secret,' he said) – has written a poem entitled 'A Prayer.'

• Kempton's Journey

> *'Oh that frisson of excitement*
> *When you meet someone new,*
> *God please let it last forever;*
> *I'll even remember to say amen at the end of my prayers*
> *Instead of falling asleep half way through.'*

The other is a 'chic' type of card with a painting by Millais on it. The message inside – my place or yours? – bears the hallmarks of Annie.

He reads Suzanne's again and feels slightly heartened. It was her birthday two days ago. No excuse to forget the date as it is the same as Cat's. He spent ages on Saturday searching for the right present for her, browsing in the various departments of Dickins & Jones; then ended up in the antique emporium as usual, where he always finds something. He bought her a pair of nineteenth-century nail scissors with moulded and engraved handles, in their own little tortoise shell case. He thought she was going to cry when he gave them to her. Then she made a funny of it instead.

'You'd better be careful what I snip,' she said, snipping them in the air near his crotch. 'Your loss,' he countered.

He had sent Cat a cheque inside her card. A hundred pounds. She had phoned him to thank him. The beeping of a call box, and her sweet husky voice: 'Kempton . . . ?' She had got an A for her essay, she told him with pride and a certain smugness. OK, point taken. That's brilliant . . . So what was she doing on her birthday . . . ? Going to a university play written by one of her friends, she said – and thanked him again for the money. He was far too generous.

And that is one of his better traits: generosity. He loves giving presents. But he'll have to rein back soon. Become one of those shoppers who race into the supermarket just before it closes, to purchase the reduced tomatos, or job-lot of specially priced broken gingerbread men, and the last loaf left on the shelf, slashed by half. No matter that it is wholemeal, and he detests wholemeal. Being virtuous will give him an appetite.

'Must go. Doesn't do to be late on one's last day,' he tells Pluto, stooping to pat him and receive his goodbye lick. He leaves the puppy in the kitchen nowadays; he has become to big to squeeze through the cat flap – the last time he tried he became stuck and Kempton had to force-feed him through amidst high-pitched squeals and struggling limbs – and the worst he ever does is upset the vegetable rack. Except for a few wizened, sprouting potatoes, this is empty anyway. Soon Kempton will have all the time – if not money – in the world to go shopping, and to walk the dog. The days, weeks, months stretch ahead of him, and he has started to make a list of how he will fill them.

Spike is lying on the table and Kempton strokes under his chin – feels the vibrating of his purrs. He grabs an apple – cochineal ripe – from the fruit bowl, buffs it against his jacket sleeve (tonight he will hang up his pinstripe for the last time), and puts it in his pocket to eat in the car.

Draws up in the yard, next to Pitman's red BMW. Gets out; but he does not immediately enter the building. A sudden tide of emotion whooshes over him. This was the building he took on with such pride eleven years ago when the old premises became too small. And from that window he is now peering up at, where Pitman's invisible shadow looms, Kempton used to gaze out: containers with French number plates being unburdened of pallets of boxes, and then one of the 'lads' would rush up with a fork-lift to ferry them into the warehouse. The cheerful yelling out of male voices drifting up to his slightly ajar window. A radio blaring. And his two vans being loaded for the day's delivery. Jaunty whistling. A thumbs-up sign from one of the drivers to Hamish, the cellar manager. Kempton's empire. Oh such hopes he'd had. And he had enjoyed every minute of every day. In his own way, mundane though it might have seemed to others, he felt as though he had created something. And when Cat was still a child – no indication what she might do with her future – he had even harboured hopes she might come into the business. Envisaged them, the pair of them, working alongside each other. Prévot and daughter.

And now it has come to this. Semi-voluntary exile. His grandfather's pear brandy has long been forgotten, and soon the name of Prévot will be erased from the company and Pitman the builder's will blaze triumphant.

'There's no room for nostalgia in this game Ke-empton,' Pitman said.

But he and Saunders have more or less agreed to Kempton's terms.

Inside and upstairs he lopes. And the girls are artificially chirpy, as though he has three ears and one eye and they are pretending not to notice. Their awkwardness is almost tangible. How *is* one supposed to behave on an occasion like this? And there is no leaving party, no gold watch as appreciation for his years of service. Not even a planned luncheon. And it occurs to him he could take Julia out to lunch.

Jim Masters appears. Pit's bull about to stomp snorting into Kempton's arena, bypassing Tim Isaacs.

'Don't forget to brief me on those "dead" accounts, which I intend to resurrect,' he says. Rubbing Kempton's nose in his failure.

Kempton sails past him without acknowledgement. Jim Masters' satisfied grin leaves an imprint behind his eyes.

Julia brings him coffee in his room as he is in the middle of clearing his desk and drawers. Filling his briefcase with stationery – envelopes, pencils, pens, notepads, photocopying paper, a stapler, glue, Tippex, jumbo paper-clips.

Anything, in fact. His last-ever perks. And the dictaphone. What the heck.

'Thanks.' As she pushes papers aside to clear a space for the mug. 'Don't tell anyone.' Caught in the act of pilferage.

'I wouldn't dream of it,' she says, surveying the haul in the open briefcase. 'It'll never shut. I'll give you a carrier. What on earth are you going to do with all those elastic bands?'

'I don't know. I'll think of something. Make catapults? Hey come to lunch with me today. I'll run it up on expenses. A splash-up fling as a grand finale.'

'You're on.'

'Tim Isaacs could come too, if he's free. And Hamish, if he can tear himself away from the cellars. We can all lament the passing of better days.'

'Don't. You'll start me off.' And there really are tears in her eyes.

'Hey – I didn't mean – look I'm really touched.'

'I'm leaving, you know. So's Tim. We'll tell you over lunch.'

He hugs her. Smells perfume that may be Revlon, or Coty. The softness of her polyester blouse under his hand. He is quite choked by her loyalty and doesn't trust himself to speak. He raises his mug in a mock salute – slopping coffee over a pink computer printout and grinning ruefully.

He has no intention of briefing Jim Masters on the dead accounts.

He takes the photograph down from the wall, of Vanessa and Cat. A virginal square is left behind, a halcyon testimonial. And he takes a red biro that he had just flung into his briefcase, to draw a minute red cross in the centre of it. In memoriam.

Lunch is at a Greek restaurant. It is decorated with posters of alluring beaches and blue horizons, others of ruined temples. Ill-matched rugs partly cover an old lino floor. One wall is taken up with bottles of Greek wines and miniatures of liqueurs. Kempton loves this place for its unpretentiousness and eccentricity. Odours of garlic and spices and slowly roasting lamb permeate the air and evoke a wanderlust in him – the urge to run barefoot along that beach, into the aquamarine line of the sea, stroll round the ruins under the furnace of the sun, and sip ouzo at a rickety table under an olive tree. And why not?

Dmitri, the owner who knows Kempton of old, brings saucers of huge black olives swimming in oil, and plates of mezze without being asked. He sits with them over a bottle of retsina. From the kitchen his wife's singing rises above the Greek music playing on the old-fashioned tape-deck next to the restaurant's till.

'Business is slack this time of year,' he says gesturing to the empty tables. Only two others are occupied.

'What about the evenings?' Kempton asks.

'Better. Saturdays are good still. But Mondays and Tuesdays it would be cheaper not to open. But you have to, don't you? Customers – they've changed. I've seen it in the twenty years we've been here. They want the glitz. All them things – you know. They don't want good, honest food and authentic atmosphere no more. Sometimes I think I'll do the place up. But that's not what I believe in. Know what I mean? And then we may never see a return on what we've borrowed.' He shrugs. His accent is curious, an amalgam of guttural Greek and Cockney. His daughter, who is one of the waitresses, resembles her father – dark, thick beaked nose, liquid eyes, heavy-set; she could not look less English, yet she cannot speak a word of her parents' tongue, and her accent is pure Cockney, which always strikes Kempton as strangely anomalous when he looks at her.

He tells Dmitri about leaving the business, and Dmitri is shocked. 'But it's yours. You started it. Eh – that's dreadful.

Blimey that's really shook me. I mean you and I goes back a long way.' He looks glum and embraces Kempton on either cheek.

People are continually surprising Kempton today. A reward of a different kind. He is always faintly astonished that people should care about him. He does not see that he has any particular characteristic that should draw them to him.

'I'm feeling quite positive actually,' he says. 'Well sad also, obviously. But quite positive about the future. I feel like I'm entering another phase in my life, clichéd though it might sound. Well I am, aren't I? It really is another phase.' He turns to the others at the table and they nod encouragingly.

Dmitri's daughter comes over. 'Mum wants you in the kitchen.'

And Kempton, Julia, Hamish and Tim are left on their own. Tim, it transpires, has applied to a brewery for a job and has been shortlisted.

'But I'm leaving anyway. No way am I staying with you gone. And as for that insufferable Jim Masters . . .' Leaves the sentence unfinished and stretches his lips into a grimace of revulsion.

Julia plans to hand in her notice this very afternoon, as a grand gesture.

'You'll get a job easily,' Kempton says. 'You're a fantastic secretary. And I'll give you a glowing reference – "She massages my neck like no one else" – No, seriously, I shall heap praise on you. I suppose I still count as a referee, even when I'm on the dole.'

'Of course you do. Are you really going on the dole?'

'Why not?' he asks teasingly.

'No, no reason,' she answers, flustered.

'But I'm not,' he says. 'It would be morally wrong.'

Hamish is staying put in the company; looks embarrassed

as he confesses this. 'What would I do?' he asks. 'Where would I go? At my age. And jobs are scarce.' He has an upside-down, narrow-foreheaded, jug-jawed face; a tiny, incongruous moustache.

Kempton, sitting next to him, lays his hand on his arm. 'Don't be daft. I wouldn't expect you to do otherwise. You'd be mad to leave.'

'But I want you to know – well, it's been a real pleasure working with you all these years.' Red creeping up his neck into his cheeks. 'It's not the same now. The others are . . . And once you've gone . . . well, it'll be odd not to see you about. I remember the day we moved into that building and you and me was doing the racking system together by candlelight. Well, so anyway, I hope the future holds good for you. You deserve it.'

A tight band seems to be coiling like a boa constrictor round Kempton's throat.

'I want to, oh shit . . .' His eyes are filling, nostrils blocking, and he swallows hard several times, his words stuck. Julia has tears streaming down her cheeks and she is laughing through them, apologising. Kempton gets a handkerchief from his pocket and trumpets his nose into it. He recovers a bit and gives a shaky laugh. 'God what a showdown. I was *going* to say that I wanted to tell you how much I appreciate your support. All your support and your loyalty. And we'll keep in touch. We *will*. That's not some sort of vacuous statement. I mean it.'

Back at the office in the afternoon for his last goodbyes, and everyone is gathered awkwardly for the send-off. From behind the reception Tim and Julia bring out an enormous bottle.

'We had a little collection for you.'

It is a salmanazar of Volnay, 1988.

And so with a short speech of thanks from him, a few

hugs and handshakes, a tight smile from Pitman and nervous giggle from Saunders, The Blot leaves that particular landscape and drives away for ever in the Carlton which he has purchased from the leasing company and intends to sell at a profit and buy something else.

'Things achieved today,' Kempton writes on his life list, underlining the 'today' twice. Tapping his foot on Pluto beneath his desk, to Glenn Miller's 'Moonlight Serenade.'
'He died without a trace Pluto. That's really sad. The greatest trombonist that ever lived.'
Suspends his pen thoughtfully in the air for a few seconds.

> '1. Estate agent and assistant came round. Usual fawning type. Told me would have no problem selling. Well he would say that. Claims to have several potential buyers wants to show round immediately. Assistant took measurements. Giving him sole agency for couple of months; then will slap house with at least one other firm.
> 2. Tallboy, chiffonier and sofa table picked up by Sotheby's. Bought some rubber plant things to fill gaps.
> 3. Spoke to Tony (stockbroker) on phone about selling a few bits and pieces; also about investing my lump settlement, which should receive by end of week.
> 4. Spoke to Chris (accountant). Discussed new pension scheme. Keep life assurance policies going if poss.
> 5. Bought a couple of car magazines. How can people get so excited about cars? Think will buy a hatchback job for Pluto. A Honda? Want something problem-free.
> 6. If worst comes to worst, could rent small flat and exist for rest of my life without a job, albeit very simply and thriftily. Hopefully—' thinking of his father's lonely, joyless last two years, '—it won't come to that. But one must be realistic. I shall never work for anyone else again. It is out of the question.
> 7. There are several ways I could scrape a living to back up my income: teach French? History? Do translation. Dabble in selling Art Nouveau. Import wine in a small way. Lecture in wine. No cleaning

windows! At least I am in charge of my own life. It's important to fix on that.

8. Received brochure about caravan/horse holiday in France. Admit looks v. appealing.'

Now, without a number against it, he writes, 'Buy easel, oil paints, etc. tomorrow. Phone Minnie – check OK.'

Pauses, then, 'Am I getting too involved/dependent Suzanne? Go Pissarro's. Chat-up potential Friday eves.'

Pauses again, and lays down the pen. He wishes he had someone to talk to about all this.

I really miss Peter. No I don't.

Remembering the last time they saw each other as friends. After a game of squash they ate in Peter's restaurant: warm salad and tiny quails served pink; a redcurrant sauce. Cooked by Peter himself. Peter was in serious mood for once (guilt?), drawing a parallel between the problems in Ireland and those in Israel; sceptical about a long-term solution, and citing historical facts to give weight to his argument. This had led to a discussion between them about the instability of other countries that had been divided up and 'recreated', particularly those which had belonged to the Ottoman Empire before it had crumbled in the First World War. Naturally, this led on to Yugoslavia.

'But really you have to go back to the Roman Empire,' said Kempton.

They went back to Peter's to watch a video he'd recorded of Sunday's football. Sat in front of the television, eating chocolate-covered coffee beans, half watching the football and simultaneously playing a game of chess: '. . . What a goal! Did you see that? Check, by the way . . .' Consumed the best part of a bottle of port. He had ended up staying the night, not wanting to risk the breathalyser. In the bathroom, on a glass shelf, was a box of Tampax and a hair-slide. He had teased Peter, who was unusually evasive.

Now he realises they must have been Cat's.

'The house is up for sale,' he tells Suzanne, walking by the river in the snow; Pluto, on his lead, trailing a passage with his nose; Suzanne's woollen scarf wound round her head; Kempton with his logger's hat.
'Where will you live?'
'I don't know. Rent somewhere? I thought about bumping off your husband so I could move in with you.'
'You'd have to learn to put the loo seat down after you. I've noticed you never do that.'
'Three years of living on my own,' he says. But Vanessa had always criticised him about it.
'When I was an undergraduate I dreamt of living on a houseboat. You know. A narrowboat. On the Oxford canal.' And as he says it the dream is suddenly recaptured and a little nerve leaps in his ribcage.
'Wouldn't you be worried by rats?'
'Rats? No I wouldn't mind. Ping – I could catapult stones at them with all my elastic bands I nicked from the company. Anyway you don't necessarily get rats.'
'It's a long way to go for a fuck. Oxford.'
'Well perhaps I'll moor it here instead. You do put things so delicately.'
'In which case let me recite some Walt Whitman to you. OK:

"There was a child went forth every day,
and the first object he look'd upon, that object he became,
and that object became part of him for the day or a certain
  part of the day,
or for many years or stretching cycles of years . . ."'

He is beginning to know her; trust her; to laugh where once he was irritated; to listen where there might be sense; to rely on her phone calls and miss her voice in between; to understand that beneath her humour are her own insecurities and sorrows; that when she made the joke about Oxford being a long way for a fuck, she was making light to conceal her fear at his going. And he wants to reassure her. Yet that is not his right.

'I like your hand in my pocket . . . I wish you weren't married,' he says, interrupting her recitation.

She stares at him, a startled expression in her hazel eyes – sage green flecks in them he only now observes. Her lips are shrivelled with cold and she licks them. He has never seen her lost for words before.

'Sorry. I'll never say that again. I promise.'

'Know thyself, Kempton.'

'What?'

'Know thyself. You're not ready for any relationship yet. You might find yourself latching onto a woman for the wrong reasons.'

'So then it's lucky you *are* married.' His turn to jest, even though he doesn't mean it.

She makes no comment. He squeezes her hand in his pocket.

'Well done Kempton. I'd say that's pretty fair. Pretty fair indeed. You're really progressing.'

It is Kempton's fourth lesson, and Simon, who runs the art classes in his home, rests his arm across the back of Kempton's chair and leans over his shoulder to inspect his likeness of the still life arrangement on the table: a box with an untied ribbon half round it, bowl, jug, and two very green apples, on a blue-and-white checked cloth. Kempton has used heavy blocks of colour and quite a lot of black, influenced not a little by the Cézanne exhibition at the Tate he went to just the day before.

He had no idea he would take to drawing and painting

the way he has; how therapeutic and engrossing he would find it. He completely loses all sense of time. It is pure delight for him, the splurging and daubing and experimenting with shapes and colour.

He is one of a group of only four – two middle-aged women and an elderly man besides himself – and Simon is encouraging of them all; ever the diplomat. But Kempton knows, without self-bluff, that he is the best. Takes an almost childlike pleasure in what he is creating, what he sees emerging from his own fingers; nor does he have any false modesty, so that if one of the others praises his work, he agrees in surprise, 'Yes it *is* rather good isn't it?' Because it doesn't seem that *he* was responsible for doing it.

Simon has told him he is an instinctive artist.

'What birth sign are you?' he asked, their second lesson.

'Libra. Why?'

'Oh well, that explains it. Librans are often artistic.'

He is a portly man, white-haired with a pitted, ruddy complexion, rosebud mouth and noisette eyes, as Kempton describes them. Has exhibited quite widely in galleries in provincial towns, and in Richmond itself; also in a small gallery off Regent Street.

At the end of this fourth session Kempton lags behind. He packs away his own stuff and helps Simon clear up.

'I've been practising quite a bit at home,' he confides. 'I've set up a room in the house.'

Where Vanessa did her china restoration. Her ghost watching over him. His over her. And her fingers painstakingly slotting a tiny jigsaw piece into the rim of a dish. 'There,' she announced triumphantly. 'And when the glue's dry, who would know?'

'Well, I've got time now,' Kempton continues. 'Now that I've quit the company. You know I quit?'

'You did mention something.'

There is something almost spiritual about Simon. But he

has a curious smell. Musty. As though he has just surfaced from between the covers of a dusty, crumbling book.

'Anyway, I've been doing a bit of copying.'

Helping Simon move the table, deliberately trying to sound casual.

'I know it's not art. It's just imitating someone else. But it's great fun.'

'Do you have anything with you?'

Simon, setting down his end of the table, wiping his forehead with his shirt sleeve.

'Well I do, actually.' And from his portfolio Kempton takes out a couple of canvases and lays them on the table.

'Good gracious.'

Simon frowns, smiles, frowns again. Makes no further comment for several minutes. Kempton's gaze rests intently on him, for some indication as to what he is thinking.

'You don't like them.'

Simon stands back and thoughtfully pinches his upper lip and releases it a few times. 'No, no, it's not that I don't like them. They're very good. You've definitely caught something. No, I'm just surprised. Van Gogh eat your heart out, eh? Look, as you say, they're not out of your own head, but you've an excellent eye. How long did they take you?'

'I don't know. Half a morning maybe. I have a problem with people though. I can do landscape or buildings. Still life. I really enjoy doing something involving perspective. The more angles the better. But people and animals . . . When I tried drawing my dog it was disastrous.' He had done Pluto asleep – who had ended up looking like a coiled string of sausages.

'I'm sure you could learn. It's only that the other comes more naturally to you. So where did you copy these from?'

'I've got several Impressionist books.'

Puts his version of Van Gogh's 'Landscape near Auvers' and Manet's 'Regatta at Argenteuil' back in the portfolio.

'I could frame them for a tenner each,' Simon offers.

And with that the seeds of an idea are born in Kempton. At any rate, something to add to his list of Possibilities For The Future.

It is Monday night, snowing again. For a few days it had looked as though winter was over. Monday the 26th. And tomorrow evening, at six o'clock, or thereabouts, it will be three years since he found her in the garage. Choking his way through the fumes. Dragging her out. His mouth on hers trying to breathe life into her although she must have been dead for God knows how long. Hurtling into the house and phoning 999. And then back to his wife, because surely he had been mistaken, surely, surely . . .

'My mother was abused by her father,' Suzanne told Kempton on their recent walk. 'She was so elegant. She used to despair of me. I felt like an ugly gawky duckling next to her. So I cracked jokes. My father worshipped her. He went to pieces.'

'I think you're lovely,' Kempton said.

'When she died I didn't have to worry about how I looked anymore. I could be myself. Now I think, how selfish. How appallingly selfish. There was this poor, distraught woman and I—'

'I'm so sorry,' he said.

'You and me both.'

And now – strains of live folk music coming from the Rose and Crown, and for want of anything else to do Kempton wanders inside. An Irish group are playing. He gets chatting to the landlord. Has a few pints, and a jacket potato that oozes butter and shreds of Cheddar through its crisp, split skin; scalds his lips. He becomes lost in the swirling smoke – 'Oh he was lost at sea,' the singer's voice rings out. And through the safety net of smoke Kempton flirts silently with a sloe-eyed girl young enough to be his daughter.

11

The Track

Every available minute he has, Kempton spends in his studio. Can hardly wait to go in there in the morning and install himself for the day. Wakes up with a sense of purpose to the alarm which is set religiously at six thirty each morning.

He has positioned the easel so that it is in front of the window (he read that the Impressionists favoured a north light; too bad that this is south), which looks out onto his own and neighbouring gardens. Starlings lined up on the telegraph wire stretching across, like musical crotchets on a stave. And Pluto, safely and expensively fenced in after months of finding every conceivable escape point, sniffing about amongst the weeds and forget-me-nots. Sometimes the only glimpse of him is his wagging stern as he dives into the laurel.

Beside the easel is a round chipboard table, which had previously resided in the sitting room with a chintz cloth covering it and the Sèvres vases on top. Now it is scuffed and stained, home to his tools of trade: palette – already satisfyingly patterned with oil colour, jar of assorted

- Kempton's Journey

brushes and palette knives, turps, linseed, rags, another jar containing charcoal sticks. And his box of paints.

If he could rescue only one possession from a fire it would be this. The last time he took such a delight in anything was when he was thirteen and had saved enough from pocket money, newspaper rounds, cleaning cars and odd-jobbing to buy a second-hand full-sized bike. He recalls the red mudguards that he buffed till he could see his reflection; and a two-tone horn that he attached to the curved handlebars. He is that child again. It was an awful extravagance under the circumstances, a real self-indulgence, but as soon as he saw the box in the shop, tantalising with its sleek rosewood lid open, he had to have it. And within, in sentry slots – rows of metal tubes (he is careful to squeeze them from the bottom upwards), their bands denoting the colour. Every conceivable colour with evocative fecund names: burnt umber, sepia, yellow ochre, croceate, indigo, mazarine, malachite, cochineal . . . The very names inspire him to paint.

Kempton is prolific. He has compiled quite a little stack of Van Goghs, Monets and Gauguins, besides his own original landscapes which are not to be ashamed of. And he has learned, with Simon's encouragement, to do people that don't look like aliens. His three-month-old hobby is becoming something of an obsession, And if for any reason he misses more than a day he gets quite twitchy. His hands are beginning to look the part – hardened palms, dark-rimmed nails, paint engrained in the cracks of his fingers. He inspects them regularly with pride; believes the evidence of his artistic toils has plucked him from the coy ranks of the bourgeoisie and elevated him to a more Bohemian status.

Kempton dropping out. Does this mean he is no longer classified as middle-class? Of late one can hardly put on the radio or the box or read the paper without someone carping on about the middle classes. To tell the truth he has never been sure what precisely is meant by the term, but is starting to develop a complex about it. If it means simply that category of people between lower and upper class, then is it his fault his father was neither a miner nor an aristocrat? Yet he is forever sneeringly branded because of it. Everything seems sneering or menacing nowadays, and that depresses him. Young people are menacing, the way they strut and swagger about, the way they jeer, the way they dress; their haircuts, their stance, their attitude. So call him sentimental, but sometimes he hankers for a milder, vanished era. And if that makes him middle-class, then *tant pis*.

On a wall of his studio are two of his pictures. Framed by himself. Very fair first efforts, considering his usual ineptness at anything connected with DIY. And he likens the sense of satisfaction he derives from seeing them there to an angler who catches, kills, guts and finally eats his salmon. A process taken from beginning to end. Not that he could kill anything; and he would be squeamish about the gutting; but in principle . . .

Over the last few weeks he has become more experimental with materials; has painted on hardboard, which he treats with a primer, cardboard and plywood. Recalls that in the garage are some sheets of wood, But he is not going in there. The death chamber. Let the next owners discover for themselves what they will. And will the ghostly traces of a car motor running sometimes thread their way into the newcomers' sleep?

A couple want to buy the house at the asking price. But it is one of those chains: they have to sell their property first. And their potential purchaser has to sell *his*. And so on. Nonetheless it is reassuring. The wife phones Kempton on a weekly basis to let him know they are still keen. She is beginning to sound agitated. She is Californian

– 'I just adore all the drapes' – clapping her hands at Vanessa's flounces and frills and flowers. And Kempton felt suddenly possessive of his home; a jolt that it, too, is soon to be consigned to the past. His links with Vanessa are becoming ever more tenuous. He cannot rid himself of the sense that he is betraying her in a way by selling the house; wiping his hands of their shared life. Their home into which she had ploughed such energy. And he would come home after work in the evenings to find tiny swatches of fabric attached to chairs and Vanessa gazing at them with head tilted in serious consideration. Her voice, her presence are everywhere at the moment. The walls burn with her aura. Never has he felt more strongly that she is somewhere, beyond the zone of contact, reproaching him. And when he is gone from here what will be left of her accomplishments to remind him? Nowhere else will bear her imprint, be stamped indelibly with her personality. His next place of habitation will not shed her laughter from behind its doors, or her rages or tears. Another bedroom will not reverberate with her vixen cries while making love.

'I adore you,' he said.

'Why? How? How can you adore me? Do you adore the witch, the madwoman, the depressive, the—'

'Stop it.'

'Well?'

'I don't know. I'm not analysing it. I just love you. I can say that.'

But she exhausted him. Pulled him down with her.

'It's horrible being me sometimes,' she said.

And of all her remarks that one has stuck more than any. So poignant. So sad. It's horrible being me.

'Is there much other interest in the house?' the American woman asked the other day.

'Well really you should ask the agents,' Kempton said

with just enough ambiguity, so that she groaned. 'Oh no. We're going to lose it. I feel it in my bones.'

In fact there has been considerable interest, but not at the asking price. And Kempton is in no hurry. Not, at least, until he returns from France.

He is increasingly excited about his trip. Away from the school holiday hordes, away from the gloom of British news: Scottish children massacred, a mother and her two babies trapped in their torched home, mad cows, cloned sheep, tedious by-elections, the government's xenophobia, Tony Blair's grin. Away from Annie's unwanted attentions. But away, too, from Suzanne. It was all very well at the onset of their affair to say one would not get involved. But how do you prevent yourself? He is not a callous human being. Certainly Kempton has his failings, but callous he is not. He has a heart that is unswervingly loyal and romantic beneath his pedantic, sometimes clumsy approach. So – his concern is growing about this relationship which started out in a mood of flippant lightheartedness. He is even starting to resent Suzanne for the casualness with which she seems to juggle with her dual life. She is, it appears to him, entirely without guilt or conscience, and this bothers him greatly. He almost feels defensive of the cuckolded husband.

He has made a list of things to take on holiday he might otherwise forget: swimming trunks, bag of bran, bag of washing powder, adaptor, camera, binoculars, backgammon, Euro-card, books: biography of Thomas More, the Rousseau, *Techniques of the World's Great Painters*, *Understanding Life Drawing*. Photos of Vanessa, Cat, Pluto. And Suzanne.

She teased him when he asked her for one, prompting his usual hackles-up reaction.

'To hell with it,' he said. 'I don't know why I asked. You really have a knack of dampening things.'

And she had looked so crestfallen at that, that *he* had

ended up apologising. The photo is great. Has perfectly caught that mischievous expression. Of course he cannot give her one in return. Which is no bad thing as he is decidedly unphotogenic. Nevertheless it would be nice to know she had something to remind her of him.

Cat is accompanying him for the first week. He expects it will be their last ever holiday together, just the two of them. Tries not to dwell on this.

The Friday after Easter – and thank God that's over with. He deposits Pluto at Minnie's just before seven thirty in the morning. The birds already twittering away invisibly as he unloads the dog's luggage from his new car – well, four years old but new for him and with a low mileage. One lady owner, the advert said. He had thought those discriminatory little asides were outmoded. He knew plenty of women drivers who hammered their cars and were more aggressive than men. He bought a Citroën in the end. An unstartling dark blue. Can never remember what model it is, and can only remember the registration – H 985 GJO – by thinking: H for Harry. 985, like 1985 – a great vintage year. GJO, like Jo-Jo. And now he recalls that that was her name: the girl at Oxford he was so mad about. Joanna, nicknamed Jo-Jo.

Pluto, sedately beside him one minute, darts off, nose to the ground, having caught a whiff of some scent. Oblivious to Kempton's whistling and muted shouts (too early in the morning to let full rip). Kempton sets down the dog basket with everything in it and tears after him. Captures him and yanks his head up from the ground by a spare bit of neck flesh; clips the lead to his collar.

'Naughty boy. Bad. *Bad*.' Lightly smacks his rump. Pluto, half grown, gazes at him with pulled-down, dismal eyes whilst his wagging stern lashes against Kempton's shin like rope. His domed, judge's head, his permanent air of tragedy, are at complete variance with his character, which abounds with joy. But he is daily becoming more wilful. His intelligence – or is it wiliness? – is remarkable. He seems to work things out calculatingly to his advantage; usually with the effect of maximum inconvenience to Kempton. He already has a vast vocabulary to which he responds according to the situation and to his own inclination.

Kempton hauls him back down the road and rings Minnie's bell.

'Pluto,' she greets him effusively as he levers himself at her. 'Hello Kempton,' she adds.

'Hello. I'll get his stuff. There's rather a lot of it I'm afraid.'

He fetches the basket and bears it aloft inside, into the kitchen. She has had locks fixed on all the windows, he notices. His mother has changed since that evening. She is subdued. There is a bewildered manner about her. More oddly she has stopped saying 'Hmph'.

'Do you want a cup of anything?' she offers.

'I haven't really got time.' He feels awkward with her. He can't help but be rather sorry for her. And this more mellow woman blunts the edge of his ancient hostility, with which he was familiar. Without it he is unsure how to behave; is gentle towards her, the way one is to an invalid. It feels unnatural. He misses the old sniping.

The day after the break-in he had helped her put the house back in order – he had also enlisted Mrs Jakes' assistance. Minnie had shuffled about helplessly, repeatedly rubbing the fourth finger of her right hand. It was, he thought then, and it occurs to him again now, almost as if someone had died and she was in mourning.

'Who's looking after Spike?'

'A neighbour's coming in twice a day to feed him.'

'You could have brought him here.'

'I didn't think of it. But anyway he'd run off. You know

what cats are like. He'd have tried to make his way home and got run over.'

'Butter,' she says.

'Butter?'

'You grease the pads of their paws with it and shut them in. They lick their paws, and the action of grooming themselves makes them feel at home. Cats love butter.'

'How do you know all this?'

'We had cats when I was a child.'

'Oh.' What does he know about his mother's childhood? He never met either set of grandparents; they died before he was born. 'Right, look I should be going. Now – Pluto likes to have a couple of biscuits in his basket at night. Actually feed them to him. And a cuddle. He really expects that. You know – a tummy rub. If you say it to him "Tummy rubbed" he rolls over on his back in readiness. It's an instant tranquilliser. And don't let him charge round directly after eating. I'm afraid his eyes have to be bathed daily and his ears cleaned. What else? Oh, of course no chicken bones. And for Chrissake don't let him out without a lead. He's got no road sense, and if he catches a whiff of anything interesting he's off. And he's just discovering he's male. You know. Becoming interested. And a flea—'

'Go.'

'What?'

'Go.'

'Oh. OK. Yes. Well. Thank you for having him. I mean it's really good of you.'

'I've been looking forward to it.'

And it strikes him: years of living on her own. The dog will provide some friendship and entertainment for her.

'I'll miss him. Well, look after yourself.'

'Yes. Have a good time.'

A last hug for Pluto. A hesitant and brief kiss on her cheek – dry as a lizard's skin – and he is off.

The front door to Peter's house is ajar and Kempton wanders in, bolstering himself for the encounter.

'Anyone about?' he calls.

Peter appears in his monogrammed dressing gown from the direction of the kitchen, sleep crumpled still. He looks his age. And he is wearing glasses.

'Hello there.' That amused lift of the eyebrow. 'Looking forward to the life of a Romany, then?'

'As a matter of fact I am.' Bristling, ready for battle. Hears himself sounding pompous and humourless. 'Where's Cat? Isn't she ready?'

'I'll be five minutes. You're early,' her voice drifts downwards. 'I'm in our bedroom.'

Where he has no intention of venturing.

'Want a coffee while you wait?' Peter asks.

'No thanks.'

'Suit yourself. I've just made myself one. I'm going to have it if you don't mind.'

'Go ahead. I'll hang around here.'

Peter's house is light and minimalist with a few choice pieces of modern art. Hanging from a coat hook are his polo helmet, crop and a pair of spurs. The emblems of a man with leisure time on his hands and the wherewithal to enjoy it.

He reappears beside Kempton, who moves stiffly away and stands at his distance like a sergeant major at drill.

'I want to tell you something,' Peter says softly, so that Cat should not overhear. 'Every day that passes I love your daughter more. She is quite exceptional. In the end, if anyone is going to be hurt it will be myself, not her. Please God that won't ever happen, because I don't think I could bear it.'

His eyes shine pink behind the glasses and he disappears into the kitchen again before Kempton can make a retort, leaving him nonplussed, with a lingering sense of unease.

His daughter descends, carrying her coat over one arm. She always tackles stairs sideways on. She is wearing a long cream shirt over black leather jeans – Peter must have bought them for her – and her tummy, that had been girlish-flat, is starting to to bulge visibly. It gives him the oddest sensation witnessing her body altering. When she was going through puberty – Oh God it doesn't seem very long ago; it isn't very long ago – he had been objectively fascinated by her developing body. Now he is fascinated anew as she moves into another area of womanhood. Too early. Too soon. And sometimes he has to avert his eyes from her: illogical or not, her pregnancy is to him such an overt declaration of her sexuality. He plays with words in his head: puberty . . . pupa = larva = baby. Pupa derived from the Latin for doll.

He waits in the porch while she and Peter embrace. Tries not to see them.

'Look after you both,' he hears Peter say. And is taken aback. Both? Himself? Then he realises Peter means the baby.

Peter turns to him. 'It's daft. I could've taken you to the airport in the van. I still could. You could leave your car here. You'll pay a fortune at the long-term car park. A taxi would've been cheaper.'

'I'm not parking it at the long term. There's a car park a couple of miles away where they charge £6 a day and ferry you to and from the airport. It works out at ninety quid, which is only about twenty more than a taxi both ways, by the time it's done Richmond and Wimbledon. And Ham for Pluto.'

As he finishes speaking it strikes Kempton that this is the longest civil exchange he has had with Peter for months. And fleetingly something flickers within him. For an instant his antipathy seems on the point of dissolving. And does Peter observe anything? A softening of Kempton's expression? A light in his eye?

'And you look after yourself, old chum,' Peter says, taking his glasses off, swiping the air with his fist and tossing his head in that remembered roguish way that takes Kempton back to countless drinking sessions, chatting-up-women sessions, chess games, slamming matches on the squash or tennis court, long discussions over a meal; and more unusually for men, frank barings of the soul. No one knew Kempton better than Peter. And Kempton liked to think the reverse was also true.

The taxi from Bordeaux airport deposits them near the station. The quay is a hive of sound and activity, a cacophony of jangling chains, tapping masts, rattling rigging, water slapping gently against hulls. Brown-armed men load and unload wooden crates from cargo boats – *'Mettez-le ici.' 'Allez, allez, dépéchez vous.' 'Cretin, que faites-vous alors?'* Hammering, banging, whistling. A fisherman mending his net – and feet skirting past him. Warm southern faces. The reek of fish and spilled wine, of soot and traffic. And beyond the tangle of boats and the irregular line of warehouses and factory chimneys, the regal sweep of the Garonne.

Kempton, chest thrown out, breathing it in, gazing about him. Shockwaves zipping through him. Oh God it's like yesterday. Why has he left it so long? Memories of school holidays spent in nearby Arcachon with distant elderly relatives; a Whitsun alone with his father in a guesthouse – Minnie digging in Crete. And he remembers chasing up and down the sand dunes. Then, years later, that summer as a student.

'Kempton,' Cat touches his arm. 'I'm parched for a coffee or something.'

• Kempton's Journey

'Oh of course darling . . . God this brings back the old memories, I tell you.' Shaking his head to clear them.

And in the station buffet, drinking coffee with his daughter at a plastic-topped table, tucking into some sort of flaky bun, he keeps repeating, 'Isn't this fun? This is such fun.'

Cat thinking it is months since she has seen her father so relaxed and enthusiastic. He is really endearing when he is like this.

At the table nearest them a group of French people are having lunch, talking and laughing noisily over carafes of rosé. The plates in front of them are heaped with oily haricots, pommes frites and some kind of meat. In between mouthfuls they smoke Gitanes and wipe their plates with coarse bread. Everything, marvels Kempton, is done with such wholehearted gusto.

'I mean a few miles and you're on another planet . . . Did I ever tell you about my grape-picking days?'

'Only a hundred times.' She smiles.

'Sor-ry.' Pulls an apologetic face. 'It's just, well, you've no idea how great it is to be here. I feel my roots are here, somehow. And with you. The icing.'

'You're cute when you're like this Kempton.'

'*Ferme la bouche, enfant.*'

Only minutes here and he has impatiently discarded the constraints of his British skin. Is acutely conscious of his French genes, and immensely proud of his ancestry, which he can trace back to the Huguenots.

Almost time for their train, and they drag their cases to their platform. Kempton's bucking along on three wheels. A TGV draws up – a sleek monster – then dashes off. A couple of minutes later their train draws up more leisurely and they climb inside.

'My *gad*,' comments Cat. 'First class. *Quel* luxury.' Settles herself into the red-and-blue seat. They are alone in the compartment.

The train stops at Libourne, then St Emilion – where a ticket collector demands their tickets. And it was here, on the outskirts of St Emilion, he passed most of that summer. In the evenings sat outside a *tabac* in the square, beneath an acacia tree. Drank Pernod, even though he hated it. And the sonorous tolling of the bell from the clocher every half hour.

Cat engrossed in her book: 'Criminal case-histories.' Kempton's eyes riveted to the window and the pretty, undramatic countryside unfolding with the clacketing-clacketing rhythm of the train – which cruises in and out of various small rural stations on its route to Bergerac.

He pictures them both, trundling along the country lanes with the wagon and horse, singing stupid old songs, the sun beating down; though the reality at the moment is drizzle from a granite sky. And now he observes that the countryside has evened out to become flatter than ever, and the interminable vineyards with their gnarled stumpy vines have given way to farmland, with smallholdings dotted amongst the patches of green. He can see goats tethered between trees.

Adèle, the business proprietor, is there to meet them from the train in the ancient Renault she refers to as the Flying Pig. She is half French, half English, and veers seamlessly from one language to the other, apparently without realising. Kempton has spoken to her several times on the phone and had imagined her as tall, dark and in her early thirties. He had fantasised about falling in love with her – to take his mind off Suzanne; had half mapped out a romantic future with her. In fact she is a small pigeon of a woman in her early fifties who doesn't stop prattling. And lives, so she informs them almost immediately, with her female lover and business partner.

Her farmhouse is a half hour's drive or so from Bergerac, near the small Bastide town of Monflaquin, and as they clamber out of the car several dogs rush through the yard towards them, scattering chickens. A woman follows at a less hurried pace. Also short and stout, with cropped grey hair and white teeth bared in a smile; a broad, rosy face like a French peasant woman. But when she speaks it is in an exaggeratedly upper-class English accent. She introduces herself as Elspeth.

'Brought the old weather with you I see. Been fine up till now. Tea? I'll make some.'

Low beams that skim Kempton's head. A fire snapping in the cavernous fireplace. And Elspeth massages handcream into her hands while she waits for the kettle to boil.

'I've been tiling the bathroom.'

'Yourself?' Cat asks her.

'We've done up the whole place ourselves,' Elspeth says.

'Except for the plumbing and electrics,' Adèle adds.

'It's never ending.'

'Six years so far.'

'But it's finally taking shape.'

They speak alternately, like a coin bouncing along, tossing from side to side.

They discuss arrangements: the first week, when he and Cat are together, they will stop at various farms, hotels and auberges for the night; the second week Kempton will sleep on the *roulotte*.

'You'll only ever be a maximum distance of twenty miles from the farm,' Adèle says. 'In effect you're doing a circle via the Bastide towns.'

He is impatient to get going. A late afternoon sun emerging, and patches of washed-out blue in the sky. Cat looks weary, he notices with concern. And at that point she catches his eye and grins at him. She is all right. Of course she is. One day he will stop worrying. He gathers his lips into a kiss which he blows towards her, over the women's heads. Sometimes he imagines that a line of love runs invisibly between himself and his daughter.

Bella is a white Percheron mare.

'An arse the size of a buttress,' Adèle says, leading her from the field.

And Kempton, snapping with his camera, has his first misgivings when he sees the size of her. Her hooves are like cymbals. She seems docile enough though, standing in the yard without being held or tied while she is harnessed. And now he is beset with another lot of doubts, at the sight of all the paraphernalia involved.

'For Chrissake I'll never remember how all that stuff goes on.'

He hadn't considered this aspect: the technicalities. Fixed in his head had been a naively romanticised image, as portrayed in the brochure. This is daunting. And he and Cat exchange glances that are similarly aghast.

Adèle positions the saddle pad on Bella's back.

'Like a ruddy great table,' says Kempton. His face is scrunched up in alarm.

The mare lowers her head for the neck collar. Bridle next; and the metal bit slips neatly into her mouth. Kempton despairing as piece after complicated piece of equipment with endless straps and buckles, all looking indistinguishable from one another, is fitted to her. And how, for Chrissake, is he expected to make her open her mouth for the bit without getting his hand yanked off by her huge yellow teeth?

'Now to attach her to the wagon,' Adèle says cheerfully. And Elspeth winks at Kempton, rubbing her hands gleefully. Like a sadistic assassin, he thinks.

First Bella has to be lined up with the *roulotte*. This involves several attempts, circling her until she is exactly central, then guiding her backwards – backwards, for Chrissake – by means of Adèle pressing her body against the horse's chest, steering her blinkered head, and speaking coaxingly. Pace

• Kempton's Journey

by snail's pace Bella reverses her hulk until she is between the shafts. All that remains is for these to be fastened to the harness, and the straps hooked beneath the footbridge of the wagon.

'*Et voilà*,' exclaims Elspeth.

'*C'est tout*.' Adèle.

Kempton is exhausted from watching. And knowing his luck, horse and wagon will be bound to part company. Envisages Bella galloping off into the distance, harness trailing, themselves in the *roulotte* rolling backwards down a hill and crashing at the bottom. He seeks out his daughter's hand.

'Your faces!' Adèle shrieks.

'They think we're going to dump them,' Elspeth says.

'And leave them to it.'

The pair of them chortling in girlish mirth.

It transpires Adèle, followed later by Elspeth in the car to fetch her, accompanies them to their first port of call, and returns every subsequent morning and evening to help with the harness until they are fully competent.

'It's in the brochure,' she says. 'We explain that in the brochure.'

'I didn't read that bit,' he says, feeling foolish.

'Poor Kempton.' Cat puts her arm round him.

'And there's no way I'm letting you do any of it in your condition,' he says severely.

'Don't be so bossy.' Elbows him affectionately. 'I'm not made of china.'

But to him she is.

The caravan itself is painted red with a swirling blue and yellow design beneath a rounded metal roof whose overlapping sides form a protective shield against the weather. Within, is compact but fully equipped – with gas stove, small sink, lighting, kitchen equipment, blankets and pillows. The seats also serve as bunks. There are drawers, shelving, and a folding table that metamorphoses into a double bed. At the rear is storage for Bella's oats, her tack, and the calor gas cylinders. Everything has been thought of. The only slight problem is that it has been designed for gnomes: they cannot stand upright. Kempton visualises costly sessions at the osteopath as a result of this trip.

They pile in their bits of luggage, along with Bella's grooming kit, a bundle of white tape and large block battery – electric fencing; and a rock which Adèle explains is to prevent the wagon from rolling when parked on a hill.

'It's an extra safeguard besides the brake. You wedge it in front of a wheel.'

'Don't believe it. It's to bash your husband with when he misbehaves,' Elspeth says.

Cat stares at her in puzzlement, then starts laughing. Kempton is aghast, speechless; blushing.

'Kempton's my father,' she says.

Apologies. More laughter all round. But his is strained.

Kempton settles into the driving seat, Adèle beside him issuing instructions. Cat crouches just behind as there is only room for two.

'*Alors, on est prêt. Allez-y,*' Adèle shouts joyfully.

He has never met two such hearty women. Are they always like this? It would send him insane being in their company for too long. They set off. The reins feel strange in his hands. His arms feel strange. The swaying motion of the caravan feels strange. He had assumed that the driving itself would be easy. But Bella susses instantly that here is a novice, and takes advantage of his inexperience, his feeble contact and weakly iterated commands. She meanders along lethargically, at one stage completely stopping to graze from the verge. He cannot pull her head up. Is sweating and angry and humiliated. Ready to abandon the whole project. What on earth possessed him to do something like this? It is Cat's fault. He can sense her laughing. Turns round to glare at her. She mimics steam with her hands. Mouths the word.

Adèle springs nimbly from the seat to the ground, wallops Bella and leads her away from the verge. Jumps back on board.

'Shorten the reins.'

'How the hell do I do that . . . ?'

Gradually he begins to relax a little, to feel some contact with her head – which seems a very great distance away. Her enormous white rump in its cradle of harness lolls from side to side rhythmically. The steady clopping of her feet. The creaking of the *roulotte*. The undulating countryside. And at the back of his mind the slight apprehension that if Bella stops for more than a second on an incline the vehicle will roll. He shifts his position nore centrally, but still within easy reach of the handbrake – which he keeps making a grab for. Now he can see ahead more easily and the perspective between Bella's ears and himself forms a straight line. She plods along, beginning to respond to him, ears twitching back and forth as he issues instructions vocally or with his hands; and as she starts to respond so his confidence grows. He is beginning to enjoy himself, to appreciate the countryside and mild breeze.

But then they come to a precipitous downward hill with a T-junction at the bottom of it. He finds it impossible to pull back the horse with only one hand, yet needs the other for the brake. There again, he must somehow steer her over from the right towards the centre of the narrow road in order to turn left (and another thing – he keeps forgetting which side of the road he should be). The *roulotte* has only frontways visibility.

Adèle hops out at the foot of the hill to check for any traffic, and holds Bella's head to prevent her going on. Kempton's hand wrenches the brake upwards. He can feel the weight of the roulotte behind it. A lorry hurtles by.

'Shit,' he says. Whistles through his teeth.

'That's why you need two people unless you're more experienced,' Adèle says. 'A man came on his own once. He was a real misanthrope and had come away to be completely by himself and not have to speak to anyone. He actually told me this. Well he was a liability on his own. Useless. And I had to accompany him for the entire fortnight. It was disastrous. I don't know who resented who more. I'm amazed murder wasn't committed.' Chuckles in retrospect.

The second thing to happen is that a group of horses in an adjacent field suddenly start charging about. Bella seems to concertina into herself and performs a small leap. The caravan itself jolts forward and bucks.

'Shit,' Kempton shouts. 'Bloody hell.' He has stopped caring about his language. Cat laughing behind him.

'That'll remind you she's an animal not a machine,' Adèle says.

After this they settle back into an uneventful plod and he regains his confidence, can sense Bella's responsiveness growing by the minute; starts actually to feel good – more like he had imagined it should be. Like an old hand. Raises his face to the cooling sky. The damp smell of the chestnut woods to one side of them. The occasional dilapidated stone cottage beneath a red-tiled roof. The rushing sound of water from a stream. Ah, this is it, this is it. Wellbeing seeping into him.

Cat takes over from him. Having been watching attentively for the past three quarters of an hour she has none of the problems he had. He perches uncomfortably behind her, to an angle, from where he can just glimpse a part of her cheek and mouth. It is parted wide in a smile. Tenderness at her pleasure bubbles within him. He can tell she is relaxed from the set of her shoulders and the give and take, give and take of her arms. Once she swivels round to him. Her eyes alight. 'Love ya,' he mouths silently.

It's going to be all right. Everything'll be fine . . . Watching his daughter's slender back rocking from side to side gently with the wagon's movement; Bella's rump swaying in a provocative, feminine way, tail swishing (and occasionally she farts, which they all ignore); the long line of her body tapering to the point of her ears; the creaking, rattling, chinking and clomping of harness and wheels and hooves. So strange. All so prickling, tingling, unfamiliar and strange. The sun lowering.

Kempton blood-letting his soul.

They set down in a field on the outskirts of Monflaquin. Adèle unravels the tape and stakes, and deftly rigs up the electric fencing. Attaches a haynet to a tree. 'Not much goodness in the grass yet.' Under her guidance Kempton and Cat detach the mare from the wagon and unharness her. Kempton thwacks her neck a few times to make friends. It is warm beneath his palm, sticky from exertion. Cat plucks some grass and holds it out. The horse blows down her nostrils and the long blades scatter.

'Well that's it folks,' Adèle says. 'I'll leave you to it. See you nine thirty in the morning. Don't forget to padlock the door. And panic not if you lose the key. We've got spares. *Amusez-vous bien.*' She walks briskly off, bottom sticking out, arms flapping like bird wings, to Elspeth waiting at the roadside in the Renault.

Their hotel is just a few hundred yards away but Kempton is concerned about the distance for Cat. Her leg. And tiring herself. Doesn't say anything because it will annoy her and provoke a stop-fussing-Kempton. But he keeps glancing towards her and slows his own pace when he senses she is flagging. At least they have no luggage to speak of. A carrier bag between them with enough for the night.

Le Prince Noir is a thirteenth-century inn in the centre of the town. Stone buildings cluster round a square, behind arcades from whose arches hang flower baskets. Narrow roads shoot off in different directions. There is scant traffic; a few parked cars – mostly Renaults or Citroëns that have seen better days; battered trucks; a Maserati, conspicuous among them, that everyone who passes stops to gaze at and comment on. But there are not many people about. The shops have shut and the breeze has become cooler as the sky darkens with cloud and late evening sets in. An air of somnolence suspends the town in timeless stillness.

The owner shows them to their separate rooms, next to one another. Winks knowingly to Kempton.

'*Elle est ma fille,*' Kempton says tersely. He is becoming fed up the way people keep misinterpreting their relationship. What do they think – he is a lecher like Peter?

If anyone is going to be hurt it will be myself not her. Please God that won't ever happen, because I don't think I could bear it.

The surprise of seeing Peter wearing glasses. The watery pinkness of emotion behind them. And Kempton experiencing a pang of contrition here in this garishly decorated hotel room in France.

Kempton and Cat huddled in pullovers and jackets, braving it outside one of the bar-restaurants. The place is deserted except for one other couple dining inside, and three youths playing on a fruit machine. Its zinging and clunking, their exclamations over the blaring television, carry into the street.

'Mad dogs and Englishmen.' Cat shivering.

'Mad cows.'

'Don't remind me. I'm bored with it. And no one thinks of the poor cows.'

'The government has reacted all wrong as usual. We're the laughing stock of every other European country. No one takes us seriously over anything. And you can't blame them.'

'No politics, Kempton. You promised.'

'Sorry.' Smacks his own hand. 'Are you a tired sweetie-pie?'

'No. Well maybe. Happy-tired.'

'Me too.' Entwines his fingers with hers. They are cold; and he rubs them to warm them.

She remembers something Peter said: Nobody will ever have your welfare so much at heart as him. Not even me.

'Kempton – Dad – don't flinch,' she says, retaining his hand tightly. 'I'm so proud that you are going to be Foetus's grandfather. Because you're, well – a fantastic father.'

And what can he say to that? Doesn't attempt to say anything. Stares down at their tightly bound hands and bites his quivering lower lip until he tastes blood.

Her omelette is runny with soft egg and gruyère. His lamb cutlets are sublime: succulent and rosy. The *pommes frites* thin as fish bones. The bread honey-sweet. God knows what they are drinking, but it is the right temperature and dark and full.

Like the night. And they sit on. Not a star, however hard he searches. It doesn't bode well for tomorrow's weather. But he is unconcerned.

In their respective rooms they prepare for bed. Cat's is narrow and single, and her feet immediately form a triangle at either corner. Since the accident she has had poor circulation in that leg and on her own she always wears socks. She can hear her father loping about next door. Dear Kempton. Smiles, imagining him cleaning his teeth in that ferocious way of his whilst peering ruefully at his mirrored reflection. Draws her hand in a caressing gesture over the knoll of her tummy. Peter's hand there. Misses it. Him. And creaks as her father climbs into his double bed.

Kempton lying there, staring up at the purple ceiling.

Thinking of Bella alone in her field. And the vivid little caravan in one corner. Do horses get lonely on their own? Funny room, this. Ghastly colours. Vanessa would have had a fit. It would not have been her type of holiday at all. Suzanne would appreciate it. His daughter just a thin wall away – he can hear her shifting about in her bed. And in three and a half months she will be a mother. Suppose something were to go wrong? Don't even think about it. It doesn't bear thinking about. And she was so sweet, wasn't she, driving that ruddy great beast? Her face was blissful. God, and that remark at dinner . . . All he wants is her happiness. Really, isn't that—

Kempton befuddled with tiredness. Too sleepy to read the Thomas More beside him. Only just able to switch off the lamp. Flops over onto one side and flings his arm outwards to the empty space beside him. Happy-tired.

12 ∫

Blinkered

He can tell it's dull and raining even with the thin curtains closed. There is that Edward Hopper sweatshop-grey thrusting between the gaps and needling through the yellow whorls of fabric. The insistent bird claws against the window. What can one expect in April? He is remarkably unbothered. *Tant Pis*. His father's expression, uttered with Leibnitz optimism in every possible circumstance: 'All is for the best in the best of all possible worlds.' Kempton recalls his father quoting that, mindless of Voltaire's gleeful wielding of the axe to that particular theory. Can hear his mild, scholarly voice. In the end optimism had not served him well. What a strange amalgam of genes he has inherited from his parents. With hindsight he doubts his father was a good teacher. He was too close to his subject; less on a wavelength with the young persons to whom he taught it. So learned and perpetually surprised that a world should exist outside his learning. Apt to drift off and waffle tediously when on a pet theme. Kempton is certain his pupils must have played him up badly. And he probably never even noticed. Whenever anyone spoke with his father they automatically lowered their voice. His gentleness evoked that kind of respectful response. Except from Minnie, whose peremptory blasting took no account of his sensitivity and the pain that would come into his eyes at a raised tone.

An incident: his father, wearing a scarlet silk waistcoat, touching the hand of a street accordionist who had a wreath of cowbells and plastic flowers on his head, before stooping to place a coin in the cracked plate.

'I like your waistcoat,' said the beggar.

And his father promptly took it off and put it tenderly round the man's shoulders.

He is often in Kempton's thoughts. His father quietly, unobtrusively, ambling along until the cataclysm rent his existence in two. Did his mother ever reflect on her actions and feel a blip of remorse? A picture of a bowed Minnie comes into his head. And she was kind to him over Christmas, wasn't she? And one or two little hints over the last few months have suggested that there is more to her than he suspected. Behind closed doors and all that. Kempton lying in his foreign bed, feet poking out like pale cod – except for a few incongruous dark tufts – wonders now not the usual recriminatory refrain: how could she do it? But: how did their marriage last so long?

A knocking through his wall. 'Morning Kempton.'

'Morning darling.' Smiles as though no barrier is between them, in the direction of his daughter's sleepy voice, at the spot where he envisages her early morning face.

Downstairs for breakfast. The local paper – *Le Sud Ouest*. Coffee, thick and dark as tar. And small flaky pastries threaded with chocolate and embedded with fat raisins. There are a few other couples in the room, and several well-behaved small dogs. He cannot imagine Pluto will ever be so sedate and obedient. The owner's pekingese is curled by their table. And Madame herself, fully made-up as if for an evening at the opera, pours them more coffee and tells them how this had been her father-in-law's hotel, and his father's before that.

'*Et mon mari – c'est lui qui est le chef. Il fait toute la cuisine lui même. Les pâtisseries, les petits pains – tous.*'

And at that moment her husband appears from the kitchen, portly, perspiring-browed beneath his tall chef's hat, bringing with him the bouquet of warm yeast and baking clinging to his apron. Sets a basket of croissants and various buns in front of them, and Madame's own *confiture de prunes*.

'Oh no, I'm stuffed,' Cat protests, sliding back in her chair, laughing, and making a vigorous gesture with her hand.

'*Mais non!*' And he picks out a croissant with a pair of tongs and puts it on her plate, beaming.

The temperature is more like February than mid April, the rain a thin constant line; and despite the overhang it lands on their faces and hands. The foot-rest is not under cover and their feet squelch uncomfortably in their shoes.

'Just as long as it's not sunny in England.' Kempton is in excellent spirits regardless of the weather. 'Anyway, the countryside's still very pretty. I feel rather sorry for Bella though.' Leans forward to slap her wet rump.

'She doesn't seem to mind it.' Cat, who is driving, shortens the reins as the lane suddenly forms a steep descent.

'I suppose she hardly notices it through that hide ...' Kempton, reaching for the handbrake and lifting it to slow the *roulotte*. 'God, the size of her.'

Every inward feeling or outward detail which once would have evaded him, he now notes: for a start he is consciously aware of his own deep contentment, likens it to the removal of an elastic band from round the wrist; then he notices other things: flowers littering the banks, a pair of darting swallows – their mewing cry, the angle at which the rain slants, how it forms globules on Bella's harness, the pink boniness of his daughter's knuckles, the shapes and textures of the trees, the straining power of Bella's glistening sides. And with his eyes closed he has a perfect picture of her in his head, the perspective as observed from where he sits. He knows he could draw her from memory and that it would come out right – commencing with the triangle formed by the wagon shafts, and tapering into the point of her ears. In his mind he can visualise every line, curve and angle.

They turn down an isolated track, making for the farm marked on Adèle's map, and between them partially unharness the mare. Already there is a logic to the sequence. They slip the nosebag of chaff over her head and tether her to a post; Kempton jams the rock behind the rear wheel of the *roulotte*. Straightens up and turns to his daughter, the light of success in his eyes – Hey, we did it. He holds up his hand to her. She holds up hers also, and they slap palms in a gesture of victory.

A collective bleating directs them to the farm. In a vast pen, jostling and shoving each other, are dozens of young goats.

'Oh God how cute. Oh Kempton I want a goat.' Cat poking her finger between the wooden rails, and a goat in the front sucking it with soft gums. The others crowding round for attention.

'Get Peter to buy you one.' Spoken grimly. One of the blessed creatures has got his scarf – his cashmere checked one, his favourite – between its teeth and is refusing to relinquish its hold. A battle of wills ensues until Kempton finally manages to unclamp its jaws.

'Bloody animal practically throttled me.' Rubbing his neck. 'And it's probably ruined my scarf.' A Christmas present from Vanessa.

The restaurant is in a converted barn attatched to the farmhouse. At the far end is a huge open fire, and above it an old tapestry, perhaps ten foot high, depicting a pastoral scene.

'God, that must be worth a fair bit,' Kempton remarks to Cat.

The farmer's wife shows them to a table, laid with pristine white linen. She reminds him of Minnie, with her faded gingerish hair in a chignon; or how Minnie used to be. He cannot forget the surprise of how thin and knobbly her back was, or the frailty of her shoulders, when he comforted her that evening. Her mysterious grief over her missing ring. Her skirt flung above her knickers as she lay trussed on the floor; and the flesh of her thighs hanging like shreds of clothing from a washing line. All his life, or for as long as he could remember, he had been held in the grip of some power by her, and the events of a single evening had dissolved it. What exactly had been her hold over him? It was so hard to pinpoint and define. He had always had the sense that she had been laughing at him, and yes, she did used to put him down; seemed to revel in his discomfort. And her Hmph. Her peremptory dismissiveness. Her pipe. Her disregard for all convention. But he remembers when he was tired at the races, leaning against her body – tough and pole-straight in those days; and, yes, her arm round him, shielding him from the excited crowd in the grandstand . . . 'He's jumping well. If he can stay the next half furlong then he's won. Then we'll go home pet.' Pet? Did she really call him that? Seems to recollect it. And the soft dark saucer of her trilby's brim, the smell of her pipe's tobacco tickling his nostrils, his tummy heavy with smoked salmon sandwiches.

The goats in the pen are female kids, the farmer's wife tells them. Bred for dairy use. So what happens to the males? Cat asks. Don't tell her, Kempton beseeches. But just like the dead bird and the stone incident from childhood, of course she knows. Then why ask? Confirmation? Does it help her confront the reality? Funny girl. In reply to Cat's question the woman draws a line across her throat with her forefinger.

Kempton orders goat for lunch. It arrives unrecognisable, cubed, in a thick blanquette sauce surrounded by salsify and thinly sliced potatoes. His daughter regards him in contempt as he eats. Then can no longer contain herself and berates him for his lack of conscience.

'But it's been killed already,' he points out. 'Almost everyone here is eating it. It's a goat farm, for Chrissake. The farmer's livelihood.' Pale creamy sauce round his lips.

'You could just wait a couple of days.'

'We won't be here in a couple of days.'

'Well one would think you'd be a bit turned off.'

'I can't say I've noticed your being put off your chicken.' Motioning to the half-eaten grilled poussin on her plate. 'What about the dreadful fate of those sweet feathery creatures you saw clucking away in the yard, eh? Poor little things. Fancy ending up being coated in mustard and herbs.' Deliberately goading her.

'They're less intelligent.'

'I wouldn't say eating my cashmere scarf smacks of a very high IQ.'

'I don't want to discuss it anymore.'

'Because you know you're being illogical. Your argument is based on sentimentality and Beatrix Potter anthropomorphism' – he is oblivious of her blank, closed expression. '—It's not as if you don't eat meat yourself. In *autres mots* it's only the timing of my consumption you object to, not the consumption itself,' he finishes jubilantly.

Cat getting up with regal dignity, without a word.

'Hey, what are you – where are you going? – hey darling,

don't be like that. I was only teasing,' as she heads off in the direction of the Ladies.

Sits there alone, the jest gone from him, in front of his half-full plate which he pushes away; no longer hungry.

When she returns – how he loves her as she makes her valiant uneven passage across the restaurant – she slides into her seat without glancing at him. For a few moments the atmosphere crackles between them. Then her face becomes red. At first he thinks she is fighting back tears. And then he notices the corners of her mouth twitching, and realises that in fact she is trying not to laugh.

'Sweetie-pie this is—'

'Silly. Yes it is, isn't it?' She stretches across the table and pulls his head towards her, kissing him on the lips, as she has done ever since she was a child.

'Yuk, I tasted a bit of goat.' Rubbing her mouth violently with the edge of her sleeve.

The refectory table behind them is occupied by an entire family; several generations, all dressed up in their weekend best, napkins like bibs round their necks. The old man slurps his nettle soup with audible hissing noises. His face is cracked like a dried out river bed, thinks Kempton; rather pleased with his analogy: must remember to tell Cat. The father, pouring wine into the smallest child's glass, catches Kempton's eye. '*Santé,*' he says.

Kempton raises his glass in return. 'Down it darling,' he says to Cat. 'Red wine's good for Foetus.'

She feels a jolt of surprise. It is the first time he has referred to the baby like that. Bowing to the inevitable? The wine warming her throat, her tummy. Life.

She feels unique in her pregnancy, as if no other woman has ever been pregnant before her. And sometimes she imagines herself as part of a network linked to an amorphous source of power from which shoot millions of tiny threads, each supporting a sphere. Within one of these is herself, as

• Kempton's Journey

the inner circle; and within that, another: her baby. Circle within circle within circle; each nurtured by the other.

Remembers a school play she should have been in – she was six or seven. Her mother was supposed to make her a pair of wings (she cannot recall what the part was: a sprite? an angel?), but was going through a depression and never made them. And Cat would not remind her. Her punishment. It was her fault her mother was unhappy. Senga Gowon got the part. Now reading law at Cambridge.

Dessert is arrayed on a trestle table, between tall church candles either end: *tarte aux pommes*, its surface glistening with caramel; *îles flottant* – snowy peaks surrounded by a pale custard; chocolate terrine. And an assortment of cheeses on a wooden board, the soft ones running into one another. Their sweet-rancid odour.

'What a spread. What a place,' Kempton says, helping himself to a selection of cheeses, while Cat takes a small portion of each of the desserts. 'I mean can you imagine anywhere like this in England? Really, the French have such *style*. And it's not expensive, either.'

As a treat to himself he has a locally made dessert wine, from which he takes slow long sips, savouring the buttery sweetness. He makes a note of the name of it on a scrap of paper, which he puts carefully in his wallet. Ends up buying two bottles, and a round of goat's cheese. The farmer's wife gives him their business card.

'*Pour la prochaine fois.*'

'*Bien sûr. Merci.*' Puts this, too, in his wallet.

'*Combien de mois?*' She smiles at them both, jerking her chin in the direction of Cat's tummy.

'*Cinq.*' Cat's proud reflex nowadays is to smooth her clothes over her belly to emphasise its shape.

'*Le premier?*'

'*Oui.*'

'*Et – le papa – vous – vous êtes excité j'imagine*?' The woman's eyes sparkle.

'*Oui. Mais elle est—*'

'*Excusez-moi Monsieur.*' She is beckoned to another table and breaks off; and Kempton doesn't have the chance to explain he is not *the* father, but Cat's father. The grandfather. Gives his daughter a small, resigned shrug.

Almost four o'clock. Bella has somehow discarded her nosebag and has grazed a perfect orb around the pole to which she is tethered. She makes a small whickering noise when they approach. They go through the rigmarole of harnessing her once more; double check straps and buckles. Remove the rock. And set off again. Bella striding out smartly, at one point breaking into a trot.

The wine, the aftermath of the delicious meal, his daughter's nearness – she is leaning against him while he drives – and the surprise appearance of the sun, combine to enrich the sense of wellbeing within Kempton.

'Dad,' Cat says quietly. 'It's moving.'

'What is?'

'Foetus.'

She takes his free hand and places it on her bare tummy, beneath the layers of her clothing. The smoothness of his daughter's skin, the convex tautness of her body. And a rippling like a fly running just beneath the surface.

'Feel it?'

'Yes.' Whispers it, as though he does not want to disturb the baby. Oh God he can remember when it was *she*, Cat, the tiny unknown person moving about inside Vanessa – Vanessa similarly laying his hand on *her* tummy; and for the first time it had really registered on Kempton that this was a living being in there, not merely a meaningless protuberance. And now it is Cat's turn. And it will go on and on. Change and sameness.

'It's fantastic.'

'I know.'

Catriona. Sire, Kempton Prévot. And Peter the sire of his offspring's offspring. So extraordinary. Peter's time, twenty years after his. He feels slightly tipsy from all the wine.

'Has Peter felt it moving?'

'Yes.'

He nods without saying anything.

Bella plods on sedately – past plum orchards in blossom, and a small château set squarely in its walled grounds; the red soil of newly harrowed fields; stone houses beneath steeply-pitched roofs with attached *pigeonniers*; woodland thinning out into glades, then becoming denser again – and the pungent aroma of wild garlic pricking their nostrils. And Bella suddenly shies sideways at a snake lying dead in the road.

After a couple of hours, during which the sun has abandoned itself once more to rain, they reach the edge of Villereal and the assigned field, near the hippodrôme. Elspeth and Adèle are already there, waiting by the Renault and sheltering under a golfing umbrella; arms unselfconsciously linked. Immediately they begin firing questions at Kempton and Cat, not waiting for answers.

Villereal, viewed through a sheet of rain, seems a dour, grey little town. Their hotel, the Continental of all names – conjuring up pictures of a multistoreyed glitzy kind of establishment – turns out to be a fifties' dump. The blousy-looking proprietor, swollen feet stuffed into carpet slippers, greets them desultorily in a rasping voice, cigarette fixed to one corner of her smudged red mouth. Her son – at least Kempton guesses by her attitude towards him that it is her son – a sullen man in his early thirties, shows them to their rooms, which are at either end of the corridor. The light switches are on a timing device that is obviously faulty, because they keep going off after a matter of seconds, plunging the staircase into darkness.

'*Merde*,' the man growls, whenever it happens.

Kempton's room has a central lampshade hanging from a polystyrene-tiled ceiling. The large bed, covered with a sludge-green candlewick spread, dips in the middle. The remaining furniture comprises a bentwood chair, formica-topped dressing table, and a wardrobe – a huge ugly thing whose handle immediately comes off in his fingers. The shower room has a bidet but no toilet. He'll just have to pee in there if the urge takes him in the night. He has no intention of groping his way blindly down the corridor, past Cat's room, when the lights suddenly fail. And as for the shower itself, behind a torn plastic curtain: when he turns it on full – it squeaks painfully – a rusty trickle is discharged.

The floor creaks beneath Kempton's exploring feet. And he can hear the proprietor's hacking smoker's cough below. What a ghastly, dismal, depressing place. And the rain that looks as though it will never let up.

Downstairs the bar area is a riot of multi-coloured mosaic, mirrored tiles, more polystyrene, and fake teak. But there is a cosy fire – and a pair of dachshunds asleep by it. How is Minnie coping with Pluto, he wonders? And this leads him to think of Suzanne. Fondly, but without that worryingly intense feeling that had rather been disturbing him. A group of locals in peaked caps, waterproof jackets and felt slippers they must have brought with in their pockets are gathered round the bar, talking amongst themselves in thick accents. They stare at him while he orders a Pernod for old time's sake: perhaps he'll like it better now; takes a fistful of nuts from a bowl and pours them down his throat. The group of men – they are all diminutive – follow his every move with suspicious eyes. The sullen young man thumps down his glass in front of him. Cat appears – is he glad to

• Kempton's Journey

see her – fresh and pretty in something flowery and long that skims her ankles. Her rather frizzy hair is scraped back from her longish face. Her skin is almost transluscent, her eyes clear.

'You look pretty, pretty, pretty,' her father says.

'Thank you.' A mock curtsy. She turns the full radiance of her smile on the staring men; and immediately the spell is broken. Their faces are suddenly wreathed in bonhomie – B'soir, b'soir – and they resume their conversation.

'God that's a relief,' Kempton says to Cat. 'I tell you they were giving me the creeps. What a dump, eh? It's all right. They won't understand.' Repeats it loudly, 'Dump, dump, du-ump. See? They're all grinning.' And they are; grinning and nodding at him.

But he doesn't like Pernod any better than he did as a student.

Over dinner, which is surprisingly good – rillettes of duck followed by grilled escalopes of salmon, and a Sauvignon to drink – Cat watches her father as he attacks his food with gusto. Eventually he becomes conscious of the laser drilling of her eyes and sets down his knife and fork.

'What is it?'

'Kempton – Dad – I need to talk.'

'That sounds ominous,' he says lightly. But he can tell the mood is set to change. His fingers curl into tense nodes on his lap.

And she doesn't correct him or try to put him at his ease. Her gaze is steady and solemn as though she is assessing him and pondering on the best way to express whatever it is she has to say. It is bound to be connected with Peter. They're getting married, that's what it is. And would he mind now?

'Peter?'

'No. This is about me.'

He is mystified. And inexplicably afraid. Pours himself out

• 228

more wine – and as an afterthought, some into her glass. But she covers the top with her hand before he can fill it.

'Dad, have you ever considered – I mean, when I was growing up you expected me to cope with things without ever really talking about them? I mean none of us spoke of them.'

'Well you did cope, didn't you?' Pinching and massaging his chin.

'No. I didn't. But because it was expected of me to do so, I had to pretend. Look, it's not meant as an accusation. But when Mummy was going through all her moods . . . And then later, after she, you know, died. Nobody asked me what I was feeling or thinking. You didn't.'

'No. I suppose I didn't.' A chill in the room. A chill within himself. His ears picking out strange noises that he realises come from inside his head.

'Please Dad, don't feel bad. That's not the purpose of this. I just need to tell you one or two things about me.'

'Of course darling.' Falsely cheerful; worms of foreboding in readiness for some unpalatable truth about to be revealed.

She has barely touched her food. For the last couple of days she has been wondering whether it would be wrong – and indeed pointless – to broach the issues. He has been so good humoured and relaxed that several times she thought, why? Let him have his illusions.

They are sitting on a bench-type seat next to one another. Is that an advantage or not? She cannot look at him without swivelling her body. But their shoulders are touching. And she could hold his hand – at present in a fist on his knee. But what she has to say is far removed from the cosiness of intimacy; it is alienating and harsh and cold. And it is essential she remain calm and detached while she imparts it. She does not take his hand, therefore, and moves a couple of inches to her left so that there is a slender gap between them.

'When I was nearly fifteen I had therapy,' she tells him, staring directly ahead, keeping her body very still. 'I've had it on and off ever since.'

Shock waves sparking through him. A humming in his ears. His nails biting into his knees. He doesn't know what comment to make; starts, 'I—' and is prevented from continuing by his daughter's vehement shaking of the head.

'No. I want to talk.' The words come out harshly, and she adds, softly, 'Please Dad.'

'Of course,' he says. Fearful.

'Look, none of this is against you. You must understand that. I do love you.'

'And I do love you. So that's something.' A flicker of a smile. His hand moving from its position on his knee, falteringly towards Cat's face. And gently he turns it towards him so that she has to look at him. Her eyes meet his only briefly, with a flinty remoteness he cannot fathom. And when she pulls away he has a sense of isolation.

'Yes. But you have to know the *real* me to love.'

'I do,' he insists.

'You don't. I'm not this perfect creature—' Voice high with frustration. '– I'm not the sweet, virtuous, Snow White corrupted by Evil Incarnate. You have to accept *me*. And love *me*.' Her fist comes down on the edge of the table with a small bang.

If only he could hug her. Can he help it that to him she will always be his baby? But he is bad at dealing with emotional issues, and that he is about to find himself embroiled in a sack-load, he has no doubt. Why, when things seem to be going on an even keel, must they be disrupted? He craves equilibrium in his life, yet it perpetually eludes him. Teases him puckishly, so that for a while he is fooled. Then – wham – let's go for Kempton's goolies now.

'You have to accept me as I *am*. Not as you think, or want to think, I am. That's spurious. Worthless. A sham. I'm fed up of shams.' Flinging her arms in the air. Her calm has deserted her.

'OK, OK.' Glancing nervously at the man and woman at the next table, an obese pair. But they are devouring garlic snails. An apricot poodle is snoring loudly by the woman's feet.

And Kempton recollects thinking – oh, only a few months ago – that he didn't really know his daughter in any true sense of the word. They were in the pizza restaurant after going to see *Babe*. But then the thought had not had any profundity attached to it. Now, in this brightly-lit dining room with the vile brown and gold wallpaper, he is about to be enlightened.

'Do you remember you told me you went to the doctor, and had some kind of crisis?' she says.

'Yes. More of a watershed, in retrospect.'

'When I was nearly fifteen I was at school one day, and in the middle of the English lesson I suddenly started screaming for no apparent reason. I screamed and cried for hours and hours until a burning rash started all over my body. My teacher asked me what was wrong. But I couldn't answer because I didn't know. The head tried phoning Mummy but she wasn't there. I was glad. I told them – her and the English mistress – I didn't want either of you to know what had happened. They recommended I see a counsellor, and I said I would on condition neither of you ever knew. I mean you have no idea what it was like – a whole lot of gunge locked inside me that I didn't understand. Like pus.'

Kempton's head in his hands, fingertips drilling into his temples. He feels as though he is being carved slowly upwards from the solar plexus.

'You seemed fine . . . You seemed so fine . . . Why didn't you tell us?'

'I didn't want to upset anyone. I knew it would hurt you. All my life I've always been worried about upsetting people. And that was part of it. Mummy's depressions. When I was a kid I felt guilty because I thought they were my fault. I should be able to cheer her up and I couldn't. Or, worse, that they were *because* of me. I thought, when I was little, that maybe I made her sad . . . All this came out gradually, after months of therapy . . . And the quarrels between you – Mummy shrieking – and sometimes I heard my name in them, and I thought maybe I was the cause. I used to shut myself in my room to get away—'

'I remember that.'

'—and pretend I was an orphan. And I was angry with you that you couldn't help her either and make everything all right. Or maybe you'd hurt her in some way . . . Look a child's mind is very fragile and susceptible, very fertile. It receives what it sees and hears and the rest it must invent. I longed to be close to Mummy – she was so pretty, I idolised her – but as soon as I started to rely on her I'd be let down. And you were working. And then, as I got older I started to want to protect you both from each other's moods. I wanted to diffuse the atmosphere. I felt I was expected to be the one always to be calm and happy and cheer you both up. The mediator. So all this came out in therapy . . .

'My escape was climbing. Being out of doors. I was incredibly reckless because I didn't care what happened to me. I had no sense of self-worth. I felt dirty and flawed . . . And I longed for attention, to be the centre of it. Mummy was always the centre of attention and I really resented that, yet hated myself for resenting her . . . And when she was well she was so adorable . . . Look Dad, what I'm trying to say . . . I'm not the innocent you think, Dad.'

She breaks off to peer at him out of the corner of her eye. He is hunched forward, haggard, clutching the table. And the couple from the neighbouring table get up and leave; and this is her cue.

'I first slept with a boy when I was fourteen and a half. You remember that boy I met on holiday in Portugal who it turned out lived near us? Him. And went on sleeping around. His friends. Their friends.'

Kempton's head is reeling. His world, it seems to him, has effectively been blown apart. He doesn't want to hear any more. Can't take it. Can't. Can't.

Into his hands Kempton says, 'Cat, I really don't think I can just sit here and listen to all this. Why? Why do I need to know?'

And the same harshness that was in her voice earlier, he now hears in her laugh: 'You see? The ostrich syndrome. Burying your head. Kempton, get *real*. I had problems because of the way things were. I have largely, thanks to therapy, understood and exorcised them. But it's taken years. Why should you get away with covering your ears to what I went through? You thought I was coping. And no I wasn't. You simply *have* to learn to see the imperfections around you without running from them or blocking. I kept everything back from you because I didn't want to upset you. And perhaps I thought you wouldn't love me if you knew. But you keep blaming poor Wart for this and that and blah-blah-blah, Peter, Peter, Peter, thinking he's corrupted this sweet innocent thing, when it's not like that at all.'

'Oh God, I'm—' Kempton feels utterly demolished. 'Please don't pull away. Please—' Too choked to say anying else as he grasps her hand and kneads and massages it; kneads and massages.

The rain drumming the window. The waitress removes their half-full plates. *Finis*? – Yes, *oui* – *finis*. And he is. Completely *finis*. Washed-up. *Ecrasé*.

'Dad – I have to go on.' Does he not realise what effort this is costing her? Regurgitating it. Reliving old pain. And knowing it is causing *him* pain. And Foetus leaping about within her as though alarmed by her distress which has communicated to him.

'Peter. Does he know everything?'

'Of course.'

Of course. Peter has no illusions and loves a real human being. Whilst he, Kempton, saw only the perennial child. And what is there to be gained by full knowledge? But Cat grew up with it. And hasn't he often thought that he hadn't protected her enough, and that she had been exposed to too much as a child? He had consoled himself by believing she had somehow been left unscathed. How pathetic. How could she possibly have been left unmarked by her mother's behaviour? Her upbringing was abnormal, and that he had pretended otherwise shows his lack of insight and sensitivity. In his quest for a perfect life he had spat on the jagged-surface edges and hoped they would unite. Had been fearful of probing, of asking, or even advising; shied away from discussing emotions. Self-deception. His dogged aspirations. Oh Kempton, who tried so hard . . . and what for? You can try your utmost to keep things static. You build what you think is a rock-solid foundation, only to discover you are on a fault line and the ground is shifting beyond your control.

'When Mummy committed suicide,' Cat says, 'it was the ultimate rejection. She had chosen to die. Because she didn't love me enough to stay alive.'

And wasn't this what he himself had felt? He had said it to Suzanne. The exact same thing.

'I didn't matter to anyone.'

'Me. You mattered so much to me.'

'But you were grieving. We were these separate, grieving entities, each with all the muck and guilt and anger and hurt and everything else that arises from something like that . . . Minnie was marvellous. Remember? I went to Minnie.'

'Yes.'

'I felt so bad leaving you on your own.'

'I was best alone.'

'You see I'd been acting different roles all my life. I didn't have a clue who *I* was. Me. That's why I loved physical things like climbing and sport. I didn't have to think. And sex. Another outlet . . . When Mummy died, when she killed herself, I felt so confused and hurt. And guilty. Well that's all part of it, isn't it? And of course I missed her. The normal person that she could be was so special . . . But I never trusted that bout would last; and I must have upset her terribly, always holding back . . . Look, she knew she wasn't like other people, that she was sick; and that was hell for her . . . And when she was gone, the good things kept coming back, and I wished I'd let myself appreciate her properly as she was, instead of always being guarded. I mean—'

Momentarily her features crumple as though she is about to cry; but she takes several deep, measured breaths and controls herself. Kempton aching for her. Longing to draw her into his arms and just hold her. But knows he must not.

She resumes speaking, in the same stilted, stumbling way.

'She often used to ask me what I was thinking about, but I never confided in her, and I feel so bad about that. I didn't confide in friends either. It was all too complicated to explain to anyone. It was easier just to bluff. Actually I didn't even know I was bluffing half the time as it had become an integral part of me. It all came out in therapy . . . And I wrote reams of poetry – you know the tortured kind of rubbish. I went completely off boys. Couldn't bear anyone near me . . . And then you and I became really close. I felt very cherished by you. That was wonderful. Truly, Dad. It meant a lot to me, our time together. Means a lot. Please know that.' Winding the napkin round and round her wrist, pulling it off, and repeating the process.

'I do.' The words do not come out; sound like a cow with a stomach ache. He clears his throat. 'I do know it.'

'I began to understand why I'd been a particular way and behaved as I had. And that Mummy's sickness was no one's fault. And then I had the accident . . . Anyway, that made me see things on another level. I read masses while I was laid up. I thought about everything in my life, and it was like it was all for a reason and I was following a trail of clues in order to discover a succession of things about myself. What I wanted and needed. I realised there were things I'd never be able to do again, some which I'd miss and some which I wouldn't, and I realised other things would take their place; that it was up to me to find those things. I knew I was fallible and that I wanted to live – once I didn't. I knew the value of life and I wanted to help others understand what that meant and help them achieve things that mattered. I wanted to be able to understand why Mummy did what she did . . . And Wart was in and out of the hospital the whole time. He made me laugh. We discussed books. He listened to my views. You know he's a voracious reader.'

'Yes.' A fleeting, smiling warmth at the thought of Peter.

'When I got out of hospital, whenever I saw him I felt something really strong for him. But it wasn't a desperate feeling that panicked me and stopped me getting on with things. It was just a lovely, relaxed, happy easiness . . . He wrote to me when I went up to Oxford – I was quite surprised – and I replied. Then last June I had this boyfriend, and I wrote to Wart and told him. He became quite inquisitive, it was really funny. Had I slept with him? he wrote back. I thought that was an odd thing to put in a letter. I wrote and told him, yes I had . . .'

Peter knew all this, while he, Kempton, was oblivious. Blinkered. He goes around blinkered.

'He – David – the boy wanted to marry me.'

'You never said anything. Why didn't you tell me about him?'

'It wasn't such a big thing for me. Anyway, you're my father.'

So why all the revelations now? Is he not still her father?

'He was the first guy who I'd been with since my leg thing. I was scared I was with him out of gratitude. You know – that he could fancy me . . . So anyway, when Wart got my letter that said I'd slept with David he charged up to Oxford and took me out to dinner. And things went from there.'

Apart from themselves the restaurant is now empty. Cat's voice peters out into the emptiness, and it is several seconds before other sounds snap into Kempton's consciousness, singly rather than as a combined sound: Frank Sinatra singing 'My Way'. The clatter of the waitress clearing the tables. The rain on the window. Bottles being moved about in the bar. Chairs pushed into place.

In the bright light Cat looks almost old, her complexion sallow. And now, finally she turns to regard her father – his face is ravaged – waiting for him to say something. He is slumped over his elbows, which are resting on the table, pushing his lips around between his fingers as though they are made of rubber. His eyes are bloodshot. He gives a sigh that judders through his body, and another. When still he does not speak, she becomes worried: suddenly frightened that she has done a wrong thing. That his love for her is not unconditional. And it rushes back to her, that feeling she had as a young girl: that she was dirty.

'Dad?'

'What you have been through,' he bursts out. 'What you have – what we have put you through – what—'

- Kempton's Journey

He sobs silently into his sleeve in this public room of the Hotel Continental; and his daughter cradles his head.

'I'm through it now. Ssh Dad, I'm through it. It's nobody's fault and I'm *through* it. And I'm better for it. Really Dad, it's all right. I know where I'm going.'

Does he?

'Forward, Kempton,' she says.

13 ∫

Grandstand

> '... Let me seize on this auspicious moment; it is the time of my outward and material reformation, let it also be the time of my intellectual and moral reformation. Let me decide my opinions and principles once and for all, and then let me remain for the rest of my life what mature consideration tells me I should be.'

Reads Kempton this momentous night in his monastic room in Villereal. Reformation. He latches onto the word and separates it. Re-formation. Re-forming. Of late he seems to have spent considerable time doing just that. Upturning his life, himself, his views, layer by layer. It seems that there is very little left that is as it once appeared to be. Now he is almost too numbed to think. Unbelievable that she could have harboured so many secrets. How could she have kept it all secret for so long? But then, if he'd known what she was up to – *fourteen* for Chrissake – what could he or Vanessa have done? He'd seen it in other families: rebellious, promiscuous teenagers and their parents at the end of their tether, and before you knew it, it was all-out war. And he remembers at the time thanking

God that they had a normal, well-adjusted kid who hadn't given them the aggro some of their friends had had. Oh oblivion. And such pain going on inside her: she had to shoulder it all on her own, spilling out her heart to a stranger. And at fourteen she was so thin and gawky. If he *knew* who the lads were who took advantage . . .

Anger snatches at him – before logic takes over, followed by searing remorse for her lost innocence whose departure he had believed so much more recent. He wishes he could have all their lives over again. Another chance please. Three or four years replayed, and see how different it would be.

He burrows his face into his pillow, nursing its sodden, scrunched-up shape against his cheeks, which are sore with salt against his stubble.

Eventually drowsiness settles upon him and with it the thought – as though Cat is saying it: 'Enough of wishing, Kempton.' And of course no amount of wishing can ratify the wrong. But – she claims to have come through it all; claims to be happy now. Certainly, she looks it, doesn't she? Don't do anything to upset it Kempton. For Chrissake, don't endanger it again. Don't make your problems hers. And if it means accepting her and Peter, then so be it.

It is dawn when he falls asleep – with the image of Vanessa, her head huddled into her left shoulder, which nudges into his armpit. So real is this image that he is prompted to stroke the place beside him. He can feel her. The curve of her bottom. It is not a dream. She is there.

He awakes barely a couple of hours later – to the relentless catarrhal coughing of the proprietor below and creaking footsteps overhead – refreshed, his mind lucid. And from outside comes a sudden burst of song. He recognises the aria as from *Tosca*; gets up to open the curtains. And there is the sullen young man in the yard, tying up dustbin bags and giving an astonishing virtuoso performance in a powerful tenor.

There's nowt so strange as folks, Kempton, his father used to say.

'Take care Kempton.'
'You too, sweetie-pie. I love you. Never, ever doubt it.'
'I don't. I won't . . . Dad? It's been a great week.'
'It has, hasn't it?'
'I'll always remember it. It'll stick in my mind for all time.'

Chewing on her finger. She seems reluctant to leave him, and hovers almost shyly. Their last ever holiday and they both know it. They are entering another stage in their relationship. It will be no less rewarding than the one they are just relinquishing, Kempton realises.

'You're the most wonderful daughter a man could wish for,' he says thickly. 'Come here.'

She goes into the umbrella of his arms and he presses her to him, feeling the warm exhalation of her breath against his chest, through his jumper; and the bump of her tummy.

'Ditto, you're the greatest father.'

Adèle, waiting in the lane in her car, gives a small toot and makes a show of looking at her watch.

'You must go,' Kempton says.

'I know. Here, this is for you.' Hands him an envelope. 'It's from Minnie. She asked me to give it to you when I left.'

'*Minnie*? Why? What is it?'

'I haven't a clue.'

A final quick kiss on the lips, more 'take cares', another toot from the Renault, and she is walking away from him.

'Give my regards to Peter,' he calls as she is climbing into the car.

And she smiles one of her broadest smiles, waving both hands gaily in a wide fan before shutting the door.

Kempton stands waving his handkerchief until the car is out of sight, missing her already, but not sad. More a wistfulness. And he is looking forward to phoning up Peter on his return and to seeing him. OK, not on quite the old basis; that will take time. And certainly it will be strange for Kempton seeing him and Cat together as a couple. Soon to be parents. And himself a grandparent.

Adjustments and re-adjustments. Do they ever cease? Only, it occurs to him, with the cessation of life itself.

So his daughter has departed. And Kempton is left with a week to himself: the two women trust him to drive the *roulotte* on his own and will meet him each afternoon to check he has arrived at the relevant destination. One man and a horse. And a letter to read.

And this sunny, mild evening, with the mill house in sight whose facilities he is using, he sits on his jacket in the meadow, glass of white wine beside him, and his picnic: a feast of coarse bread, strong creamy cheese, fat radishes picked that day, rillettes of pork; and to finish – wild strawberries. A hoopoe cocking its crested head at him. The chiming of a cuckoo. And a few feet away, Bella grazing – the peaceful pulling and munching sounds she makes; the smell of grass. The 'plipping' of the river. Beads of moisture on the overhanging willow branches. Late sunshine diffused between the greenery.

'*Dear Kempton,*' Minnie has written.

> 'So, shortly you are to become a grandparent, and myself a great grandparent. It does not seem such a long time ago that I was carrying you, and my sudden awareness of the accelerating years made me feel this was an opportune moment to write to you, in order that you may

perhaps understand a little more about me. I do not wish to be on my deathbed with regret on either of our parts.

Let's get some stuff out of the way immediately. I know full well that you have resented me over the years and believe that I have let you down in many ways; also that you hold me responsible, at least in part, for your father's death. Certainly, I was not a conventional mother for a boy to be lumbered with. I never attempted to be an elbows-in-yeast type and I will admit that maternal urges did not come naturally to me. I would agree, too, that I expected you to fit into my life and made, so it seemed — I use that word deliberately, as you will see — few concessions. In retrospect I should never have married, let alone borne a child. However, I should like to say at this point that, contrary to what you think, I do have a great fondness for you and am very sad that you have had to endure so much sorrow and tragedy over the last few years. I have tried to help in small ways, but you made it clear you had no wish for my assistance or advice, so I have respected your wishes.

Have you ever considered that perhaps our rift has bothered me? Or that I minded the fact my son was plainly antagonistic towards me? I have, I know, a sharp tongue and a strange humour, but sometimes an outward brusqueness can be a façade behind which dwell other sentiments. Sometimes I have teased you because you can, you know, be a little pompous and self-righteous, if not downright judgemental. I suppose I was trying to get you to take yourself somewhat less seriously. Even as a young man it struck me sometimes that you behaved then as though you were already middle-aged. This, I think, was your way of proving your sense of responsibility and was perhaps a reaction to what you saw as my lack of it. Am I correct? I am, you see, more perceptive than you give me credit for. I also knew of your wife's illness; I realised it was more than an ordinary neurosis and my heart went out to you. She was not a bad girl, and I am sorry I could not take to her. But frilly women have always set my hackles rising. Nevertheless I apologise belatedly to you for my attitude.

You are a good, decent man, Kempton, who deserves a little happiness (I greatly liked your new lady friend by the way). It is as though the events of the past few years have been taking you over beyond your control, but now I have the impression you are beginning to take charge and strike out and back. Certainly I admire you for leaving the business, especially as I

• Kempton's Journey

recollect how hard you worked, starting it from nothing and with virtually no money. Cat also tells me your painting is coming on well. Marvellous girl that. You should be proud of her. I know you are. She is a credit to you. By the way, did you know that I painted once? No you wouldn't. Then I lost the urge. Maybe one day I'll take it up again. I'd better hurry!

About myself. I grew up in an enormous house in many acres close to Shaftesbury in Dorset. My father, a splendid and rather stern figure of a man, was a very wealthy landowner, art collector and investor, whose favourite spectator sport was horse racing. He had always wanted a son. Instead he had five daughters of which I was the youngest. In case you are wondering about the others, my oldest sister died of TB when she was fifteen, the next died at just a couple of months old; Edith, the third girl was very prim and proper and never married. She was killed in a car crash nearly fifty years ago. My sister nearest to me in age, Joan, and myself never got on. She married when she was nineteen to a South African and as far as I know still lives out there in that country.

By the time I was born my father, understandably I suppose, was fed up of the whole female household. But I was different from my sisters. I was tall for my age and preferred the rougher sort of games that boys played. I had no respect for my mother, a weak, snobbish woman, and idolised my father. He, however, had no more time for me than the others. There was just one occasion. I accompanied him on a walk to see a badger's sett and he let me smoke his pipe. At the end of the walk, in the only gesture of generosity or affection I can remember his showing me, he gave it to me. It's the one I have now. The next day I was packed off to boarding school in Sussex. I think I was twelve. As you can probably imagine, boarding school and I did not mix. Suffice to say I fitted in nowhere there, and rebelled in every possible way. It was there I was given my nickname of Minnie, instead of Millie – intended as a sarcastic jibe against my height and general size. But I preferred it – which of course diluted everyone's pleasure.

After school I went to Cambridge to read archaeology, and met your father, who had been teaching since his MA and gone back to do a PhD in modern French history. I found him rather interesting. He was half French, which made him seem a bit different, and was quite handsome in those days. He posed less of a threat to me than the other boys who frankly frightened me with their swaggering, cocky attitudes. I had no friends. I did not trust other people, and in return they found me aloof. I think I was an attractive girl, but I was gauche and had no social graces whatsoever. Your father seemed to accept me as I was, and when he asked me to marry him I couldn't think I'd like anyone better, so I accepted. It seemed preferable to going back to living at home after university.

We were married on my twenty-second birthday, when I had graduated. My father gave me a generous dowry, and a few months later he died and I inherited a further sum. Not long afterwards my mother died also.

Your father. What can I say about him? He was all the things you knew and a few things besides. He was penniless but loved luxury and beauty. I bought for us the house in which you grew up. Did you never question where the money came from which we lived off? Your father earned a pittance as a schoolmaster at a second-rate public school. Your school fees (I could never have afforded boarding costs, and we decided it would not be a good idea for you to attend the school where your father taught, despite the carrot of reduced fees), most household bills, etc., came from my inheritance – my security for my old age. It was not long before our differences became apparent; and the intervening war years did nothing to bring us closer. In fact, for the last two years of the war your father was at home. He contracted glandular fever, and then seemed to have one ailment after another. During that period I supported us entirely financially.

After the war he eventually got a lowly teaching job, and then was given the post you know about, where he remained until he retired. I developed an interest in racing, and it quickly became my escape. Cultural stimulation was provided by archaeological trips and meetings, where I met like-minded people. I was beginning to learn about myself as a human being, but because I was married I could not fully explore that self. I felt trapped. Painting, gardening, even writing, all helped to give meaning to my days, but within me was a constant restlessness and a sense of solitariness.

Despite our many disparities, your father was a man with a healthy sexual appetite, and I must tell you at this point, without wishing to offend you, I was repulsed by the act and by his body. As you know I became pregnant many times – only to miscarry. My final pregnancy *was with yourself. After that we ceased relations. I really could not bear him to come near me, and by then my resentment of him was very great. Money was increasingly a problem, and it seemed wrong to me that your father was not making more of an effort to look for a better job. With his qualifications I am still convinced he could have lectured anywhere. He was verging on brilliance academically. But he was lazy, and that to me is unforgivable. When I discussed the possibility of selling and moving to a smaller house he looked so mortally wounded (you recall that particular 'afflicted' expression) that I abandoned that idea. And I must admit I loved the house — quite apart from its convenient proximity to a certain racecourse.*

You were a placid, well-behaved child, which was fortunate as I could not afford any help, even to clean that big house; and I was by then writing weekly articles — one for the archaeological magazine I still write for, the other a gardening magazine. Occasionally, I sold my watercolours (landscapes or flowers). From time to time I dabbled in buying and selling antiques at auction. I had inherited my father's keen eye. And so we scraped by. And if things became particularly bad I sold a family heirloom. However, almost as fast as I did this your father acquired possessions: silver, his books. And as for his waistcoats! They cost the earth. Once he gave one to a tramp, would you believe? And he sounded so proud of himself when he told me, as though it had been a real act of philanthropy. My money; and a tramp in a hundred-pound waistcoat!

However, I do not wish to taint your recollections of your father. Poor Edmond. He couldn't comprehend my anger. He was definitely a kind and sensitive man; only lacking in worldliness and any sense of practicality. But I don't believe he was entirely without guile, and I am fairly certain that he married me for money. Nonetheless I do not hold that against him, and I speak now from exasperation rather than malice. Whilst he sat whimsically daydreaming or immersed in his books, I sat worrying over bills.

Then, when I was in my early forties and you were eight or nine, my life changed. I was on a dig in Crete and I met someone with whom I fell desperately, wonderfully in love and who, even more wonderfully, fell in love with me. Her name was Viola Tomassi, and she was Italian. She was the same age as me and married to an Englishman, a London banker, from whom she led a completely independent life. She had such guts, that woman, such beauty, humour and spark, besides a great musical talent. Oh, and the conversations we had! I had never known such conversations. I had never known such a friendship. I wanted to pour myself, my mind and my body, into her. And she to me. We really were two halves of a whole. It was the most incredible thing to happen to me after everything I had been through, and so unexpected. And I felt an immense relief – it explained so much about myself – and such joy. I did not feel any guilt, even though lesbianism was so taboo at that time. Certainly it did not feel wrong or unnatural, and I could not think of it like that.

Over the years we saw each other several times a week and spoke on the phone each day. We took trips together and she came racing with me (you may remember her? She had very beautiful dark eyes and long black hair). And now you will see that I made a bigger sacrifice than you would have believed of me. Two years after I met her, Viola and her husband divorced and she tried to persuade me to live with her. Do you know how tempted I was? How I longed to? How I imagined and dreamed what it would be like? But I knew I could not do it. You were then about eleven, and to be told your mother had gone off with another woman would have been an impossible thing for you to come to terms with – Besides being both humiliating and embarrassing for you. You were doing well at school and I did not want you be taunted because of your mother. Also, you were far too young to comprehend what it all meant. There was, at the time of your youth, a very different outlook from today, and a boy of your age then was far more innocent than a comparable boy today. So, Viola and I decided that when you had left school and were old enough to cope with the scandal, we would live together. Meanwhile, we would continue on the basis we always had. Your father assumed she was just a casual friend. Not a soul knew about us. That was the worst of it. We so hated not being able to be open.

We bought each other rings, and longed for the day we could live together; spoke often of the home we would buy, where it would be, the possibility of emigrating, the things we would do. Did we ever quarrel? Naturally we did, like anyone in a close relationship. And the situation itself led to tensions. Also, Viola was Latin, with the temperament to match. And I am stubborn with that sharp tongue! But Viola never

> sulked. That wonderful smile would start slowly and flood her face – and her anger would be gone.
>
> Then, when you were leaving school, preparing to go to university and finally Viola and I were making our plans, the most terrible thing happened. Viola started getting appalling headaches. It was a brain tumour, and it was inoperable. She died within three months of the diagnosis.
>
> I had no one to turn to. Not one single person. She had been my only friend. My grief was almost unbearable.
>
> Afterwards, I simply could not countenance remaining married to your father. The rest, you know.
>
> So there you have it, Kempton. We all have our skeletons and our crosses; some an unfairer share than others. But then, what is fair? I want your happiness and fulfilment, and I should like us to be friends. Of late I began to see the possibility of that happening. I could treat you to lunch at the Turf Club sometime. You would have the privilege of ascending the main staircase to the dining room. I as a mere lady have to use the side stairs.
>
> Enjoy your holiday. I shall be having fun with Pluto.
> Love, Minnie.
>
> PS I can picture your face when you have waded through this lot. It is shell-shocked.'

And she is right. Reading in the deepening grey light, he is utterly, totally shell-shocked.

The sun appearing intermittently through the yarn of cloud; but it is mid-winter cold again. The lane cleaving through forested escarpments of pine, birch, hazel, scrub and sweet chestnut; early wild strawberries like garnets spangled amongst the undergrowth. The forest thinning out, revealing glimpses of russet soil and fields of maize and wheat; past a strawberry farm, with long alleys of fruit in open-lidded cloches. To the right, a reservoir, its dark surface teeming with water birds. And shortly after this, a meadow in pink-flowering clover.

He comes to a village – children haring out from behind

wrought-iron gates, shrieking, pointing, and waving at the caravan. Kempton waves back, and doffs the panama hat he purchased the previous day. The lane starts to descend steeply. Bella's hindquarters sink into the cradle of her harness as she checks herself, and Kempton applies the brake and shortens the reins. The mare's ears twitch in acknowledgement. Message received. The *roulotte*'s undercarriage clanks like a ghost's chains. And the rain comes down.

A small rainbow whorl on the tarmac startles Bella, but it is several seconds before she gives her predictable side-hop.

Kempton leans forward to pat her steaming rump. 'The trouble with you is you're so big your reactions take a while to reach your brain, don't they old girl?'

He talks to her freely now, and judging from the activity of her ears, she seems to appreciate it. And who would have imagined a week ago that he would have been able to handle her by himself? He is really quite tickled. The sense of independence is tremendous. Have horse will travel. Last night he slept for the first time in the wagon, on the pull-down double bed. He cannot recall ever having slept so well: an owl hooting, unfamiliar night-time noises gently butting his consciousness as his eyes closed. He had left the door ajar and in the morning had woken up to a whickering and Bella's hairy white face peering in.

Well, hi there.

Late afternoon, and he 'parks' on the outskirts of Monpazier and strolls to the town. Once again the rain has abated and the central square is occupied by a small band of men playing boules, or just hanging around watching. Fierce concentration scratches into weathered skin. Outside a café-bar another group are playing cards, drinking beer and smoking. Where have all the women gone? And Kempton starts humming in his head: 'Where have all the flowers gone . . .'

• Kempton's Journey

He wanders into a *tabac* to buy some postcards and stamps, and the local rag for a laugh, and goes to sit outside the café-bar near the old men. Some sort of argument is going on, and he gathers that it concerns the recession. One old boy with a face like tree bark, and nicotine fingers he keeps jabbing at the table with, is becoming quite heated.

Four cards.

'*Darling Cat,*' he writes on the first.

'Hope you arrived back safely. I enjoyed our week so much. It was such a pleasure to have you with me and I am glad of our "talk". This is my second day on my own and I must say I am quite chuffed with myself the way I've managed so far. I could become addicted to this kind of life ...'

'Dear Minnie,
'Am sitting outside a small café-bar in the pretty Bastide town of Monpazier while penning this note. I must say this life is certainly very therapeutic. One finds oneself ambling at a very different pace from the normal frenetic one. The tribulations of modern living seem a long way away ... I have been doing a lot of reflecting ...'

Pauses, pen dangling in the air. Unsure how to continue. How could he have failed to guess about his mother before? Does Cat know? It is so obvious. And her revelations have cast light not only on many aspects of his childhood, but also on her attitude towards him; and he remembers that often he had felt wounded by her peremptory manner. Now that he has grown used to the idea – his mother a lesbian, for Chrissake; forget all the coy words: gay, butch, whatever; forget about his own fantasies about beautiful women having sex together; this is different: this is his eighty-year-old *mother* – now that it has sunk in, and the shock has subsided, he just feels tremendously sorry for her, that her chance of real happiness was snatched away after years of patience. He respects her honesty. He sees her finally for what she is, as someone of immense courage and, yes, integrity. There are things she has done which still rankle, still cannot be excused, but they are comparatively trivial in retrospect. And what of his feelings towards his father, now that he has been shown a blemished side to that man's character? These, too, have had to be reshuffled along with the balancing of allegiances towards his parents. And again, his own lack of insight dismays him: that he had never even *wondered* – as Minnie remarked in her letter – about the financial situation at home. Or perhaps he had, but did not want to know the truth; opting, as he would always do, for the least hassle route.

It is the only explanation. And now he thinks: I suspected all the time – as the startling disclosures cease to be startling – It was always there in my subconscious. I just didn't want to confront it.

'... *Thank you for your long letter. I was astounded to say the least, and was also immensely moved. I should very much like to take you up on your offer of lunch at the Turf Club (will accompany you up the side stairs). Meanwhile I hope you and Pluto are fine.*'

Pauses again. Love? Yours? Kind wishes? Settles on 'Yours Ever.'

Number three.

'*Dear Peter,*
'*Sitting outside a typical café-bar in the quaint old town of Monpazier. A bunch of wizened-faced men playing cards at the next table. Another lot playing boules in the square. Recognise the scene? Had a great time with Cat – hope she reported back the same. I learned a few home truths and am a wiser man, I hope, for it. As for you and I – bygones, etc?*
   A bientôt, Kempton.
   PS Am seriously considering getting a horse and wagon.'

• Kempton's Journey

Of course he is not seriously considering it. Tosses this in as a light aside. But after he has written it there is a tiny tweaking at his brain. And the idea, which throughout his trip has been gestating and developing, takes an interesting turn. On the cardboard beer mat he jots: horse/wagon? Incorporate into idea? Where keep?

The fourth card;

> 'Dear Suzanne,
> 'You would love this trip. Get-away-from-it-all tranquillity with a huge white Percheron horse plodding sedately in front of you, through charming countryside and quaint villages. My daughter has left and I am sleeping this week in the caravan itself, rather than in auberges. Quite an experience. Plenty of time and space in which to get to know oneself a little better. Weather patchy, but it doesn't matter. Hope you're well.
> Love …'

Oh God, he wishes he could put a bit more. But her husband might see it. And then he is inspired. Finishes with a bold flourish: 'Kay.' And now changes the 'love' to 'with lots of love,' and adds several x's.

Wishes she was with him. No, not because he is lonely; but because he is happy and he wants to share it with her.

Evening has set in and Kempton turns off the road up a small lane. A boulder at the corner is his 'landmark'. They continue along here for a few hundred yards until they come to an ancient bridge spanning a small river. Here the lane splits into two, one climbing steeply and becoming a track running along a ridge of hills, the other winding out of sight. He takes this one and comes to a hamlet. In a small paddock are several loudly snorting pigs. Bella goes rigid when she sees them and stops dead, refusing to budge.

Kempton bounds off the wagon to lead her past. Strokes her nose and eyes behind the blinkers.

'Poor girl, it's OK. Good Bella. They won't hurt.' Pulls on the reins. She is snorting herself now and sounding exactly like the creatures she is so frightened of. Still she will not move. In the end he resorts to thwacking her rump with a willow branch and yelling at her. Fifteen minutes, it takes him to make her walk past, and he is quite het-up by the end of it. Bella, sweating and trembling, deranged-eyed like a Stubbs painting. Kempton full of remorse at losing his cool with her.

The gate to the field he is using for the night is marked by a large red cardboard arrow. He opens it and leads Bella and the *roulotte* inside. As soon as he has unharnessed her she immediately falls to her knees and rolls, rotating from side to side, itching her back and grunting. It is a curiously human noise. Kempton leans against the *roulotte*, watching and smiling at her antics. There are certain things, certain moments which snare his throat because of their specialness – and now Bella is struggling to her feet and shaking herself, before charging round the field bucking – and this is one such moment: seeing this immense creature reverting to her natural wild state at the end of a day of servitude to him.

Later, after Adèle has visited and left again – 'Well done, you're coping brilliantly'; after he has washed and smartened himself up a bit, in so far as this is possible, with his body cricked like a gnome, he walks to the farmhouse and knocks on the door. The young woman who answers, and the elderly man behind her, welcome him and introduce themselves as Ninette and Claud. When Kempton speaks to them in fluent French they invite him inside for a glass of wine.

The interior is a showpiece for their ceramics which they make and sell, and for Ninette's needlework.

• Kempton's Journey

'We've built up quite a reputation,' Claud says. 'People come from miles nowadays to buy our work. And it complements Ninette's other business very well.' Pinches her cheek fondly.

'Ouch.' She feigns crossness. She is perhaps twenty-five or thirty, a pretty woman in a small, plump, dark way. Her father is in his sixties, Kempton guesses, stocky and silver-haired. A widower probably, and his daughter looks after him. Lucky fellow.

So what is her other business? Kempton asks her, taking a subtle sniff of his white wine: a full, fruity nose.

'I sell home-made produce,' she says. 'Rillettes of pork – Did you see? we keep pigs up the lane.'

'Yes I noticed. I—' About to relate the incident with Bella.

But she continues, striking off items on her fingers: 'I sell *confit de canard*, jams, dried mushrooms – we have ten different types in the area, you know. And bottled fruits. And I have someone make up unusual basketware. There's so much willow around. Even small chairs with rush seating—'

'And I make a superb plum brandy,' Claud, not to be outdone, interrupts her, smacks his lips in a kiss. 'Believe me, a sip of that takes you through the roof.' Laughs, hugging his arms round his belly. 'Anyway, the business is really taking off. And the beauty is we're our own bosses. None of that rat-race rubbish.'

Kempton's mind churning. Doesn't believe in fate, and yet here he is, in this house in the middle of nowhere, and these people are his best contacts so far.

They insist on his having dinner with them. Ninette sets a casserole on the old wooden table in the beamed dining room.

'Eel in red wine with lambs' tongues,' she announces proudly.

Lambs' tongues? Maybe he misunderstood. He looks alarmed; and she notices, gives a squeaky, girlish laugh.

'Oh not real lambs' tongues. It's the name of a mushroom.'

He bends his head reverently towards his plate: the rich blend of aromas titillating his nostrils.

'You're fortunate to have a daughter who's such a good cook,' he says to Claud.

There is an awkward momentary pause, and they glance at each other.

'We're husband and wife,' Claud says quietly, taking Ninette's hand possessively. She gazes into his eyes with blatant devotion.

'We've been married for nine years,' she says. 'We've got two children. They're with their grandparents in Toulouse for a few days.'

Touché, Kempton. But he had been determined to avoid the same annoying mistake that had pursued him the entire week with Cat. And the age gap between these two must be thirty years.

He apologises profusely, in a bumbling, cheek-reddening way. Explains about his own situation.

'*C'est rien, c'est rien,*' they tell him, laughing at his embarrassment, Claud thumping his back to reassure him, and pouring him more wine.

Over *tarte tatin* and the sweet-fiery plum brandy – which has to be the strongest thing he has ever drunk, and that's saying something – he discusses his business idea with them. Is aware of slurring his words slightly, yet he feels sober. They are as enthusiastic as himself, and Ninette scribbles notes as he talks, and afterwards makes further suggestions.

They say their goodnights with much backslapping and kissing on cheeks. And the cool damp air hits him as he ventures outside, zipping up his waterproof jacket. *Le Style*

• Kempton's Journey

Français. It could work. It really could. And as for that plum brandy ... Kempton can still feel it smouldering in his tummy and chest; its sharp sweetness on his tongue.

A few yards on from their house is the small whitewashed church, dominated by an open *clocher* with an immense bell set inside. A lantern over the door illuminates it and a notice informs the casual tourist that the building is thirteenth-century. On a whim he goes inside – first has to unlock the door with an old iron key left trustingly in the lock. He enters hesitantly, feeling rather like an intruder.

Within is eerily silent and empty; several lit candles cast shadows across the white plaster-work, alight on marble statues, pick out Jesus's agonised face on the cross, spill like water over the stone fonts and project spectre shapes on the tunnelled ceiling. There are no pews, which strikes him as odd. His feet echo. He feels alone. He is alone. Yet it is an exciting feeling. The atmosphere is both light and solid.

'*Everything*,' wrote Jean-Jacques Rouseau,

'is in constant flux on this earth. Nothing keeps the same unchanging shape, and our affections, being attached to things outside us, necessarily change and pass away as they do ... Thus our earthly joys are almost without exception the creatures of the moment ...'

Kempton is tugged by an overwhelming emotion he cannot define, nor does he have the need to. He does not pray. Just stands there in the nave of the church, listening to his own breathing. He continues to stand there for perhaps ten minutes, not moving. Has the sense that his feet are growing from the ground, that some sort of magnetic energy is drawing him from himself.

He turns eventually, to go.

'Thank you,' he says in a strong voice.

And his voice rebounds off the walls, is thrown back at him from the coved ceiling: 'you, you, you, you.'

Locks the door behind him. Is startled by the caterwauling of a pair of cats which streak across his path. Lopes thoughtfully back to the field for another night under the stars. Except there are none.

14

Last Furlong

'*Le Style Français,*' Kempton writes on the plane. 'Business Plan.' The nun next to him reeks of garlic. It is quite overpowering; he feels almost nauseous with it. A sublime expression on her smooth-wax face as she gently beats time with her two index fingers on her lap to whatever it is she is listening to through the headphones. A French religious magazine open on her lap.

'A French way of life imported to Britain,' he writes in the specially purchased hardback book he found at a stationer's in Bordeaux this morning. 'An entirely new concept with a novel and fresh approach.' Or perhaps, 'Have horse will travel. Produce from the glorious Perigord region of France delivered to your door by horse and old-fashioned romany caravan whose interior is a cornucopia of temptation—' yes, that's good; he likes that; '—from ceramics and small pieces of furniture to regional gourmet delights and unusual wines and liqueurs.' It sounds evocative, he thinks, fills one with the sense of yearning one gets when one reads a travel brochure. The important thing is to whet the potential customer's appetite.

Literally. Perhaps make more of the art aspect? 'Private orders and commissions taken?' he jots down. 'Have really alluring leaflets printed, well-illustrated and with photos. Cover with horse and *roulotte* and yours-truly.

MARKETING—' he underlines this heavily. 'Should be able to get plenty of free publicity in view of originality of idea. Phone number etc. painted on *roulotte* beneath *"Le Style Français"*.

CUSTOMERS/OUTLETS: All my old customers, plus tap private homes, shops, pubs, hotels, etc. Mail order? Hampers?'

Ideas bombarding him like tumbling hail – speaking of which, it has begun to do just that outside. Over the speaker the captain's languid voice warns of turbulence, and simultaneously the 'no smoking' and 'fasten your seatbelt' signs illuminate.

'INITIAL OUTLAY (stock not included): Horse. *Roulotte*. Refrigeration. Van for when weather conditions bad, or urgent deliveries. Printing costs. Harness –' he suddenly remembers. That could cost a fair bit.

'ONGOING COSTS: All the usual, but – no rates or rent! Grazing for horse. Upkeep of horse per week?

'RE-GRAZING: Phone Petersham Farm as first choice. Ideally placed. As far as I know, no other farm in area. Find out common grazing rights in locality as second choice.

'GOODS/ITEMS STOCKED: Food: rillettes, confits, dried chestnuts, pâtés, dried mushrooms, walnut oil, goat's cheese, three kinds of cow's cheese, sunflower honey, jams, bottled wild strawberries and other fruit, cured pork, smoked eel. EXPAND LIST WITH TIME.

'Wines: Three excellent local reds. Splendid sauvignon; two equally good dessert wines (muscat, and semillon). Strawberry liqueur. Plum brandy(!) COULD REALLY PUSH ALL THESE.'

A mental V-sign to Pitman.

'Non-food: Ceramics, basket-ware, chairs and boxes,

embroidered linen, cushions, needlework, herbal face creams. My own paintings.'

And this had been his original idea, conceived in Simon's studio: to frame his 'impressionist' paintings and hawk them around to pubs. From that dubious seed had sprung *Le Style Français*. Which could take off and escalate into something quite substantial; he is certain of it. Kempton, the itinerant entrepreneur. Has a cartoon image of himself in eighteenth-century gypsy's garb.

He lists his suppliers and contacts with their addresses alongside – referring to the cards he has collected, and jots down a few other details as they come to mind. Rings salient points. So much to do. But there is no hurry. He will not slip backwards into that old pattern, nor will he attempt to be overly ambitious. His pace and nobody else's. Nobody else to whom to be beholden. All the time in the world.

If he survives the flight. The plane is bucking disconcertingly. An insignificant metal cocoon being tossed about. The sky ragged blacks and shades of grey outside the window beside which he is sitting. Hail the size of sugar lumps battering it. And now – streaks of lightning interspersed with the resounding booming of thunder. The lights inside the plane flicker. A child wails from the back. Scared whimpering of a woman just behind Kempton – now trying to drink his red wine, which leaps out of its plastic glass all over him and splashes his cords. And next to him, the beatific-faced nun quietly holds the heavy black crucifix that lies across the blue plank of her bosom, as though it is the key to heaven.

Does not blink as her co-passenger repeatedly mutters, 'Shit, shit, shi-it.'

Kempton ploughing his way with an impressive crawl up and down the fast lane of the pool. Goggles protecting his eyes. He does so wish the dawdlers would stick to the middle or slow lane. And here is one making towards him, cleaving a slow, lumbering passage. There will be a head-on collision.

'You're going in the wrong direction, for Chrissake,' he yells, ducking round her and grazing his side against the blue rope, drenching her blonde bouffant carefully sticking out above the water as he flails around her. Realises belatedly that he knows her. Beth Turner. He is going to her and her husband for dinner tomorrow. Also realises that it is he, not she, who is going the wrong way. Ignores her irate, water-choked cries and prays she will not recognise him behind his goggles. Does a Duncan Goodhew spurt away from the scene of crime, head glued doggedly to the pool surface, swivelling it occasionally under the crook of his arm for air (a flash of himself at fourteen going up to collect the swimming cup from a lesser MP at school prize-giving). And as he turns he glimpses Beth – now out of the water – in agitated conversation with the pool attendant, obviously issuing a complaint. Slinks out while her back is momentarily turned and makes a dash for the men's changing room, yowling as he slips on the wet tiles in his urgency and stubs his toe. Eye-watering agony.

Kempton, red-eyed, combed wet hair, toe bound up in loo paper to alleviate the pressure of his shoe, panama hat – it and he have become inseparable – on his head, sits in the sports centre bar nursing a pint of lager. Still recovering from the shock of his near-miss – it could have been really embarrassing – and pain from his toe, which he is certain is broken. It has come up like a plump cocktail sausage.

At the other occupied table a green-haired girl gazes into the piglet eyes of a spotty youth, blowing smoke rings at him which he pretends to catch. He has the biggest pectorals and biceps Kempton has seen; a neck the circumference of an elephant's leg. They are, he decides, a particularly repulsive pair. The boy's pumped-up body and arms are an elaborate mapwork of tattoos, the most eye-catching being a pair of breasts peeping over the rim of his sleeveless black T-shirt. 'I love Sharon-big-tits,' blaze the blue-and-yellow words rippling above. And is the green-haired, smoke-blowing girl the subject of his public declaration? Her tits don't look big to Kempton.

He has finally acknowledged to himself that he is a breasts man. Thinks greedily of Suzanne; plunging his face between them. Soft, blue-veined waves surrounding his cheeks; his lips and tongue lost in them. Vanessa's were tiny and he can truthfully say it didn't matter. He adored her body. Sex with her. Vanessa the entirety, not just an isolated part of her. But she had a complex about them, and woe betide him should his gaze occasionally stray inadvertently towards a more generously endowed woman.

'Have implants if you're that bothered,' he said to her once, to calm her down.

It was the wrong thing to say.

'You don't fancy me the way I am. You want me to be something I'm not.'

That familiar feeling of helplessness. 'I don't. I meant for *you*. If *you* want to. I don't care. I love your boobs just the way they are. They're sweet.' Tried to put his arms round her.

She pushed him away. 'Oh you're such a liar. You're so transparent. You're pathetic. Men are so pathetic about breasts. It's insulting. If you want a cow go into a milking parlour.'

He had laughed then. Why hadn't he tried to soothe her? He could have held her forcefully until she relaxed. That nearly always worked. But her remark had struck him as genuinely funny. His laughter served as a trigger and she started throwing things, before marching into the kitchen. The next thing he knew was that she was running from the house with the car keys in her hand – although at that point he did not realise it. He only realised when he saw her dash towards her car parked in the road and heard the engine turn over. Chased frantically after her – it was a Saturday morning – and could only watch, powerless and horrified as she drove a few yards down the road and repeatedly rammed the bonnet into a wall. The grinding of metal. The barking of dogs. The appearance of neighbours. Vanessa ranting. Oh Vanessa. So impossible. And afterwards, so repentant and remorse-filled.

And the day she was finally diagnosed, after several weekly sessions with a psychiatrist: manic-depressive. The despair afterwards. I don't want to be manic-depressive. I want to be normal. Why can't I just be normal? Why did you marry me? I destroy everything.

Lithium was waved in front of her. The bright orange-beckoning carrot promising quasi normal life. Oh and her relief as she grasped it. So excited. Lithium, the panacea. She had such optimism, such faith that it would work.

'I'm glad now that I know what's wrong with me, as at least now I can *do* something positive about it . . . I'll make you so happy,' she said to him. 'Everything will be wonderful.'

Her optimism was heartbreaking in retrospect. Vanessa dragging herself about with no energy, heavy-eyed, drowsy and lethargic. Tummy distended with indigestion.

'It's not fair. Other people can take it. Why can't I?' Weeping. Her hopes dashed – and raised again as the dosage was changed. And for a while it looked as though the drug was working. But the dosage was too low; insidiously the symptoms of her illness began to affect her once more. And he was so sorry for her. So very sorry. Watched as one evening she ceremoniously flushed her supply of Lithium down the toilet. And then downstairs uncorked a bottle, a treasured bottle worth God knows how much, of Château Ausone '83 and proceeded to swig it back.

'At least let me have a glass,' he said. But could not wrest it from her.

Punishing him because no one could help her.

'I'm a lost cause, I'm a lost cause . . .'

And so sorry for himself too. Sometimes he felt battered, hoovered dry. Sometimes – yes he admits it – he wanted out. But he could never have left her. He was trapped. Hates himself for thinking that her death freed him.

She fades from his thoughts. He finishes his lager. One last look at the green-haired girl and tattooed boy. And hobbles out, towards his car in the car park, and Pluto, who insists on accompanying him everywhere nowadays.

'Poor toe.' Suzanne rubbing it with hers.

'Thank God she didn't recognise me. I mean it would have been awful. Me going there to dinner tomorrow. I tell you, I wish I wasn't going. I know it'll be deadly.' Kissing her nipple and tugging at it gently between his teeth, feeling it extend like a little twig.

'How do you know it'll be deadly? It might be all right.'

'It won't be. Trevor is so . . .' He chances it. 'He's so middle-class. And it's one of these spare men things. I've already been warned. Served up like meat. And I know just the type I'll be paired off with.'

'What type's that?'

'Oh the usual – bored divorcée. Kids. Probably training to be a counsellor or therapist – sorry, nothing personal, you're different – standard pretty. Pretty standard. Good tennis player.'

'She sounds ideal.'

'I don't know why I accepted.' But he does. Because for sure there's nothing better to do this Saturday night.

'You never know. You might meet the love of your life.' Moving closer to him and leaning slightly over him to make her breast more accessible.

• Kempton's Journey

'For Chrissake.' Glances up at her face: red patches on either cheek after their love-making. Her bright eyes. 'You're laughing. Why are you laughing?'

'You're tickling me.'

'Rubbish. Tell me why you're laughing.'

'I'm not. Really.'

'Yes you are. *Really* you are. *Now* you are.' As he begins tickling her all over. Suzanne shrieking and writhing. 'Stop it. I can't stand it. Stop it.' Grabs his penis.

'Pax,' he says.

Kempton painting in his studio. But the house is no longer his. The garden – immaculate since Minnie took charge of it in his absence – is no longer his. The American woman can finally sleep at night. He has six weeks to get out. Actually he can't wait to leave; the place holds no appeal for him anymore. In fact he should have sold it three years ago. And he has seen something he would like to buy. It is perfect for him. He has not been so excited about anything for years. The realisation of a dream. The phone rings just as he is applying azure blue to his latest Pissarro. He runs downstairs and just makes it to the one in the bedroom before the machine cuts in.

'Oh,' says the voice when he answers. 'You're back. It's Annie.'

'Oh hello. Yes I know. How are you?' Leave me alone, leave me alone. He is already tensing.

'Extremely well. I've had a wonderful week of golf. When did you get back? I thought you were still away. I only phoned to hear your voice on the machine.'

She is becoming obsessive. The woman sets his teeth on edge. He wishes he could be rude to her. He wishes she would stop hassling him.

'Just over a week ago. I got back last Friday.'

'But I thought you were going for three weeks. You said

you were going for three weeks.' Inquisitor's sharpness in her tone.

'Two. I'm sure I said two.' Knowing full well he hadn't. He had fibbed in the hope that a space of three weeks might cool her adour. 'You must have misheard.'

'I never mishear. Why didn't you phone, if you were back?'

She is relentless in her pursuit of him. And he has partly himself to blame. After a stream of excuses every time she phoned, he finally ran out of imagination and stamina. Ended up seeing her twice before his trip. Worse. He went to bed with her on the second occasion. Can't bear to think about it now. She'd cooked an amazing meal, plied him with Chablis then Château Montrose, then led him, lamb to the slaughter, upstairs to her room. He didn't know how to refuse without offending her. Later, when he thought about it, he was reminded of the joke about the man who suddenly didn't fancy the woman he'd brought home: You wait downstairs. I'll bring the etchings down to you.

In Peter's promiscuous days he had had a maxim: *Dans les nuits tous les chats sont gris*. But for Kempton this didn't work. As soon as he was inside her he wanted to slither straight out. It was all he could do to stay erect. But a man's reputation was at stake. The onus on a man to perform was very unfair, he often thought. So all the time he was giving a credible imitation of his usual performance he was fantasising about Suzanne.

'I'm sorry. I've been terribly busy.'

'That's no excuse, darling.' He hates the way she calls him that, in her power-jewellery voice. 'You don't just ignore someone you've slept with.'

He wishes she would not remind him. Mutters another apology. Wishes he could be more brutal, tougher. 'The house is sold. I've been busy with that,' he says.

'Well that's good news for you. Have you found anywhere to live? You can always come and—'

'Yes.' And he tells her. Also tells her about his business idea.

The silence her end is followed by a laugh like breaking china. A Kensington laugh, is how he described it the other day to Peter.

'You can't be serious.'

'Why not?'

'But darling. You – I mean, with respect it's so – new-age. If that's the right word.'

'I think you mean Bohemian.'

'You won't be happy living like that.' Disenchantment has seeped into her tone. The man on whom she had for some reason set her sights, is about to become Unsuitable.

'I assure you I shall be.'

She persists for a bit longer. Jokes about the male menopause, about trying to reclaim his youth, about shedding his responsibilities. And finally she has said something worth responding to.

'Responsibilities to whom?' he challenges. 'My daughter's happily shacked up. With my best friend, if you want to know. What about responsibility to myself? This is what *I* want. Not what someone else wants for me.'

'Well I'm afraid it would be hopeless as far as our relationship is concerned.'

'Annie—' he says it at last. 'We don't have a relationship.'

He can hear her intake of breath.

'You have be-haved a-bom-in-ab-ly,' she enunciates, separating each syllable.

A click as she hangs up, and he is left with the dialling tone. Halleluja. Free of her. He is freeeee of her.

Bounds back up to his studio. No, azure blue is wrong. It should be lilac – peering more closely with his glasses at the book from which he is working. That's what was lacking. Short brushstrokes of lilac in the sky between the poplar trees.

Remembering France.

The house in Putney Heath exudes prosperity. As Kempton crunches his way up the gravel drive towards it he feels a slight sense of condescension. A quick peep through the illuminated dining-room window reveals candles flickering in silver candelabra, and a lot of cut glass. He has never much cared for cut glass, even when it was at the height of fashion. Trevor Turner is a Thatcher babe. Man-thrives-in-the-eighties and goes on thriving. He is a successful surveyor and land agent: shiny red face, shiny balding crown, *bon viveur* belly. A man who never questions what he has achieved and whose aspirations are straightforward.

Opens the door to Kempton. '*Good* to see you. *Glad* you made it. *How're* things, eh?' Effusive emphasis on the first word of each sentence.

'You too. Yes. Fine thanks.' Kempton steps into the hallway.

'*Come* in. *Come* in.' Trevor waves Kempton towards the drawing room, putting a glass of Champagne in his hand on the way. 'I think you'll know nearly everyone.'

And he does. Knows two out of the three couples. The other he is introduced to on his way over towards the hostess – who is talking to another woman he also knows. Too well. Grinning broadly at him now as she spots him. He feels momentarily giddy as he limps his way across the room, and stops for a moment in his tracks. Can feel himself blanching, then the blood roaring back into his cheeks and ears. She *knew*. Why didn't she tell him? Just look at her smirking as though it is the biggest joke since the mouse ate the cat. He has the urge to turn and run. If only he were a doctor: my beeper's just gone off I'm afraid. An emergency. He knows someone who does that. The man, a surgeon, has a low boredom threshold and can pre-set his beeper in readiness. Kempton wracking his mind for an instant excuse as Trevor pushes him – finger on his spine – towards the two women. Everything is in slow motion: her grin, the hostess's welcoming little wave, the other two couples interrupting their conversation to mouth hello, his own propelled passage across the room – which dimly he notices seems to contain rather too much blue. He could kill her for this. She goes too far. This is nothing short of warped. There is no way he would have come this evening if she'd said yesterday that—

'Kempton, *lovely* to see you. Why are you limping?' Beth plants shimmering lips a millimetre above his cheek in the air. Her blonde bouffant is immaculate.

Kempton arranging his lips into a social shape. 'Lovely to see you too.' Avoiding looking at the grinning woman next to her. 'I sprained my ankle. It's nothing.'

He should have bandaged it for effect. But right now he is too preoccupied with fury and embarrassment to care about anything else.

'Oh poor you . . .' Turns back to the other woman and makes a small gesture – a flick of the hand. 'You know Suzanne Harrison.'

'No I – How do you—' he starts to say as though he has never met her before in his life. Eyes glinting out rays of antagonism.

'Hi Kempton.'

'I hear you bought one of Suzanne's puppies, Kempton,' Beth says.

'Oh yes. I forgot.' Oh you idiot Kempton. What an *idiot* thing to say. How could you forget if you bought a dog?

'I mean I didn't recogni—'

'We bought one as well. A bitch. I've shut her in the boot room. We must swap doggy tales – pun intended – later.'

He smiles politely. 'Yes that'd be—'

'Excuse me, I must tend to the food.' And leaves them.

'Well, well,' says Suzanne.

'For Chrissake what are you doing here?' he whispers angrily at her. 'Why didn't you tell me you were coming? It's going to be really embarrassing.'

'I don't see that it need be.'

'Oh don't be trite. For once – please – just don't be trite. You really are the limit. Well this is *it*. Let me tell you, after this little trick this is *it*, as far as I'm concerned.'

And she looks bloody good. A bit of make-up. Some grey stuff round her eyes. Red lipstick. Her breasts. Oh God, and doesn't he know those breasts swelling above the dark green of her dress, or whatever it is she's wearing? The out-of-sight mole. He really fancies her. Yesterday in bed was amazing. And they had talked for hours as well. It only shows you can't trust even someone you think you know. Shit what a farce. And where is her husband anyway? Come to that, where's his partner for the evening? Ten of them already present, and ten place-settings in the dining room, he realises as they all traipse in.

He is put between Suzanne and the wife from the couple he didn't know previously. An attractive, loquacious woman called Wendy. Manages to ignore Suzanne almost totally throughout the starter – a rather good terrine of turkey and veal – and devote all his attention to Wendy, who is certainly knocking back the wine.

'—And this hairy ape was coming straight at me in the pool,' he overhears Beth saying at her end. 'Head-on, in the wrong direction. He had the *nerve* to shout at me. Obviously fancied himself as another Duncan Goodhew behind his poseur goggles—' General amusement. Kempton's earlobes tingling. His own forced laughter. He can sense Suzanne's mirth next to him. 'Anyway, so this hotshot obviously didn't think I spotted him sneaking off, but he slipped and stubbed his toe so badly I thought he'd got his desserts. I told the attendant to leave him. I mean the guy's toe was probably broken. I reckon that's retribution enough for a ruined hair-do.'

More laughter. Trevor pouring out the decanted red wine now in readiness for the next course. 'A decent Gruaud Larose,' he says when he comes to Kempton. 'Got to try and impress a wine merchant.'

'Ex-wine merchant.'

'Well, you know.' Trevor anxious to gloss over that. Not at ease with redundancy.

'I'll tell you about my new business venture later.' It has just occurred to Kempton that Trevor and Beth could be good customers.

Trevor looks relieved. 'Didn't know you had anything up your sleeve. *Looking* forward to hearing about it.' A bead of sweat travels diagonally across his forehead and drips onto his plump, manicured hand holding the decanter.

The conversation round the table moves via science then Stephen Hawking onto God. Wendy, who it transpires is a nurse, announces loudly that she is a panentheist.

'You mean a pantheist,' her husband chimes in rather scathingly across the table.

'No I don't.' She sounds very drunk. 'I mean pa*nen*theist. They're two different things. My beloved husband loves nothing better than to show me up in public. It's one of his more charming traits,' she informs the table.

Kempton cringes. A quarrel, begun at home, exported to a dinner party and vented after a few glasses of wine. And doesn't he remember what that was like?

Wendy explaining in a belligerent tone that the pantheist doctrine identifies God with the entire universe, whereas with panentheism the universe is a part but not the whole. 'So there,' she tells her husband. And proceeds to elaborate on her theme.

Kempton suddenly aware of Suzanne's silence beside him. He is acutely conscious of her closeness.

'So where's your husband?' he mutters into the ear poking through her hair. Her ears stick out slightly. He finds that rather sweet. Her perfume is nice, whatever it is.

'So where's your dinner partner for the evening?' she whispers back.

'I haven't a clue. Maybe they didn't bother to try and match me up after all. Maybe she was ill or couldn't make it for some reason.'

'Or maybe she's here.'

'What are you . . . talking . . .' His voice petering out. Suzanne's laughing eyes, teasing mouth. Glinting little teeth.

'You haven't answered my question,' Kempton says, his face a few inches from hers.

'As far as I know,' Suzanne rubbing her foot up his shin beneath his trouser leg, 'my ex-husband is in Iceland at the moment on business.'

Next to him and opposite him there is a full-scale row being conducted. Trevor is attempting to be peace arbiter. 'Ladies, gentlemen – this is not the right forum for a quarrel,' he pleads to no effect.

'I don't think I quite caught what you—' Kempton says to Suzanne.

'Yes you did. Perfectly. I said my ex-husband is in Iceland at the moment on business. Word for word that is what I said.' Her bare toe caressing his knee beneath the floor length table cloth. Himself with a massive erection under his napkin.

'You're divorced,' he says stupidly.

'Mmm.'

'When?'

'About six or seven months ago.'

'Why didn't you tell me? I mean all this time I was thinking . . . Well why didn't you *tell* me?'

'You didn't ask.'

'For Chrissake.'

She removes her foot from him; stares at him penetratingly.

'I've had my own finding out to do, Kempton. I don't want to be anyone's crutch. You weren't ready for a relationship.'

'And now?' he says softly.

She doesn't reply.

He won't – can't – let go of her eyes. His are riveted to hers, drawing them into his own and simultaneously being drawn by hers. Whilst the rest of the table is degenerating and everyone is squabbling, and marital disharmony is being exposed, something is happening being these two and the air is fog-thick and magnetic. Except for Suzanne flicking her tongue round dry lips, neither of them moves. The flecks in her hazel eyes are like flames, he notices. Her lipstick has come off and her mouth is childlike-pale. A small crumb of food in one corner. Freckled chin. And now the flecks in her eyes are merging. She is beautiful. How could he not have seen before that Suzanne is beautiful?

'You're beautiful,' he says tenderly.

Her eyes fill and spill over, and he lifts his napkin from his lap to dab at them. Revealing his huge hard-on making a pyramid effect of his trousers. She sees immediately and starts laughing through her tears.

The pair of them laughing; clasping hands openly now and laughing, impervious to the rest of the table.

Yes, of course I love her.

15

Kempton's Journey

'Though I fled into the depths of the woods, an importunate crowd followed me everywhere and came between me and Nature. Only when I had detached myself from the social passions and their dismal train did I find her once again in all her beauty.'

'Well I never thought I'd find myself back here.'

Kempton, peeling a garlicky king prawn and taking a bite: the satisfying crunch and dense texture between his teeth. His treat, this lunch in the Paddock Suite of the clubhouse. And a bottle of Veuve Cliquot. He is smart in light beige gaberdines, pale blue shirt, striped silk tie, and a new navy blazer – day-member's badge attached to one of the brass buttons. Binoculars round his neck. And his French panama hat which, granted, is a bit summery for today's twilight gloom. He also sports a new hairstyle: the side bits down his ears left longish, and the wispy pieces on the crown cut short so that when they are blown about they look less as though he has been electrocuted. From the window he can see the parade ring and winner's enclosure on one side and the racecourse on the other;

and in the centre of the course, the lake. The clubhouse didn't exist when he was a child, but otherwise everything is more or less as he remembers. He is taken back, the years swept away; and nothing has happened in between. His eyes glued to the window as Minnie alternates between consulting the race card and *Sporting Life*, and explains some of the fundamentals to him – interrupted constantly by people coming up to her.

He is impressed and amazed by her popularity. Everyone seems to know her: jockeys, ex-jockeys, owners, a veterinary officer, a clerk of the course from thirty years ago . . . One old boy, a retired trainer with slicked-back hair and an Irish accent, remembers him from when he was a child; immediately launches into nostalgia, throwing out names of people and places that mean nothing to him. His mother animated as he has never seen her; in her element, this Saturday, 25 May at Kempton Park.

He has to admit there is something heady and titillating about the atmosphere that is infectious. There is nothing relaxed or leisurely, and even as he walked from the members' car park, past the hospitality marquees and through the members' entrance, he felt the zing of excitement within him; a real thrill running through him. They arrived early, and as yet the place was not crowded. The life-size bronze of Desert Orchid near the paddock was new to him.

'We'll meet there if we get separated,' Minnie said, leaning heavily on her shooting stick as she walked.

He has noticed her walk has slowed over the last months, and her breathing is laboured. Now, across the table from him, her bent face falls into folds and flaps. From this angle her chignon looks, he thinks, like a soap pad. She suddenly claps her hands.

'Here look at this. Well I never.' Passes him the race card.

He puts his glasses on. 'What am I supposed to be looking at?'

'Where my finger is. The fifth race. The main one. 4.05. The Crawly Warren Heron stakes. Entry number ten.'

'Good God.'

And there it is: a colt running called Kempton's Journey. Three years old. Ridden by Alan Dermot; trained by Peter Graham of Newmarket. Owned by someone with an unpronounceable Arab name.

'We must put some money on it,' he says. 'I mean we can't not.'

An omen of some sort? The fact that the form reveals a less than startling career to date only goes in his favour, as far as the horse's namesake, now reading avidly, is concerned. Both their fortunes about to change. The courses of their lives about to converge and be redefined.

'Has not been heard of since finishing down the field at Epsom last September,' he reads out loud. 'Prior to that won a couple of small races and came second at Newbury in his maiden race. An inconsistent horse who may improve with experience. Definitely for the speculator.'

He has absolutely no doubt that it will win; says so to Minnie, who gives a tolerant little nod without commenting. He is anxious to put his money on directly.

'Don't be absurd, you've got two and a half hours,' she says when he tells her. And he feels suitably flattened by the old put-down manner. But he is restless now; over the last hour the crowds have steadily been building up and people are milling about everywhere. He wants to be among them.

'The – SP – might change,' he says defensively.

'I doubt it very much,' she replies dryly, smiling to herself at his use of the initials, which she knows he has looked up in his guide and which hung unnaturally on his tongue.

'The odds on him will be pretty fancy,' she adds.

'Perhaps I'll get the bill anyway. If you don't mind.'
'As you wish.'

He pays, while Minnie scrawls a few relevant notes on her folded over paper, sucking the ebony end of her pipe handle, bifocals down her nose as she concentrates and grunts. The veins of her tanned freckled hands are like entangled worms. Her writing is shaky.

'Thank you for lunch,' she says, getting up and putting her hat back on, patting it over her chignon.

'*De rien*. My pleasure.'

They are still awkward and stilted together, inhibited by a lifetime's habit of sniping at each other that cannot be reversed in a matter of a day or week. But the good intent is there and they are both aware of this. Creeping their way towards establishing some sort of bond.

He helps her on with her jacket and is reminded again of her thinness as his thumb rests on the base of her neck.

Outside into the drizzle. He is a bit concerned about his panama hat getting ruined, but can't do much about it. There is quite a gathering of people around the Thames Suite, where the jockey John Reid, Graham Dench, of the *Racing Post*, and the trainer Gay Kelleway are talking to the public and marking race cards. Banners everywhere with the sponsors' name. All that money blasted on bunting – and does anyone really take any notice of it? Kempton wonders. It's another world. The cigars. The pearls. The hats. The endless rounds of Champagne. The trophies. The big time. He can't conceive what it must be like.

Minnie concentrating on the horses being paraded by their grooms. In the centre of the ring a cluster of men and one woman stand about: owners, trainers and officials; and a representative of the sponsoring company to award a prize for the best turned out runner.

'The horses look really small,' Kempton remarks.
'Well they're only two-year-olds.'

'It seems a bit cruel, racing them at that age.'

'Well, for a start many of them are in fact nearer three; a thoroughbred horse's year is taken from January, but the real birth date could be before that. Secondly, don't forget they only race half the year. Thirdly, they're not carrying a great weight they're not up to. Fourthly – it's only a six-furlong sprint. And they love it.'

Who is he to argue with an expert?

'Now, what you must watch for,' she says, 'is a horse that's sweating. Bad sign that. Over-excitable. Out of control, more often than not . . . There, look at her. She's nice. Good long stride.' Points to a bay filly wearing a visor. 'Alert head carriage. Nice round leg action. Don't be put off by the visor.'

'Are you going to bet on her?'

'No. Too hit and miss. I'll put something on the 3.05. The Handicap stakes.'

The jockeys appear on the scene – diminutive, and sprightly as terriers. They saddle up and spring lightly aboard their mounts. Their jack-knifed legs make Kempton wince. And God knows how they stay on with their knees virtually resting on the horses' withers. And the horses themselves, bottled-up, imploding with energy and tension, sideways-stepping, leaping and plunging. Minnie points out a couple of jockeys and a trainer. The Tannoy constantly blaring out with information. The atmosphere charged with expectation as the race is shortly to begin. People hurrying about with urgent expressions. The queues at the totes and general swarming around the Tattersalls Enclosure . . .

He can see why people get addicted to the whole thing: feels himself being sucked into the keyed-up excitement and rushing adrenalin. Almost on a high.

The horses make towards the course, and Kempton follows at a run; ends up joining the crowd and finds himself hemmed in by the railings. Jostling, flag-brandishing bodies pressed against him. Beer and raw onion breath. Too late, realises he is about as far away as he can get from the winning post. And he'll never find Minnie again, for Chrissake. The hubbub of voices, a screaming flailing-armed child directly behind him; and the rain comes down heavily. Through the network of umbrellas springing up, with his binoculars raised, he can glimpse the horses going into the starting stalls – several of them playing up. Finally they are in position and the starting gun cracks out, flag comes down. Out into the open shoot the horses, diagonally across the main circuit. The commentator's voice gathering pace. And he, Kempton, gripped with all the old feelings he'd forgotten: the tingling suspense, the thrill as the horses approach in a tangle of legs, the jockeys pitched forward over their heads, faces partially concealed by goggles. And there is the filly Minnie picked out with its blue-and-red visor – and then they are flashing past – thundering – which reminds him of his nightmare: the one that finally sent him to the doctor. Within seconds they are gone and there is just a view of disappearing streaks of colour, and barely a minute later the race is over.

He is forced to remain jammed to the railings until the solid block of the crowd gradually breaks up and people converge in different directions. He himself lopes off in the direction of the paddock – shielding his hat with his arms – in case he might find his mother there. In the ring the three exhausted winners are being unsaddled and walked around. Cameras trained on the shining young faces of the jockeys. No Minnie to be seen. He needs the loo. All the Champagne. And of course! The beautiful dark woman with the accent, who had come to his rescue that day: she was Viola, Minnie's lover. How sad. How terribly, terribly sad. And now not even a ring as a memory. His mother thwarted by a small boy and by protocol. How she must have wished sometimes that he did not exist.

The weather brightens, and for the next hour and a half he wanders about, re-acquainting himself with the layout of the place and with the procedure. And as he retraces the steps of his boyhood and resurrects images, smells and sounds; as incidents surface from a forgotten nook and topple one upon the other, a wistful smile flits across his features and there is a tugging sensation in his gut. His childhood bouncing back gleefully to confront him in his going-to-seed middle age. Hey look, the past calls out, it wasn't all bad. Do you remember you quite enjoyed some parts? Do you remember sitting on one of the horses after a race?

And yes he does. He could have been no more than five. Can see himself, a rather good-looking little boy with smooth skin and grave eyes beneath dense, dark hair, being led around. For an instant can recall his happiness, pure happiness. And the coarse mane between his gripping fingers.

And meanwhile, where has Minnie got to? The main race due to start in twenty or so minutes. And Kempton, never one to leave things until the last second, heads briskly for the 'rails' bookmakers lined up in front of the steppings. Not for him the tote or the 'board' bookmakers. No. Kempton will be up there with the big boys for his bet. £25 is not to be sniffed at.

He goes to William Hill's first. An elderly man is quietly and unhurriedly giving his instructions, and Kempton begins to shift about restlessly. The time ticking by. There is a woman behind him now. He shrugs at her and rolls his eyes, and she looks back at him with a frosty smile. Kempton ostentatiously consulting his watch, clearing his throat. Eventually can contain himself no longer: 'Excuse me,' he says to the bookie, who looks more like a lawyer, 'there are others waiting.'

• Kempton's Journey

'If you would be so kind sir,' the bookmaker says, writing.

If you would be so kind. What kind of grammar is that? Another couple of minutes pass. Kempton rocking back and forth on his heels, beginning to boil.

'I shall take my trade elsewhere,' he threatens.

'You do that then sir.'

And he does. Fuming, outraged. To Ladbrokes – where he has the fortune to nip in smartly just as another man arrives. He has simmered down a bit. And this bookmaker looks a genial, smiling sort of chap. But time is running short. According to his calculations the horses have been in the parade ring for several minutes.

'What are the odds on Kempton's Journey in the Heron Stakes?' Kempton asks him importantly, and leaning forward confidentially.

The man refers to a sheet: '58–1 as it stands at the moment, sir.'

Fifty-eight to one! Kempton does some protracted mental arithmetic and works out he will be £1450 richer by the end of the race. Excitement spiralling through him, quickening his heart. He'll take Suzanne to Thailand.

'I'd like twenty-five pounds to win please.'

'Pardon sir?' The bookmaker looks less rosy-genial. 'Did you say twenty-five pounds?'

Sounds of restlessness from the man behind.

'Yes that's correct. Look, I'm not rushing you or anything—' he looks at his watch. At this rate he'll miss everything.

'With respect sir, you'd be better with one of the board fellows, unless you've got an account with us.'

What a cheek. Doesn't this chap want his business? Casts his eyes towards the congestion round the 'board fellows.' A yelled 'Take 6–4' from one of the tic-tac men over the hub.

He stands firm. 'I'm not going into that zoo.'

'With respect sir—'

'Hmph. It's all right Frank,' a familiar voice behind him says (and did he imagine the Hmph?). 'Put it on my account. He's my son.'

'Oh right you are Mrs Prévot. You should've said, sir,' to Kempton, who gives a curt nod of acknowledgement. Tingling neck. Humiliated.

The bookmaker takes a form and starts filling it in. Minnie signs. Kempton pretending to peer around him with an insouciant casualness. He waits with his mother, itching to be gone, scalded like a child hauled up before the class, and fearing that he is missing all the activity in the paddock – while the man who had been behind him places his bet. A staggering £2,500 in total. Then it is Minnie's turn. Her bet is a more modest but still staggering figure of £175. How can she afford that? And nothing on Kempton's Journey.

'I thought you were skint,' he accuses her, striding towards the paddock. His mother trying to keep up with him.

'I had a fair bit of luck in the third and fourth races. Now don't look all pious. Hmph.'

He didn't imagine it. Her Hmph is back. Extraordinary. And he is oddly glad. Like seeing an old friend.

'Oh well, I'll give you your twenty-five pounds back with interest later. Incidentally, why didn't you back my namesake?'

'One of us has got to come out tops, Kempton.' She gives a teasing little chin jerk, and just for a fleeting second he is struck by something in her expression that is faintly reminiscent of Suzanne.

He can hear her wheezing, and slowing his pace, takes her arm. She does not resist, and he thinks how strange it is walking along with her arm tucked in his; and, once he becomes accustomed to it, how pleasant. It is like a seal of affirmation; and he feels within him the strange pricklings of something hitherto unknown: affection.

The jockeys have been aboard for some minutes, and Kempton immediately seeks out number ten and the identifying red-and-black diamonds of the jockey. The horse concerned is a liver chestnut who appears to be walking out well, glancing around him keenly, without panic; nor is there a tell-tale glint of sweat on his neck or hindquarters. If anything he seems to be too calm compared to the others.

'He looks good, doesn't he?' Kempton says to his mother, whose head is swivelled towards Regal Archive. 'Well-grown for a three-year-old,' he adds loudly, for others to overhear, and with a knowledgeable head-tilt.

'What? Oh not too bad. Carrying a bit too much of a belly on him. He's obviously been laid-off for a while.'

He doesn't say anything. Nettled. Watches as the horses make for the course.

He accompanies Minnie back to the members' enclosure and they climb up the clubhouse steppings towards the top, where a friend of hers has kept a couple of places for them. There is barely time for a hurried introduction – Ted Browning, my son Kempton – before the horses are being positioned in the stalls. Kempton hardly able to suppress his excitement. Binoculars close to his eyes. The commentator's laconic voice over the Tannoy. And they're off. Through the powerful lenses he can distinguish the individual horses and riders. The red-and-black diamonds of Alan Dermot on Kempton's Journey, who is running well, somewhere in the middle of the field. Row upon row of spectators, all with their binoculars trained. Heightened tension. And Kempton's horse is moving up, away from the middle, towards the front. The commentator's voice gathering pace: '... And now it's

Regal Archive in the lead, closely followed by Sorbie Tower. Then it's Kempton's Journey . . .' The crowd becoming carried away; the roaring-out of different names, stamping of feet, waving of fists, jigging up and down on the spot (It sounds like 'Today in Parliament,' he thinks). And himself, yelling with the rest of them, mindless of everything else, 'Come on Kempton's Journey,' till his throat is raw. And for a few moments it looks as though his horse is about to put on a spurt and advance upon the two leaders – Kempton's heart pounding, adrenalin coursing through him, waving his hat, bawling his head off; and then something happens: Regal Archive performs a sudden acceleration, with Sorbie Tower closely on his quarters gathering speed, and Kempton's Journey slips back again and another horse overtakes him into third position.

'. . . And with just half a furlong left to run it's Regal Archive, and Sorbie Tower's almost alongside him now . . . They're neck and neck . . . It's going to be a photo finish as they approach the winning post . . . Yes, and it's Regal Archive just in front of Sorbie Tower. And Regal Archive ridden by John Reid has won by a neck, against Sorbie Tower, followed by . . .'

The commentator's voice running down like a gramophone in need of winding. And Kempton lets the binoculars drop against his chest. Staring bleakly ahead. His horse finished fourth. Not atrocious. Just mediocre. He feels as though it is indicative of his own life. Mediocrity. All the zest has gone from him in contrast to his elation of a few minutes earlier.

Minnie's sympathetic eyes rest on him.

'Tea, I think,' she says briskly.

He trails after her – she is chatting away to Ted Browning, a ruddy-faced, bald man with cockroach eyebrows and a green tartan waistcoat (his father had a red tartan one).

• Kempton's Journey

They end up in the Paddock Suite again, from where he can see the winners being led around. The ear-splitting smiles of the jockeys. The presentation of the trophies. He watches the crowds thinning out. He is as exhausted as if he had ridden in the race itself.

Minnie pouring out Earl Grey.

'Ted may be able to help you out with your wagon and horse,' she says.

'Really? How come?' A spark of revived interest. Turns his gaze from the window onto the man opposite him. He has a thick, pitted skin, small blue eyes buried in pouches of flesh.

'Well, happens I buys and sells old carts and carriages and does them up,' he says. 'Got a couple of old Romany caravans I'm doing right now.'

'I don't believe it!'

'Thought that might perk you up.' Minnie smirking at him.

'Well it has. Where do you live?' To Ted – who is cramming Black Forest gâteau into his mouth.

'Near Reigate. Got a small place there.' Crumbs round his mouth.

'Now don't be modest Ted,' Minnie says; and to Kempton, 'He's got a manor house in fifty acres.' Taps her pipe into the ashtray.

He tries not to show surprise. The man looks like a scrap metal dealer. Perhaps he is. They can make a fortune.

'And I've a gelding might suit. Used to be a tinker's horse. I knew the guy. Died a couple of months back. Couldn't see his horse go to the knackers. A piebald about sixteen hands. You know the sort. Nine or ten year old. Your mother says it's for a business. Well I tell you, you could smarten him up real nice. You know, plait his mane and tail with red ribbon. I'd teach you how. Or 'course you could hog him. I've a couple of others. Suffolk Punches.

Magnificent beasts, but they'd cost you. You're talking thousands there.'

'I couldn't afford that. There'd be no point.' Kempton leaning keenly across the table. 'When could I come over?'

'Any time that suits you.'

'Tomorrow?'

'I could come with you,' Minnie says.

So it is arranged. He is no longer despondent. It had been absurd to attach so much importance to a race. And after all, he thinks – back to his normal, rational self – Kempton's Journey is a fairly obvious name for a horse. But the taste of almost insane excitement: he will not forget that in a hurry.

His mother collects her winnings – generously waves aside the twenty-five pounds he owes her and pushes the notes back at him when he tries to press them into her hand.

'Don't be ridiculous. If I can't treat my son after an extremely lucrative day, hmph . . . And by the way, your horse ran very well. Very valiant. It was the jockey's fault. He looked behind him at a crucial point. Horse lost its attention. He could certainly have been up there in third place, if not with the two leaders.'

She hangs on to his elbow as they walk back to the car. In her other hand is her shooting stick. Familiar leather bag over her shoulder. She seems to tire quickly, and he is anxious. Suddenly he doesn't want her to be old.

He unlocks the passenger door for her, and as she is about to climb inside the car he prevents her. He smiles awkwardly at her, tugging at his chin, and she wonders what is to come.

'Minnie, you never hugged me as a child. Give me a hug now?'

She stares at him dumbfounded, a smile breaking over her features, pale eyes becoming moist. Cannot maintain the smile, as her mouth quivers. Her arms form an open-ended loop; and he goes into them.

It has been a good day. Yes. A bit of a flutter, a few wins. A hug with her son.

'And you never gave me a party,' he says.

16

Winning Post

Cat clearing out her room. Putting away childish things. Kempton sticking red stars to all the furniture he is selling, which is nearly everything. Pluto, bemused, wandering from one dismantled zone to another, with Kempton's maroon leather slipper in his mouth like an outsize tongue. The smells of cooking from the kitchen: Peter preparing omelettes for lunch.

Half the boxes seem to comprise Kempton's record collection or books; everything is either colour-coded or indexed in alphabetical order. His painting materials are stacked alongside his easel. The dining table (sold with the house) is taken up with his Art Nouveau and Deco *objects*, and his recently acquired Clarice Cliff dinner service. A boxful of mementos and photos. Basic kitchen stuff. Not a lot else, apart from his clothes. And he has been brutal with those too. Or rather Peter has. Getting rid of clutter. Cat is taking all the porcelain; it would be out of place in Kempton's new abode. Ready for the life of a Bohemian. The actual moving date – Friday 14th – is nudging ever closer. At first he had been convinced something would happen, could not believe everything would go so smoothly. Only now, just three days away, is he beginning to think that things might just conceivably for once, proceed without a hitch. And yet despite all the evidence of imminent decampment around him – even his bed has a red sticker on it – sometimes a wave of unreality will come over him, as though a black-cloaked figure has brandished a wand and shattered the glass globe that allowed him to glimpse the illusion of his future; and there he is stuck for ever, as he always has been and always will be, still working for Pitman, unable to tear himself away from a memory-drenched house and his roots; the same routine-bound man who never sought beyond his rather bumpy nose. Is still at loggerheads with Minnie, and Suzanne doesn't exist. Unreal. Unreal.

His daughter stands up from her crouching position, and arches her aching back so that her tummy sticks out like a proud peacock's chest. And this, if nothing else, drives home the true facts.

She smiles gently at her father. 'Our lives,' she says simply.

'It's the right thing,' he says with certainty.

Her soft toys packed into a suitcase. And one day she will say to her child: Those were Mummy's when she was a little girl.

'Of course it is.'

'I know it's a bit late – but you really don't mind?'

'Being honest, I think you should've done it ages ago.'

'Yes. I thought the same thing myself a while back. And you and Peter, you're still ... Listen, I want you to know if ever you need a roof over your head for yourself – and my grandchild – there is one. I don't mean that negatively. Only that you should feel secure and wanted. Shit, I put things so badly, don't I?' Legs planted wide in the middle of her room, a rueful small-boy grin.

'Hey Kempton, I know just what you mean and I love you for it.'
'You too Sweetie Pie.'
'Then aren't we both lucky?'
Peter calling upstairs that the omelettes are ready.
'Yes, I dare to think we are.' Kempton mentally touching wood.
'. . . Come on you two sloths, They'll be ruined.'

'I haven't played Blindman's Buff since I was a child.'
Suzanne being guided along Duck's Walk by Kempton from his car, which is parked in The Avenue, St Margarets, a few yards away. A couple of passers-by staring and smiling at adults' antics. Pluto straining at the lead in his other hand.
'Why all the secrecy?' Suzanne, one arm outstretched in front of her in an exaggerated way.
'Revenge.'
'You could be leading me to my doom.'
'I could indeed.'
'I think this must otherwise be known as blind faith.'
He steers her and Pluto into a small entrance way, stops, and begins to unfasten the knot of his handkerchief tied round her head, pretending for a moment that he cannot undo it.
'Blast.'
'Don't be horrible.'
He pulls off the blindfold with a flourish. *'Et voilà.'*
They are in a tiny garden edging the river.
'Meet William.'

'William?' She pretends to scan the area for a third person.

'Of Orange.' Gesticulates to the unwieldy houseboat moored just below, between Twickenham Bridge and the railway bridge. 'He's a Dutch barge.' The name boldly painted in red-and-yellow lettering along the slab side of the great hull.

'I thought boats were supposed to be female.'

'Too bad. This one's a bloke.'

Thursday, early evening. A low fat sun ejecting yellow ochre, squelching in its own yolk. Tiny moth shimmering in the heavy air. A low-flying plane lumbering noisily towards Heathrow. Shadows and swirling silver patterns on the brown water. Crescent leaves from the overhanging willow boughs. And Kempton in his panama, Suzanne in a wide straw hat, stand hand in hand surveying his new property. Her arms are bare, freckled, and rather sunburnt. On the end of a very short leash Pluto stares worriedly into the water; cringes as a train clatters past at tremendous speed over the railway bridge. And as always when he is anxious, he squats and pees. Hasn't yet learned to balance on three legs.

'So,' Kempton says proudly, 'what do you think?'

'I think—' His face is positively glowing. She was about to crack a funny, but a glance at his transported expression has changed her mind. 'I think he's splendid.'

'He is, isn't he? Yes, that's the right word. Splendid.' He tightens his grip on her hand, lifting it to his lips and kissing it.

She relaxes against him. 'And very macho. Look at the size of him.'

'Sixty foot by twelve, to be precise.'

'However will you drive him?'

'Well I won't at first. He's semi-permanently moored. This little plot of land goes with him, by the way. But there's an engine should I wish to go for a jaunt. You don't need a licence to go downstream. Up-river you do, because of the locks. But you can get one on a daily basis. It's not that hard to drive. The old owner showed me what to do. I mean, of course it'll take a while to get the hang of it all properly. But I've got loads of bumph to read—'

Never a man to do things by halves, Kempton's reading matter now ranges from *Living on a houseboat: The Pleasures and Pitfalls*, to *How to Look after Your Horse*, and *One Man and His Wagon*.

'—And the guy at the marine place, Doug, says he'll help me out whenever I need it. People are very helpful. I've already met a couple of other boat owners. It's like a club. Very friendly. River gypsies they're known as.' We are. Himself about to become one. 'So then – I'll have a volunteer skipper, I hope.'

'Five. Four females and a bloke.'

'Great.' He has met her children several times. He gets on with them all, but Julian, in particular, he has a rapport with. He is reading botany and horticulture at university, and is a serious boy with a slow, gentle smile; the sort of boy that once he might have hoped Cat . . .

'And two bloodhounds,' she says.

He envisages parties on board, jazz blaring out. The boat chugging down the river on a fine day. Gershwin. 'Summertime and the living is easy, fish are jumping and the river is high . . .' Playing his upright piano he part exchanged for the baby grand. And Richmond just across on the opposite bank. And if he wishes to stroll there on foot, then it is barely five minutes: down Duck's Walk into Willoughby road, across Richmond Bridge – and straight into the Odeon cinema. Perfect. What more could a man want? And then, just another five minutes away by car, grazing in a meadow belonging to Petersham Farm: his horse. He is taking delivery of it and the wagon in a fortnight's time; he thought it better to settle in first. He could even get interested in gardening; this one is so pretty and manageable, about twenty-five foot square, with a shed he intends to pull down and replace with a larger log cabin where he can paint.

A ramp leads to the boat deck, adorned with flower tubs, and Kempton helps Suzanne aboard. They have to push Pluto, who has slid to his haunches.

'He'll get used to it,' Suzanne assures him. 'Let him off the lead. He's hardly going to dive over.'

'Are you certain?'

'Absolutely.'

He unclips the lead and Pluto bolts off to explore, stern wagging.

The driving cabin is a dark green box-like construction over the front deck. The steering wheel is immense. Suzanne stands behind it and pretends to drive. She looks dwarfed. The interior, on two levels, is as spacious as a bungalow, with two double bedrooms, and an open-plan living area and galley kitchen running almost the entire length of the hull.

'The result of knocking out a warren of passageways and cabins,' Kempton explains. 'The old owner was an architect.'

A third tiny room with bunks, which Kempton will use as a study, is huddled into the stern, and one bathroom, a quirky hexagonal shape and comprising a hip bath, basin and loo, is in the bow. The main bedroom has its own shower and loo. Everything is gleaming wood – the stripped floor, beams, panelled walls.

'It's fantastic.' Suzanne opening and shutting cupboards and drawers, shaking her head, laughing delightedly. 'It's really fantastic.'

'You see! And there're all mod cons.' He is boyish in his enthusiasm.

He takes her hand and shows her everything: the solid fuel fire and heating system, the generator for emergencies and cruising, the mains electricity lead that runs into his garden; the sewage system which consists of a holding tank that has to be pumped off once a week into the main drainage; the telephone connection on a flexible lead, the water hose with which he must fill the tank, also once a week. The diesel engine.

'And I've learned a whole new vocabulary pertaining to boats,' he says with pride.

Suzanne has never seen him so happy; looks at him with a mixture of indulgence and tenderness.

'So tomorrow's D-Day. I must say I'm not looking forward to the move itself.'

'I'll be with you to help you.'

'Yes I know.'

Thank God for that. For Suzanne.

'We could christen the bed now if you like.'

'How would you feel if we didn't?' she says, surprising him.

'Is this indicative of anything sinister?'

'No. The contrary. The first night should be the first night.'

'OK.'

'You're not offended?'

She is beginning to learn just how easily he can take umbrage; but it is more than that: he gets genuinely hurt. And she is learning to tread lightly where once she would have jumped in with four hooves. He, in turn, is learning about her many insecurities and complexes.

'How could I be, put like that? No, I agree.'

They climb back up the staircase onto the deck and sit on two fold-up chairs side by side. He opens a bottle of chilled white wine he brought with him. A Tourraine. Pours it into two glasses. A pair of swans gliding silently in the channel between the arches of the two bridges. Less silently another train hurtling past, then another plane overhead. Traffic. Hooting. Modern-day sounds contrasting with timelessness. A symbiotic blending, and each oddly comforting.

They sit on in their own silence for a bit, sipping wine. Pluto lying at their feet, calm now, watching the swans laconically. The plip-plip of water. Drifting conversation of people wandering along Duck's Walk. Voices from the opposite bank.

From out of his pocket Kempton pulls a small book: the Rousseau.

'Would you mind? It's just the tiny passage almost at the end,' he says.

'No, I'd like you to. I'll get my own back with Sylvia Plath later.'

It has become a pleasant and intimate little evening routine: reading small pieces to one another.

'OK, so – "I enjoy the kind of happiness for which I feel I was made. I have described this state in one of my reveries. It suits me so well that I desire nothing other than that it should continue and never be disturbed."'

He stops reading and puts the book down on the ground. Turns to her.

'That's it. That's how I feel.'

'Me too.'

Pause. 'We could make it legal.' Tracing his finger round and round the rim of his glass.

'We could but—'

'Is that a yes or no?'

'A yes. But not yet.'

'So it's conditional.'

'No. It's not conditional. It's a definitely one day, but just not yet.'

So he must be content with that.

'I love this woman,' he says, staring out at the river.

'I love this man.'

That's fine then. And he hopes and prays that it will 'continue and never be disturbed'. Can see no good reason, the way things are, the way *they* are, that this will not be the case. Tilts his hat at a raffish angle, then hers.

But he will never be complacent. You learn that.